Rach

Novels

The Serial Dater — 31 dates in 31 days

The Serial Dieter — 31 dishes in 31 days

with other 'Serial' titles to follow

Oh, Henry — the first in the Henry Houdini series

Short Stories

Various Henry Houdini long short stories

The Serial Dieter

ISBN: 978-1-913633-20-2

Published in 2020 by August Publishing UK.

The locations are or were real, although Rachel has taken 'artistic licence' in some instances, especially given that some were closed for the duration of the final edits! She's ever grateful for her friends Messrs Google and Wikipedia for the research materials including maps and mouth-watering menu photos.

www.augustpublishing.co.uk

Cover design/co-editing by Caroline Vincent

The Serial Dieter

The second in the 'Serial' series

– 31 dishes in 31 days

Rachel Cavanagh

Dedication

This book is dedicated to my tireless septuagenarian uncle Michael, to whom I owe a lot and will be forever grateful. He lives not a million miles from Donna's mum, Lesley. Or would… if she were real.

And fond memories of my father who would have turned ninety-one on the day this novel was released.

Where we are…

Following on a year later from the end of *The Serial Dater*, where Northampton-based technology journalist Isobel MacFarlane had to date thirty-one men in the thirty-one days of May, her best friend and health and beauty colleague, Donna Evans, takes the helm, with challenges being thrown at her from her colleagues and life!

Chapter One – A Year Later

Monday 23rd April

"Busy?"

I look up and there's Izzy. My BFF. She looks happy. Not that that's a rare thing, she's often happy, more so since William asked her to move in. Can't believe they've been together nearly a year.

"Donna?"

I shake my head to snap myself out of Wizzy… or is it Willizzy. I laugh.

"Come on. Share the joke."

I shake my head again. "Oh, nothing. Just my brain, you know."

Izzy goes all serious. "I do."

I may come across as a dizzy blonde but she knows better. Knows all about my semi-photographic memory. Normally.

Izzy's my colleague, best mate (in reverse order). She does the technology column (this time last year, a dating column!) and I do health and beauty. So you see that's why I have to be the way they expect me: healthy and beautiful. It's hard though.

Anyway, enough self-pity. I am happy… most of the time. Duncan's lovely, really lovely. He's the 'one' and I couldn't be… well, happier. He was Izzy's first date so we've only known each other about a year. We met at a speed-dating event Izzy invited me to, but I've known about him, via Izzy, for a bit longer. And he's gorgeous. Tall (not that difficult when you're five feet two and a half), dark and… I know, a cliché. And my soulmate. There, another cliché.

"Busy?" Izzy repeats and I laugh again.

"Sorry. I have so many balls in the air, it's like being at David Beckham's training camp."

"Golden Balls." Izzy smirks. I blush.

"Someone said that," I say. "About David Beckham's training camp. Can't remember who. Funny though." And if I can't remember maybe no one did.

"Too busy for a drink?"

I look down at my empty mug, sitting on my desk next to my empty green Coke glass, and shake my head. I think of the brain cells I'm killing with all this shaking but reckon I've got plenty to spare.

I did some research on this fact some months ago when I was doing an article on brains vs. beauty (using celebrities as examples mostly) and remember that the BBC, amongst others, quashed the only-use-ten-percent myth.

"Quash," I say, then lisp a 'myth', only to realise that Izzy's gone… probably to the kitchen.

"Keeping brain tissue alive consumes twenty percent of the oxygen we breathe, according to cognitive neuroscientist Sergio Della Sala," I quote under my breath as I walk, with mug and glass, to the kitchen.

Sure enough, Izzy's there, kettle rumbling, two mugs, probably with hot chocolate powder covering their bottoms. I smirk.

Izzy smiles. "It's so lovely to see you so happy," she says as she pours water into the mugs. "After…"

I shake my head, put my previous mug and glass in the dishwasher, and take the new mug she offers me. I go to wrap my hands around it but know it will scald me so I change my mind.

The elephant in the room is the baby I lost… or rather the baby that I may have lost. I was 'late', you see, and got all excited because I thought Duncan and I were going to be parents. We'd not talked about timing but we both wanted one, a boy or girl, it didn't matter. I'd even bought a pregnancy test, three actually, but hadn't needed any of them as late turned out to just be late and not stopped, so it wasn't meant to be. I told Izzy, of course. I tell her everything.

Izzy points to one of the empty tables. It's ten in the morning so too early for elevenses, everyone else being studious at their desks but we work on Izzy-and-Donna time, taking breaks whenever we like. Not that we don't work hard in between but we prefer an empty room, easier to discuss sensitive topics.

I don't really want to talk but Izzy looks like she has something on her mind so we sit.

"Are you okay?" she asks and I give her a weak smile. It's the best I can do but it seems to satisfy her.

"And you?"

"Yes, good, thanks," she says with an equally weak smile so I wait for her to speak again, and she does. "I'm a little worried about moving in with William."

"Oh?"

"I don't want to burden you…"

Part of me wishes I hadn't said anything but I know it was the right thing to do. It feels like we're both at the same stage… Duncan and I have talked about living together but not made any firm plans. Izzy and William aren't the baby type, unless it comes to parrots in William's case, but I know Izzy feels badly for me. It's not easy being happy all the time. Sometimes I wish I was like Izzy; no pretence, take her as you find her.

"It's fine," I say. "Really, it's fine. It would have been too soon anyway."

She smiles sympathetically and changes the subject. "We've booked a holiday."

I grin… and mean it. I love holidays, even if it's not me going on them. "Ooh… where?"

"Larnaca."

I catch my breath. It's one of my favourite places. "You're so jammy. I love Cyprus."

"You should come with us!" She's Cheshire catting. "You and Duncan."

Though it's a great idea, it's bad timing. We're not exactly… what's the saying? Love's young dream. We're actually younger than Izzy and William but you know. We're finding it difficult to talk at the moment, which is strange because talking's one of my favourite things to do.

"Next time," I say. "So why are you worried?"

"Worried?"

"About moving in."

"Oh, yes. Too used to my independence, I suppose."

"Can't say I blame you. I'd be the same, although I'm only renting my flat so it's easier. It's a big step regardless."

Izzy nods.

"Have you found someone to rent yours?" I ask.

"Yep."

"You're still doing the rooms thing?"

"That way if it doesn't work out…"

"Do you think it won't?"

She shrugs. She's always been the cautious one of the two of us. But she's taking the leap first. "That way I can come and go whenever I like, if I need to, and I'll still have the box room for my stuff, and the loft."

"It makes sense."

Izzy's the logical one. If I owned my house… flat, I'd probably rent out the whole thing but she's getting lodgers for the two double bedrooms. "Monday to Fridays or full-time?"

"One of each actually. Amanda's full-time. Works at St Andrew's Hospital. Tom's Monday to Thursday – doesn't work Fridays – at Barclaycard. Married, two er… three children maybe, from Harrogate."

"Nice. I love Harrogate." I do. Duncan and I went there last year for a music festival.

"It does look lovely."

Izzy and I don't usually struggle for conversation but I can't think of anything else to say. Thankfully, William appears in the doorway, his head not far off the top horizontal beam. Izzy's facing me so she hasn't noticed. I tilt my head, pointing my chin at the door. She turns round.

"Oh hey. Did you want me?"

William opens his mouth to say something but closes it again. I'm guessing he doesn't want to say no and is thinking of something more tactful.

"Me?" I offer and he smiles.

"When you're ready."

Though Izzy's dating him, we both know William's 'when you're ready' means now or thereabouts so I pick up my mug, whisper a 'catch you later' to Izzy and follow William into his office.

Chapter 2 – Mission Possible

William stops by the door and points towards his visitor chair. It's not an annoyed point, I note, but a 'please will you sit' point. My sunken heart lifts a little.

He closes the door and sits opposite me.

I want to ask him if everything's all right but decide to let him go first.

"Donna…"

I want to say his name back but again, I wait.

"How's work?"

I'm not sure what to say to that. Of course I'll be positive, I always am with William, with pretty much everyone other than Izzy when I'm feeling low, but it wasn't quite what I was expecting. I put on a semi-broad smile. "Enjoying it, thank you."

"Busy?"

"Uh huh." Then feel irreverent. I want to apologise but say nothing.

"I have a… er…"

I raise my eyebrows in anticipation of what he's going to say next. Favour? I look down at his desk. Cold cup of coffee? I look back and semi-smile again.

"A project I'd like you to do."

Knowing Izzy's 'thirty-one men in thirty-one days project', my heart re-sinks. I think he won't be getting me to date anyone though because he knows I'm seeing Duncan and they get on almost as well as Izzy and I do. I raise my eyebrows again. "Absolutely, William. Happy to." Happy might be stretching things, certainly until I know what he has in store for me, but he's my boss so I don't have a lot of choice. Besides, it'll take my mind off… things.

"Following on from Izzy's successful er… project last year, the board…" He points to the ceiling. "Wants something similar. Don't worry, not dating." He laughs, and I smile and shake my head. "No, something in keeping with your usual column. With…" He looks down at a copy of the paper, turned, I see, to my page. The one on… I look closer… the hot-stones back massage treatment. Not William's usual reading material, I think.

"There's been a lot done about beauty so probably not suitable for the kind of thing I have in mind."

Izzy had dated thirty-one men in thirty-one days… or that was the 'brief'. She, and I, actually went speed dating in the middle so it was forty-something. I try to recall. Sixteen that evening so forty-seven. Doesn't quite have the same ri– Then I realise William's waiting for me to speak. "Sorry?"

"Any suggestions?"

"For..." I feel particularly dumb as I'm not sure whether I've missed anything since he dismissed beauty. So it's got to be health-related. "Spa treatments?" I blurt without really thinking they're more beauty than health, although some can fall under both categories.

"Erm... not really the kind of thing I was thinking. Got to be a bit more substantial. Something more regular, to fit in with the thirty-one theme."

I nod, unable to come up with anything helpful.

"No, something food-related."

"Oh, okay, sure." I must admit that is more appealing. I may eat relatively sensibly, more salads than Izzy's ice cream and Disaronno, but trying out different food to what I might normally eat, especially if the paper's paying for it, is something I could do for a month. Then it dawns on me. It's the twenty-third of April. May has thirty-one days. Izzy's project happened in May. "When..."

"I'm giving you a bit more notice than I gave Izzy... Seeing as it's been done before it was easier to come up with the concept, but again, the order's only just come down from on high so..."

"No, that's fine. I can do that. Yes, I can absolutely do that." And I can. I know my stuff. I know my stuff but I need clarity. "So are you asking me to try different diets or different dishes, only it's not really possible or practical... practical or possible... to do thirty-one different diets in thirty-one days. You need to do one for at least a week to show any..."

William's nodding so I stop.

"Thirty-one dishes in thirty-one days?" I suggest. "Low calorie, under... say, five hundred, a bit more of a challenge." *Because the concept in itself isn't enough.* "Healthy eating in preparation for the summer, something like that?"

"Sounds perfect."

"Is there any other remit than that?" I ask, hoping he says 'no'.

"Not really."

I wait for the explanation of 'not really'.

"There is... one slight complication."

Here we go. All the food needs to be white – popular with those who've just had their teeth whitened. Or green... veg, smoothies. I could easily do that, as long as it's not the powdered shakes. They're nice but not for a whole month.

"I need you to cover for Veronica."

"Ver...?" Veronica? Who's Veronica?

"Your counterpart. Down in Hemel."

I remember. We've never met but I've spoken to her a couple of times, emailed back and forth more often. Lovely, from what I can gather. "Oh, sure. Will they email me her files or something?" I'm hoping it's not what I think it is.

"Ah no. I need you to be in situ. Just for a month, *the* month. Would tie in quite nicely. Can you hold your workload that long?"

I'm not sure but nod all the same. We seem to be doing a lot of nodding between the two of us. I want to look outside William's office to see if anyone's watching us, imagining that we're like those dogs on car dashboards – those old English bulldogs, Churchill types – but William would see so I resist.

I just say a blanket 'yes, no problem' and let the whole concept sink in. So I have to live in Hemel Hempstead for the whole of May? Then I realise William's not a mind reader. Izzy is when it comes to me but… and I wish she were here. I wonder why she didn't say anything. "So I have to live in Hemel Hempstead for the whole of May?" I repeat but aloud this time.

"Please."

Again, it's not the kind of please that is a request. It's a you-have-to… or rather I-have-to kind of please.

It could be worse. Hemel's not the most salubrious of places but I have family nearby so at least I can stay locally. William will likely know this from Izzy but it still all fits in a little too neatly and I begin to think that it's a set-up somehow but I'm not sure why.

A week isn't long to make arrangements. My mum will be delighted as it'll mean I'll stay with her during the week. Her twin sister and my uncle live in the next road so I'll get to see them too – it'll make up for the once every three weeks currently.

"We'll pay reasonable expenses, of course," William adds then looks towards the door as if the conversation's over.

I go to speak but am stopped by William's desk phone ringing.

"Thank you, Donna," he says, hand hovering over the receiver.

So I leave his office.

I then realise I won't have another weekend with Duncan, not a full one anyway, before I leave Sunday afternoon. I'll be back every Friday, or he can visit and stay at my mum's, but it won't be the same. He doesn't often work late on a Friday, because he tends to during the week, so we get quality time but I suspect I'll be spending some of that on the M1 motorway, going north with all the other commuters, albeit from junction eight rather than the heart of London.

Londinium, I mouth without saying the word aloud and it reminds me of the TV programme *Time Team*. I don't watch it – not a fan of history – but my mum loves it. I think she has a crush on Tony

Robinson. I loved him as Baldrick, with his very uncunning cunning plans, but no, it was Blackadder for me. Bearded series two rather than geeky gawky series one. Izzy's the geeky of the two of us.

With project assigned, my first instinct is to speak to my oracle but she's on the phone when I get back to my desk. I wonder if it's to William but when I look at him, he's striding towards his door. My eyes follow his path as it leads to my desk.

I smile and wait for him to speak. Like nodding, I feel I'm doing a lot of smiling today.

"Someone from the Hemel office is going to ring… actually more likely email you with all the details. You'll simply be Veronica for the month. I don't know if she's got anything else that needs to be done but they can always reallocate. One column, one project is probably enough. It'll take you a while to settle in but it's only temporary so don't worry if you don't get everything done. The project's the most important. Izzy will help, I'm sure."

With that, he looks over at her. She's still on the phone, chatting away, smiling. William looks back at me. "We have a few days so…"

"We do," I say and he wanders off towards Izzy but when it's clear she's not coming off the phone any time soon, he veers away and walks into the kitchen.

I look from Izzy to the kitchen. I can't see William through the half-glass wall from the angle I'm sitting, which is weird as he's super tall. Six feet four, I think. Anything above five feet four for me is tall, over five feet ten – Izzy and Duncan's heights – is semi-super tall.

I sigh, wiggle my mouse to reactivate my screen, type in my password, and open up a new Word document.

Chapter 3 – Sharing The News

Izzy finally comes off the phone. She looks in William's direction then mine. I think she's deliberating who to speak to first but comes to my desk.

"Is everything okay?" she asks when she's still a few feet away.

I want to say I'm not sure but I'm more upbeat than that. "Sure."

"What did William want?"

Straight to the point. "He's got a project he wants me to do."

I can almost see her gulping. "Oh?"

"Thirty-one dishes in thirty-one days… I think."

"Oh," she says quite noncommittally. I can't decide whether it's a good thing or not, this project, but if anyone can help me, Izzy can. She's good at taking charge, stands up to William more than I can, always has.

"In Hemel. Hempstead."

"Hemel? Why Hemel?"

I shrug but I'm not sure why as I do know the reason for Hemel. "Sister paper. My equivalent's on holiday."

"For a month?"

"Apparently. Or at least, I think so. He's just asked me to fill in so I'm not sure."

"When have you got to go?"

"In the next few days. He wants me to start May first so…"

Izzy laughs. "May again?"

"Yep." I do a slight swerve as there's not much more I can tell her. "And I get to stay with my mum."

"Oh cool. How is she?"

"She's fine."

"Delighted to have you back home?"

"Will be. I've not told her yet but she always hints that she'd have me back like the proverbial… even if she doesn't actually *say* so."

Izzy laughs.

"Did William not tell you?" I ask.

"About…"

"Transferring me?"

Izzy looks horrified, almost mortified. "Transfer?"

"For a month."

The smile returns. "Phew. I thought… he wouldn't do that to me, to us."

"So he didn't tell you."

Izzy shakes her head. "Keeps work and home very much

separate."

"Of course."

"So have you met your equivalent…?"

"Veronica. No. Spoken to her a couple of times."

"What's she like?"

"She sounds very posh, glamorous, I think, which you'd expect from a health and beauty columnist, not that I…" I laugh when Izzy blows a raspberry. "They're going to email me with the details. It's all a bit much to take in."

"Of course. I'm sure he wouldn't have asked if he didn't think you'd be okay about it."

"It'll be good. I know the area already so it won't be totally alien." I was born in Chesham, which, according to Google, is about seven miles from Hemel and Tring, in different directions so sort of a triangle with the A41 along one side. Ish. I was young when we moved to Tring though but still have a soft spot for Chesham. Chesham Glass. The Wagon and Horses. Waggon? But my focus is Hemel.

I know the Plough roundabout – the 'magic roundabout' according to the locals – a large roundabout with five, no six smaller ones around it. It's a nightmare if you don't know where you want to get to but treat each separately and you're fine. As I said, I know the Plough but everywhere else in the town is a bit hazy.

There's a nice park somewhere near the road along from the old Kodak building, which is flats now, Living Well, or something that's like the gym chain. Carry on from there and you get to the old village, which I suppose Hemel was at one point. I think the town centre is similar to any other; a shopping centre or two with other shops dotted around it. It'll be fun getting to know it.

Then I realise I don't know where our offices are down there. Maybe they're on one of the industrial parks out of town. That won't be so much fun but I'm not there to have fun. Am I.

"Donna?"

I realise I'm staring at a small ant crawling across my desk as I'm thinking… miles away. About forty miles from Northampton. I make a mental note to google that too. I leave the ant to negotiate one of my coasters and look back up at Izzy. "Huh?"

"You said, 'It'll be good. I know the area already so it won't be totally alien.' Or something like that."

I think it was exactly like that. "Yes. It'll be fine." Then there's Duncan. Things aren't particularly rosy between us at the moment and I don't know if this'll help or hinder.

As if she's reading my mind, she asks about him.

"He's fine." Fine. Everything's 'fine', which it isn't. But it will be. I'm half-glass-full Donna. I see the best in everyone and everything. I know I'm really lucky. I have Duncan, Hunky Dunky, a wonderful caring vet who everyone loves. I adore him. It's just circumstances. We'll be fine, more than fine. The lady doth protest. No. It will.

I sit up a little straighter in my chair and smile. Until an email pings into my inbox. "Ooh."

Izzy's still looking at me, waiting for me to say something. She points at my screen. "Is that from Hemel?" She can't see from where she is and is far too polite to lean forward and… She leans forward. "What does it say?"

I open the email and scan the contents. "Oh."

"Oh? What does it say?"

"Nothing about why she's off."

"But you're just there the month, yes?"

I scan a bit more of the email. "It doesn't say. William promised… well, not promised but said it would just be a month."

"Do you want me to have a word with him?" She looks at the kitchen but, like for me earlier, it's not possible to see anything much. As if by instinct, we turn to his office and he's there, drinking a cup of something, coffee probably. We turn back and give each other the 'he's made himself a drink!' expression and laugh.

I love Izzy. Most people don't 'get' her, she's serious on the outside, but I know inside she's like marshmallow. Not as soft as me so I guess I'm like melted marshmallow but…

"I'll have a word tonight."

I blow her a kiss and mouth a 'thank you'. "He did say you'd help me though I'm not sure what I need help with yet."

"At least he gave you *some* warning."

I think back to the previous May. William had told, instructed, Izzy the morning of the first of May, the first day she was supposed to meet someone, and another thirty. The speed dating ended up being a bit of a bonus, in more ways than one for Duncan and me.

She's right; at least I have a week's notice. Seven days to plan thirty-one dishes, or at least the first one, and move two counties… Buckinghamshire's between Northants and Hertfordshire, not counting the brief flirtation with Bedfordshire as I bypass Leighton Buzzard. Some would say not a bad thing but the rare occasion I've driven through there it looks really nice.

"And will Duncan be okay with it?" Izzy asks.

I shrug but she continues.

"Absence makes the heart grow fonder."

I want to say 'out of sight, out of mind' but fortunately resist. It's not like me to be half-glass-empty but it's not like her to be quite so positive. William really has changed her. No, that's not fair. She's always been adorable, it's just her skin's more porous these days so the adorability exudes somewhat easier. Adorability. I like that.

"Better get back," she says and points to her desk.

I mouth another 'thank you' and turn my attention to the email. It's quite official with the office's address – not one I recognise so will google it – together with parking arrangements (on site, fortunately, which makes me think it's not town centre), details who to report to – Hazel in HR – who will provide me with my ID badge, computer log in etc. I'm surprised I won't be using my own but remember that I'm Veronica for the month. I make a mental note to ask William whether I'm to pretend to be Veronica or whether this project will be under my own name but I can ask Izzy to ask him that.

I feel sorry for Duncan. In a way it's perfect timing, but in another respect it's lousy. What's to stop him going off with someone else when I'm not home? I don't often feel insecure but I'm feeling it right now. It's only a month, I tell myself, but a month is a long time in a relationship of less than a year. And I'll be away for our anniversary. Not the day, evening, we met, that was the fifteenth, but our first date, when we 'got together'. Ooh, it's warm today, I think, as I fan myself with a 'Maybelline' coaster.

On the 'Calendar' on my computer, I skip forward to May the eighteenth and see it's a Friday. Mmm. Could be worse; a mid-week when I can't see him, but could have been better; a weekend. We'd do something in the evening. Maybe I could leave work early… or have a work-from-home day. Counting just the weekdays, it's only twenty-five days away. A lot can happen in twenty-five days.

I decide to tell my mum before Duncan. Good news before bad. I send her a quick text and have only just put my mobile back on my desk when it quacks. I forgot to put it on silent so some of my colleagues look at me and I can feel my face flush. I put up a quick hand to Karen, my fashion colleague, and Keith, our agony 'aunt'. Fortunately it didn't penetrate the glass between my desk and William's office, and his PA, Janine, is on the phone so didn't hear it.

Mum's just texted a 'yay' which is typical of her. She's only in her sixties but not the biggest of technology buffs. She left that all to my dad. My uncle's more the whizz when it comes to iPods, iPads and everything 'i'. As is Izzy. She's my number one go-to in most respects, but hey, you know that by now.

Chapter 4 – Talking It Through

Izzy's back at my desk and tapping her watch. I look at the tiny clock bottom-right of my monitor and it tells me that it's not only lunchtime but ten past lunchtime. Where's this morning gone?

I know the answer to that one. Reading and re-reading the email from Hemel. From someone called Ian. I look at his email address and it's iedwards@... Ian doesn't admit to being a job of any description so I assume he's also human resources or maybe security... or perhaps IT. The only Ians I know are Ian Beale from EastEnders – who doesn't exist – and Ian Botham, the cricketer – one of my mum's favourites, and of course, I don't actually *know* him.

Izzy's hovering, not tapping her watch anymore but I can tell she wants to.

"Sorry, yes." I grab my bag – it looks too nice outside for a jacket – and follow Izzy down the hall. Sometimes she forgets that her legs are so much longer than mine that I have to skip, not quite hop or jump to catch up but not far off.

Frosty's on reception and engrossed in something or other. Marion's surname is Frist but Izzy nicknamed her Frosty (just to me) and it stuck. Her being busy lets us off the hook from her steely glare, which is always a blessing. You'd think she'd lighten up given that she and Mike, our usual daytime security guard and my one-time beau, oh Lord, are an item, and have been for months. They think we don't know but they're not at all discreet. To start with, other than William – because he's the boss – Mike is the only person Frosty's nice to, and not just nice but gushy. It's quite stomach churning.

Speaking of which, he's got what looks like jam on his jumper as we pass him down in the main foyer. I'm hoping it's jam. Either that or he's killed something or someone, and while he's not the softest person on the planet, that would be beyond him. Terminator Two's Arnold Schwarzenegger Mike is not.

We exchange the briefest of smiles, much to Izzy's chagrin, and head out onto the main road. I assume we're off to do the usual Market Square Boots meal deal trip and I let Izzy go slightly ahead, which isn't difficult because again she's forgotten that her steps are like Bigfoot compared with my... whatever the opposite of Bigfoot is. Littlefoot? Lightfoot.

That reminds me of an author my mum likes, Freda Lightfoot, and I make yet another mental note to see if my mum's got her latest book. Knowing her, she'll have bought it on publication day, she's that big a fan, but without the technology to hand she may not have received 'the memo'.

Yes, again, we patronise Boots and I go for prawn. I usually go for chicken but I fancy prawn today. Prawn in a light – of course, I am the health and beauty columnist (just don't tell my readers about the huge bar of Galaxy chocolate lurking in my desk's top drawer) – Marie Rose sauce. It makes me wonder who Marie Rose actually was, assuming she exists, and I add that to the 'to google' list.

"My treat," Izzy says and takes my lunch from me.

"Ahh, thank you." I step from the queue so I'm not in the way. I take the time to dig out my mobile and hit the multi-coloured 'G' app square. I search for 'Marie Rose sauce' and up comes a helpful link to Wikipedia. I stab on that and I'm told:

Marie Rose sauce (known in some areas as cocktail sauce or seafood sauce) is a British condiment made from a blend of tomatoes, mayonnaise, Worcestershire sauce, lemon juice and pepper. A simpler version can be made by merely mixing tomato ketchup with mayonnaise. The sauce, as well as cocktail sauce, were ('was', I mentally correct) *invented in the 1960s by British cook Fanny Cradock.*

There's a little '1' after Fanny's name and I click on that, smiling at the difference between 'fanny', as a noun, in England vs. the United States. "Fanny pack," I whisper then smile as I add, "bum bag." The one takes me to *'The origins of 10 modern classic foods.' Channel 4. Archived from the original on April 6, 2014. Retrieved 6 June 2014.* I hit the back arrow as it's gone a little too off track. As have I.

Izzy joins me and we head out into the Market Square. We wander through the market, much of it second-hand on a Thursday, and I stop at a toy stall that also sells DVDs, music CDs and audiobooks. It's the latter that grabs my attention as they remind me I don't read enough.

Duncan's not a big reader and we tend to watch box sets together but there are times when he has to work late, or is called in for an emergency; a run-over pet or flea-ridden hedgehog. It's just as well he doesn't bring his work home with him. Not that Buddy, Duncan's... our beagle, would like it if he did. He barely tolerates me despite me often feeding and walking him. A one-person dog.

I squeal as I spot an Anna Jacobs audiobook. It looks very much Freda Lightfootesque and I think my mum will enjoy it. It's not her birthday for several months and Mother's Day was a while ago but she'll be putting me up, or putting up with me, for a month so it'll be a small contribution to rent. Three pounds fifty. Very small.

Izzy's flicking through the DVDs and has already picked out a couple which are lying flat on a row next to her. I crane my neck but can only see the top one. I smile at the picture of Will Ferrell in front of a post-9/11 New York 'cursing the heavens in futility'… as Emma Thompson put it. *Stranger than Fiction* is one of my favourite films and I'm surprised Izzy's not got it already but I'm more surprised that I don't know that fact for sure. I have no clue what the other DVD will be.

It seems that it's just the two for today. She usually buys at least one – she's a DVD hoarder is our Izzy despite our love of Prime and Netflix. As the woman, one of two sisters I think but have never asked, takes the DVDs, I see the other cover. It's *The Hitman's Bodyguard*. Being another film I love, I want to cheer. With the market surprisingly busy, I resist, but my stomach is doing flips on my mouth's behalf. Still, I know, it's only a film but my brain's not right at the moment. It's too full of William's project, Duncan, and what could have been. I need to clear it so I shake it and it just hurts.

"You okay?" the woman serving asks.

I smile sweetly and say, "Yes, thank you. A wasp, I thought."

She appears horrified and looks around. I think she must be allergic, no, anaphylactic. When she gets stung. I look around too but there's no sign of wasps. Not that I actually thought there was. "Sorry," I say as if to appease her and go to wander off but realise I've not paid for the audiobook. And that I've not finished looking through them.

I do so and buy the Anna Jacobs along with a James Patterson Michael Ledwidge combo. *Step on a Crack*. It's the only one of his I've read in its entirety, in paperback version, and I was exhausted. It was brilliant but edge-of-your-seat stuff and I'm looking forward to listening to it. I'm normally a chick flick… no, chick lit… actually both… kind of person, I love romance, but every now and then you just need a bit of thrilling. I giggle and the woman giving me my change smiles. She probably thinks I'm completely deranged but so be it. She wouldn't be the only one.

Izzy and I spend the rest of our break sitting on a bench on the edge of the market square eating our lunch and talking about 'Project Donna'. We've not thought of an official name but that's because 'Project Donna' so far only consists of the concept and a strategy for breaking the news to Duncan. He'll be okay because he's so busy with work and I'm probably worrying more than is necessary, but apart from the 'blip', the no-baby blip, things are great and I don't want to change that.

We, Izzy and I, have agreed that I'm not going to sugar-coat it, it's only a month after all. No favourite meal, soft lighting and wham! Maybe we'll do that anyway, because we do, but I'll tell him while we cook or before we get engrossed in the TV or something. The sooner the better. Like pulling off a plaster. That was Izzy's idea.

Chapter 5 – Breaking The News

Duncan takes it better than I'd expected. I break the news as soon as we get inside his house. We'd already arranged for me to go over there and we arrive at the same time so rather than faff about talking small talk, I do it.

"And you're really okay with this?" I ask as he's tucking his car keys into his jacket pocket hanging up on the rack above the hall radiator.

He turns round and plants a kiss on my right cheek. "Of course. William's asked so..."

"Not really asked but yes, I suppose I have a choice."

"But you want to do it."

Although I'd thought of little else the whole afternoon, I really wasn't sure. Part of what was holding me back was Duncan but as he's taking it so well, I didn't need to worry. So why am I? Out of sight, I tell myself then go with Izzy's more positive 'absence makes the heart' and all that. I guess we'll see one way or another.

He pulls me towards him and kisses me passionately. I feel myself melting as if the radiator behind him is turned up to full. "I love you," he whispers into my ear and I'm almost a puddle as I whisper the same.

We walk hand-in-hand into the kitchen and set about making dinner. It's lasagne, and regardless of how busy he is, Duncan always insists on making meals from scratch. I should be like that, being a 'health expert', but I'm not and feel all the more of a fraud for it. I'm a convenience queen and think that if Messrs Asda, Tesco and Sainsbury want to help me out by doing all the work for me, why should I resist? I'm like Izzy in that respect.

But Duncan's right. It means we spend more time together and it's fun. And there's no doubt it keeps the flame alive, not that there should be anything to dampen it, not after only a year. I think too much.

The meal cooked, the conversation returns to Hemel Hempstead as Duncan pours me some Merlot. It's a McGuigan Bin, which isn't overly inspiring as it makes me think of the Irish boxer and 'bin'? But it sounded nice when Duncan bought it from Amazon.

"Rich and full flavoured," I recall as Duncan pours some into his own glass. "Aroma of red plums with herby notes to balance. This Merlot shows great fruit flavours of blackberry, raspberry, cherry and ripe red plum. These are nicely integrated with soft caramel and vanilla oak characters to create a smooth, soft and easy-drinking red wine."

Duncan laughs and takes a sip. I should know what I'm talking about because any kind of food and drink comes under my 'health' banner, and there's been enough speculation about whether red wine is good for you or not over the past few decades so it's a column I can repeat, updated of course, quite often. Not that I do; there are always plenty of other topics to talk about.

Like Izzy, I write six columns a week. Again, like her, I can do them in advance. I can cheat easier than her dating because I could carry over a lunch or dinner to another day. While she had to be very careful about not giving away what she was doing, I can be very open about mine and for that I'm grateful.

"And you'll be back at the weekends," Duncan says, picking up our earlier conversation.

"Or you could come to Mum's." He could. She adores him and vice versa. She's as pleased as anyone that I'm finally 'off the shelf', not that I wasn't when I was dating Mike but she didn't like him at all. And on reflection, I can't say I blame her.

"I could. I'd like that."

"Are you rostered to do any Saturdays next month?"

He purses his lips and squints as if deep in thought. It's his practice, so technically he can work whenever he likes, or not, but he's a very fair boss and of course, who really wants to work at the weekends, especially when they have families?

It's so easy to come back to that topic. Families. Children. Babies. However hard I try, I can't help thinking about it. It's really silly but… No, I'm going to keep busy. I will be busy; planning and doing these thirty-one dishes. I smile, a grin almost, and Duncan puts down his fork, lasagne barely touched. He stands and my eyes follow his. He walks around the table, holds my hands in his, lifts me from my chair and leads me upstairs.

Chapter 6 – Preparation, Preparation, Preparation

We resurface an hour later, both grinning. It's not only patched but I think cemented any cracks there were in our relationship. We did a lot of talking in between… I blush.

We know we want to be together, we've talked plenty about our future. We'll leave it to fate. I'll go off to Hemel for the month then we'll resume life thereafter. We'll both be busy; Duncan's reminded me he had a couple of seminars in London in May, as well as training a new senior member of staff so the month will fly by. I hope.

So, I'm back to being bouncy Donna… no, Tigger D, as Izzy so fondly refers to me, and I'll make the most of the new experiences the temporary relocation will bring.

A list. I need to write a list. Not quite a shopping list as Izzy did but I will have to make sure I have everything I need. Other than a toothbrush, there's nothing of mine at my mum's house.

Duncan's gone to work early but we had breakfast together so I'm sitting here, still in my pyjamas, surrounded by empty dishes which I'll pop into the dishwasher but first things first. I grab a notebook and two pens, one blue, one black, in case I need to split the list for some reason. I don't know why but girl scout and all that.

What do I want to achieve this month? That's a good place to start. A balanced reportage. Interesting places without it being restaurant reviews; Izzy was very careful of that with her pubs. For her it was all about the dates; for me it'll be the dishes. So I start my list… of lists:

– List of things to take: suitcase, laptop, phone, chargers, clothes etc. Enough for a week or the whole month?

– List of pubs and restaurants in Hemel Hempstead: lunch (alone or with colleagues) and dinner (with Mum? With Aunt Jan and Uncle Pat?). Breakfast?

– List of pubs and restaurants in Tring. Definitely with family. Not breakfast unless the weekend, not practical.

– List of types of dishes. Not as mad as it sounds. Aunt Jan and Uncle Pat are vegetarians so something to bear in mind.

– List of places around the area. Why stick with Hemel and Tring? Repeat places or go somewhere just once? It would make the project more interesting but possibly more complicated.

I draw a little arrow to the left of the list of places to point to underneath Tring then think how much easier it would have been to make this list of lists on my computer. I have to type it up anyway – but I've started so I'll finish, like a dog with a b– Buddy. What's going to happen to Buddy while I'm away? Of course Duncan managed before I came on the scene but he'll be away too at his seminars.

Then my brain takes me to images of skinny skirt-suited professional women flocking around him, talking about the things that make sense to him: diseases… aspergillosis for example. Poor William. He was heartbroken when his parrot, his Baby… I sniff. I have to think of something else. When did I become so insecure?

Come on, Tigger D. Bounce. I think of Duncan and our interlude last night and my smile returns. A big… no, huge grin in fact. It always does the trick.

So… back to the list. What have I got so far? Things to take… places… dishes. What else? I have no clue. I'll just wing it. That's what Izzy did and she was fine.

I look at the microwave's clock. Oops.

Not really time to dump everything in the dishwasher but I do it anyway. Duncan prefers the place neat and tidy (don't they mean the same thing?)… clean and tidy then, and it'll only take a few seconds. His house, you see, is very much a bachelor pad. Lots of black, grey and white. He doesn't have many possessions, or rather he has the usual amount but lots of storage so everything's neatly hidden from view, unlike my flat, which is… well, not.

I look around the open-plan lounge / dining area and nod. Possibly not up to Duncan standards but I'll probably be home first anyway. Home. I like the sound of that. I have an ongoing lease on my flat and only have to give six weeks' notice but if I'm away for a month… No, too soon. Wait for life to return to normal.

After a shower, I feel much better, almost back to normal. It does that. Not sure how but it does. It's like it washes the blah away. PMA. Positive mental attitude. Yes. PMA.

Chapter 7 – Tick, Tick, Tick

Tuesday 24th April

I'm whistling when I get to work and Mike gives me a strange look. I stop whistling as I stare at his jumper. The jam (I'm hoping) stains are still there so he's not only wearing the same jumper – not very surprising as it's his security uniform – but he's not noticed it needs washing. I had such a lucky escape.

I give him the briefest of smiles, and walk on, whistling again. The last track to play in my car was Queen's *Somebody to Love*, one of my favourites, and it's become my earworm. Izzy and I used to sing it at the top of our voices whenever it came on at Chicago's. Happy days.

We were both single then, and looking, and it was very much our mantra. Everyone else in the bar… club?… was singing too, and it was such a wonderful experience. Strangers became friends for a few minutes, a couple of hours – we didn't just stop at Queen – then were lost again as we all went our separate ways. It's a shame really that life's like that but there we go.

I get a smile from Frosty when I walk past reception. She's on the phone, sounding her very professional self, so it was probably a slip… or leftover wind from breakfast.

Izzy's at her desk but on the phone. There's no evidence of a drink in her vicinity so I go to the kitchen and make something for both of us. She likes chai tea – her own – work doesn't do anything other than cash and carry PG tips, so I make one of those and a coffee for myself.

She's off the phone by the time I rejoin her.

"Eh up. How are things?" she asks me in a fake northern accent. Northampton's a dozen or so miles south of the Watford Gap, a service station known as the unofficial north / south divide, so we're still considered the south.

I think about last night and give her a goofy grin.

"Oh… like that? Good on ya."

I can feel a blush flooding my face. I open my mouth to speak but shut it again.

"I'll see you later," I finally blurt and scuttle to my desk.

I'd forgotten to print off the email from Hemel and hadn't taken my work laptop to Duncan's… because I had no intention of doing any work, so couldn't remember everything it had said. I thought it would help me with compiling my list, the paper version of which I dig out from my bag as soon as I've deposited my mug on my coaster.

I log onto my computer and bring up the email without looking for any new ones. I print it double sided and highlight the important things: the collecting ID, log ins etc. I google the address and am relieved that it's on the edge of the town centre, not far off from the gardens whose name I can't remember and the Kodak-building-cum-nice-apartments. Not that I know whether they're nice or not but the building's blue and it can't have been that long ago since it changed.

I google it. Wikipedia tells me that Kodak vacated in 2005 and that it's called the K D Tower – no relation to the singer Lang presumably, and converted over a decade ago so longer than I thought but I only drive past… ish; I see it when I get to the bottom of the long hill from the M1 motorway, before turning left so I don't actually go that near it but it cuts an impressive figure nonetheless.

As you can tell I'm easily distracted but I'm going to have to be focused for the next month… or rather the next few days then next month. So checklist. Ah, one thing I didn't put on my list is who I have to tell. Right…

Duncan. Tick.

Izzy. Tick.

My mum. Tick.

Er… I do have other friends but no one I absolutely positively have to tell right this instant. I look at the list of three names and I feel quite sad. This really isn't like me. I'm usually the life and soul and that in itself makes me feel sad. I then come to the conclusion that this 'thirty-one dishes' project couldn't have come at a better time.

It's nearing the end of April yet I'm feeling as if summer's been and gone, and I have only a cold harsh winter to look forward to. I need the proverbial slap round the face and I know just the thing.

Chapter 8 – Izzy Pick-me-up

Unlikely as it may seem, because she's more sensible and serious than I am, Izzy is the cure for all my ills… she and Duncan usually. So I abandon the list and head over to her desk.

I can feel my brow furrow… as my dad would have put it; he was quite old-fashioned, more so than my mum who's a young sixty-six. "Clickety click," I whisper and laugh. Izzy's on the phone, for a change, and she's smiling. She's looking at me so I don't know whether she's smiling at me, or laughing or to whoever she's talking to on the phone.

The reason for my brow furrowing, by the way, is an object Izzy has in her left hand, her right is still cradling the phone. The 'thing' is quite difficult to describe. It looks like an animal, no a large bug. I shiver.

I stand by her desk and wait. I'd offer to go to the kitchen and make a drink but it's too warm for a hot one and we had the last of the Cokes yesterday. We have to supply them – work gives us water and two flavours of cordial but they get a bit repetitive after a while – so I can nip to Sainsbury's on the way home, or better on the way in tomorrow or I'd be taking them back to Duncan's and knowing him, and me, they'd probably stay there.

Izzy finally comes off the phone and grins broader.

"Everything okay?" I ask.

"One of my suppliers. I usually email them when I receive something but this…" she points to the 'thing' "arrived with no instructions. I thought it was easier to give Renu a call to see if it's similar to the one they sent me last year."

I'm torn between asking what the 'thing' actually is but am now more fascinated by the name she's just mentioned. "Renu?"

"Yes. My contact there. She's really sweet. Product development for the tech company who supplied this. Never met her, of course, as they're based up in… Newcastle, I think. New something."

I wasn't expecting a 'she'. Interesting. I want to rack my brains for other possible 'New's in that part of the country but the only one I can come up with is America's New Hampshire so I'm now back to the 'thing'. "And what is 'this'?" I point to the bug.

"Oh, a grasshopper."

I wasn't far off then.

"Except this one, Renu tells me, isn't wind up but USB generated."

"And you've got to test and review it?"

"Uh huh."

Although I'm not technology minded… at all, I'm a little green. More fun than testing a new shade of lipstick, 'boldest' mascara, or revolutionary diet that everyone who's A-list (or Z-list) is following. "Drink?" I ask and point towards the kitchen.

"Erm…" she says and looks down at her almost-full glass of summer fruits squash.

"No problem," I say and debate whether to have the same or orange.

"Can't really join you at the moment, sorry." She points to her screen. I'm guessing she has too much work to do.

"No problem," I repeat and stand there, not sure whether I do actually want a drink or if I should just return to my desk with my proverbial tail between my legs. I really don't know what's got into me lately but not even my Izzy-pick-me-up is working… probably because she didn't actually pick me up.

I don't have a drink on my desk so I head for the kitchen to get one anyway. It won't be the end of the world if I get half a glass and it sits on my VW campervan coaster until it goes warm… which would be a lot quicker without the air conditioning turned on.

"Come on, Donna," I tell myself as I crack into action. "You've got less than a week until you have to go AWOL."

"Everything going well with that?" a voice behind me says and I squeak.

I turn round and there's William, waiting in line with a mug in his hand. I move back, squash in my left hand, glass in the other.

"Don't let me stop you," he says and smiles.

Janine, his PA, used to get most of his drinks but he seems to have been more liberated, or at least capable, since he started dating Izzy. She's a good influence all round. There are still professional boundaries of course but his rougher edges seem to have softened. Hoorah for that. Not that they were really ever that sharp. I'd never heard him shout but more formidable, you might say, forthright…? No, garnered respect. I sound more like my parents, my dad anyway, every day.

"Thank you, yes," I reply, to his earlier question. "Arrangements made, plans drawn, that kind of thing." Despite me having no clue as to what dishes I'll actually be eating, or where, I figure I still have plenty of time to make, draw, those plans.

Boy, am I wrong.

Chapter 9 – All Systems Go

Sunday 29th April

The rest of the week flies by and it's the day of my 'move'. I'm not ready. I am but don't feel it.

I stare at the toaster, waiting for the cinnamon and raisin bagels to pop up, but more staring than waiting. Despite it being Sunday, Duncan's nipped into work – something to do with the new trainee – and it feels as if we (Duncan and I, not him and his trainee) haven't talked very much since we got home, his house, last night. I wanted to have breakfast together but fell asleep again and by the time I'd got up, he'd gone. He left a lovely note, with extra kisses, but it's not the same.

So Tigger D is a little late coming out of her shell this morning but surface she will. I'm keeping my PMA to the fore and seizing life. That lust that Izzy... er, no... I shake my head... Iggy Pop sings about. "Alexa, please play *Lust for Life*."

Alexa, Duncan's Amazon Echo, blue rings and announces *Lust for Life by Lana Del Rey on Amazon Music*.

Not what I was expecting but okay. Ooh, it's very slow. Nice but no, too slow, too... not quite depressing but not what I need. Another time for sure.

"Alexa stop."

And she stops. She's my second, no third favourite female. I have to put my mum before her and Izzy, don't I. But there's my aunt Jan, so fourth.

"Alexa, please play *Lust for Life* by Iggy Pop."

Lust for Life by Iggy Pop on Amazon Music.

That's more like it. It immediately gets me tapping my toes, my shoulders wiggling and before I know it, I'm bopping around the kitchen. I've forgotten all about the bagels and look over to the toaster only to see they popped up ages ago and have probably gone cold and hard. I shrug. Not the worst thing in the world. I pop them down for a few seconds to at least warm a little, even if it makes them harder, and bop while not letting them out of my sight.

I tap the stop button when I feel they're probably done enough and frown as two black rings appear. Fortunately they're not scorched enough for the smoke alarm to crack into life but the bagels certainly don't look particularly appetising. I shrug again and pull them out anyway. They're not hot enough to burn my fingers so I can carry them across to the plate, which I'd normally bring to the toaster. It's a fine art, this eating lark... as my readers are going to find out over the next month. Eek.

I've already packed – I did that yesterday morning when Duncan was at work... the joy (not) of being the boss – but there are the last-minute things like laptops (mine and work's), mobile (mine – no one other than William has a work mobile) and all the gazillions of cables that accompany them… okay three but I also want to take my Kindle, CD drive (because I have some audiobooks I've not transferred onto my laptop yet), then I have a spare USB plug for my step-counter watch because the lead for my Kindle is one unit, ditto the mobile and laptop cables.

It's very complicated living in the twenty-first… twenty-first? Yes, it's only the twenty-first century. Not that the likes of Izzy would think so. She loves technology but that's her job. I'd last five minutes as a technology columnist and probably four of those minutes would be trying to work out how to switch on whatever I was supposed to test and review!

No, I'm being hard on myself. I'm very capable. Just ask Izzy and Duncan. He always says how proud he is of me but that's more general rather than technology specific.

So, packing. Be ready for when Duncan comes back. I hope he comes back.

I look at the clock. It's only just gone ten. I don't have to leave until four. I decide to make the most of my time and power up my work laptop. I could use my own but I try to keep everything separate. I have nothing personal on my work laptop. William wouldn't appreciate it. I can access my work emails on my phone if I need to, which I try not to, but no, I compartmentalise.

With Google ready, I bring up my saved list of restaurants and pubs in Hemel Hempstead. I know Tring much better and given that I'm starting work on Monday… tomorrow… eek! I'll at least be having lunch out somewhere then. Even if it's not 'out' and it's a van in the car park or canteen meal… I don't know if they have a canteen. I've seen from Google maps that their building is smaller so they probably do the van thing with more snacky options in a vending machine or kitchen. But I can't do snacks for the next month.

And oh, I'm going to have to weigh myself… aren't I? I've really not thought this through. I'm hoping I'll be given more instructions. I should speak to William, or at least William via Izzy. But he didn't seem too sure himself. No, I'll wait. I'll see what Hazel, the HR lady, and company tell me as I settle in and just go with the healthiest options of whatever there is on offer and start some kind of report. An interesting one though. It has to be interesting. Gulp.

Chapter 10 – And I'm Off

Duncan doesn't get home until three… an injured cat making him late apparently. He's normally a tough cookie when it comes to his patients but I can see his hands shaking when he hangs his jacket up in the hall. I don't say anything but give him a hug. He sniffs, says he's getting a cold, but I know better. That's why I love him.

Speaking of which, I won't go into detail – sparing all our blushes – but we go straight to the bedroom and I'm pleased I've got all my stuff ready as we don't come out until three fifty and then my mind isn't on travelling, but travel I must so I gather my bags into the hall and double-check I have everything.

I have a quick look around Duncan's flat, which is a little pointless as I'd brought everything over from mine already packed but have convinced myself that I'd unpacked something while waiting. Of course I haven't but I'm a little OCD like that. I'll be back on Friday. As long as I have enough clothes, my work laptop, mobile phone and money… oh, and car keys, I'll be fine.

I'm only just on the M1 and I can feel my eyes drooping. I've fallen asleep before (on the M6 coming back from Manchester after a party at 3am in the middle of winter, a couple of decades ago, well before Duncan) and it was no fun so I turn up the music – Heart FM – the start of the Vodafone Big Top 40 with Marvin Humes. The songs will probably be quite fast so I should be okay.

Way down at forty is what sounds like a love ballad for penguins. Marvin hasn't said who it's by but I can see why it's at the bottom of the chart. I feel old to think it's dreary but it's not helping my drowsiness. I'm grateful that my entire journey is around forty-five minutes, which I roughly calculate – allowing time for adverts and some chat – will get me no more than eight tracks. So from number forty to thirty-two… no, thirty-three inclusive. Not necessarily a great forty-five minutes but hey, it'll probably include songs I've never heard of as I'm not usually in my car, or near a radio – one that's on anyway – at four on a Sunday afternoon. It makes a change.

I'm not halfway to Milton Keynes, junction 14, when the traffic slows. That's saying something given that much of the journey has been fifty mile an hour roadworks. They're making the motorway 'smart' and I've encountered other 'smart' and my heart sinks. Someone, a boffin somewhere, has concluded that having everyone slow down to sixty, fifty or forty will make everyone's journeys quicker because there won't be so much slowing as speeding. Go figure.

I get excited when we go over thirty but only a hundred feet or so later we're crawling again. The electronic '50' signs are teasing. The hard shoulder is open, mostly containing lorries, so we have four lanes at our disposal but it's the 'sheer weight of traffic' as reports often call it. I'm London bound, albeit only to junction eight, as is the rest of the UK population it would seem. I don't know how anyone could do this day in day out but this will be me for the next five weeks; work down south, travel back to the cheaper north for the weekends.

I usually drive over the M1 at junction 15, bypassing Grange Park industrial estate on the outskirts of Northampton, and head down the A508 through pretty villages (Roade and Grafton Regis amongst them) before hitting the A5 then another A-road whose number I've forgotten – or possibly never known despite it being on the signs I'm absentmindedly following, skirting around Leighton Buzzard, and smiling as I drive through Horton and pretend to be Jim Carrey in the animated movie where he hears a 'who'. This time, however, I want to go through Hemel so it's M1 all the way to the A414 then down the hill to the magic roundabout and Kodak.

I use the word 'want' loosely. We've come to a halt and I look at the clock. It's heading for five pm quicker than I am. I frown as I realise that doesn't make any sense but my head's so scrambled that it's probably logical somewhere in the universe, like Arthur Dent's comment about having tremendous difficulty with his lifestyle. Crazy as it sounds, I know the exact phrase but don't want to say it, even in my head, in case there's a Vogon ship captain in the ether who misinterprets it and sentences the Earth to destruction… not until I sort things out with Duncan anyway.

Apparently there's going to be a new *Hitchhiker's Guide to the Galaxy* film… or whichever is the next instalment of the franchise. I love Douglas Adams's humour but even can never remember the order they come in. Izzy knows it – her brother Mark is a huge fan. As with most things to do with her family, it's come up in conversation at some point.

Is it the one about fish? I don't know but I'm a huge… no big, I don't specifically follow what he's doing so big… medium-sized Martin Freeman fan. I love the film he was in with Amanda Peet about serendipity, not the Kate Beckinsale serendipity with John whatshisname… Cusak. Oh no, that was Simon Pegg. Not with Kate but Amanda. And it was… *I Love You, Man*? No, that was American with… the guy with the nice smile. *Man Up*. That was it.

I need the traffic to be moving as I'm thinking way too much but smile as I spot a lorry in the outside lane – which I don't think should actually legally be in the outside lane – for Wetherspoons. I thought it was a government lorry with its huge green sign with white 'Running Clean & Green' heading but spotted the non-capitalised wetherspoon underneath it. wetherspoon singular, I note. Journalists, columnists, are like writers, we're both of course, in that we're grammar er… Nazis. I hate using that term these days but we are sticklers. Yes, sticklers, that's better.

So rather than put a picture of something delicious on the side, it's green and white. Probably just as well as my stomach's rumbling so at least I don't have anything other than that reminding me I'm supposed to be at my mum's having lovely smells wafting across her kitchen diner. This, the two-tone, albeit very planet-friendly (other than the fuel it emits) lorry, I've got it across from me for goodness knows…

Ooh! We're moving. Yay!

Chapter 11 – Familiar Territory

I finally reach my mum's at ten past six. Not a happy bunny. Me nor my mum. I did warn her before I left that it wouldn't be the usual forty-five minutes, though I'd convinced myself with the calculation of the Top 40 that it would be, and had left double that time. "No problem!" she'd chirped, though I know she dishes up on time when she's cooking. Five thirty. Very early but she prefers a structured day. When she's home. And who likes being late?

We're having lasagne and I can't help smiling. Duncan and I had to reheat ours the other night because we got a little heated. I cough. I'm glad I'm only thinking these thoughts and–

"Are you okay?" Mum asks.

I realise I've been staring at an embroidered poppy and matching ladybird on the tablecloth. I look up and laugh at Mum's apron. It's a picture of a sexy body. A man's sexy body. Needless to say it's not my mum's but my dad's – the apron not the actual bod… I feel a little sad but remember when he'd opened it one Christmas and howled with laughter. And I mean howled. Tears and everything. That had set us off, not that it takes much with my mum. She's the hyper version of me, and that's saying something. I might be Tigger but she's the Duracell bunny. When you're not late.

"Yes, thank you."

"Set for tomorrow?"

A stone plummets in my stomach as I'm reminded of what lies ahead. I've done scant research and other than Wetherspoons with a capital W and ending s – I'm a rebel, I've got no real plan.

I'm only hoping that the editor at Hemel knows more about this project than I do. William said he's leaving it to me but I'm pretty sure there'll be some kind of structure. If not then I'll wing it. No I won't. I'm not a wing-it kind of person. I admit I like to know where I'm going, what I'm doing. Izzy's more a fly by the seat of your pants. A pantser? Whereas I'm more of a plotter, though you wouldn't think it by what I've arranged already. Barely more than nada. Maybe I can be different here, spread my wings a little. For work, anyway. "Yes, thanks, Mum."

"It'll be fine." She knows me too well.

Dinner was scrumptious. Mum's had a couple of decades' more practice at lasagne than me and for something so generic, you'd almost guess that our two versions weren't even related. Melt in your mouth is an understatement. I wonder if it's the type of mince she uses but I saw the packet and it's not. The pasta's supermarket own too, as is the cheese so it must have another 'secret' ingredient. It certainly wouldn't be the vegetables in the sauce.

Honey. Sometimes people add honey to things you wouldn't expect. Is my mum that crazy? Yep.

We spend the evening chatting and it's lovely to catch up. Normally we speak a lot, text more often, FaceTime sometimes in between visits; me to her, rarely her to me, but it's never enough to just 'chat'.

"Hottle wottle bottle?" she asks and I look up. As if I were to say no, she has it all done and it's between her outstretched hands. It was quite a warm day but it's got cooler. The heating goes off at eleven and with the blinds down, it feels positively arctic. Okay, slight exaggeration but it's a welcome offer nonetheless.

"Thanks, Mum." I take the bottle from her. 'Hottle wottle bottle' was what my dad used to say. He's the unspoken topic of many conversations. We go on but it's not the same. I have to think nice thoughts. It's been too long.

Oh, we solved the Buddy problem. Duncan's beagle. Off to Mark, Izzy's brother, his wife Ellen and their fabulous daughter Lola… L O L A Lola. I can't help it. Every time I hear the name I hum the Kinks song… Anyway, back at the ranch. I smile as I think of spaghetti westerns. My dad loved them. We'd slouch on the sofa when I was younger on rainy, the rainier the better, Sunday afternoons and watch them back to back. One movie after the other. Us back to back would be silly. One of us would be facing the wrong way.

So yes, they're going to have Buddy whenever Duncan needs him to. Mark thinks he's fabulous… Duncan rather than Buddy, although Buddy's a huge fan of Lola and vice versa but there doesn't seem to be a lot that L O L A doesn't like.

She wants a dog but Mark and Ellen have said she'll have to wait. They had horses for a while but I think they cost too much, as they do. We had an Irish Wolfhound when we were younger and he ate more than I did. Paddy, not named after my uncle Patrick, was a rescue. Too big probably, certainly nothing else 'wrong' with him. Lived to be twelve. Almost unheard of but it's not long at all and not when you don't know him until he's five. Or six. So he could have been thirteen.

It's one less thing for Duncan to worry about. Buddy. Not that he would. He's very level headed, way more than me. We're alike in so many respects but in others we're yang and yin. Or is it yin and yang? Whatever the opposite of chalk and cheese as our differences complement each other.

So upstairs I go with my hottle wottle bottle and only mildly panic about tomorrow. What's the worst that could happen?

Chapter 12 – Settling In

Monday 30th April

I arrive nice and early. Too early it seems. There's only the security guard on duty. I get on well with security guards, or used to, so it doesn't faze me, and Phil seems lovely. Only a few inches taller than me, he's not what I'd expect from a security guard… until he opens his mouth.

He should do voiceovers. He has a voice deeper than, oh I don't know, the Grand Canyon. That's deep, isn't it? Treacle. Or is that rich? Sticky. And my brain's back with Mike and his jam-splattered jumper. I shiver at the thought.

"Are you cold, honey?" Phil asks and goes to switch on a heater. It's not yet eight but almost May and certainly not arctic.

I smile and say, "I'm good, thank you." And he smiles. His teeth should also do adverts as they're more pearly than pearls. I wonder about the phrase 'pearly white' because I thought pearls were cream and think perhaps it's an East London cockney thing. Mike would know. His dad was a king. Not royalty or anything but occasionally dressed up in the black and white, cap and all, that the pearly kings, and queens, wear. I don't suppose he did it for charity but he was tradition through and through.

I want to ask Phil where he's from but figure that "Where are you from?" is a little impersonal although having known him for less than twenty minutes doesn't exactly make us bosom pals. So I settle for a more tactful, "Do I detect a hint of an accent?"

Phil smiles wider. "You do, honey. Phoenix."

"Arizona?"

"Uh huh."

As in the US, I want to add but fortunately stop myself because I feel foolish. Where else would it be?

"Isn't that Grand Canyon territory?" I ask and get another 'uh huh'. Had Phil been one of Izzy's dates she probably would have thought him dull but I think I'm going to like him. What am I talking about? He offered to put on a heater for me. He's practically Romeo.

That makes me think of Duncan and I get sad. Not because he makes me feel sad but I know I'm going to miss him. I'm looking forward to Friday already and hope the week will fly. It's rather scary how much I have to do between now and then but I'll get it done. If there's one thing I'm good at it's–

"Penny for 'em," Phil says from the periphery of my brain.

"Oh, sorry. Monday morning."

"Blues?"

I laugh. Had there been any ice, Phil would have just cracked it.

He points behind me and there, in the doorway of the security office is the most gorgeous man I've ever seen. *Apart from Duncan of course*, a little voice inside my head reminds me.

This one is Idris Elba meets Denzel Washington meets Jamie Foxx meets erm… whatshisname Johnson. The Rock. Okay so they're the only black sex gods that spring to mind but that's not a bad list for… I look down at my watch… ten past eight on a Monday morning. This Elba-Washington-Foxx-Johnson… ooh, that would make a great porn star name… has the most amazing almond eyes. They're like that super-rich doctor's from *Grey's Anatomy* who's probably been in plenty of other things since then – assuming he's gone, I've not watched it for ages – but will always be known for the hot young doctor from *Grey's Anatomy*. Not McDreamy, as… what was her name Grey, Meredith? Yes, Meredith Grey called him. Patrick something. Dempsey.

This McDreamy's mouth has moved but his words haven't registered. I'm still transfixed above his nose rather than below it but I can tell by the fact the rest of his face moved that he said something.

"Sorry?" I say and wipe the side of my mouth to sweep away the drool that I hope I'm only imagining.

"Good morning? You must be Donna aka Veronica."

Good morning definitely sounded like a question but yes, it most certainly is. I can almost feel the sun rising, the birds tweeting, and half expect Mary Poppins to appear in her blue attire, never-full bag and umbrella, and burst into song.

"James Norton, like the bike manufacturer," Phil says from beside me. "He's going to be shadowing you."

I picture me and this god standing next to each other, his shadow casting my easy-to-swamp-a-five-foot-two-and-a-half… I look at the space between him and the top of the doorframe. It's very Williamesque, so Adonis, sorry, James is probably also six foot four. I usually find really tall men intimidating – I do with William but William would, unintentionally, intimidate anyone, he just has this 'air'. And I wonder how thin the air actually is that high up. I get the wobbles just standing on a chair. I can't imagine being that tall all the time. But when you're used to nothing else…

"Donna?"

I'm not sure who's actually said my name as I'm still staring at the couple of inches between the top of James's head and the white strip of wood that looks newly decorated. My brain is in a world of its own and instead of thinking of work, I'm thinking of standing on chairs. Old brown wood with green plastic seating. Heaven help me. Or James can in the meantime, and by the sound of it he's going to.

I think I'm in heaven already.

Snap out of it.

I'm hoping that's my brain and not Mr Arizona or Mr… wherever James is from. He doesn't look like Hemel born and bred. Local yokels certainly weren't this hot when I lived in Tring.

I lower my eyes to his and his eyebrows are raised. Mighty fine… I shake my head. "Sorry. Got stuck in traffic on the M1 coming down here… to Tring last night, and it's sort of had a knock-on effect."

That's my excuse anyway. Or the best one I can come up with. I couldn't get to sleep last night so Mum and I were actually up till midnight finishing a jigsaw of a tiger by the edge of a river. It's a really famous picture, or I thought it was until I went to google it and found everything else but and had to click on 'Show more results' three times until the screen refused to show me any more. I did giggle at the picture of artist Bob Ross's hair on the way though so it was worth it. So did Mum, especially when she said hers was just as mad 'back then'.

I of all people know that there are more important things in life than getting frustrated at not knowing who painted a picture but it's still grating. As are Phil's teeth by the sound of it.

"Our very own Walter Mitty," James says and laughs.

I must be back in the room because I heard that word for word. And yes, something, or someone, snapped me back.

"Very pleased to meet you, James," I say, then to Phil, "And you, Phil. Thank you for the offer of a heater."

James pulls a 'but it's quite warm' face, or it's how I interpret it. I just smile and shrug.

"Ready, m'lady?" James asks, steps away and holds out a bent arm as if he's a Victorian gent offering to help a damsel across a puddle.

I look down, not sure why as I can't expect to see his jacket on the floor between us. I shake my head then realise that he'll take that as a 'no'. I'm feeling crazily foolish so I straighten up, smile and say, "As I'll ever be."

Chapter 13 – Mirror Image

The office is scarily like ours back in Northampton. It'll certainly make life easier when finding my way around. James takes me to a desk which, I work out quickly, would be Karen's back 'home'. That would make me next to Izzy's and I wonder whether this is the right way round but we're split up at our office because we'd talk too much. I've answered my own question.

This desk is incredibly tidy, almost as if someone's been fired and removed their belongings, no personal touches at all. Having spoken to Veronica a few times, I'd not got that impression of her but sometimes work is work and I admire her obvious clear-desk policy.

"Hazel will be in shortly," James tells me, "so she'll give you all the basics. Other than an initial password to get onto our system, your log in will be the same. She didn't see the point of setting up a new one. Veronica sorted out her workload before she went on leave so there shouldn't be any overlap. She does what you do, I'm assuming, so she's just paused it while you take over then she'll resume when she returns post bump."

"Post bump?"

"Baby. Didn't anyone tell you?"

I shake my head and feel the tears looming. I can't believe I'm being so emotional but I'm not in my comfort zone. It's a replica comfort zone but I feel like I need my people around me. I need Izzy. I look at the clock and it's not yet half past eight. The open-plan office is weirdly quiet. Ours is usually busy from six till six and later. Either they have less work to do or there's something going on.

As if reading my mind, James adds, "And I don't suppose anyone told you that it was a staff training morning today. They've all gone off to Boxmoor Hall."

"Except for you."

He half nods then shakes his head. "I offered to hold the fort."

I look in the direction of reception and James continues. "Phil's just external. You know, the actual security. We usually have Owen on reception but he's helped organise it all so…"

I smile at the thought of Frosty being replaced by a man, or more accurately how she would feel about being replaced by a man. The words 'balloon' and 'lead' spring to mind, although we do have Jason when she's not there.

"The phone system's automated. Apparently you don't have that yet so we're not quite mirror images."

"Automated?"

"Saying the name of the department or person or keywords, that kind of thing. I never actually ring the main number so I don't know but it's why Owen gets involved in other stuff. Apart from face-to-face there's little for him to do, although sometimes there's a mad moment on the phone so… Ah, there's Hazel."

A sixty-something woman with bright red hair and a terribly clashing tartan two-piece is unlocking an office opposite the kitchen. She's not how I'd pictured a Hazel at all, but I'm learning to expect the unexpected around here.

Mike would have shouted over to her but James is far more sophisticated. He walks… no, sways… no, sashays over to her. She's already in her office and is facing James so a large smile is plastered on her face by the time he reaches her. I can't see what he says as he has his back to me but she's fiddling with her hair. I find it endearing and know, or suspect, that she and I are going to get on. The thought reminds me of the scene in *Notting Hill* where Alice Tinker – or whatever the *Vicar of Dibley* actress's name was in *Notting Hill*… Honey, yes, it was Honey. William… Thackeray's sister so Honey Thackeray follows Julia Roberts aka… nope it's gone.

Anna Scott. Julia Roberts was Anna Scott. I smile as I remember the scene in the restaurant where she and William Thacker, not Thackeray, overhear a group of rowdy men putting Anna down and William offers to defend her honour. Anna says she would have done it herself but hesitates before giving them a piece of her very intelligent mind. Classic.

So, yes I'd be Honey to Hazel's Anna only not in the toilet underneath the stairs. That would be way too weird.

James turns and beckons me over. I don't feel them move but my legs take me to Hazel's office. I feel numb everywhere, not in a pins and needles way but that the world is revolving and I know I'm part of it but everything's surreal.

Hazel is as Scottish as her tartan, which she tells me is the Mackinnon before I've even asked – I am staring at it – but she says she's been a Smith for "longer than you've been alive, dearie". She reminds me of the television character Supergran who I struggled to understand when I was younger but Hazel's words seem to trip off her tongue and into my ears as easily as if I were wearing a babel fish. Good old Douglas Adams.

James leaves, doffing his imaginary cap and walking backwards as if he's a Shakespearian character, perhaps William himself. Just the thought of 'my' William, my boss, brings me back to the now and I return my gaze to Hazel who's sitting behind her desk and is holding out a piece of paper.

I smile and take the proffered sheet. It's a personnel form. The kind where they want to know your next of kin should something happen to you. I'm confused and it must be evident because she apologises.

"I'm sorry, dearie. Wrong one." She takes back the sheet. "We have that already." She opens a file and, like a bank clerk but without a rubber thimble, licks her right index finger and flicks through a few sheets. "This…" She holds out a sheet which this time is a security questionnaire. "Only the bits relevant to your car… er, I think that's all we need. And your name at the top."

"Of course." I take a pen that's lying between us and fill in my details, still a little confused that they don't have this information already. I hand it back and Hazel reads it.

"Just as well."

I wait for her to continue.

"We still had the Peugeot."

"Oh. That went a while ago. I'll let Chloë know." She's our HR lady, Hazel's equivalent, or one step down. I don't know yet if Hazel has an assistant. I figure she does but that she… or he… this is the twenty-first century… is at the team bonding thing.

"No need. We have a shared system. I'll update it now and that'll be job done."

"Excellent," I say and feel a bit lame. Izzy's the techie but I can appreciate how wonderful it all is.

Hazel taps a few keys and grins. "There we go. Now…"

We chat about why I'm here, my life history with the paper (which didn't take long – health and beauty columnist is the only job I've had there) and go off at several tangents along the way. Yes, Hazel's definitely my kind of woman. She does however explain why I'm there.

"Veronica, as you know, is on maternity leave, back June fourth. I think you're just here until the end of the month but it's fine to not have a handover. If you could leave her some notes it would be appreciated. She can log in from home and get the electronic files so she can see what you're up to…" She pauses. "Oh dear, that sounds very big brother but it's not, I assure you. She'll have her hands full with Ethan."

"Ethan?"

"The baby. Had him last week. Quite a big boy by all accounts, given that she's so trim and he's her fourth."

My heart's breaking but I try a smile. It seems to be genuine enough as Hazel doesn't react until I sniff.

"Sorry, a cold coming, I think."

Without speaking, she passes me a box of tissues. I don't need it but take one to be polite. "Thank you."

Four children? Veronica has four children? I've always had the impression that she's around my age, but how can you tell from a voice. She sounded mature. Yes, actually, that's not me but sensible. Yes, sensible. Grounded.

"And you have everything planned? Your 'project'?"

I nod despite the answer not being a complete 'yes'. I have a list of some venues, a handful of downloaded menus, some of which look perfectly suitable, the others maybe just starters for less than five hundred calories. The instruction was 'dishes' rather than 'meals'. It'll add to the variety and I can always skip a sauce or two. I don't have to know exactly how much everything is as long as it doesn't go over. My head starts calculating five hundred times thirty-one and I've got to 15,000 straight away and add the other five hundred. So 15,500 calories max in a month. Peezy.

"There is something I want to run past you but we can come back to that."

It sounds ominous but she doesn't look worried or scary so I shouldn't be either. Scared, that is. I don't think I could look scary if you covered me in spikes and gave me a megaphone. Okay, that's weird.

"Right then…" Hazel pushes back her chair. "Let's get you settled."

I'm about to stand, meeting over, when I hear what sounds like a herd of elephants coming down the corridor. I look round, hitting my elbow against the chair. I want to say 'ow' but feel foolish. It's more surprise than pain. And pride, perhaps.

"They're back." Hazel sort of states the obvious. My new colleagues, and there are loads of them. The open-plan arrangement is similar to ours so I wonder where they're all going to sit but Hazel senses my query and explains. "Most are freelancers. Everyone, other than a trickle of us, went. Only half of them live in the area but Billy wanted them to all come back here as some have only been in the office for their interview. A couple never. They live too far away, Scotland for one, Devon for the other. Not quite Land's End to John O'Groats but still. We did Skype or Zoom video interviews. It's not so important for the freelancers."

"Oh," is all my brain and mouth offer as I'm half seated half standing. I want to add something else but backtrack to the name. "Billy?" I sit back down.

"William Tyler, our editor, most people's boss. But he hates being called William. Too stuffy, he says, so Billy it is. Suits him better actually. No shirt and tie for our Billy, not unless he has a meeting with the board. Very down to earth. You'll like him. Everyone does.

Respect him too, of course. Anyway, I'll introduce you now he's here. He might even do a speech. He does love his speeches, especially with a captive audience. He had high hopes for the training. Helped Leah and Owen with all the arrangements."

"Leah?"

Hazel laughs. "Sorry. I forget you don't know everyone."

Anyone, I think then correct that to James, Phil and Hazel but don't say anything.

"Leah's my assistant. I think the training was her idea but Billy loved it so much that he kind of took over. No malice, just enthusiasm."

William, our William, has gone up in my estimations over the past year, having got to know him better via Izzy, but enthusiasm isn't something that comes naturally to him. By the sound of it, his namesake got our William's share. I'm looking forward to meeting him.

Chapter 14 – Being Veronica

We come out of Hazel's office and she points towards the far end of the open-plan sprawl. "Après toi?"

"Merci," I say and Hazel giggles. I'm not sure why I'd not put her down as a giggler, given it's a work environment, but my heart bonds to her that little bit more.

I follow and immediately feel intimidated. I'm not the world's most confident person and am out of my depth. I shouldn't be because we're all part of the same company but the only person I've ever spoken to before, and that was a long time ago, is possibly the only one who's missing... on maternity leave. So probably at least nine months ago.

Hazel heads straight for Billy's office, aka William's office. Both of them. As I said, the building is pretty much a replica of ours, on the inside at least, or this part of it. The offices. Even in my head I'm rambling. Nerves. My dad always said I should think an idea through before I verbalise it but I just like talking so I guess I talk as I think and vice versa.

Billy stands. He's not as tall as our William, around five eight maybe, so still taller than me. That's not difficult. He's also around our age. Mid-thirties tops. He's very sweet looking, not sickly like banoffee pie – Izzy's favourite, but 'nice'. I've never liked the word 'nice'. It's too insipid. But yes, Billy looks like a nice guy and from Hazel's description of him and his enthusiasm, he's going to be.

He gives me a broad smile and sticks out his left hand. It's tilted like a normal handshake but I catch a glint of wedding ring. I'm neither disappointed nor pleased. I'm not sure how I should feel but he's my boss for the next month so I shake his hand, with my left which feels odd as I'm right handed, and match his smile, or a level or two lower. I don't want him to think I'm taking the mick.

I laugh. That's the kind of thing Mike... our Mike, my security guard ex-boyfriend, he of the dubious jam stains on his jumper, says. Taking the mick. Mike.

Billy's speaking but I'm a few words behind so just keep smiling. "...meet everyone."

Fortunately I don't need the missing first part of the sentence as he's already come out from behind his desk and is walking towards his door. I take it as a cue to follow him and notice that Hazel's been outside the whole time, that or she moved and came back.

I feel like a celebrity between two bouncers as they escort me into the middle of the open-plan office. Billy, without any warning, shouts an 'Oy!' almost loudly enough that I feel my eardrum reverberating. It does the trick though and everyone pays attention.

He almost skips to a neighbouring desk and retrieves a chair, pulling it back into the office. My first thought is that he's going to ask me to stand on it because I'm so short but he hops up onto it. It's not quite a leap but it's done with almost as much enthusiasm as the skip. "Can I have your attention please." As if the 'Oy' didn't work. "Good. Thank you, everyone. I'd like to introduce you to our newest member of the team, replacing Veronica for the month."

I'm listening but beginning to panic. I'm pleased this isn't day one of my 'project' and I'm not yet having to eat anything that could be classed as a healthy 'dish'. I should get in the right frame of mind though. I had porridge so could have included that but I added so much golden syrup that 'healthy' it most certainly was not. It's a wimpy thing to start on anyway. I should go with something safe. I'm relying on Wetherspoon for its under five hundred calories range but knowing how varied Izzy's month was, I'm going to have to be a bit more imaginative. I don't know the town very well, much less than Tring so it'll be fun exploring.

My brain veers me in a different direction as I realise that they're all waiting for me to speak. I look up at Billy who's still standing on the chair. He and everyone else are staring at me.

Confident Donna finally kicks in. "Hello. It's lovely to be here. This is my first morning so please be gentle." That produces a few chuckles from across the room. I'm glad it's broken the ice, not that it felt like there was any that needed to be broken.

I'm almost immediately swarmed with people coming up to chat with me. No one introduces themselves, which is a shame, although I think even I would struggle to remember them all, but they welcome me, 'to the madhouse' one says.

They finally disperse and Billy hops off the chair, puts it back where it belongs, then takes me to a desk tucked round a corner I'd not noticed earlier. Unlike the desert of a desk, probably one used for the freelancers, this one's amazing. It's swamped with what must be free samples; top brands plus some own labels. There's a photo frame at an angle, which I expect to be Veronica's family but I see when I turn it that it's Veronica and Beyoncé. Of course it is. And it doesn't look like Veronica's caught her as she was passing by. No, they look like they know each other. So, Mrs 01442-with-six-digits-thereafter, do you?

Veronica, who could be mistaken for Beyoncé's younger sister, is as gorgeous as I had expected. She looks like a natural beauty, and I want to think she's a diva but she's always been lovely when we've spoken on the phone.

I still can't help liking her, Veronica, jealous though I am. Who wouldn't be? I look around but there are no other photos. On the shelf behind the desk there's nothing. There is 'stuff' everywhere so there's no room for anything else but you'd think with three other children and presumably a husband lurking in the background that there would be at least one photograph of her family.

Amongst all the goodies though I spot an envelope with my name on it. The handwriting, all five letters of it, is almost calligraphy and I assume it's from Veronica as I figure everything's classy where she's concerned.

I'm not wrong. *Welcome and good luck*, it reads. *Hazel and Billy will guide you but let me know if you get stuck.* Veronica provides her phone number which is the local 01442 code so I think she could always pop in if I got desperate but she'd have to bring Ethan with her and I'm not sure I'm ready for that.

Considering Duncan and I weren't planning to have a baby so soon, I'm shocked at how badly I'm taking not having one... or rather thinking I was, then it not happening. I'm not a spring chicken, as Mike once told me (nor an oil painting – thanks, Mike!), so I can't leave it too long. A friend of my mum's had her one and only daughter when she was forty-five so I've got, in theory, a decade and a half but...

Chapter 15 – Exploration

Despite me having to come up with a meal, as well as a report on it, tomorrow, twenty-four hours away, I'm far from panicking. The normal, Northampton, Donna would be but I'm beyond crazy so I take a few minutes to settle in. There are drawers either side of the desk. I'm spoilt for choice. I plump for the right-hand one.

I open the top drawer which is about an inch deep. I'm not surprised when it's only full of pens, pencils… It breezes shut, soft closing, and I smile. I remember Izzy saying she'd played with her kitchen drawers when she'd first had them. Simple things. Next drawer down is normal depth and before I open it, I challenge myself to guess its contents. Given the amount of clutter… sorry, merchandise samples, on Veronica's desk, I'm assuming that the drawers will be full of them too but am surprised when they're almost empty. There's a tray at the back and while it's again only deep enough for pens and such, there's one solitary item in it; a picture.

"Ah ha!" I say as I retrieve it, as if it's the fountain of youth or some other long-lost treasure. I then realise that I said it aloud and look around but no one's paying me any attention. The office seems emptier and it looks as if the freelancers have gone. As I'm only there for the month, I don't think it matters but I love people; the more the merrier.

Anyway, this photograph. I'm still holding it sort of aloft so bring it back down to studying level and that's what I do. *Wow.* I can almost feel my bottom jaw drop open. Veronica and her children, or rather baby Ethan is represented by a medium-sized bump. The children's eyes are stunning. One's are bright blue, as are Veronica's whereas the other two's are hazel, almond really. Just like James's.

There's no father but I assume he's the one taking the photograph, especially as the youngest child is sticking her tongue out in his direction. The other two are boys and clearly look as if they're going to break a few hearts.

A thought leaps into my head and I turn to Veronica's stack of letter trays. I remove a handful of the sheets and it only takes a few seconds to find her surname. Her email wasn't initial and surname like iedwards but veronica@ and her signature didn't have it. I guess she's that kind of person; unstuffy, natural.

I breathe a sigh of relief as it's not Norton as I'd been dreading but Abbott. I wonder if she's married to a Russ or whatever Costello's partner's first name was. Relief and dread? Really? Was that what I was really thinking? I nod silently to myself and know I'm in trouble. *He'll have a girlfriend*, my brain tells me, and for a fleeting moment I don't care. I'm mortified, my mum would be mortified, Duncan would be worse, and I shake my head again and tell myself to switch back to work mode.

I pull a sheet that Hazel had given me from my bag, switch on Veronica's computer and type in the password to get through the firewall, or whatever the first barrier is. Hazel had probably told me but I'd not really been paying attention.

It does the trick as the familiar company logo flashes up, along with the homely ID and password prompts I know and love. I type in my usual details as I want to check my emails and so on before becoming Veronica, and the usual 'Hello Donna' appears. I feel comforted by familiarity and check my emails. I'd already told all my regular contacts that I was going to be incommunicado for the month and the stragglers have replied wishing me luck with my thirty-one diets project. I had actually told them it was thirty-one dishes but had no inclination to correct them. Unless you're a dieter – which I often am – you wouldn't know that you have to stick with a diet for at least a week.

Being a health and beauty columnist sounds glamorous and it is – food's a curse in this job. I get as many food samples as Veronica gets makeup, although I get plenty of those too, and I promise to eat them all… the food that is, not the makeup! I know some girls can spend chunks of their wages on new cosmetics each month but I'm super lucky in that I get it all for nothing… unless there's something in particular I'm after but I'm really naughty and drop not-too-subtle (at all) hints and hey presto, first class post later.

Izzy's the same but more subtle. You wouldn't think of it as she's more outgoing than me in some respects, some think forthright. I know she's a pussy cat. Her freebies are usually worth a lot more than mine though. I don't know how much cosmetics cost to make… ooh, another potential article … but they're going to be pence, albeit millions spent on advertising, versus Izzy's laptops, tablets… which is why Veronica's desk is the way it is. Izzy donates all her 'finished with's to charity shops, hospitals, hospices, schools. William's idea, or protocol, I don't know. But it's different with my freebies; who'd want used cosmetics or half-eaten chocolate bars? Not something I want to think about.

Speaking of Veronica's desk, I have things to do. I'm being allowed to work a day behind for this month as there's no way I could get a 'dish' piece written for today's issue so I submitted a piece on chemicals in lipsticks on Friday. Izzy didn't have that luxury and dated her first guy… Duncan, my Duncan, at the Picturedrome… the first evening so she did the same; submitted on the second of May. She couldn't exactly have been set the task in the morning and be expected to have dated a guy and written the article by the two pm cut-off. That would have been crazy. Instead she had… eleven to eleven, twelve, met at eight so… nine hours' notice. I got a week. Easy breezy.

He should be with me tonight, Duncan. But it'll probably just be me, as Mum will be out somewhere – she is most evenings. I have my list of eateries but I'm going to make it easy and plan to visit the nearest Wetherspoon (singular), The Full House at nearby Marlowes, the shopping centre I'm looking forward to becoming acquainted with. I wonder how many charity shops there are here? Then I wonder why I hadn't searched that online before.

So I set to work…

Chapter 16 – An Unexpected Offer

I'd done little of the donkeywork before I left Northampton but I have my plan of eateries and low-calorie dishes, all courtesy of Google.

I'm lucky really, especially compared with Izzy – she didn't have much choice when her dates where concerned; other than the weekend, apart from the odd one, she could only really meet them in the evenings whereas I have the choice of breakfast: a healthy porridge perhaps, lunch, good old Boots meal deal, or supper, dinner, tea… And I can eat anything I like pretty much, as long as it's 'healthy'. But next up is lunch.

Hazel has filled me in on what people do. I saw from the huge fridge in the kitchen that most bring in their own, some name labelled, most not. It doesn't strike me as the kind of place where people steal their colleagues' lunches but nothing surprises me these days. Actually that's not true, everything does, but I like to keep an open mind.

I snigger at the thought of my brain being like a western saloon with swing doors so busy they never really shut for long. The other alternatives are town or a van that turns up mid-morning with a horn claxon thing that sounds like a cruise ship, apparently. I've never been on a cruise ship so don't know but I imagine it'll be impressive. I picture the whole office clamouring to the window just to get a glimpse. I'm convinced I was Walter Mitty in a former life.

"Penny for them."

"Huh?" I look up and there's James in all his gloriousness. I clamp my mouth shut to stop it from drooling. The relevant emoji replaces the saloon doors and I grin, lips still clamped but desperate to pull apart and show my pearly whites. Or rather, I thought they were pearly white until I met James, but his skin is that much darker. Oh my.

"Just thinking about lunch," I whimper.

He pats his taut stomach, he's wearing clothes, sadly, so I can only assume it is; he doesn't look like he has an ounce of flab and with a hint of a gym bunny, I wonder the size of his triceps. I want to look down at them but know that I'll end up being Helen Hunt to his Mel Gibson in *What Women Want* – haven't seen that for way too long, must make a mental note – where she ends up staring at his crotch, so I resist.

"A girl after my own heart."

Never a truer word.

"The van's going to be here shortly. Want to pop down for a bite?"

It's too late to stop myself and I burst out laughing, probably as much my lips wanting release as the rest of my body does. I apologise but he just smiles.

I go to stand but he continues.

"Actually. No. Let's wait. If you don't mind."

I shake my head.

"Let's go somewhere proper. It's your first day, we have to celebrate. Unless…"

"Unless…"

"Unless you have other plans."

I shake my head again.

"Let's do that then. Half twelve for one?"

I nod. I don't trust myself to speak as I know I'm going to gush.

"See you later."

I nod again and feel so dumb. He doesn't know I'm not but I'm being a typical dizzy blonde. I'll show him, I think, and it feels like a challenge but remind myself that I'm here for a month, five full weeks, then it's 'Sayonara, James' and back to my ordinary life.

Maybe that's the problem. It's become a routine. A year after meeting Duncan, we've 'settled'. There's nothing wrong with settling but not when it's become too familiar and your eyes start wandering.

Those eyes. Those almond-coloured eyes.

Chapter 17 – Change Of Plan

I look at my list as a distraction and the morning soon passes.

"Ready?" I hear and look up. It could have only been one person really – the one I've been thinking about all morning – and I'm not wrong.

"Hi, James."

"Okay to break for luncheon?" he asks in a very stern Shakespearean accent. I expect him to doff an imaginary cap and say 'forsooth' or 'm'lady'.

"Anywhere in mind?" I ask then realise how stupid a question that is because I know nowhere in Hemel other than the aforementioned magic roundabout and ex-Kodak building.

"Just a little place I know," he says and winks.

Oh my god. I think I'm going to turn into a puddle and slither off my chair. I cough to retain my composure and he points at the box of tissues.

"Hazel said you were coming down with a cold."

I sniff to complete the pretence, pull a tissue from the box, and stuff it in one of my trouser pockets. I'll use it at some stage, or it'll be retrieved when Duncan does the washing at the weekend – did I tell you he's Superman?

The thought of Duncan brings me back to earth and I breathe.

"You sound okay to me," James said and stands a little straight as I leave my chair… fortunately not slithering but walking like a normal human being, albeit a five-foot-two-and-a-half one.

Okay is fine, I think as we walk away from my desk and back out into the main area of the office. Fine really is all I want between us. James may be a sex god but he's a colleague, and only a colleague for a month. Duncan is where my heart lies, not James. James is a stranger and I'm not going to be swayed by his charm. It doesn't normally work on me, so why do I feel like this?

I cough again and it does the trick of clearing my head, making me see sense.

James stops walking and turns to me. "Oh dear, maybe not so okay. Will you be all right to be Veronica for so long?"

I want to do a Dawn French's *Vicar of Dibley* schoolgirl laugh as she's confronted by the chap who played Robin Hood's Guy of Gisborne. Richard Armitage. Tall dark and handsome. And James is most definitely those.

I become very adult and say, "Yes, thank you. Just a summer thing." Knowing it isn't. Or more accurately a summer fling it most definitely won't be.

He goes to touch my cheek then seems to think better of it and looks around the office. He then pretends to remove a stray hair from my top and drops it into a nearby bin, belonging to one of the many people I haven't met yet.

"Ready?"

"As I'll ever be."

As I imagine what his touch would have felt like, I crumble again. My head may last the month but I'm not sure my heart will.

Chapter 18 – The First 'Dish'

After a gentle stroll alongside the River Gade and through Gadebridge Park, James takes me to a lovely little Italian in the heart of what used to be Hemel Hempstead village. It's been swallowed up by the town but forget that's looming and you could be back in the past. It's lost none of the charm I imagine it's always had and this place, and Ristorante Alberto looks like a jewel. It is, however, closed.

James peers through the front door glass then turns to me. "I'm sorry."

"That's okay. You weren't to know."

"I should have. I love the place but do only tend to come at night. In the evening. Evenings. Not that it's my… not every night."

My heart races at him being flustered. It's enormously endearing.

I point to a sign on the door. "Closed Sunday, Monday, twelve to two fifteen, six to ten the other days."

James nods. "Should have spotted that."

Izzy would have probably checked in advance, on Google or something, but I'm not her and I didn't know we were coming here. Didn't know we were going anywhere until James suggested it and this wasn't on my list which is silly as it looks lovely.

I want to state the obvious and say we need to find somewhere else but he'll know that. I'm tempted to suggest Wetherspoon but I've planned to go there tonight so I think twice in one day would be too much. I only have to eat healthily once a day though.

"McDonald's?" I jest.

"Okay," he says a little too readily as if he's not only a fan but also a regular customer. Of course sophisticated men who frequent probably mid-price Italian restaurants can enjoy Ronald McDonald too. I shudder. Not quite the image I wanted to conjure.

"Cold?" James asks. He must know I'm not as it must be twenty-something degrees but I love that he cares.

"Oh no, just…" I don't know what 'just'. Of course I'm not going to share my Ronald McDee and sophisticated men and their children with James, so I leave it at 'just'.

"Let's wander and see what takes our fancy, shall we?" he suggests.

I'd not realised until recently, actually today, since meeting James, how much of the English language lends itself to innuendos. The makers of Shrek must be eternally grateful.

As we walk towards the more modern area of Hemel town centre, James points out places of interest. Most are signed or signposted but I like listening to his voice so don't interrupt.

Nor do I when we stop at Subway on the edge of the main shopping centre, The Marlowes. He gives me a goofy grin, or as goofy as he gets with those fabulous teeth. "Didn't think I was serious about McDonald's, did you?"

I laugh and shake my head.

"It would be a bit difficult actually as there hasn't been one here since 2011."

"Really? Why's that?"

"I don't know. Not profitable, I suppose."

"But that's crazy. Shoppers always want a McDonald's."

He shrugs and I stare at his broad shoulders, wishing I could rest my head on one of them for just a few–

"There are two out of town. One Apsley way, took over The Bell, lovely old place. The other's in the leisure park top of the hill... Jarman's, do you know it?"

"I do. I go to the Tesco there for petrol. Not stopped at the complex other than that but quite fancy the snow centre, and I'll definitely do the cinema while I'm here."

"Want someone to go with?" he asks then immediately backtracks. "I'm sorry. That's very presumptuous. I'm sure..."

He stops and I want to know what he's sure of. That I already have a boyfriend. Yes. That my mum would go with me. Yes, especially anything with Tony Robinson in it. That I have better things to do. No, I don't. Okay, yes I do. I have thirty-one reports to write about thirty-one dishes and our lunch break is ticking along a little too quickly. I then remind myself though that the clock's not actually started so I can have whatever I like.

"Shall we?" He points to Subway's front door.

"Love to." I'm melting. And it's not because of the weather.

We stand side-by-side and look up at the choice. They do salads, which I'd not realised, although I know they put plenty in their rolls. Not rolls, subs. Doh. I'm torn between the chicken tikka and Italian B.M.T.(R). The B.M.T., not forgetting the (R) trademark, is only two hundred and forty-five calories. I expect the tikka to be more but it's a mere one hundred and forty-one. This is noted as an easy option for one of my dishes but think perhaps it's too easy. Where's the challenge in salad?

The picture of the B.M.T., not forgetting the (R), makes it look very nice with lots of green (lettuce – definitely dull, sorry lettuce), red onion (not conducive to lunch with a colleague, one you would definitely snog had you been single, assuming he wanted to), tomato – of course, that's the 'T', peppers (yuk), olives (formerly yuk but growing on me since Duncan made me try them on several occasions), grated cheese (yum), cucumber (meh, as security guard and ex Mike would say), green chillies, I think they look like chillies, and flat cubes of meat. Flat cube sounds like an oxymoron but they're squares. Okay flat squares.

I always carry a notebook and a couple of pens in my bag, in case one of them runs out, and am making notes. I then realise I'm being quite rude. "Sorry," I say to James who is still studying the board and doesn't appear to be noticing me let alone hearing me. His head moving left to right makes me think he's not a regular here until he nods and smiles.

I follow his line of sight and think he's going for a Meatball Marinara like the guy in the advert until the man changes his mind and settles on turkey and ham, which I always thought a little dull. On the way, he goes for… cogs in place… yep, chicken teriyaki and envies a lady who orders… grey cells, grey cells… tuna. Again, a little dull. Got to have lots of mayonnaise and sweetcorn on that one. No, not turkey and ham. He goes for steak and cheese. Better, but still no. I watch too much TV.

We settle on a turkey, bacon and guacamole wrap (me) and a chorizo flatbread pizza (James), accompanied by a bottled water and Pepsi max (bottle not tap) respectively. I know. Not sure how we got there either.

"Shall I?" I suggest, spotting a table in one of the front window corners.

"Absolutely," James says and joins the queue to be served.

I go to pull my purse from my bag but James shakes his head.

"Wouldn't hear of it. I always treat the newbies."

I doubt it very much but laugh and thank him all the same.

I make a few more notes while I wait for James and next thing I know he's arrived with the tray and puts it between us, sitting opposite. I'm not sure I can concentrate if I have to look at him for what's left of our lunch break but better that than having to sit next to him as I think the spark between us would probably burn the place down.

"So," he starts, "turkey, bacon and guacamole wrap. Is that allowed?"

"Sorry?"

"Turkey, bacon and guacamole wrap," he repeats.

"Allowed?"

"Aren't you supposed to be within the five-hundred-calorie mark?"

I hadn't looked by the time I got to this one on the menu. I'd almost lost the will to live from all the choice, and I'd not started on the Subway Savers, one of which is James's chorizo flatbread pizza, which is a shame because it almost looks as edible as the person who's going to be savouring it. I feel the inside of my mouth liquefy and I swallow before I've eaten or drunk anything.

I give a hesitant, "Er... yes."

"Five hundred and fifty-eight."

I blow a raspberry and James laughs. He's so perfect that there must be something wrong with him and I feel like I've set myself a challenge. Another one. Because three in a month isn't enough already. But I realise I've forgotten what the other two were.

"Challenge, challenge, challenge," I mumble, then realise that mumbling is actually speaking aloud, albeit quietly, and it turns out that James has supersonic hearing. Of course he does.

I take a bite of my wrap, swallow then go to speak but I remember. "Veronica's desk drawer, not ditzy."

"Er... okay. I'm sure it isn't."

I laugh, not a normal laugh but a schoolgirl laugh, and blush. This is going so well.

Chapter 19 – Colleagues

"So how long have you been at the paper?" I blurt to James so there are no pregnant pauses. Pregnant. Not a word I particularly like yet so many women… no, tears, stay back. I cough again and reach for the tissue in my pocket.

"Is it that hot?" James asks, pointing to my wrap.

My mouth isn't burning. I shake my head. "Is yours nice?" I ask before blowing my nose in as ladylike a way as I can muster.

I've asked mid-bite and he's chewing away like an otter but with much better manners and less buckier teeth. He nods though so that answers the question but he answers it anyway. "Not had this before but often seen it on the menu and wondered."

Often. So he is a regular.

"Not that I *do* actually come here often. As the saying goes."

And here was I wanting to have an intellectual conversation but it feels like it's my fault and I'm not on my way to proving to him I'm not ditzy, not that it really matters. Like Izzy with not falling in love with dates, I remind myself that I'm here to work but can have fun in the meantime, as long as that's all it is.

Being reminded of work, prompts me to ask my next question. I want to ask James again about his time at the paper but figure he'll remember and tell me at some stage. I go for, "Would you tell me about 'our' colleagues?" I emphasise the 'our' because they are while I'm there.

He goes to speak but I interrupt. "Sorry. Do you mind if I jot it down?" I hold up my notebook.

"Not at all. Wouldn't want to get in the way of progress," he says then frowns as if he doesn't know why he's said it. Nor do I but don't mention it.

"Thanks."

My pen poised, he starts. "Billy, our editor, you've met."

I write: *William = Billy.*

"His P.A. is Nathan."

I write *Janine = Nathan* then look up. "Oh."

"I know. A male P.A. Very twenty-first century. I'd say that Billy does like his boys but it's not true, not in that respect. He's happily married, to a woman, Cassandra. Been so for a couple of decades, I think. Two boys … twins, IVF I think, but can't remember their names."

I write all this down.

"Agony Aunt. Vacant at the moment. Been for a while, which is a bit of a surprise. You'd think they'd be queuing up to give advice but Billy's very fussy. Needs to be qualified. I think he'd do a good job himself but… Then we have, going round the room… you aka Veronica for a month in the corner." He pauses for breath and his eyes go up as if retrieving the information. "Then on the other side, there's Frank, the money guy…" James puts a hand up to his mouth and leans forward as if about to impart a great secret and he does indeed whisper. "Accountant, but actually he's really nice." James smiles and sits back.

Speaking normally, he continues. "Second of the trio is Greta, our everything else reviewer: books, films, whatever doesn't fall into any other remit. The third is me, James, the technology guy. The same as your Izzy, I believe."

I grin at the mention of my best friend. I jot all the names along with our respective equivalents.

"Then there's Leah, Hazel's assistant – who does much more than just personnel, human resources, call it what you will. She's like our office manager really. Leah sits next to the kitchen sort of opposite Hazel's office. They like to be opposite each other so they can talk without actually speaking.

I can feel my eyebrows rise and my mouth opens a little. My brain chugs.

"Oh," he explains, "they have some kind of code. Not exactly lip reading but they can communicate just by looking at each other. Not ESP because their lips do actually move but… No one's managed to figure it out but it works. The job gets done so that's all that matters. Speaking of which…" He taps his watch and takes the last bite of his pizza.

I lean over to look at his watch and I'm horrified when I see we've been out for over an hour.

"Don't stress, little one," he says then looks equally horrified. "I'm so sorry. I didn't mean that in a… erm."

"It's fine. I didn't take it in a… erm."

He blows me a kiss and I flame as if I've not only had the hottest meal on the menu but someone turned up the heat in the shop. I look around and see no one's paying attention. As if they would.

"What about fashion?" I ask, meaning their fashion journalist. Karen's equivalent.

"Fashion?"

"Columnist. Journalist. Fashionist," I say then laugh rather inadequately.

"Uh huh."

"The fashion journalist? Or do you not have one?"

"Yes."

I feel like we're going round in circles but say, "We really should be…" I hurry down the rest of my wrap despite James assuring me that Billy won't be bothered, and probably won't notice that we're not there because he's too busy, but it's not exactly the impression I want to make on my first day.

We take our drinks with us and stroll quicker back to the office than on the outward journey. Although Hemel isn't particularly familiar territory, it actually never has been, it doesn't feel alien either which I like.

We arrive at James's desk first, it being nearer the entrance than mine. Although the office's layout is almost a replica of Northampton's, not everyone's sitting in the same seats. That would have been too much to ask.

"Thank you again for lunch," I gush then roast as James pats my arm. Not really a pat, more of a soupçon of a touch. It's all too much and I decide I need to either steer clear or set ground rules. We've not mentioned partners but it feels as if he's assumed I'm single. I've not exactly been fighting him off but it's not fair to either of us to not say anything.

I will. Next time we talk, I will. I'll make it clear I'm with Duncan, and while I'm very flattered, nothing can happen. Nothing at all. We're only colleagues, James and I, and that's all it can ever be.

Period.

End of.

Thank you but no.

Now, what did I say about the lady protesting?

Chapter 20 – Another Walter Mitty Moment

My mobile's ringing as I approach my desk and I only just get to it before it rings off. I grin as Izzy's face appears. It's not her live face but her photograph. A normal twentieth-century phone call.

"Hey!" we say in unison.

"How's it going?" she asks.

I shrug.

"Donna?"

"Sorry. I shrugged. I forgot you can't see that. I'm too used to FaceTiming my mum."

"You and your FaceTime. How is she?"

"Yeah, good."

"So…"

"So…?"

"Why the shrug?"

"Oh. First day, you know."

"They being nice to you?"

The image of James and his soupçon touch leaps into my head. "Yes," I squeak.

"You okay?"

I can't see her but I can picture Izzy frowning. She worries more than I do… or rather she did until recently. We seem to be roles reversed.

"Oh yes," I say with more conviction. And I am. I'm going to Wetherspoon singular… literally; on my own, by the looks of it. It was all a bit of a rush this morning so I didn't get much of an answer on whether Mum was free but I'm pretty sure I know what it would be. She has a hectic lifestyle, such as it is being retired; too many clubs, fitness sessions, other stuff. Chess is the latest thing. I didn't know she even had a board! She seemed to get more involved in anything that was on offer when my dad died. He was a workaholic so she was on her own much of the time, after I'd left home especially, but there's a big difference between being alone and lonely, and I only really appreciate it being here.

"Hello…?"

"Sorry, Izzy. Having a bit of a Walter Mitty moment."

"So they're all being nice to you."

"Yes. Really nice. Hazel, you know, the HR lady, is as batty as a fruit–"

"Which is why you get on."

I can feel warmth running through my body again. Not a James warmth but an Izzy warmth and I love it. She always knows how to make me smile. I wish I could bottle her.

"Yes. You'd *love* her." She would. Izzy thinks I'm a bit mad, okay batty, but only because she's serious. Of course I don't think that because she's my BFF and I really know her. It's everyone else. Whereas... hark me. Whereas... Hark! How old am I? Thirty going on twelve going on sixty-something, my mum. Not even my mum says 'hark'. Maybe only at Christmas.

My ear's itching. Someone's talking about me.

"Donna!"

I look round the office but it's Izzy again. "Are you there, Donna?"

"Sorry, Izz."

"Yes, Walter."

"Huh?"

"Walter Mitty?"

"Oh yes. Sorry."

"Are you really okay?"

"Absolutely. There's just a lot to learn in a really short time but no, everything's fine. Everyone's being lovely. They're leaving me to it pretty much but I'm used to that. I... er..."

There's a slight pause on the other end of the phone. "Donna."

"Sorry, yes."

"What's going on?"

"Nothing. Really. It's fine." Tears threaten.

"Donna..."

"There's this guy." I look around the office and although no one's looking at me, they're too near for me to 'turn on the waterworks', as Mike would say. Damn Mike. My brain should be full of Duncan but Mike's in it? I shake my head, put on the broadest smile I can imagine – just as well as someone's coming over – and I say to Izzy, "It's all good. He's being really nice to me. I miss Duncan, that's all."

Izzy sounds hesitant. "If you're sure."

"Yep." And I nod to prove it but of course she can't see that. "I have to go. Someone's..."

"Of course. But you're okay, yes?"

"Yes. Love you."

Izzy giggles and it kills me. She's gone from the serious one to carefree. I should be; I have everything I ever wanted. I put on a smile, blow a kiss into the receiver, and we say 'speak soon'.

Nathan, as the person turns out to be, is Billy's P.A. The twenty-first century male P.A., not that there weren't any in the twentieth but I've never come across one before. I'm not sure why it should make me feel any different but…

"Donna, right?"

I nod and try to place his accent. It sounds a little Swedish. Nathan, I suppose, could be a name to fit a multitude of nationalities but anyone can have a foreign relative they've been named after, or like me… one of my middle names is Diana, the other Dawn, yes I'm double, treble D! – just because my mum liked it, them. She studied classic Greek literature at university. I was lucky I wasn't Desdemona or Delilah.

I realise I've not answered Nathan's question and it needs more than a nod to make me look anything other than rude. I stand and hold out my hand. I'm about to say, "I am. Lovely to meet you" when he lunges at me and gives me a bear hug.

"Snap out of it, Donna." I think I hear as Nathan releases me.

"Sorry?"

"Wanna get out of here?" Nathan points towards the kitchen. "Hot choc or something?"

I still can't place his accent. It's somewhere between German and Scandinavian but with a hint of French. My head hurts. But it hurt even before he came over.

I follow him to the kitchen.

I wondered after the hug, which, though lovely, feels as if it's bruised a rib or two, whether he'd lead me by the hand but fortunately he's spared me that. I do think though that I'm really going to enjoy working here for the month. Nathan, Billy, Hazel… and James.

James.

James, James, James, James, James.

And look. Guess who's in the kitchen when we arrive.

Chapter 21 – Companions

"Hey, Jamie poppet!" Nathan screeches as the two men see each other.

'Jamie' laughs but I stand there open-mouthed.

"So you two've met then," James says looking from me to Nathan and back to me.

I can't speak. My brain has Etcha-Sketched itself clean. Nathan. James. Donna. Phew. Not clean completely. I'm in Hemel Hempstead on a thirty-one dishes in thirty-one days project.

"I know," James says.

"Sorry?"

"You're in Hemel Hempstead on a thirty-one dishes in thirty-one days project," James repeats. "You're our Veronica for the month."

I blush. I'd said that aloud? James nods. My mouth isn't moving yet he understands what I'm saying. He's a superhero, just like Duncan.

But Nathan returns my sanity. "And isn't it going to be fun!" He claps. Billy may not be gay but Nathan most definitely is. Oh yes, this really is going to be fun.

I don't quite know what to say when Hazel joins the 'party' and James explains that this rendezvous was planned. That they've got something to tell me. My stomach takes an immediate nosedive but they're all smiling so it sweeps northwards just before impact.

"We couldn't let you do this all on your own," Nathan blurts and it's clear he's been struggling to keep the secret.

"This?" I ask.

He makes a circling motion with his right index finger as if he's swiping a bowl full of cake mix and I half expect him to stick his finger in his mouth and lick it. It wouldn't quite have the same effect than if James had done it and at least I'm spared that embarrassment.

"Your project," James adds and the room does seem a degree or two warmer all of a sudden. There was I thinking I'd come to my senses.

Hazel takes over… thankfully. "We have a cunning plan. To come with you."

Ah, Baldrick. "Thank you, but I'm quite happy to do it on my own." That sounds really ungrateful. "I mean, I wouldn't want to put any of you out. It's meals so breakfast–"

Nathan laughs but Hazel ignores him. I'm not sure what James does as neither of us is looking at him.

"Breakfast," I continue, "and supper… dinner, tea." I'm still not sure which to use 'down' here. "Which is obviously not work time. Company for lunch would be lovely." I can't help looking at James but he's tinkering with something in a cupboard. Hazel jumps when he lets a door slam accidentally.

"Sorry. Was looking for something." I can't think what that would be but it goes unremarked.

"Thank you though," I add. Normally, at home, I'd be telling the truth; I'm *more* than happy going to the cinema on my own because I know I have Duncan at home, or I'd see him the next day. Friday's only four days away. I'll be fine. I smile but she can see straight through me.

"Frank's wife knows your mum," Hazel says, "and they're never at home. All those clubs they belong to, which is why Frank never tends to be in a hurry to leave here. Mad when you've got satellite TV showing box sets like *Suits.* Anyway, yes. We've come up with a rota."

I sit – they'd pulled me up a chair when Hazel said they were taking over – open-mouthed. I really don't know what to say. They've created a rota so I never have to eat any of my dishes alone, not when going out (café, restaurant – the choice is completely mine).

"James," Hazel continues, now sitting opposite me, "and my Leah will accompany you any lunchtime of your choosing. Not if you want something from the van or bring in your own… unless you want the company, of course."

We all look at James who shrugs and nods simultaneously.

The only desk I can see from the kitchen is Hazel's, and Leah's not there so I'll speak to her, thanking her in advance, when she is.

"Then in the evenings we have…" Hazel pulls a note from a pocket in her top. "Mondays – that's today, isn't it." She looks up at Nathan. "Mondays is… are?" She shakes her head. "Whatever. Mondays are Nathan here. Who's Swiss, in case you were wondering, although he's lived here so long he's more of a native." How did she know?

Nathan smiles but Hazel's on a roll. "Tuesdays Frank. His wife's chessing, I think, that night… with your mother, I believe." Hazel looks up at me. I shrug. She looks down again. "Greta's Wednesdays. She can't do Thursdays as she has guitar lessons. Something I've always fancied actually so I should have a word." She pulls a pen from the same pocket and circles Greta's name. "Thursdays are Billy."

That should be fun. Other than looking at Nathan when he was mentioned, I've not been reacting throughout this list, concentrating on Hazel but I look at James when Billy's mentioned. Nathan would have been more logical, being Billy's P.A. but it's like I'm seeking some kind of reassurance.

"Fridays are Phil – we have a night-time security guard and another for the weekend. Apparently Phil never goes straight home after his final shift of the week – he's six to six but can leave early if you need to. Very good of him."

Hazel's still staring at the piece of paper. I don't have the heart to say I'll be going straight home. To Northampton. Phil struck me as very accommodating so I'm sure he won't mind. I'd be quite happy to spend a lunchtime or two chatting to him in his office, as long as it doesn't distract him from his work. We'll sort something out.

"I figure you'll probably want to do your own thing at the weekend."

I would so I nod. I definitely feel like the Churchill dog but I'm not complaining as I'm eternally grateful that they – or Hazel at least – came up with the idea of chaperones. Duncan and I have agreed that I'll go home or he'll come here most weekends. There are only four because I'll be going home for good on June first, so we'll sort of alternate, with me going home or him or Izzy, or both, coming here. I get to see her anyway when I'm back home as Duncan has his surgery. Even if he's not rostered on, he's often summoned to work.

Hazel hands me the list.

I take it and murmur a very grateful, "Thank you".

"So," Hazel summarises for me, "we have James or Leah for lunch." James is about to agree but Hazel's not looking so continues. "Nathan, Frank, Greta, Billy and Phil in the evenings. I'm backup as I'm dog sitting on and off, more on than off – he's very old, very poorly, injections." She shudders. "How does all that sound?"

"Wonderful. Apart from your poorly dog, sorry to hear that. But thank you so much for arranging this." And it does sound wonderful. It sounds glorious.

Nathan's going to be a hoot. I've not met Frank yet but if my mum likes his wife I'm sure I'll like him. Greta. Not met her either but I'm intrigued. I wonder if she's Swiss too. Again, I can't see her desk from the kitchen but imagine her to look like Heidi. Perhaps not in full regalia in the office. Just at the weekends. Wednesday nights, hopefully.

Billy. Oh, Billy. I'll have to be on my best behaviour but yes, again, very interesting. Another hoot perhaps. Then Phil. I'd like to. Maybe Duncan will miss a Friday on his weekends coming here. No, I shouldn't think like that. And I'm sure Phil wouldn't want to play gooseberry. Maybe we could meet for one drink, to show my gratitude. Yes, that sounds like a plan.

I hear the scraping of a chair and Hazel's standing. I do likewise. She's mouthing something and I lean forward to see if she's only mouthing or whispering.

"Greta," she says at normal volume and I pull back. "I have to remember to speak to Greta about her guitar lessons." Hazel points at the piece of paper.

"Ah, yes. Did you…?" I offer her the note but she shakes her head.

"Better get on," she says and heads back to her office.

"Me too," Nathan says but that'll mean either I have to say likewise and jump in front of him or be left in the kitchen with James. Fortunately my heart's still on its normal rhythm but I don't want the temptation. No, not want. Yes, not want… and not need.

Although my companions have been sorted in a very Doctor Who orderly fashion, I don't know exactly where I'm going when. And what if any of them are vegetarian, vegan, or they don't like the venues I've chosen? Maybe I should let them choose, they're the locals. I could but what if there's nothing on the menu under 500 calories.

While I'm Walter Mittying, James mouths a 'see you later' – I think that's what it was – and takes himself out of the picture… literally.

My brain continues whirring while I walk back to my desk. I've gone past James's – his back to me, thankfully, Greta – on the phone, Frank – ditto, Billy's office – empty, and Nathan – another back, facing his open filing cabinet.

While I was hesitant at first about the whole project, and being in Hemel Hempstead wouldn't be my first choice – no offence, Hemel, I'm really looking forward to it now. If nothing else, I get to meet most of the regular colleagues for more than a chat at the kettle.

Fun with a capital F. Yes, I'm up for that.

Chapter 22 – None So Queer As Me

I spend the rest of the Monday afternoon preparing my first article. I start, exactly as Izzy did, explaining that I've been given this project and what it entails. I assume my colleagues won't mind being mentioned but this is only a draft so I figure it doesn't matter. I can check or Billy will pick it up when he goes through it with me, which he'll want to before it goes anywhere near a printer; my desk's or the 'final' one. It'll be funny seeing my picture on a different sheet. Or will they use Veronica's? For a month, it doesn't matter. Probably better if I'm incognito if I'm going to test out these establishments' food. A Beyoncé lookalike, I am not.

I sense someone standing by my desk so look up. A very sweet twenty-something with trendy-black chunky glasses is smiling back.

"Hello," she says and offers her hand. I take it and shake it. "I'm Greta."

I go to stand but she shakes her head and points to a visitor chair her side of my desk. I nod a little too vigorously.

"Hi, Greta. I'm–"

"Donna, yes."

I laugh. "Of course you know who I am. Thank you so much for offering to be my chaperone on..." I desperately paddle swanlike trying to remember which day she was mine.

"Wednesdays," we say in unison.

"It wasn't really an offer but I'm happy to do it."

Oh great. My first subject and an unwilling one.

"It's a great idea!" She smiles and I'm relieved. If she's unwilling under the surface it certainly doesn't appear that way on top. "Drink?" she suggests and points in the vague direction of the kitchen. My desk is tucked in a corner with a vortex behind me above the main entrance. It's the same at our offices and I've always thought a complete waste of space but I suppose it saved on the cost of extra bricks, carpet, walls, wallpaper, extra desk, chair, and all that stationery for the person they can obviously do without. I think too much.

We chat as we walk, and Greta's delightful. She's like a younger version of me; Tigger G. That reminds me of Honey G, that really weird rapper on... what was it...? X-Factor? Britain's Got Talent? One of those. It doesn't matter and it's not important enough to look it up, especially as my desk is several feet behind me, the space growing.

Frank smiles and mouths a 'hello' as we go past. I feel a bit rude for not stopping but Greta's on a mission so I smile and mouth back. I wave my hand around in what's supposed to be 'see you upon my return' and it obviously does the trick as he nods. Or he's just being polite.

Greta's already at the kettle and I can hear it rousing. She's got out two mugs and is spooning coffee into one of them. She tilts the jar as if to offer me the same. I shake my head. "Hot chocolate please." I'm fortunate they have the same low-calorie version, about a third of normal, as we have in Northampton – the same suppliers presumably – and I'm in hot chocolate mode. It's the end of April and really warm yet here I am wanting chocolate. None so queer as me.

Greta soon has me in stitches. She's reeling off loads of jokes and could give Jeremy Vine a run for his money. No, not Jeremy, his brother, the funny one... obviously. Tim. Something about a vacuum cleaner unused yet still gathering dust. I chuckle.

"So, how are you finding day one?" Greta asks, getting back on topic.

Is it really only day one? And not even day one proper. "It's been fantastic," I answer honestly. It really has. "Everyone's been so nice and if those I haven't spoken to yet are half as nice I'm going to have a... er... fantastic month. And I get paid to eat. What's not to like?"

"I know. I heard that. I can't complain though. I get sent more DVDs and books than I can handle. I read and watch movies, and TV boxsets, for a living. Everyone has to eat but who gets to do all the rest of it and get paid?"

"You must see things you don't really want to see, read things not of your genre."

Greta pulls a face. "Ooh. You know your stuff, Donna."

"I love reading. Don't get much time but I like a chapter or three before lights out."

We spend the next few minutes comparing reads – Alan Bennett's *The Uncommon Reader* a mutual love, Arthur from Julian Barnes's *Arthur and George* is another matter.

"It's fascinating how made-up people, the characters," Greta says, "can endear themselves... George... or not. I found Arthur fascinating but not likeable, but I don't think he was supposed to be, although he was helping George."

I struggle to recall what, or rather why, I didn't like Arthur. "I was listening to the audiobook so maybe if I'd had the words in front of me."

"Maybe, but the fact that neither of us warmed to him must say something."

I could talk about books all day, although way less read than

Greta, but I am there for a reason… and that reason's going to start with Nathan in… eek, a couple of hours.

"Sorry. You're busy," Greta says when I look at my watch.

"Just settling in, finding my feet, you know."

"I do. This is month two." She points to her chest.

"You're a newbie too?" To use James's word.

Greta and I smile like mirror images. Yes, I'm definitely going to like it here.

I never did ask what nationality she is.

Chapter 23 – A Million Miles Away

I'm ready when Nathan calls for me at five. I did have the Wetherspoon in mind but I'm hoping he's going to suggest somewhere as he's a native, and he doesn't disappoint.

I don't know whether he's a car driver or lives near enough to walk but I know from Hazel that my car's okay for the duration. Like Northampton, the Hemel Hempstead office has twenty-four hour CCTV security, only one guard but the police station isn't a million miles away; the other end of the shopping area rather than on the same road as our building but near enough to come to our rescue.

Oh God. Why do I keep thinking of James?

"Hello?" a voice says from a million miles away.

We're walking, yet I can't remember leaving the office. "Sorry." I shake my head as if to clear everything except what we're doing right now.

"It's just up ahead. I'm sure you're going to like it. It's a popular place so I booked a table but if it's not your cup of tea…"

I can't imagine anywhere not being my cup of tea. If he took me to whatever Hemel's equivalent of Northampton's Boston gay bar would be, it wouldn't matter. I remember what a good time Izzy had. And that's putting it mildly. An explosion in a Dulux factory, I think she called it. She certainly had the hangover to show for it.

I feel a little nostalgic as I think of my best friend. I should be seeing her at the weekend but I miss having her around. I wonder if Greta will mind being my Izzy for the five weeks. Greta doesn't give me the impression of minding much. Health and beauty may not be her thing but we both have the best jobs in the world. I see how much my suggestions can transform people's lives – I only have to look at my Instagram feed to see that. Yes, Izzy's the techno nut but I'm not far behind. Okay, maybe a few hundred kilometres but we both need technology for what we do.

We're here and I can't help laughing as we stand outside the restaurant. Ristorante Alberto again. It's still Monday so it's *still* closed. Nathan had said he'd booked a table yet how can he have done.

"This isn't where we're eating, obviously, but I brought you here so you know it. I only have you Monday evenings, you should get one of the others to take you."

I smile a broad warm smile and want to give him a hug.

He points over the road. "Chiangmai Cottage is our destination of choice. We're…" He looks down at his watch. "Right on time." As he speaks, a little Chinese lady comes to the door, turns the 'sorry, were closed' sign to 'welcome'. Nice touch. The missing apostrophe from 'were' doesn't escape my attention but I don't mention it to Nathan or the lady. She looks far too sweet and I don't want to hurt their feelings by starting with a criticism.

"Best Thai Restaurant. Unique. Has no equal. That's what Chingmai is to customers who are over-whelmed by the ever-evolving cuisine, according to Google," Nathan whispers to me as we follow the lady to a secluded table near the back of the restaurant. Being so early – half past five – there's no one else waiting to come in so we have the pick of the place, but the table she gives us is lovely. It's quiet so we can chat.

The lady returns with two menus. "Drink please?" she asks with a lovely soft Oriental voice.

"I'm driving later," I tell Nathan then turn to the lady. "Just a lemonade please." I look back at Nathan and he appears sympathetic but orders a Singha Premium Thai Lager. The lady smiles and leaves us to it.

"Are we having starters and mains or mains and dessert?" I ask, hoping for the former as the starters look really interesting and an 'assorted fresh fruit plate, tea or coffee' isn't overly appealing as a latter. I love fruit but my mum keeps loads at home, and I like to go for something I'd not normally have when I'm out.

"Starters and mains? I'm not really a sweet person."

I laugh. "Oh, I don't know…"

Nathan grins and blushes.

We spend a few minutes looking at the menu and thank the lady as she brings our drinks. My glass is a standard size but Nathan's lager looks huge. The label professes it to be 630ml, so about twice mine. I drink slowly so we'll probably be about the same speed.

"I love the names," I gush, returning my attention to the menu. "Ped Ron, Goongthalay, Pla Murk Yang. Ooh, it's calamari. I *love* calamari."

"I'm more of a Goong Hom Sabai fan myself. Or Pla Goong."

That's next on the menu. He said it like a native. "You come here often?" I say then twig the corniness.

The corners of his mouth crease. I thought he looked a bit geeky earlier but only now I realise, because he's slim. Without an ounce of fat, though not gawky thin or gym-bunny buff like James, Nathan has a very good figure, if you like football rather than rugby build. I go with the latter every time and lovely though Nathan is, he's *so* not my type. Not that I'm looking. *Yeah, like that stopped you with James*, my brain tells me but I ignore it and look back at the menu.

"You could say that," he says.

The lady returns with a notepad and pen at the ready but when it's clear that we've not chosen, she turns to leave after flashing a brief half smile – a be-pleasant-to-all-customers smile rather than a recognising Nathan, so either she's new or doesn't work very often.

As if reading my mind, Nathan says, "She's always like that; not really dour, just not much either way."

"Oh. I'm not sure I could be like that but she must see so many customers that we all blur."

"I like that: blurring customers. It's quiet so she'll be back soon. She'll be spying behind a curtain somewhere."

I smile. "We should get on and decide then really."

"We should," Nathan agrees and when the lady returns he does indeed go for the Goong Hom Sabai ('prawns with a sash', he tells me) and Pla Goong (spicy Thai shrimp salad, the menu tells me), clearly a fish fan.

I love chicken so go for the Lab Gai Yang followed by the Ped Yang. I probably shouldn't mix chicken with duck but it looks like they don't come with much sauce so I'm keeping the calories down. The project hasn't officially started yet but it doesn't hurt and I could always cheat and use it if I need a spare.

It's not actually going to be as easy as I thought. Maybe snack lunchtimes are the way to go. I don't suppose readers really want to hear purely what I thought of the food but more my overall experience, especially the people I meet and anything funny. I should have spoken more to Izzy. Of course I read her articles but it's been a year and I've forgotten the finer detail. I know, I have a good memory but even so.

I laugh as I think of Nigel the Day-Glo cyclist.

"Penny for them?" Nathan says, not quite as sultry as James but it reminds me nonetheless.

"I was thinking about something a friend, my best friend, back in Northampton did last year."

Nathan leans forward. "Ooh yes… tell Uncle Nathan."

Nathan's slightly younger than me, and while he could technically be my uncle, in a soap opera kind of way, had we been related, he'd never feel old enough to be so.

In between bites of Lab Gai Yang, which is even more delicious than it looks, and less spicy hot than its redness would imply, I tell him all about Izzy's project and I don't think I've ever seen anyone with eyes wider. He claps and I look around the room. There's another couple almost as far away as they could be to us and they seem engrossed in their conversation.

Nathan leans in and whispers, "What fun." I'd not noticed his aftershave before but I recognise it.

"Is that Guilty?"

His eyes dim a little. "Sorry?"

"Your aftershave. Gucci Guilty?" I cover aftershaves in my column occasionally but the last time was a while ago. I then realise how personal I'm being and can feel myself blushing. I go to apologise but he smiles and the brightness returns to his eyes.

He nods and stabs an errant prawn that had fallen out of his Goong Hom Sabai and pops it into his mouth, swallowing it whole. "You're a dark horse, Miss Donna."

No one's called me Miss Donna, other than my doctor and that's always superseded by my surname, before but I love it, Nathan's version. Miss Donna to Uncle Nathan. Part of me doesn't want this evening to end, and having ordered, we're still waiting for our starters so it's not going to finish in a hurry. I feel more relaxed because there's no romantic spark between Nathan and me so there's no pressure. It makes me realise what Izzy must have gone through during her forty-something dates. I laugh as I think of the speed dating, where I met Duncan, Izzy's first date initially and he'd been as lovely as she'd said. I sniff as I realise I'm welling up. I'm such a baby. Oh god. Why does everything come back to babies?

"Donna?"

I look up.

"Are you okay?"

I smile, marginally matching his but it's nowhere near as genuine and I'm sorry for that. "Sorry. Just missing–"

"Ooh… do tell."

So I do as I'm told. I start with Izzy's project and how she'd met Duncan the first night and really liked him but he wasn't for her but she felt strongly enough for him to then compare everyone else.

"Didn't she mind you having him…? So to speak."

I cackle. It's been a while since I've done that. Nathan's such a tonic.

"She's delighted. She has her own man so…"

"Ooh, one of the forty-something?"

I should shake my head but instead I tap my nose as if it's a state secret.

Nathan laughs and we tuck into our main course.

Nathan's Pla Goong does look scrummy for a 'salad' while my Ped Yang appears more innocent than it is; I finish my lemonade before I'm halfway through the dish.

Nathan, like the gentleman he is, orders me another drink and the rest of the evening is spent chatting about more general things; current affairs (not that kind!) and the like, without resorting to the weather. We do chat about writing and we both like pretty much everything so that's an easy topic to talk about.

We've eaten all the food when it dawns on me that I'm supposed to be making notes on at least one course. Or rather will be from tomorrow. Tonight would have been great practice. I can remember what it looked and tasted like but not in enough detail. Writing articles doesn't faze me but… *Pull yourself together, Donna.*

"Dessert or shall we head off?" Nathan asks.

I'm torn, not about dessert; I have no space, even for fruit which is mostly water anyway, but if we head off it runs the risk of the evening ending. My mum's at some club or other so no rush to go back to her house.

Nathan clearly senses my hesitation. "Guided tour of our lovely town?"

"That would be fabulous!" I say a little too eagerly.

Nathan catches the eye of the lady who had let us in and taken our order. He rubs his fingers together indicating he wants the bill.

I get my bag and go to fish out my purse but Nathan tuts. I look up and he's shaking his head. He goes to speak but I butt in. "I can't let you. It's far too generous."

"Don't worry. Billy's paying."

"He is? I er…"

"Oh yes. He's paying for the whole thing, the whole month. He didn't tell you?"

I shake my head, although William, my William, said something about covering expenses.

"Yep. Up to a certain budget but I know what that is and Frank's approved it all so you'll have no worries, especially on his night, which is… tomorrow, right?"

"Yes. You, Frank, Greta, then Billy Thursdays. Hazel did say Phil was doing Fridays but I'm going home then or Duncan's coming here. Maybe Izzy but I'm not sure. She's rather engrossed with moving in with William so it's all a bit up in the air."

"No problem. And Duncan sounds lovely."

I must admit that I had gushed about him, how I really feel, and all's right with the world again.

Chapter 24 – Chats Like This

Bill paid, receipt taken to include a small tip, and we're on our way.

We head back through the town centre, wandering and chatting, little faster than the proverbial snail but I'm in no hurry. I've still not remembered what club it is my mum belongs to on a Monday. It's only courtesy of Frank that I know she's at chess on a Tuesday.

As if reading my mind, Nathan asks about my mum.

"She's lovely," I gush. "I'm very proud of her. As soon as she retired, she filled her life with so many things. She loves evening classes so she's always out and about, although she does get time off for good behaviour: bank and school holidays and the weeks in between each ten-week block. You know."

He nods. "What kind of thing does she do?"

"Pretty much everything. Sewing, pottery, darts, d–"

Nathan laughs. "Darts as in the sport? Arrows?"

"Yep. For a while anyway. And dancing, ceroc, ballroom, anything that moves."

"And pottery. That's useful."

"She'd done some really nice pieces. Her house is full of things she's made, in the lounge mostly, but she spends most of her time in her kitchen diner as it's warmer and she has the table to prop her books on. She's a bookworm, reading much more than me. We used to swap before I met Duncan and got a life but knowing all the stuff she gets up to, she's probably never around to read."

"I love books."

"Me too, although… Book. Book club. That's where Mum's at tonight. They're doing Alan Bennett's *The Uncommon Reader*. Her suggestion so she wouldn't miss it. It's one I'd lent her, Izzy having lent it to me yonks ago." Greta and I had mentioned it so I'm not sure why the penny didn't drop.

"I love Alan Bennett. I've read…" Nathan's eyes head to the top-left of his brain to retrieve the information. "Pretty much everything he's done. All the books certainly, less so the plays, although I love dialogue more than description so I've read a couple. *The History Boys*… I didn't know that was his until I spotted it in Waterstones."

"Me neither… until the film."

"Ah, yes."

"And the other one?"

"Sorry?"

"You said two plays."

Nathan laughs. "*The Lady in the Van*. Book, film and play. Read, seen, read."

"Me too, although not the play. Just the book and film. Once and several times. I have it on DVD."

"And of course his *Talking Heads* are genius. So so funny."

"They are. And really clever. And how they remember all the words. I have a really good memory but don't think even I could remember however long it is that they have to monologue for. Of course in the TV version they can cut whenever they want to."

"I don't think they do though."

"No. And not on stage, of course."

"He can come across as dry, Alan, but *The Uncommon Reader* is so funny, and while he's probably met the queen on a few occasions, it's an insight that likely no one but Prince Philip really knows. Not that *The Uncommon Reader* is real of course."

I laugh. I really like Nathan and it's sad that I'll only get to chat like this four times while I'm here. Maybe he could sneak a lunch or two. There are likely to be times when James or Leah aren't available. Hazel won't know… or mind, I'm sure. I still can't get over how kind she is, and everyone else is being. I don't know that my colleagues back home would do the same; sacrificing not only their lunch breaks but their evenings too for a 'newbie', as James called me… and I called Greta. Newbie. I don't use it often enough.

Nathan and I find ourselves outside Asda. I'm about to ask why when Nathan explains.

"I forgot to get some milk and the one I have at home is probably full of blobs."

He cracks me up. Duncan's the same, although he'd still use the blobby milk. Men.

"No problem," I say and we head inside.

"Do you want to come with or wander?" Nathan asks.

I don't want to be a pest so say, "Wander's fine."

"Cool," he chirrups. "See you at the tills in ten or thereabouts?"

"Cool," I repeat, actually feeling quite cold as we're by the refrigerators with bagged veg, and the store has air conditioning so it feels almost arctic.

As he wanders along the dairy aisle, it's a great opportunity for me to see what low-calorie dishes there are available. I head back to the fresh vegetables and fruit.

Most of the salad boxes are less than 500 and the 'Meatball Marinara' makes me laugh. It's like Subway all over again without the bread 'sub'. At 405 calories, it's near the top end… well, four-fifths, but that's fine. If I have a Diet Coke or something with it, that's okay, but Diet Coke's minimal so I can have that anytime. So it leaves me with 95 calories, 94 if I'm sticking to the letter of the 'less than 500' for a packet of crisps.

This is probably taking it all a bit far but it's supposed to be a meal, and a salad on its own is a tad dull. Not that a salad and crisps equates to a meal. Ooh, Spicy Butternut Falafel, Rainbow Grains and Houmous. That's certainly not dull. It's a meagre 268 calories so I could have a fat Coke. There are 139 calories in a standard 330ml or 210 in a 500ml bottle – I did all this for a project a few months ago and I don't suppose they've changed since then – so I'd be pushing it to have the latter and a bar of chocolate or crisps. Being a health and beauty columnist, I shouldn't really have crisps, chocolates, or any kind of fizzy drinks but I do a fair amount of exercises… and sexercise. I can't help but grin, and a man standing a few feet away, on the opposite side of the aisle, having too good a feel of a melon, stares at my chest.

"Hello…" I say and he flushes red, puts down the melon and shuffles along to the sliced meats and fillers. I shake my head but can't help laughing. "Venus and Mars, Venus and Mars," I say not too loudly. The thought of a Mars bar makes me hungry. The meal was lovely but seems ages ago. 229 calories in a standard Mars so I could have the Butternut salad and a Mars but a bit of a waste.

I have all these figures going around my head when I hear a voice.

"Ready?"

I look up from the salad box I'm holding – this time a chicken and bacon pasta salad, coming in at a whopping 505 calories so that goes straight back, and I nod to my companion. He's already holding a carrier bag, clearly containing more than milk.

"No queue?" I ask and he smiles. "What else did you get?" I realise that's not only nosey but rude. I feel we've hit it off but I've known him less than twelve hours so not enough to be that personal.

He opens his bag and moves it towards me.

At the invitation, I peer inside. "Ooh."

"I know," he says.

Accompanying two plastic containers of green topped, semi-skimmed, milk is a huge bar of Galaxy chocolate, my favourite. It could only be bettered if it were fruit and nut but I don't know whether Galaxy does that. I should. I'm such a slacker.

I can't see the weight of it but it's probably about three times the normal 100g. "Do you mind?"

Nathan, who shakes his head, and I retrieve the chocolate. There's a receipt in the bag and we're miles away from the confectionary aisle so I know we won't be accused of shoplifting.

That wouldn't go down with either William.

I turn the bar over and my heart sinks, albeit not too far as I'm familiar with the breed, as I read the nutrition content: 2275kJ per 100g, 545 kcal per 100g. So less than a third of the bar and I'm over my meal's allowance. Not that I'd be doing my readers a service by suggesting that anyway.

I buy a couple of the salads, a six-pack of Walkers Light Ready Salted crisps (although my favourites are a non-light cheese and onion, these will go with anything) and an eight-pack of Nestle Pure Life still spring water. The tops are in four different colours so they look like flavoured water but this pack features 'their favourite DC Super friends characters', whatever they are. I don't have time, or inclination if I'm really honest, to look as I've kept Nathan waiting long enough. So plain ordinary water. At less than 20p for a 250ml bottle, that can't be bad.

The walk back to the office car park is filled with chat, more about my mum and Duncan. I can talk for the whole of the UK, not just England, and again we've covered my nearest and dearest but I know nothing about Nathan. We've only talked generally about him, work mostly, and putting the world to rights.

It's too late to ask him anything new as we get to the car park barrier so we wind down our conversation, currently about Donald Trump's latest spats with Russia and North Korea. We took all evening to get there so that's not bad. Neither of us is really interested in politics; it ends up being a fairly short topic.

"Where are *you*?" I ask, meaning Nathan's car.

He looks around him, pats his body and laughs. "Sorry," he says and points ahead. It's the same direction as my car. I'd gone green – literally – at a green BMW Z4 convertible next door but one to mine when I parked up this morning. I only know it's a Z4 because every time we drive past the Wollaston BMW showroom near the junction of Cliftonville and the Bedford Road back home, Duncan drools. I'm not sure what he'd make of this one as he's a blue boy whereas this is a slimy green. I was letching at the car rather than colour… which is very unlike me, or most girls probably. The first question we tend to ask about cars is 'what colour is it?', unless you're Izzy; she'd want the spec first.

I can't remember what was between us earlier but the Z4 is now next door, being they're the only two left.

I laugh but I'm not surprised. Although he's on a PA's wage, he is, it turns out, the owner of the aforementioned Z4. And it's barely a year old.

On second viewing, I'm still a fan, although not a colour I would choose.

"Urban green," Nathan states, as if again reading my mind. "Not to everyone's taste but I love it. Camouflages itself very well when I go for country jaunts."

Yes, I can imagine Nathan as a jaunting kind of person.

My Swift looks quite large by comparison, albeit shorter. It's technically a small car but one of the biggest, widest certainly, small cars on the market, or was in 2008. I fancy a Vauxhall Mokka and while that's bigger, it's only an inch wider. But that's another story.

We press our unlock buttons in unison and his sounds 'exclusive'.

"It's been such fun, Donna," Nathan says as he leans in to give me a peck on the cheek.

"It really has. Thank you. I'm looking forward to next Monday already."

He tuts. "Don't go wishing your time away."

He's right. I've got another six days and however many hours, including two days with Duncan and some time with my mum. I hadn't expected to be honoured with her presence for much of the duration and am all the more touched that Hazel had gone to the trouble of finding out and ensured I'm not lonely.

I have a warm fuzzy feeling as Nathan and I part ways, and even the A41 is nice to me so I'm back in Tring in no time.

Chapter 25 – Catching Up With Mum

My mum's smiling as I enter her hallway. I wait to be told her good news.

"They loved it!" She claps and looks like me when I've had too much caffeine, which is very pre-Duncan Donna.

"They loved…?"

"The book!" Mum looks at me as if I've forgotten who she is, not where she's been all afternoon and evening; with Aunt Jan and Uncle Pat, then book club. They like books, my aunt and uncle, but the club is really just my mum's kind of thing. They're more gardeners and historians. Monday mornings for Mum are a book and a bath… sometimes the same book she's meeting about later in the day. 'So it's fresh in my mind,' she says. Not that her mind is particularly ever stale.

Most book clubs meet once a month so there's plenty of time to read the whole thing but her group, of six at last count, mostly devour a book a day which makes once a week easy. Not that I imagine my mum being one of the 'mostly's because she's always so busy doing other things. They therefore don't pick massive tomes for their agreed choices, so those who don't have so much time, can at least get the one done.

"Tea?" she asks.

"Mmm, please."

She flicks on the kettle which she normally only puts the exact amount of water into so she must have been (a) expecting me home and (b) expecting me to say yes. I am rather a creature of habit; never saying no to tea.

"Have you eaten?" she asks.

"I have. A really lovely Thai."

"Neck tie?"

I stick out my tongue. "Thai, like Chinese but more flavoursome. No, that's not fair, just different."

"Nice."

"You?"

"Oh yes. Pat cooked us a lovely veggie pie before I went out."

"Nice." My mum and I are like twins in lots of respects. She's an inch and a bit taller – five feet four – but blonde too, although hers is a colourant, and bubbly. It's lovely being 'home', my third home if mine's technically first and Duncan's second, but they've been reversed for this month. In theory I'm getting to spend more time with my mum than at my flat or Duncan's house but most of that will be sleeping because she and I will probably be out most evenings.

"So," I continue as she puts our teas in front of us on the table, "remind me what you're doing when."

She rolls her eyes, not in a rude way but as if to recall what she does actually do each day. "Book club Monday evening, as you know..."

I *had* forgotten earlier.

"Tuesday morning: Pilates. Can you get time off? Join me?"

I shake my head. It's not really my thing anyway. Should be as I am a health columnist after all.

She shrugs and sighs. "Tuesday afternoon: the garden centre with Jan and Pat, so I'm home in the morning. Then in the evening it's chess with Frankie then–"

"Frank? You mean with his wife."

"Yes, Frankie."

"Huh?"

"Frank's wife is Francesca but everyone calls her Frankie."

"That's not confusing at all."

My mum smiles again and continues. "Wednesday morning, your aunt and uncle and I go to Costa. It's a shame you can't join us. It's really nice in there. Yes, there are babies squawking and children running around but they're usually at the top end. And the babies are so cute..."

Hint hint. It's not like we're not trying. "And in the afternoon?"

"Home," she says matter-of-factly as if it's the most natural thing in the world and she couldn't possibly be out doing something else like saving the planet for the WWF... or is that the wrestling organisation? That wouldn't surprise me; she's so fit these days. Fit as in... ew...

"Wednesday evening is needlework. Guitar for beginners Thursday evenings, with Pilates again that morning, and your aunt and uncle in the afternoon, Beechwood or The Cog. We tend to alternate or vary depending upon how busy and if the schools are off or not. Pilates is such fun. Jan would love it but she says it's not really her thing. Probably not. She's the quiet one. You should meet Clandestine, our Pilates teacher. She's such a hoot!" Mum rolls her eyes towards the ceiling again.

She'd have to be fun if my mum thought so. She should meet Hazel. Or the three of them together. Maybe too much. Clandestine, pronounced, Clan-dess-teen, sounds very hippy, French perhaps, so probably the perfect person for Pilates.

Hang on. Mum mentioned guitar. "Guitar? You're learning to play the guitar?"

Mum points upstairs to the front side of the house, the box room, her everything-hobby room.

"Does someone called Greta go?"

Mum purses her lips and looks serious. "Greta… Greta, Greta, Greta. Yes! Really sweet girl. German or something. Do you know her?"

"A colleague. Yes, very sweet. Not German, I don't think. Not pure enough."

My mum laughs, a dribble of tea leaking out of the left side of her mouth. She's nothing if not class.

"Do you think you might continue with it?" I ask as Mum retrieves the dribble with her right thumb. Yes, class personified.

"Probably. I sound like a cat screeching at the moment – it's only the second lesson – but so do most of the others. I think Greta's been before though, somewhere else if not here, with Bernard, because she's really good. She should be in intermediate but seems a bit lacking in confidence."

I laugh as Mum says 'Bernard'. Her eyebrows are down to the tops of her glasses – we're alike in that respect too – as she says it low voiced, baritone? I like him already.

"Why?"

"Oh, because the HR lady at work, Hazel, is interested."

"Sure. It's a ten-week course but it's revolving. Not revolving… evolving. What do I mean?"

"Ongoing? Continuing, continual, continuous?"

"Something like that. There's a break of a week or two then it starts again until the longer holidays. Bernard's said he's happy for us to repeat the course, we don't have to move to intermediate. I think that's just him being nice. Not actually saying that we're all so terrible that we'd have to stay in the beginners for the rest of our lives."

"It's only week two."

"True." Mum takes another sip of tea and swallows. "Nice. So you're getting on okay in the new office."

"I am. They're all lovely. Veronica's a lot to live up to so it's just as well I'm not replacing her."

"Maternity leave, wasn't it?" She winks at me but I ignore the gesture and question.

"You know I'm doing this thirty-one dishes in thirty-one days…"

Mum nods.

"Hazel, the HR Manager who's interested in guitar, has arranged for her colleagues to accompany me each evening. She's even set up a rota. Frank, Frankie's wife… husband. Frank's tomorrow night when you and Frankie are at chess."

"Bless him."

"I know. And going back to you… So we're up to Thursday evening? Guitar."

She puts down her mug. "Friday mornings Dunsley Farm, you know, opposite Tesco."

"I do."

"Dunsley Farm, Tesco then home, probably a trip to the charity shops after lunch, or the hairdresser comes, and erm… what do I do Friday evenings?" She blushes. "Oh yes…"

"And…"

"Saturday is–"

"Don't change the subject, Mum. What do you do Friday evenings? Come on, spill."

"Okay." She'd be no good as a spy; she folds too easily. "Bridge."

"You play bridge?" A WWF panda campaigner or wrestling participant, WWW, I've remembered, yes but not a bridge player. She'd always said it was too boring.

"Saturday is–"

"Mum." I can always tell when she's fibbing. The blush is still there.

"O… kay. I see this guy called… Charles."

"Guy?"

"Man."

"Age?"

"Sixty-seven. A few months older than me. Why?"

"That's okay. Guys are usually younger than men."

"You think I've got a boy toy?"

"You do have a new spring in your step, Mum, so I wouldn't put it past you. Actually, wouldn't put anything past you. WWF. WWW."

"Huh?"

"Oh, nothing. Where did you meet… Charles?" If that's even his name. It probably is Guy the guy, thirty-seven looking for a cougar. And with Pilates, my mum certainly is.

"Crossing the bridge over the A41 to the park with Elliott."

Elliott is my aunt and uncle's dog.

"Like Heathcliff and Cathy. Star-crossed lovers," I suggest, hinting at more information. It may not be subtle but I'm past that.

"Not exactly."

"Oh?" I straighten a little then wiggle in my chair as if settling down to an epic.

"He was walking in front of me. Short jacket so I could see his bum."

Sometimes my mum forgets that I'm her daughter and there are lines you don't cross, and while 'bum' isn't exactly one of those lines... I indicate for her to continue.

"He pulled something out of his pocket – tissues, but I didn't know at the time – and a clump of dog bags fell out. Clump. I like that word."

I smile. My mum's a wordie too. Us and our onomatopes. Thank you, Noah Webster the lexicographer (1758–1843). And Wikipedia of course. "Go on."

Like me, my mum gets easily distracted. She's staring at the Radio Times crossword. She and my aunt do it together but apart – if that makes sense – then compare whenever they see each other, which is almost every day at some point, for a cup of coffee and toasted teacake at the very least.

"Mum."

She looks up. "Yes. Energy. Let me just write that down." She jots 'e n e r g y' in the crossword then returns her attention to me. "Where was I?"

What did I say about easily distracted?

"Bridge. The non-game variety. Tissues. Dog bags."

"Oh yes. I was only a few feet away but sped up and returned them to him. I thought he was sexy from behind but corrr..." It's like the room's suddenly been engulfed in flames. This must be the real deal. But I get the sense there's more to it. I look at her in a 'what's wrong with him' kind of way.

"He's... er... married."

"Oh, Mum."

"Not happily."

"They never are."

"They live in separate bedrooms."

"Of course they do."

"He's leaving her."

"Of course he is. Let me guess: his wife doesn't understand him, she's ill, or he just needs to wait until the children grow up, although he's sixty-seven so grandchildren?"

Mum shakes her head. "No, none of that. They don't have children."

"Money then."

Mum shakes her head again. "Nope. No reason. They're in the process of getting a divorce but she's applying for jobs away from the area so they're waiting to see what happens before they sell the house."

That sounds reasonable. My mum may be scatty but she has a good head on her shoulders. It's been years since Dad died and why shouldn't she be happy, just not with someone else's husband. Pot. Kettle. Black. No, I don't know yet if James is married but he seems too… awesome, not a word I use very often, to be single. It happens though. But I'm not. I feel so hypocritical. I say a weedy, "Okay."

"Another cuppa?" she asks and I look at the clock on the microwave. I have a perfectly good watch but the microwave's in my eyeline so I go with that. It's half past ten. Where's the time gone?

"No, I'm okay, thanks."

"Hot water bottle?" My mum's keen to please. Even if I were cold, it's going to be May in an hour and a half, hopefully heralding stretches of nice weather. I shake my head. The duvet on the spare bed, my bed, is really thick so I know I won't take long to warm.

"But thanks."

I say goodnight and head to bed, my brain a whirr.

Chapter 26 – Day One Official

Tuesday 1st May

"So this project you're doing, Donna," Mum says to me as she stirs a saucepan of porridge. It's May and quite warm already but still we have porridge. It's a regular ritual whenever I stay over, which isn't as often since I met Duncan, but I can't see it happening all month. Cheese on toast for lunch, not that we're going to share any of those, but it's what I have if I visit for the day. I can feel my mouth salivating.

"Donna?"

I look up from staring at one of the silver cupboard door handles, as my brain moves to thinking about her and Charles. "Yep."

"This project. Do you have it all planned?"

"Not really. I have notes but..."

"Do you not think you ought to? Write a list of what you're going to be doing when. You're normally so organised. Are you okay?" Her face creases. "Are you and Duncan okay? You seem distracted."

James. She's not wrong. I smile. "Oh yes, just missing him."

She looks convinced. "Of course you are."

Can't make babies when you're here, I expect her to add but thankfully she doesn't.

It's Tuesday, day one of my project, and the day when my mum has Pilates, the garden centre and chess. Knowing her, she'll grill Frankie who would have grilled Frank about my first day. Mum and I didn't talk that much about it last night and there isn't really time now. I have to be at work in an hour and she's no doubt got things to do before she meets up with Clan-dess-teen and all their lycra-clad cohorts. That I would like to see.

"Thanks, Mum," I say as she places a steaming bowl of semi-liquid nirvana in front of me. I know Nirvana's a place (and a rock band) rather than a thing but porridge is truly heavenly. I'm used to the two-minute nuke from a sachet type, especially the golden syrup variety, but the start-from-scratch oat version is yummily gritty, like granary versus wholemeal bread, I suppose.

"I'll probably take Elliott out at some stage today. Your aunt's got a commission for someone's birthday. A couples of horses, skewbald and a grey. Very handsome pair."

I smile and recall a photo, taken years ago, of my aunt and her amazing paintings at an exhibition or sale. I'm not sure I ever knew which. Horses are her specialty, having been a groom for racing driver Stirling Moss's sister, Pat, back in the fifties, I think. I've not been on a horse since a teenager but I've always been fond of them. My brain's more on Elliott, although I desperately want to carry on the conversation of Charles, helpfully prompted by the mention of Elliott but my mum points at my bowl and says, "It'll be getting cold and you have to be getting on."

That's me told.

As I drive to work, I can't help but picture my mum on that bridge the day she met Charles. We've not talked about his dog, assuming he has one given what fell out of his bag. Charles is a very steadfast name but I can't imagine him being like that. Not if he's a patch on Mum.

Elliott's an eighteen-month-old cream-coloured cockerpoo but not quite. My aunt and uncle aren't sure what he actually is but that's what his birth certificate said so it's all they have to go on. He's mad, a bit too much really for them but they adore him and it's reciprocated. He loves my mum especially because she's equally mad, and it wouldn't surprise me if she treats him like a baby when no one else is around.

She takes him out when she's available, sometimes with my uncle when my aunt's busy. Needless to say there are loads of paintings of him – Elliott, not my uncle! – in different poses, many in the bedroom I use. Although it's my room rather than my mum's or the lounge or dining area, I think she has the pictures in the house for company. He's certainly a character is our Elliott.

My mum was a secretary before she retired but never went into much detail. Banks, I think, but I reckon she was a spy, still is with the amount of time she's out, but only domestic because she's home every night rather than being in a swanky hotel bedding a gorgeous James Bond type. She'd love my James. No, not *my* James. Oh, man. Now I've got him on the brain.

Duncan. Think about… Oh no. I didn't speak to him at all yesterday. I didn't text so he'll think I didn't think about him. Of course I did; Nathan and I talked about him so why didn't I call or even look to see if there were any messages. I'm driving on the A41 so I can't pull over until there's a layby and I've just passed one so there won't be another for miles. I'll do it when I'm parked up, by which time he'll be in surgery, with a patient at least or something. His phone will be off in a locker or in his bag so he won't see it until lunch by which time it'll be a day and a bit. Oh, Donna. What are you doing?

Thinking too much. I'm driving. Concentrate on driving. It'll all be fine.

Chapter 27 – Get Cracking

I arrive at work relatively stress-free, from a traffic point of view anyway, and look forward to a hectic day. Although I have a sort of plan, I'm going to play a lot of it by ear and that's rather thrilling, despite it probably being half the population's daily routine; not knowing what they're going to have for an evening meal until they go shopping or out to dinner.

Veronica's final piece runs today. I've looked at a few back copies and she doesn't have as much space as I do at Northampton. Billy's said that I can have the same or a smaller space and he'll accommodate, which is very… accommodating! He has my intro piece so I'm not panicking. Much.

I wave my pass over the security scanner and the barrier lifts. There are loads of cars so I must be one of the last to arrive, even though there's half an hour before the official start time. I suppose after yesterday's staff bonding outing – was it really only yesterday? – there's work to be caught up on.

Speaking of which, I'm pretty sure I've not met everyone yet. There are roles at Northampton that must be duplicated here – advertising admins and a sales manager at the very least – but it's only day two, day one of the 'project'.

I find a space on the second level and spot Nathan's bug (that's the name I've decided on, considering the colour) as I walk back down the ramp. The car park's tucked behind the back of the building so there's not a lot to see other than concrete until I get to the main door. There is a back door but I've been told this pass doesn't open it from the outside. Not sure why but I do as I'm told. The thought of that makes me smile… and reminds me of Duncan.

"Oh sh…" I hadn't messaged him when I arrived, not in the car park anyway, so I delve around in my bag and fish out my phone. Fully charged, I can't believe I plugged it in last night without unlocking the screen and seeing what I'd missed. Anyone would think I'd had too good a time to think about my former life… or rather my pre- and post-Hemel life.

There's only one missed call and when I tap on the recents icon, there's a voicemail. My heart flutters as I listen to Duncan's voice. "Hi darling," he says. "How's it all going? I won't disturb you as you'll be swamped but a quick message to say I'm thinking of you and… I'm thinking of you. I love you. Bye for now."

The hesitation is very Duncan. I'm not sure what he was planning to say but whatever it was it would have been nice. More than nice. Probably something naughty but he gets embarrassed quite easily. For someone so outgoing, he's quite shy – I know, an oxymoron –

but when we're together he's confident, smutty, and very bad.

Phil smiles and opens the door for me before I've had a chance to swipe the pass again.

"Sorry, Donna. I should let you do that so it clocks you in. I know you'll log in on your computer but you know."

It's not something I've given a huge amount of thought, or inclination. I'm on a flat salary so it doesn't really matter when I've clocked in or out unless I take the proverbial and swan around like I'm Lady Muck. No one here seems like that, I'm sure not even the super-classy Veronica.

"No problem," I say and hover my pass over a flat sensor. "How was your evening last night?"

Phil shrugs. "Usual. Chores, taxi service, that kinda thing."

I'm surprised after working a twelve-hour day that Mrs Phil would get him doing chores. Taxi service, yes, but although he doesn't sound too enamoured, he seems the kind of… upfront guy to not be bossed around.

"The joy of being a man," I say and wonder why but it's too late. It's out there.

"Spot on," he drawls and winks.

I smile and go on my way upstairs.

Someone I don't know, but assume is Owen, is sitting at the reception desk. He's on the phone but as we've not met, I hover, not wanting to interrupt, to wait and introduce myself. He puts his hand over the mouthpiece. "Hey, Donna. How are you?"

I'm a little taken back that he knows who I am but put on my best smile. "I'm really good, thank you. Owen?"

He gives a 'Glee' grin then points to the phone. "Catch up later, sweetheart."

I'm not sure anyone's called me sweetheart since my dad and it chokes me a little but I love Owen's enthusiasm. I wonder if there's something in the Hertfordshire water that makes everyone so jolly. If so, I'm going to bottle a load and take it home.

I wave a temporary goodbye and walk through the double doors that separate the tranquillity of the reception to the madhouse that would normally be a newspaper's open plan office. Except this one's quiet. I wonder if there's been another staff bonding half day scheduled without anyone mentioning it – not that I'd be invited being a stand-in, but no, all the desks seem to be filled with my new colleagues busy at their respective roles. I can't see my desk until I get round a final corner so I don't know what awaits me but after giving everyone on my way a brief wave, I'm greeted by an almost-empty desk. Apart from Veronica's samples.

Today is day one. Official. In the next… I look at my watch. Eight, twelve is four, one is five, five and twenty-four is twenty-nine. In the next twenty-nine hours, there has to be an article, a 'dishes' article, on the system – Billy's happy to take it off from there. I can't exactly plop it into his in tray now can I. Plop. "Plop." I say aloud and look up. No one's paying me any attention which is just as well. No one needs to know how mad I am.

So yes, twenty-nine hours for five hundred words maximum. I can do that. No problem. Uh huh. Yep.

To get me started, I pull out my plan.

– List of things to take: suitcase, laptop, phone, chargers, clothes etc. Enough for a week or the whole month?

Done and sorted. Tick.

– List of pubs and restaurants in Hemel Hempstead: lunch (alone or with colleagues) and dinner (with Mum? With Aunt Jan and Uncle Pat?). Breakfast?

Done and sort of sorted. Half tick. The 'who' is okay. I just need to expand on my list of 'where'… and more importantly really, the 'what'. There may be places on my list that don't do any main meals under 500 calories. Google's been my friend so far so I jot down 'google more menus' next to this prompt.

– List of pubs and restaurants in Tring. Definitely with family. Not breakfast unless the weekend, not practical.

That's okay. I can play Tring by ear. I know it way better. I've been almost everywhere and while not eating rubbish, I certainly wasn't counting calories. I do need to pay more attention. Okay, next.

– List of types of dishes. Not as mad as it sounds. Aunt Jan and Uncle Pat are vegetarians so something to bear in mind.

This is the crucial bit. I'm supposed to be the guide for my readers, advise where to go and what to eat. I wonder if Greta does food reviews. I should ask her. No, I'll wait until our evening on Wednesday. It'll be something to talk about, not that I usually have any trouble.

– List of places around the area. Why stick with Hemel and Tring? Repeat places or go somewhere just once? It would make the project more interesting but possibly more complicated.

It might but wouldn't the reader want to know about places they've never been? Dishes they've never eaten? Of course they would. So, within reason, I need to find places they'd not normally go to so no more Subway, McDonalds. Oh but Wetherspoon is ideal. Okay, compromise. Regular town-centre places at lunchtime – we, and those reading my articles, will only have an hour after all. Then somewhere more interesting. Brain clicks to Wiggington. The

Old Man thereof. It's a book. Can't remember who by, a local chap, I think. I'll google it.

There's supposed to be somewhere *really* nice at Wiggington but probably outside the price range, not that anyone's told me what it is yet. So yes, definitely imminently, eminently... come on, Donna... eminently sensible, Sherlock Holmes-esque, at lunchtime then a little crazy in the evenings. It's Frank's evening tonight so, being the accountant, he'll know exactly how much we can spend.

A search for *The Old Man of Wiggington* isn't helpful, not even when I add Hertfordshire, as most of the results had wanted me to go to The Wiggington at Tamworth. I try 'books about Wiggington Hertfordshire' and the closest I get is a series of local history books by Mike Bass and Jill Fowler. Clever people. That's a kind of dedication I admire; to spend probably years researching somewhere and sharing their knowledge. Even if they'd lived in the town all their lives, they'd still have to check everything. I wouldn't have the patience, not that I'm not a patient person but you know. Too much to do.

So, I must have imagined the Old Man, which is sad. I like to think there was one at some stage.

The pub it turns out is an inn, a hotel no less, called The Greyhound. It looks very nice, exclusive with its smart lemon-coloured frontage, black railings and 'warm welcome' red and white sign. Probably way beyond the company's budget for my project, so something perhaps to treat my mum to. And it serves Doombar beer and ooh, Tring Brewery's Ridgeway Bitter... my uncle would approve, but it's a pub, sorry inn, with beer so he'd be happy regardless. He doesn't get much opportunity, being the driver when they go out, so a table for four definitely, with me as chauffeur. Mum and my aunt's birthday mid-September. Mustn't forget.

And back to the present day.

Chapter 28 – The First Official Dish

I've just gone back to my list when Frank appears by my desk.

"Good morning, my dear. And how are things with you?"

I smile. I've been doing a lot of that recently and it feels good. "I'm very well, thank you, kind sir." I hope I'm not being patronising.

"All set for this evening?"

"I think so. Thank you. It's very kind of you to do this."

"Nonsense. Gives me something to do other than watch television when Frankie's out with your mum. How is Lesley?"

"She's well, thank you. I hadn't realised she was so busy. All these evening classes, subjects I never knew she liked."

"It's not everybody's cup of chai. Frankie's always been a chess fan but I believe Lesley also does the guitar and yoga, is it…?"

"Pilates."

"That's right. Pilates. That and the chess are private; in local halls rather than schools but I think the guitar is Adult Learning so in one of the local schools. It's amazing what's on offer and considering chess is supposed to be quite an intense thinking man's… woman's sport… I think it's a sport, officially, you know."

I haven't a clue but nod.

"Yes. Considering chess is supposed to be quite an intense thinking woman's sport, they don't half talk a lot."

I laugh. A round-hearted belly laugh. Frank looks a little taken aback but smiles nonetheless.

Tonight's going to be fun. He's a little serious, old school, but I can see underneath is a heart of gold, and given that he's sharing it with me, I'm honoured.

"So… how's it all going?" he asks looking at my too-tidy desk. Back in Northampton, my equivalent would be covered in white with very little brown fake wood to be seen, but I know where things are when I need them. It would be me juggling a lot of open assignments. Here I have just the one.

"Not bad, thank you. Still at the planning stage but a much easier job than Izzy had. Do you know all about Izzy, back at Northampton?"

Frank frowns.

"Izzy… Isobel, my technology colleague, had to date thirty-one men in days and…"

Frank's frown lifts.

"Write about it," I continue. "It was actually forty-something as we went speed dating mid-month. It's where I met my boyfriend actually."

Frank smiles. "Yes. Frankie did mention how you'd met... Duncan, is it?"

"It is."

"Not in context, but it makes sense now. Yes, that's tough. I'd go for the food option."

I laugh. "Me too."

"So," he continues, "has anyone explained the rules?"

Uh oh. "Rules?"

"Not rules as such but erm... oh I don't know. Terms. No, too formal. Stuffy. Anyway, you have a limit of fifty pounds a day, which I think is pretty good really."

"It's fantastic," I gush. Considering Izzy had a ten-pound daily limit, fifty is astounding but who could get a decent meal, or a half-decent one to include a drink, for ten pounds.

"Yes. Fifty pounds a day. You can go where you like. I have some ideas. I can pull up a chair if you like." He points to Veronica's visitor chair.

"That would be great but aren't you busy?"

He waves a hand down like a... I don't know what like but he pfuts. Or something like that.

"It's just figures. Everyone's still submitting all their receipts and whatnot for last month so no point in me even starting on them until they're all in."

That shatters my illusion that anyone working in finance is manic at month-end, month-beginning, but Frank knows best, and I think part of it is him being polite. He too might be swan-kicking underneath.

He pulls the chair round towards mine and I move up so there's space for the both of us at my desk, albeit with none of our four legs outstretched.

"What have you got so far?"

I show him my list.

"Okay..."

I know how bare it is. "But I've been to Ristorante Alberto with James, and Nathan," I blurt. "It was shut on a Monday though so we went for a nice walk into town. We ended up at Subway, James and I, so I got a feel for the area."

"That's right, you've not actually lived in Hemel."

I shake my head but he's still looking at the sheet so he can't see me. "I grew up in Tring and know it really well. I should therefore know Hemel but I left home years ago and I only visit every–"

"Ah, yes. Well, never fear. We'll look after you. Everyone on board is local born, never escaped like you did, so they'll be able to answer any query you have. Be good to be more about the food, wouldn't it." Great minds think alike. "So, Alberto's and Subway. That was lunch yesterday?"

"It was. Nathan took me back to the old village last night, evening, but not to Alberto's, not to eat. I thought we were when we were heading in that direction but it was still Monday."

"Of course."

"We ended up at the Chiangmai Thai."

"Nice. I do like it there. One of Frankie's favourites actually."

"It was really nice. Then Asda." I can't help smiling.

"Asda?"

"Milk. Nathan had forgotten to get some milk."

"Ah..."

"And I picked up some essentials."

"Mum not feeding you because she's never there?"

I laugh. "Not quite but no, more like research."

He waits for me to continue.

"A couple of the salads, some light... low-calorie crisps and bottled water."

"Eminently sensible." Sherlock Holmesque, yes. "So the salubrious Subway and Asda. Anywhere else as classy this lunchtime?"

I'd not thought that far ahead. I'd tried not to as it would mean thinking about James. "Not really. Just see what James fancies doing." I know that I could be going out with him or Leah and think the latter would be better to keep me on the proverbial straight and narrow. Plus she and I have talked very little so far, only because our paths haven't really crossed, so it would be nice to get to know her better.

"I'm sure he'll come up with something."

I don't know whether Frank says that because he knows James will be my chaperone today or whether it's a more general comment. Of course I'm not going to ask so don't reply.

"And tonight? Anything you'd like to do?" Frank asks.

Leaving Wetherspoon as a solo back-up, I say, "I drive past the K2 Balti House every time I come down to the hill to the magic roundabout–"

Frank laughs and I smile. "Ah yes the magic magic roundabout. The Plough, don't you know."

I don't like to tell him that I do as it may sound smug but he spots me looking at it on my notes.

"Indeed you do. So the K2, hey?"

"Is that okay? In budget? Or more importantly, something you'd like to do? Not too spicy?"

"Don't worry about that. I can do hot. Not quite vindaloo. I'm more of a Bhuna or Dansak lover myself."

I'm so pleased I'm in such good hands. "I'm not an Indian food expert but I'd rather have a bit of a kick than the ultra-mild Korma, not that I don't like sweet."

"We'll find you something."

"That's really kind." I feel like a stuck record but it is. It wouldn't bother me to go on my own but it's always nice to go with someone else, especially someone who reminds me of my dad. I get a little sad and nostalgic and Frank seems to notice.

"Now. Let's see what else you have." He looks at my woefully inadequate notes. "Oh, I knew there was something else," he says, looking across at me. "Billy *has* told you that you don't have to be office bound, hasn't he."

I shake my head.

"Nathan didn't tell you?"

I shake my head again.

"William, your boss, didn't say before you left?"

I shake my head a third time. Izzy was very much office bound there and really it wasn't any different. She met the guys on her own time. She stretched a lunchtime or two but all but a couple of her dates were in the evenings. May only have been one. I can't remember; it *was* a year ago.

"You're already giving up your evenings, twenty-something of them."

I nod. "Twenty. Twenty-five days but twenty evenings. Fridays don't count but–"

"So you shouldn't have to give up your days too."

"It's fine. I'd fully expected to come here every day but one or two off occasionally would be a bonus."

"Make sure you do. Go somewhere that isn't Tring or Hemel. Too much concrete here, and of course you're used to Tring. Do you know any nice cafés?"

"A few spring to mind."

"Do you have access to a dog?"

I laugh. "My aunt and uncle have a mad cockerpoo type."

"Perfect. It's supposed to be nice all week so go somewhere different one lunchtime. Do you know the Bluebells, Marsworth way?"

"I…"

"The bottom of the reservoir, not far outside Tring. There's a disused pub on the main road."

I know exactly where he means. “My mum and aunt used to visit a friend there. I thought it was Long Marston but yes, I know it. I’ve not been in the café but the car park’s always been busy when I’ve driven past. I think popular with cyclists especially, like The Cog.”

“In Tring.”

“Frogmore Street.”

“I knew it when it was Tringfellows. It’s such a shame they changed the name. I love play on words.”

“Me too.”

“Of course, dear. You’re the journalist.”

I’m a columnist rather than fully fledged journalist but don’t correct him. “Do you do any writing, Frank?”

“Not really.”

“Not really?” Not really in my book usually means yes but they’re too shy to talk about it.

“Everyone’s got a novel in them,” I offer.

“So they say but not me. Not that kind of imagination. No, I’m helping Frankie with hers.”

“Oh?”

“Her autobiography. She used to be a nurse at Great Ormond Street Hospital.”

“Gosh.”

“Exactly.”

I laugh, only just getting the significance. I’d meant ‘gosh’ as an exclamation rather than an acronym.

“She obviously dealt with the children but many were offspring of celebrities. I’m talking back in the day; she retired probably around the time you left home, so not the people you’d see on television these days.”

I know what he means. In the year, minus two weeks ish, that I’ve been with Duncan, we’ve watched more films and box sets than ‘live’ TV so I recognise only a few of the people on *I’m A Celebrity Get Me Out Of Here* or *Strictly Come Dancing*, even when told who they are. And having them described as a ‘TV personality’ doesn’t help.

I’m not quite George Clooney era, although he was incredibly sexy in *ER*… Duncan does like all the ‘scrubs’ type programmes… not actually *Scrubs*, other than the first couple of series as they got silly – banana-skin silly rather than clever silly – after that, but anything that features green operation-style uniforms. *Supervet*, that kind of thing. It makes me cry but Duncan’s used to it, although he is a big softie, and I love him cuddling into me on the sofa. I picture him looking up at me, doe eyed, and I smile but realise I’m ignoring Frank.

"Sorry, Frank. You'll have to tell me more when we go out tonight. Should I book the K2?"

Frank shakes his head. "Leave it to me. Or I'll get Nathan to do it. He won't mind. And yes, gladly tell you more. Frankie's a very interesting lady."

"Thank you. I look forward to it." Other than research, I don't have a lot to do. This may be a lot tougher than I expect but for now I'm going with the flow.

"I'll leave you to it," he says and wheels the chair back to the other side of the desk.

"Thanks again, Frank. You've all been really nice."

He shrugs as if it really is nothing. He's probably glad to get out. "Have fun with James at lunchtime, whatever it is you get up to."

I'm grateful that Frank has turned away and can't see me blushing. I'm not the quickest at picking up on innuendos and I'm sure he didn't mean it as such, but my brain is one step ahead this time.

Chapter 29 – Those Almond Eyes

I do a bit of googling and add to my lists. The Bluebells is exactly where I was thinking. It'll be great if I can borrow Elliott and take him round the reservoirs. It's not been raining for a while so little chance of getting him muddy, unless he jumps into the canal. Fortunately the sides of the main reservoir itself are too high and even nutty as he is, he wouldn't be daft enough to jump in. Would he?

Although he's a fruit loop, he's very road savvy – my uncle's taught him well – so I'll probably be a skinflint and park near the village hall rather than in the car park itself. I google 'Tring reservoir car park charges' and click on the first link to Tring Reservoirs Herts and Middlesex Wildlife Trust. I feel guilty at trying to save some money, especially as I'm not going to pay for any meals this month. Not very helpfully, it just says 'pay and display'. I don't suppose it's very much and like the country parks in Northamptonshire, all the money – in theory – goes to the upkeep of the park. They're like corner shops; if you want to keep them going, keep going in. I like that. It sounds like a slogan. I should submit it somewhere.

I can't believe I've nodded off. I look at the screen's clock. Midday. It's only been a few seconds but I have a couple of rows of 'dddddddd's where the middle finger of my left hand had rested on the 'd' key. DD for Duncan and Donna. I haven't had enough early nights but it always feels like my mum and I have much to catch up on. Though it's usually more her updating me on her hectic life than me with mine: work, Duncan, work, Izzy, work, Duncan, work.

Another half an hour and it'll be lunchtime. I'm assuming it'll be the same as yesterday, 12.30. Later rather than earlier suits me as it makes the afternoon go quicker but if I'm not tied to my desk, it doesn't really matter.

I'm about to google something else when a shadow falls over my desk. A big dark shadow.

I look up and it's James. I'm surprised my heart doesn't skip. I don't feel my hands getting clammy or my mouth dry. I've been thinking about Duncan a lot, although I haven't checked my phone since Frank left my desk which I should have done to see if I'd had any messages or voicemails. I can sneak a peek when I'm out at lunchtime, or pop into the ladies on the way out if James has come to collect me.

"Hi," he broods.

"Hello," I chirp. I try to sound as non-committal as possible and his shoulders slump a little. Or I think they have. I have to wear my sensible Donna head when he's around. Think of him as Leah, or Greta, or Nathan. Yes, that's the way to do it.

"Okay for lunch?"

"That would be lovely. What time?"

"Okay if we go now?"

"Oh, right." I wasn't expecting that. I lean down to the floor, grab my bag, reminding myself to check my phone at the earliest opportunity.

"Sorry but I have a two o'clock meeting so need to drop you back here before I head out again."

"No problem." Dropping me back sounds like we're going in his car. I wasn't expecting that either.

"I thought we'd head up to Jarman Park."

As well as getting my petrol from Tesco there on the way to the motorway, it's also home to the ski centre and cinema, and others. I know we don't have time for a quick ski or to see a movie, not even if we missed the adverts, so I'm guessing it's either Tesco for lunch or somewhere else I've not noticed the name of on the complex.

We pull up in the general parking area then head towards the eateries. There's so much choice. First up is Frankie and Benny's but we go past that. We also pass Chiquito and Bella Italia. Either of those would have done.

As expected, we pass Planet Ice. That would have been too much to ask of a lunch break. I'm pleased when it looks like we're going into the Pommel Horse, one of the Hungry Horse franchises as they're next up and have plenty of choice. I'm vaguely familiar with the chain as we have at least two in Northampton: one on the Sixfields leisure park and one in Kingsthorpe. I can't remember their names yet neither venue is a million miles from mine or Duncan's.

I'm confused when James walks away from the building rather than towards it.

"A little detour first," James says and I fall a step behind so I can sense where he might turn.

Thankfully he goes past the Subway next to it. I'm sure he'd not do that two days in a row.

I laugh nervously as the only other options are the DJ's Play Park, which I don't think caters for anything over a teenager – legally rather than mentally, the athletics track – I'm wearing the wrong shoes, or over the road to XC, which I think is a climbing and skate park. Although it's bound to be for all ages, again it feels a little too young and perhaps too much for a lunch break.

We do indeed stop outside DJ's. I look at the list of activities on their board and spot go karting. Duncan and I went to a track in Northampton, one in the St James's part of town ironically, for his birthday last year and I loved it, although the cars we had were particularly smelly and I did get a bit sick and disorientated as I whizzed round but he loved it so that was all that mattered.

"Have you karted before?" James asks, standing a little too close for comfort. For mine anyway.

"A couple of times. It was fun, when I wasn't feeling queasy from the engine fumes. Duncan, my boyfriend, thrashed me but yes, fun." I'm not as competitive as him, or probably most men… or Izzy. "The last time I drove a kart, I sat in the middle of the lane so Duncan couldn't get past… not actually on purpose but I didn't know the rules. While he hadn't complained as such, he had rightly pointed out it didn't make it much of a contest."

James goes to open the door but stops so I stop. "I'm only kidding," he says. "Literally. I'm sorry for teasing but the karts are tiny." He grimaces as if only now realising how short I am. I'm used to it and was teased as a child but grew to love my five-foot-two-and-a-half frame.

"It's fine," I say and give a genuine laugh. He's only being funny and he's all the more lovely for it. Help.

He points to the nearby XC, the climbing and skate park. It's a huge place so they probably do more than that. I've only just thought that when a poster shows us they also do high ropes and caving. I'm not great with heights and certainly can get claustrophobic so I'm hoping we're doing the first of the two choices. I've never skied because I like to be in control of my feet but would give a baby run a go. At least with the climbing, I assume, we will be attached to something, and ropes being easier to manage than skis I'm keeping everything crossed that it's that. I could jump off a skateboard which I couldn't with skis so that would be my preference there.

Thankfully it is my first option; the climber, a trial in fact, so pretty much as low level as it can get. The blurb says, 'Join us for a one-hour taster session where you'll get the full climbing experience with all the basics taken care of for you. Enjoy warm-up games, bouldering, rope climbing and auto belays. We also run dedicated Mini Mountaineer sessions for three- and four-year-olds.'

"Am I a mini mountaineer?" I ask James and he grins, his earlier unintentional faux pas put behind us.

I have no clue what an auto belay is but the tutor explains it's the device we're going to be attached to. It looks a bit like a gadget

Duncan has for weighing his suitcases but hopefully this one's a lot stronger. I'm not overweight, slightly curvy at the most – it's tricky for anyone five foot two (and a half) to be skinny, but I could still give a handful of suitcases a run for their money. Not that suitcases run.

It turns out James had pre-booked so we only have to wait a few minutes before it's our turn, although not before we both sign waivers.

"It's so if we die it's our fault," James explains cheerfully.

Chapter 30 – A Great Distraction

The hour flies by and it's such a great distraction. I can't remember the last time I'd forgotten everything. Needless to say, James is far more skilled than me. I'm not as competitive and have certainly less muscle definition; James's so much so that it becomes a distraction. But I hold my own and get higher than I had expected from when we'd stood at the bottom looking up.

Finally our hour is done. What he says next stuns me.

"I love what we have," James says as he removes his helmet. He does look particularly sexy in his jeans and zip top. "I don't want it to stop," he continues, "but I want more. I'm assuming we can't..." James looks at me with those gorgeous eyes and I can feel my heart breaking. Literally breaking. Part of me wants to be with him too but every time I think of Duncan, I feel worse. I won't cheat on him. I absolutely won't. But these eyes keep looking at me.

"You're married, aren't you," I say as we walk towards an area selling hot and cold drinks, not quite a café but it amounts to the same thing. My statement is not a question. And it's not a topic we've raised before. He's not wearing a ring – it's an instinctive glance that almost every woman does the first time they meet a man they fancy, regardless of whether in a solid relationship or not – but I know the answer's going to be yes.

He bows his head and stares at the floor so I can't see his eyes. "Yes," he whispers.

I feel sick, warm, I'm not sure which but I knew the answer before I asked. He's too lovely to not have been snapped up already.

"Then it's a definite 'no'. I'm sorry but I'm not only not cheating on Duncan but I'm certainly not letting you cheat on your wife, not with me anyway." I don't want to ask the next question but I need to know. "Do you have children?"

Without looking up, he nods.

"How many?"

He mumbles something. I think it's 'Two'. Or 'Oh'. He could have a dozen children, it doesn't really matter. Having a wife is bad enough but even one child is a no-no. Now I've got a picture of a bright pink defibrillator... no, not defibrillator, that revives people. *No! No!* What a stupid name for that hair removal thing. Delapidator. Come on, Donna. What's it called? I'm usually so good with words but my brain is mush. Baby brain. I shake my head. Babies are the last thing I want to think of.

James finally looks up and I see the hurt in those eyes, and realise I'm still shaking my head. I'd stand here all day doing that if it meant it would sink in... with either of us. We have an undeniable spark but I'm a decent human being. He is too, I'm sure. I can't. He can't. We can't. Oh, it's horrible. I'm horrible for thinking it.

"It's probably best if Leah accompanies me for lunch from now on," I whimper. "Or I go on my own, or sit at my desk. It's no problem, especially if I'm out every evening."

He says nothing.

"I'm very grateful though," I say, stepping forward and I hold his arm. My hand feels as if it's burning through his top. I release my hold and step away. "For such a fun time today. It was really kind and thoughtful of you."

"I can't help feeling the way I do," he says.

And I guess he can't but I'm only here for a month so…

"We should get going," he says and pulls his keys from his jeans pocket.

We walk side-by-side back to his car, past the Hungry Horse and all the other options.

We haven't eaten but I brought in the Asda salad and it's sitting in the fridge at work, right at the back with my name on it… a little childish but it's the only reserve I have.

I feel lousy but less guilty than before we'd had the conversation. I hope it doesn't cause an atmosphere as our paths will cross again, even if it's only me walking past James's desk.

The drive back to the office is wordless. The radio's not on – he'd switched it off on the outward journey. I'm tempted to switch it on but apart from being rude, it would state the obvious.

I thank him again as he pulls into the car park, into the space that was between Nathan's and my car last night. Normally I would have told James this but it doesn't seem appropriate, nor important. It's the silly kind of thing that's so insignificant there's nothing much to say in response, less this time.

"I'm sorry," I repeat as he swipes his pass to let us in the back door. It's the first time I've come in this way and we're greeted by a simple grey stone and metal staircase. It seems as bleak as I feel, and I can almost sense the cold underneath my feet.

My apology either goes unnoticed, unheard or ignored. I think the latter is most likely.

The stairs come out to a door next to reception, not the one I'm using when coming up from the front door or security office but one tucked in a corner, not noticed – by me certainly – before now. I should be more observant but my brain's been a little occupied since I arrived here yesterday morning. I can't believe it's only been a day and a half. So much has happened, and gone wrong.

As James peels off to speak to Owen, I remember I have another twenty-three and a half workdays left at this office. Twenty-three and a half with James. I'm not sure I can bear it.

I also don't know whether I should be waiting for James or make my own way back to my desk. For my own pride, I pick the latter but pull a notebook and pen from my bag and jot a brief 'Thank you again for lunch, James' onto a sheet and leave it on his desk as I walk by, having collected my Asda salad en route.

I'm grateful my desk is tucked around a corner. I can't see James's desk from mine so when he gets out of his meeting, I'll run the risk of passing him every time I want to go to the kitchen, ladies, out for lunch or home time, but I can't dwell on it and hopefully it'll blow over. He's a very reasonable chap. And I'm a very reasonable chapette. Or whatever the equivalent is.

I'm pretty sure I can't hear James from my desk either. Although there are peaks and troughs of noise and quiet, no single person is distinguishable at any one time. There's a decorum whereby everyone seems respectful of everyone else's personal space and I'm particularly grateful. But then I remember he had a two o'clock meeting so he may not have even come back through.

I have emails from my and Veronica's readers. I'm curious (nosy) so go into her 'sent' items to see her style. It feels a little creepy but my heart almost stops when I see how many emails she's sent James. And reading them, I can see why.

They're together. That or they're having an affair. It's all very intimate yet strangely detached. I can't quite work out why. Their surnames are different – I knew this already but now assume Veronica uses her maiden name for professional reasons. I stop reading as I start to feel sick. I'm intruding on a couple who are doing nothing wrong. A married couple discussing childcare, plans for the weekend, whether she still needs him to finish early on Friday. Normal couply stuff.

I shouldn't be surprised and actually I'm not. It doesn't take a genius to figure that Veronica's just had a baby, and James is… The father. Ethan's father. And the other three in the picture. So much for him having two. That was bad, lying to me. If that's what he did. *He* certainly didn't use the correct level of decorum, or whatever.

Why couldn't he just come clean and say, 'Sorry, Donna. I can't have an affair with you. I'm married to the woman whose job you're doing this month. We have four children, double what I told you. Or what you think you heard. And we're very happy, thank you very much.'

But he didn't, my brain tells me as I head for the ladies.

Chapter 31 – Being A Chicken

To take my mind off James, I crack on looking at Google maps, listing potential places to go and looking at their menus. Many, the restaurants mostly, don't have calorie listings but I figure they'll have something. I need to be more accurate than that though because if they don't, I'll be stuck with Asda or Subway salads every day. Not a bad thing for lunch, and I'm sure the sandwich van lady or gent will know the calorie content of their own selection.

It's two o'clock, the time James's meeting starts, before I finally check my mobile's messages. I hadn't expected James to be collecting me so early and seeing how that panned out, I simply didn't have a chance to look then. Apart from anything else, I get carsick at screens… or maps, or anything really. So I do while tucking into my salad and it makes my day. Duncan's one message rather than the salad, although that was nice. No, the message is a very simple 'Don't forget I love you' with a bunch of emojis thereafter which make me laugh. Apart from the face blowing a kiss, I think he hit them at random, or selected the recent few, a bit like doing the scales on the piano only less tuneful but funnier. That's Duncan all over. I can imagine him chuckling to himself.

It makes me smile and I send back an elephant and a face blowing kisses then a heart with two stars. No words but I tell him all the time that I love him and sometimes it's not what we say but how we show our affection. It's like the showing not telling in writing. Have the character do something, don't tell us how they feel. "You can't handle the truth!" I blurt then cower, hoping no one's paying me any attention. If they are, I can't see them so that's fine. Unless they know it's Jack Nicholson from *A Few Good Men*, they'll just think I'm having an argument with a supplier or something.

By the time five o'clock comes round, I've not only compiled a great list of eateries, along with some less than 500 calorie options, but I've written an article. Not the most inspiring of starts was my description of the Asda salad, but I've embellished it as much as possible, saying why salads aren't all boring and they can be welcome in the warm weather; containing hidden water and so on. I then go on to detail my trip to Chiangmai Cottage with Nathan so plenty of humour. I hope.

It's been a very strange forty-eight hours. My mum is light relief so a nice kind of strange, and the rest has been too, but they say your life can change in a matter of hours and before I met James I'd wondered… although it had when I'd met Duncan. When you think your life is on a certain course and something comes along to shake that, it really does make you wonder.

Part of me calls myself chicken for hiding in my corner but unless I need to go to the ladies – which I don't because I forgot to bring a drink with me – or the kitchen to get the forgotten drink, I stay put. I have to face James sometime but I'm waiting until Frank gets me before venturing out.

Yes, I'm a chicken.

Chapter 32 – A Couple Of Small Someones

The more I stare at the picture of Veronica, her children and the 'bump', the more curious I am about the person taking the photograph. I've assumed it's her husband but it could be anybody. But why would he not be in the photograph. She has her right hand on one of her son's shoulders, her left over her bump, which we now know as Ethan. Her wedding ring is silver, platinum more likely, simple and unassuming but the engagement ring is massive, blue with diamonds, a bit like Princess Diana's, now Kate's, the Duchess of Cambridge, as she'd more formally known. This ring is a more modern version, and Veronica looks very classy – to be expected from a health and beauty journalist. I scoff. Okay we're not all like that.

I want to know who James is married to for sure but chide myself for the nonsenseness of it all. Nonsenseness, another Donna word?

No, it makes no difference. James has someone if it's not Veronica. Veronica has someone if it's not James. I have Duncan, the gorgeous vet. Not only does James have a someone but he has small someones and that's a no…

No. No, Donna, you're a good girl.

It'll be fine. I'll go home Friday night and Duncan will throw his arms around me and…

I want to cry.

It's just as well I don't as Frank comes over to collect me. I had my bag ready, complete with recently checked phone – nothing new from Duncan – so Frank and I are away as soon as I log off my computer.

Thankfully, James isn't there when we approach his desk. His two o'clock meeting must be a long one. I strategically let Frank go first.

I can't see him as he's slightly ahead of me but think I hear him smirking as my eyes rest on James's desk for a second or two too long. I can certainly imagine it. I'm not subtle. I know I'm not subtle. It's never been one of my traits. But after a couple of days, for anyone to have picked up on my feelings for James isn't good. Has he? Frank? My mum hasn't, although she knows there's something wrong, but given things are a little strained with Duncan, that's quite easy.

I need to get home, not my mum's, but my home, Duncan's home, to see him. I can't take a whole day off but I could leave really early one morning. Wednesday, Thursday, Friday. Three days. I can't leave it three days. But I have to. I can't. It'll be fine. Oh, why is life always so complicated?

Okay. I'll make the most of it here. Apart from the James hiccup, it's going really well.

Frank and I reach reception and Owen's still there. I wonder if he finishes at six, the same time as the security crossover. I've not met Phil's night shifter but will definitely stay one evening so I get to meet him… or her. Coming in before six in the morning would be a tad mad, and of course that's not like me at all. We have Jason from six pm to six am so I'm curious but won't inconvenience Frank by delaying our trip out.

"Hello, Donna. Lovely to meet you finally, properly," Owen says with a warm smile.

I give him a big smile in return. "And you, Owen. Can't really stop but…"

"No problem. I know what Frank here is up to. I er… I mean."

Owen blushes, bless him. Frank and I laugh.

"You have fun, you two," Owen concludes. "See you bright eyed and bushy tailed in the morning."

"You will," Frank says and opens the door for me at the top of the stairs leading down to the security office.

I expect to see Phil when we get to his room and I'm not disappointed. He's watching a monitor and what appears to be someone loitering near Nathan's car. I don't remember seeing Nathan at his desk when we walked past but I was concentrating on James not being at his so wasn't really paying attention.

We're all watching the person on the black and white screen unlock then drive away the car next to Nathan's, a very grubby what-should-be-white Vauxhall Astra van. A BMW Z4 it is not.

"Oh, that's okay," Phil mumbles, still staring at the screen.

Frank coughs, making Phil jump. Considering he's supposed to be 'on guard' with a pair of eyes in the back of his head, he's not terribly observant. "Night, Phil," Frank says and gestures towards the front door.

"Yes, right, Frank. G'night. G'night, Donna Dishes."

I only just refrain from blowing him a kiss. Mike he is also not. Thankfully. There's no food in sight, not even a crumb in evidence of Phil having eaten a morsel. No stains on his impeccable uniform and only a metal cup of steaming coffee next to a huge silver thermos, the cup being the lid.

I'm really looking forward to K2 and still so grateful to Frank for taking me – I will tell him later. Sometimes I forget to say 'thank you', which is terrible. I'm not like that but my mind whirrs at a million miles an hour and I have to tell it to slow down and take one day at a time, an hour at a time, a minute. Sometimes I need to take a breath.

"Convoy?" Frank suggests as we get to his car. It's the first in the car park so he doesn't need to ask where I've parked as we wouldn't have got to mine first.

"Absolutely." We both know where we're going but Frank's the native. K2 is actually walking distance but the opposite side of the magic roundabout so tricky to get to on foot. We'd only be crossing two roads but still not advisable, especially straight after work and as some shops shut so the world and his wife would be travelling.

Anyway, I don't know where Frank lives so we could be going in opposite directions. Taking both cars makes sense. "I'm up a floor," I say and point northwards.

He nods. "I'll wait by the barrier."

I've done enough nodding for the month already so I head to my car and we're soon on our journey… all seven minutes of it, and four of those are waiting to get out of the car park. Our offices are spitting distance, almost literally, to the magic roundabout so even if people wanted to let us out one way, the other is often blocked. The joy of being close to the town centre.

Chapter 33 – A Day For Climbing

I've been past K2 umpteen times, hundreds, not thousands for sure, but never been inside. It's a treat. The staff are so welcoming and there are loads of them. Although we're early, and there are only half a dozen customers sprawled around in such a big place, there's a really good atmosphere.

It's darker than I imagined but that adds to the ambiance. There's wood everywhere, even on the ceilings, and it's very smart, very typical Indian, very Balti… if there is such a thing. I *should* know. I should be the expert; food does come under health, but I'm not normally being so specific when it comes to calorie counting. That's what a lot of people get wrong; they spend so much time counting calories that they forget about balance.

After I'd mentioned K2 to Frank, I'd Wikipediad it. They're a clever lot, these Wikipedia contributors. In this case, I'm told that K2, also known as Mount Godwin-Austen or Chhogori at 8,611 metres (28,251ft) above sea level, is the second highest mountain in the world after Mount Everest at 8,848 metres (29,029ft). Located on the China–Pakistan border between Baltistan in the Gilgit-Baltistan region of northern Pakistan, and the Taxkorgan Tajik Autonomous County of Xinjiang, China, K2 is the highest point of the Karakoram range and the highest point in both Pakistan and Xinjiang. It doesn't mean a huge amount to me but second highest, perhaps where the '2' comes in, is impressive indeed. Not that it takes much to impress me but even so…

We're given menus and for the second evening in a row, I'm overwhelmed by the choice. It helps having the English explanations and 'hot' ratings.

"Starter and main?" Frank suggests and I'm grateful.

I am normally a pudding person and the choice here is really good: ice cream, sorbet, chocolate mousse, pineapple or dumplings. Pineapple's one of my favourite fruits but I tend to have something I'd not have at home, or be able to buy too easily, when I'm out, and especially somewhere like this. Dumplings are gorgeous but ones I've had in the past can be really filling, even small ones, and I don't think I'd manage it only after just the main course. Ice cream wouldn't be so filling so I'm torn but say, "That would be lovely."

There's an astounding choice of starters. I fancy the crispiness of a bhaji so go with that. There's only a choice of onion which isn't particularly sociable but I have no plans to get up close and personal with Frank and I'm sure (hoping) he doesn't either.

I'm very much a chicken main person so wouldn't do that for starter as well – hence me having the maybe-weird combo of chicken and duck yesterday – so the onion bhaji is a compliment and I think I've settled on that and tandoori chicken but remember that the main should be less than 500 calories and with lots of lovely tikka sauce it's going to be way over, certainly if I include the fritter aspect of the bhaji. I'm about to take another look when I see Frank's chosen already.

Our waiter comes over and introduces himself. His name plate says 'Bhumi' but he gives us a small bow and says, "Bhu, at your service. May I take your drinks order?"

Frank says something but I'm not listening. I'm still staring in awe at Bhumi's name.

He leans in a little towards me and our eyes meet. "It means 'earth', my lady," and he gives a slight tilt of his head before rectifying it again. It reminds me of when my iPhone decides to adjust a picture that is perfectly fine as it is and I click on 'reset'.

I pull back a little and smile. Everyone here is so nice and Bhumi, Bhu, obviously loves his job. You can usually tell. Either that or he's a very good actor. I *could* picture him on a Bollywood movie set. "Could I have a lemonade please."

Bhu bows again. "I shall return momentarily with your lemonade, madam, and your..." Bhu turns to Frank. "Kingfisher, sir." Frank returns Bhu's subsequent bow. "Then I shall collect your food order when you are quite ready. Sir, madam."

Frank and I smile at each other as Bhu heads off towards the bar area.

"It's all very authentic," I say and look around the restaurant. The blue, red and gold chairs look like they've not long been bought, no scuffmarks in sight. The decorations, again ornate, look equally fresh. I don't know Hemel well but imagine it has a real mix of cultures. I did think for a second that perhaps Bhu originated from Luton, a couple of junctions north on the M1, where I know there's a healthy Indian population, but that would spoil the effect. So here we are in little India and I'm looking forward to getting to know Frank better.

"Where did you meet Frankie?" I ask, launching into his personal life.

"School."

"Really? Childhood sweethearts?"

Frank laughs. "No. Evening classes. Five years ago. Dance lessons."

"Oh." I'm astounded. I don't know why I thought they'd been together forever. It felt natural. There we go.

Frank just smiles. "And you? Oh yes, you were dating. Speed dating was it?"

"Yes. I went to keep Izzy company really, for her project."

"Like I am you tonight."

"Indeed. Which reminds me. Sorry." I tap the menu.

"No, of course, you must choose something."

"I had but remembered I have to be good."

"Under 500."

"Under 500, yes."

While the menu's great, it's not helpful in that respect.

"Bhu will know, I'm sure," Frank says.

I smile. "I think you're right. I'll pick some alternatives and see which I can go for."

"Maybe they could cook them a different way, for you. In peanut oil or… you're not allergic, are you?"

I shake my head. "No, very lucky. Not allergic to anything as far as I know, apart from aeroplanes."

Frank pulls a sad face. "My Frankie too. Gets very sick. We have a small camper so we tend to take that around the UK. She's a brilliant driver, much better than me, but don't tell her I said that."

I laugh. He's such a sweet guy. He really is like my dad.

Bhu's back with our drinks. He puts mine in front of me first then Frank's. Like yesterday, the glass is huge.

We both say our thanks then Frank speaks. "My lovely and esteemed colleague here is on a mission. She's trying out different recipes as a bit of research, and would like to know how many calories there are in some of these dishes."

This has put me rather on the spot as I've not yet had a chance to return to the menu.

"No problem," Bhu almost squeaks. "Fire away."

"I like, love chicken."

Bhu nods.

I continue. "Something with not too much sauce."

Bhu nods again. "Lots of calories in sauce."

"But not dry, something with flavour." I grimace at the last bit as if suggesting anything they create doesn't have flavour but Bhu doesn't appear to take it as an insult.

He leans forward and taps the menu in exactly the right spot, it turns out. "May I recommend the Lamb sikampuri or Seekh kebab or Sarson wali machchi or Shahi king prawn for starter or…" He moves his finger. "The scallops. There is the option of the seasonal salad but…" He looks around him then back at me and blows a raspberry.

I'm astounded yet again but Frank and I laugh… again. It's only day two of my short life at Hemel Hempstead and it has already exceeded my expectations, not that I really had any.

"And for main course…" Bhu moves his finger again. "The Shashlik is very nice. Chicken or Lamb, you said you love chicken.

Perhaps the Sikampuri for start then Chicken Shashlik. Grilled is your best option. Marinated soaks up all the flavour but also the..." He pats what looks like a flat stomach. "Calories. Fish is the best option for watching one's weight but, madam... no. I thank you."

I get the impression he was just about to compliment me on not having to watch my weight, which I don't do particularly but he was perhaps too self-conscious to continue. "No, I thank *you*," I sort of repeat. He bows, removes our menus, with Frank's choice of Aloo then a lamb dansak and Bhu's ultimate suggestions for me noted, in his head rather than on an order pad or handset, and leaves us to chat.

The food arrives when we've only got into our stride, talking about our respective 'squeezes': Frankie and my mum. Not that I squeeze my mum but I like Frank's terminology. It's very 1940s. He looks about the same age as my mum, mid-sixties, and I'm guessing Frankie's around the same. He doesn't say and I don't like to ask.

"So, dance classes. Ballroom?" I nudge.

He blushes a little, which is really endearing. "Salsa. Very erm... intimate."

I laugh but tone it down to a smile as he blushes even more. "That's lovely. I've never really been a dance fan. Thankfully nor is Duncan. We disco, if that's still the term used."

Frank shrugs. "It was all tea dances in my day." He winks and I know he's fibbing but I don't suppose he is a modern dance fan. Motown perhaps.

The subject changes to work, fortunately skirting James, more about how Frank got into accountancy; taking after his father. Frank actually wanted to be a doctor but doesn't like blood so was happy to change. "I can't say I do either," I confess. "I gave blood for the first time last autumn – late, I know – and fainted."

Frank gasps.

"I was okay after a while," I continue, "but felt so sick. They said they were very grateful but didn't want me back. It was such a shame because apparently I have lovely veins." I'm not sure why but I look down at my arms. I have thin skin on the backs of my hands and my veins are visible at the best of times but protrude even more when holding cutlery. I put them down.

"Oh I can do that," Frank says, "give blood. I go quite regularly, whenever we get the email. I don't look when they're doing it. Frankie and I go together. Considering how carsick she gets, she provides pints of the red stuff. She's much braver than me in that respect. I'm the bare minimum, I'm afraid."

Poor thing. I admire his tenacity though. "It's a shame I can't. I'd like to do my bit and they had one of my favourite brands of crisps.

I can't remember what it is now but I recognise the packet, more white than coloured. Anyway. The last thing I knew I was opening the top of a pack of chicken, which I very rarely have. Usually cheese and onion or plain. Next thing I'm on a stretcher. I was only concerned about where my handbag was. They'd retrieved it thankfully. The nurses were ever so nice. But it was half-term Friday and I was there for three hours. Not great. Duncan was away so even worse. I didn't tell him until it was all over. I'd walked to the venue, a local school as it wasn't open for classes, but the ambulance ended up taking me home so it was okay in the end."

"Poor thing," he says as I smile at how our brains work.

Our starter plates are replaced by full mains and I'm astounded for the third time in one evening. The restaurant is named after the second highest mountain and I can see why. The starter wasn't particularly filling – I'd only had the salad box for lunch – and I'm glad. My plate, both of our plates are heaving. Rice is in a separate stainless steel bowl but there's little room on my plate for much. I guess I'm supposed to pile it on even higher. I think doing that will certainly make it Everest but it looks so lovely that I'm sure I'm going to conquer it.

Frank and I look at each other, cutlery at the ready.

"I'm going in. I may be some time," Frank says and I want to howl with laughter. Other than the rock climbing at lunchtime, I can't remember when I've enjoyed myself so much. Yes, I can. With Nathan yesterday. Okay, not a good example but it's a day for climbing, it seems.

Chapter 34 – Reflections On The Evening

After our delicious meals, Frank and I take a break before heading our separate ways. The outside is even posher than the inside. There's a gorgeous balcony area to the rear of the building with a garden and loads of shrubs. My aunt and uncle would be in heaven.

Bhu was a joy so we gave him a reasonable tip – that's Frank and I from our own pockets, not courtesy of Billy this time. Bhu's eyes almost sparkled as I handed him a five-pound note. I'm sure people have given him much more before but he'd gone to the trouble of getting a photocopied menu and written down all the calories beside each item. A fiver is nothing for such a level of above and beyond.

I will definitely be back, with or without Frank… possibly with my aunt and uncle, even just for the garden – and I think that's what places bank on, especially with the likes of Facebook and TripAdvisor where a review can make or break.

I think unless K2 does something seriously wrong, I'll be passing their doors, and coming through them, for many years to come.

Frank and I chat about our lives, over two delicious but seriously strong coffees, and it's not long before we're both yawning. We apologise then laugh in unison. It's so lovely to be on the same wavelength as someone, especially of a different generation. I wonder if he'd adopt me but I feel disloyal to my dad. I shiver as I think of my mum finding me a new dad, Charles, even if it's not like that. I shiver at the thought which prompts Frank to speak.

"Come on, let's get home."

"It's been a fabulous evening, Frank. Thank you."

"It has and made all the more lovely, fabulous…" He dips his head and I do likewise. "Fabulous by the company."

On anyone else, especially a decade or two younger, it might feel creepy but not on Frank. He is a positive gent.

We return to our cars, wave through our windows, and do indeed, go our separate ways.

I've already decided before I get back to my mum's that I'll take tomorrow morning off. I'll make sure the article is written so I have a grace period. Walking Elliott, I've decided, will give me some space and air to breathe. Not that I feel bad but I know that next time I see James…

He never says no, does our Elliott, and being Wednesday morning, my mum, aunt and uncle will be at Costa so the hound will be home alone, which he's not a great fan of. I love the quiet so never complain.

It's a bit late tonight to ring and ask, although I'm sure they won't mind. I can call in the morning, or I pop up there before they come down to collect my mum. My mum can drive, does when doing her own thing, but when they're together, my uncle is the chauffeur. It's how it's always been done.

I reach her house and her car's not there. She has a garage but it's full of hobby and gardening stuff that's overfilled the box room and shed respectively so she always parks outside. Even if she, or we while I'm here, blitzed the garage and whittled it down to the two original storage places, I'm sure she'd still have her car on the drive; it's too convenient. I park up next to where she always goes; nearest the front door, and sit staring at the royal blue metal electric garage door. I'm not sure why but I don't feel ready to leave the cocoon that is my Swift.

Hemel to Tring is a mere seven miles but my car's heating system is fabulous, even for one that's over a decade old. I keep thinking about replacing my car and I've spent a fair amount on it in the past few months but it, she, runs beautifully so I'll wait until she's sick.

I smile and picture the green-faced emoji on my phone. Izzy was poorly earlier this year, nothing major, a bug, which I picked up after it had left her. She's a caring sharing person like that – so we were swapping that and the other sickly emojis: the one with the thermometer sticking out of its head and the head bandaged, even though we didn't need even a plaster between us.

After much deliberation, actually me thinking and going off at more tangents than the magic roundabout, I do finally get out of my car. Not that it's cold outside but it's late, gone ten, late for a school night, so not t-shirt weather. It's only the first of May after all.

I head indoors, make myself a cup of tea and dig out my notebook. The evening is fresh in my mind, and with Bhu's list of calories, I asterisk – using a red pen my mum uses for when she's sure she'd got a crossword clue correct; it's always a pencil up to that point – the ones that come in under 500 calories. Not at all bad. I can't really keep going back to K2, much as I'd like, but will try once or twice more, even if it's not under the guise of the thirty-one dishes.

Once I've done that, I start writing up my reflections on the evening. As promised to myself, if not to my readers, I made it much more than just about food. Health and wellbeing is about relationships, interactions and how kind we can be to ourselves as well as each other. I'm not spiritual or religious, they often go hand in hand with health and wellbeing, but peace of mind, or the lack thereof, can have such an impact on the rest of our lives.

I'm feeling very deep and meaningful when Mum gets home. I can't help frowning despite being pleased to see her but what she's wearing lifts my spirits. It's a black and white ensemble, not dissimilar to a checkers board.

"Do you always...? Is that your...?" I'm pointing at her top which actually more closely resembles a jockey's jersey except it's actually a jersey, knitted, rather than shiny. Her trousers, to be fair, are a simple black but her shoes are black and white checks.

"I thought it would be funny," she says all innocently.

"It is."

She smiles, not sensing any of my sarcasm.

"Not had the ensemble long then."

She shakes her head. "The shoes are relatively old but I got the top last Friday then remembered I had the shoes. Frankie took quite a shine."

"I bet."

"Said I was brave. I don't know why. They're only black and white."

That is true but anywhere else than a chess club... although better than a draughts club I suppose.

"Cuppa?" she asks, heading for the other end of the kitchen.

"Please." I go to take over my mug but she returns and collects it.

"Have to wait for the kettle anyway."

Makes sense. "Did you win?"

Mum, back by the kettle, shrugs. "Didn't play a whole game, it's only a two-hour session, but I'm in the lead."

"Oh, I didn't realise it was like that. What happens in between sessions?"

"Everything gets recorded. They're very serious about it, George especially."

"George?"

"He didn't found it, it's been going for decades I think, but he's one of the most senior there. Sprints around the hall like a bat out of the proverbial."

"Sprints? How old is he?" My mind's imagining a centenarian on roller skates.

"Not sprints, whizzes. He's in a wheelchair. Electric thing so it can go pretty quickly. He has a horn on it, gets you out of the way if you're not paying attention."

"Wow."

"Nearly gave poor Terry – that's George's number two – a heart attack when he was logging everyone's scores at half time. That's so no one cheats when we go to have our cups of tea. Not that anyone would but the kitchen hatch and serving area are at the other end of the hall. Terry was taking too long apparently, and of course George had to chivvy him up."

"Sounds like a barrel of laughs."

"It's good fun. We, Frankie and I, take it as fun but of course George and Mildred don't."

"Mildred?"

"We call Terry 'Mildred', you know, after the 1970s comedy show with Terry Scott and whatshername."

It rings a bell. "June something?"

"Whitfield. That's it. Terry and June, not George and…"

I nod, not overly the wiser. Mum watched it when I did my homework, with the sound low, she's considerate like that, so I'd look up every now and then, or hear her laughing but I wasn't really paying attention.

Mum makes the tea and I tell her about my evening. She's not at all surprised as she knows Frank well through Frankie. Finally tiredness overcomes me so I say goodnight and head to bed.

I'm only halfway up the stairs when I hear the radio blare but she swears, making me laugh, and turns it down.

After dumping my bag in my room, I head to the bathroom. It's a fire door, on a swing arm, which shuts whether we want it to or not. It cuts off the radio. I know my bedroom, equipped with the same type of door but a wedge to keep it open until I'm ready to sleep, will be just as quiet. My mum's not a late-to-bed because she's always up early, cracking on with the day before heading out, so I'll probably hear the creaking floorboards before I nod off.

Teeth brushed, mouthwash gargled – in that order tonight but I do vary. The back of the mouthwash bottle says in that order but in the process of researching this topic some months ago, I read that it should be the other way round. Red wine's good for you. No, it's bad for you. Who do you believe? I tend to be informative but vague in my column. I'd like to think this makes me a guide rather than an expert. People like Greta only voice their opinion on the films they see, books they read, they don't make the films, so likewise I can be an assistance rather than persuasion.

I finish jotting my article onto my notepad while sitting in bed. I could have dictated it all into my phone, then copied and pasted, but it misspells words: 'I' for 'are' and so on. Not sure why. I'll still have my morning off but I'm going to go in early… not pre-six am early to see who covers when Phil's not there, but just to type and submit my articles. They're not dated so I'm leaving it to Billy to accept what when. He's the editor so I don't expect he'll print them one a day. It'll be thrilling though seeing my name (and picture?) in another paper.

I feel sorry for anyone writing a novel. I've thought about it but writing about real life is so much easier, especially when it's in hundreds of words not thousands. You'd have to have a pretty good idea to be able to create whatever a novel length is, eighty thousand is it?, to know who your characters are, what they're doing and saying and so on before putting pen to paper, fingers on the keyboard. No, I'm sure that's not me. Izzy said she's wanted to but I don't think she's had the time. It's so full-on with William.

I hear my mum come up the stairs as I switch off my light. I go to say goodnight but she diverts to the other side of the landing, to the bathroom rather than her en suite. I rest my head on my pillow, waiting, but am not conscious long enough to hear her come back.

Chapter 35 – Day Two Official

Wednesday 2nd May

Day two and I'm at the office at seven. Coming in early, it turns out, isn't the smartest of moves as Phil is late – a pre-arrangement to take someone somewhere, I'm yet to find out who and where – and the nightshift guy, Gavin, doesn't know anything about me.

My pass worked for the car park and the front door but it's only temporary. It doesn't have my picture on it so I'm down in the security room, on a visitor chair, waiting for a proper member of staff to come in and confirm my identity. At my suggestion, Gavin phoned the Northampton office but it went through to answerphone. I offered him William's number as the number one but he, Gavin, refused because it was, he said, probably my boyfriend's. For a split second, I was going to say, "No, my best friend's boyfriend," but I didn't think that would have gone down too well.

He is only doing his job, I remind myself, as he looks at me with an 'I'm only doing my job' expression on his face but unlike Phil, and pretty much everyone else at the Hemel offices, Gavin is not a talker. Thankfully, he's not a Mike either so there's no food around, which actually is a shame because I left home before Mum got up so no porridge and I'm expecting to be at my desk and back home again in an hour or so.

Gavin's spending the whole time staring at his monitors. There's a bank of six black and white screens showing different aspects of the site: two of the car park – one at each end – two of the rear of the building from inside and out, two at the front from the same points of view. They are very much to check non-staff activity but it's still a little creepy… probably because they're in black and white and people walking by appear ghostlike even though it's clear they're real.

"How long have you worked here?" I ask Gavin but there's no reply. I want to try again but notice he's got earphones in each ear. White. Apple-type. Bluetooth. Cordless. I can't hear any noise so they're probably noise cancelling and yes, my noise is most definitely being cancelled. So I dig out my notebook and record events. I don't suppose I'll use it for anything other than recounting it to Izzy but it gives me something to do.

It then occurs to me that if Gavin can't hear me, he can't hear anything else. I could sneak out. I already swiped in when I arrived so I can get anywhere in the building. Other than computers, which aren't the latest high tech, there's not a lot else to nick. But I decide to stay put. Gavin may only be the eyes but I could be the ears, listen out for anyone, although he'd spot them on the monitors unless they were wandering around upstairs. Even if they came downstairs, he'd spot them from the camera that covers the entrance hall. And he'd spot me.

It's not a scenario I had anticipated on day three, day two official, and really not wanted. It's not the end of the world; someone will turn up eventually, and Gavin the Gerbil… ooh, I like that, yes, Gavin the Gerbil will spot them a mile off. Not an actual mile as the camera only goes as far as the road but far enough to spot a danger.

He's not fat but his uniform is definitely a size or two too small. Considering he never answered my 'How long have you worked here?' question, I can't tell whether it was the original uniform he was given on day one that he's grown into or one he's had to replace that for as he ran out of room.

I shouldn't be nasty, he's probably a really nice guy – he's certainly conscientious enough – and it's really not like me. No, it's much more Izzy's style. She had plenty of practice this time last year. Then I realise that this time last year, she was typing up her notes from meeting Duncan the night before. The first cog in my happiness.

And back to present day.

Gavin must have convinced himself I'm not that untrustworthy as I'm not shackled to anything that doesn't move, or anything that does, and with his back to me I could garrotte him. I look around the room and can't see anything immediately that would do the job. Here I was, only a few hours earlier, saying I couldn't write a novel, yet my mind is thinking of how I could murder someone I've only just met and who holds the security of millions of pounds' worth of building in his beady eyes.

I look down at my lap. My notepad and pen look back up at me. I could papercut Gavin or stab him with a Bic. It's not actually a Bic. Nor a Biro. It's a very classy looking three-for-a-pound-from-Poundland ballpoint. Blue. Blood poisoning. I'd stab him with a Poundland pen then he'd get blood poisoning. In about three months. No, that's not going to work. I'm rooting around my brain, and Gavin's office, for another scenario when there's a knock at the door.

I look up and there's James. Uh oh.

Needless to say, Gavin doesn't hear him. How he missed him on the monitors, I'm not sure, but with his back to me, as I said, and him not moving, there's no way of telling if he's actually awake. It's past his clocking off time – I look at my watch. It's an hour and a half past his clocking off time so maybe past his bedtime.

"Gavin, mate," James says. Nothing. "Gavin!" he bellows. I'm prepared for it but Mike, sorry Gavin, isn't. I can see the similarity more now; they even have the same haircut.

Gavin wobbles in his chair, rattling the desk slightly and the monitors with it. "Huh?" Gavin turns round. So the noise cancelling aren't quite. "Oh, watcha." He's all class.

"Gavin. I shall take charge of this lovely lady here."

"You will? Oh right, okay. She was just sitting here until you came, or someone."

"She has a pass."

"Yeah, I know that. We was keeping each other company." Were.

James, thankfully, doesn't appear convinced. It doesn't look like James respects him and I like him all the more for that. *That's all. Respect. No more than that, Donna.*

After holding the door open for me and letting me go first, James climbs the stairs two steps at a time. I struggle to keep up. He mumbles something then speaks louder, possibly loudly enough for the non-noise-cancelling ear buds. "He's such a wa… No, James, be nice. Gavin's a misunderstood fellow."

I go cold when James's hand brushes mine. That must be a good sign surely. No rush of heat, no longing. There's no apology, no comment, so it must have been accidental or I imagined it. I'm hoping for the former as it's the innocence I'm seeking. I don't want to go imagining things that aren't there.

Not sure why I thought Owen would be there considering it was clearly only Gavin and me until James arrived but again, I wouldn't put it past Gavin to hang onto me, albeit not literally, until someone convenient came to collect me. A phone call to the only other member of staff being far too much trouble, given that it was to another complex.

James and I walk through to the main office area in silence, the movement-sensitive lights flicking on as we go. It feels a bit like a catwalk except I'm the dowdy fashion designer walking alongside the supermodel.

"This is me," James announces when we get to his desk.

"It is."

"You have a good morning and I'll see you for lunch?"

We had this discussion yesterday, or rather I'd told him I wanted Leah to take me out for lunches from now on, or I'll fend for myself, but that either didn't sink in or he's trying his luck.

"No, not today. The reason I'm here early is that I've come in to type up a couple of articles before I'm having the morning off."

"Oh."

We look at each other for a few seconds and it appears to be the end of the conversation.

I head to my desk. I feel good. Not because I've killed the conversation but because I held my own. I said 'no' to James. Something feels lifted. Whatever weight I had around my shoulders has gone. It may come back. I have another four weeks of James's company whether it's a few desks or a few miles apart but that's okay. He's blurred into the distance, and Duncan and Elliott are the only males in my brain as I cross the plain blue carpet to Veronica's domain and log on my computer.

I pull my notebook out of my bag and in less than twenty minutes, I have one article submitted, the other in drafts. Both Williams have given me a free reign this month and as long as I'm not 'derogatory to any establishments' I frequent (William I's words) and keep all the receipts (William II's – Billy's) I can go, do and say almost whatever I like. It's really quite liberating.

James's desk is void of human life when I walk back past. I've already mouthed a 'hello' and 'thank you' to Frank, putting up my hands as if I'm praying – not sure why, and smile at Greta. Nathan was the only other desk I passed and he wasn't there. Timekeeping seems very relaxed here, regardless of what Phil had said previously. For the upper echelon – William and Billy's bosses – who probably do receive the paperwork for every aspect of their empire, I don't suppose the editors' PAs being a bit late features on their radar.

As long as the cogs keep whirring, the editions sell, they're happy. They must be to a point because Billy always seems to be. William, on the other hand, will always be William and seem dour to those who haven't got to know him.

I continue my journey out to reception. Owen's on the phone so I get the briefest of waves. Gavin has, thankfully, been replaced by Phil who is also on the phone and gives me a more regal wave than Owen, in keeping with Phil's heritage. Not that I know what the heritage of Arizona really is, and for America not having any royalty, that doesn't make sense but I'm going *out* through the front door rather than *in* so I'm happy.

Chapter 36 – A Snake On Speed

Making sure I've left the office before they head out to Costa, my aunt and uncle are thrilled when I call them, hands free, from the car on the way home. They're always pleased to hear from me but especially when I offer to take Elliott for a while.

So I go straight there and my uncle answers the door. "Oh good morning," he says as if it's a total shock.

"Morning. Something smells nice."

"Pies for the freezer."

"Yum. Is Auntie Jan busy?" I ask then can't help giggling when Elliott races in at the sound of my voice, his whole body shaking, and squeaking like mad. He's like a snake on speed… a very curly-haired snake. He licks my hand and I know he'd lick anywhere he could find that was naked. That conjures up a rather disturbing image so I slot it back in the 'do not retrieve' section of my brain. "Did you not hear the doorbell?" I ask Elliott, not expecting an answer.

"In the garden," my uncle explains, the day already being warm enough to leave the back door open. I'm pleased, not for Elliott's benefit, he's out there regardless, but because I plan to go to Tring Reservoir and it's invariably overcast whenever I visit the place.

"Aunt Jan's in the garden too?" I ask not sure whether the 'in the garden' only referred to Elliott or was answering my previous question.

"Painting. The horses."

I smile and wander through to their conservatory, via the kitchen where the smells are naturally even stronger. I breathe deeply then out as I stumble over the threshold and bundle myself into the stifling glasshouse.

"Nice trip?" my aunt asks as she adds a bit of white to show reflection in one of the horse's eyes.

I laugh, half-hearted. Only my pride has been dented and my aunt's known me all my life so I shouldn't be bothered but it reminds me of my dad and it makes me sad. Just for a second.

"They're beautiful," I gush as I look between the photograph – one my uncle probably took, being a professional photographer – and the painting. It's more than replicated; it's captured the souls of the horses' eyes. It takes weeks, especially part time, to do each of these paintings and she charges way too little, and this one's nearing completion.

"For a sixtieth birthday," my aunt explains. "One of your mum's friends. Her husband's commissioned it. Really sweet. And brave of him to get me to do it. You know what your mum's like at keeping secrets."

Frank. It has to be Frank. I didn't know they had horses.

"Is her name Frankie?"

My aunt turns to face me, brush poised in her right hand. "Yes. Do you know her?"

"I work with her husband."

"Ah yes. Your mum did mention something like that. That's handy actually."

"Oh?"

"Would you mind taking it to him when it's done? It'll be a few days but I'm ahead of the deadline. I can't trust your mum with it. Too much temptation to blab."

"Not at all. I'm there the rest of the month." Even if I weren't, I'd have come down from Northampton especially. Frank's been so good to me, and Frankie to my mum, I'm sure.

"Do you mind if I finish this little bit?" My aunt points to one of the horse's noses which looks complete but presumably isn't. "Only we're going to collect your mum shortly."

"Sure."

My aunt turns back to the painting. "And you're taking Elliott out, Pat tells me."

"I thought we'd go to the reservoir."

"Mmm. He'll like that." I know she means Elliott but I'm sure my uncle would too.

"See you later," I say, not sure exactly when as I plan to eat at the Bluebells café in the grounds of the reservoir which will take care of lunch then I'm off out with Greta tonight so it'll be somewhere in between. That'll be interesting as Greta will have met my mum twice, enough exuberance for anyone even remotely shy, so I'll get her take on the bath bomb that is my mother. I'll need someone to be in though to drop Elliott back as I won't be able to get in.

Elliott does his snake impression again as I walk back through to the lounge. My uncle's engrossed on his iPad so I retrieve Elliott's lead and clip it onto his collar. The noise makes my uncle look up.

"There's something interesting on eBay," he says and points at the screen. They belong to the Tring Historical Society and my uncle helps out at the town's museum, the general rather than Natural History one – the town has both, so he's forever looking for local memorabilia.

He turns the screen and I see it's a piece of Goss crested china. A sweet little bowl. It has the usual lion and unicorn picture and is only £3.99 'buy it now'. I remember at least two similar in one of my uncle's dining room cabinets but he returns the screen to face him and clicks on the blue button. "For the museum," he states and I nod.

"See you later," I say and tug gently on Elliott's lead, not that he needs any persuasion as he's already primed.

"Have fun," my uncle says while going through all the paying procedures.

"I will," I reply and let myself out.

Elliott loves going in the car. He doesn't even mind the vet as it's going somewhere and he gets to see cats up close and personal. He's funny. He goes nuts if he sees them through the lounge's patio doors but avoids them if confronted on the pavement. It's like he's protected by the glass and makes so much noise when he's let out that they're long gone by the time he could get anywhere near. I don't know what he'd do if he did.

I open one of my car's back passenger doors and he hops up. I swap his lead for the harness I leave in the car. It's a sort of one-size-fits-all but Buddy, Duncan's beagle, isn't much smaller than Elliott so I don't bother altering the straps. We're not going very far and while I know accidents can happen anywhere, it really would take Harry Houdini to get out of this harness. Elliott's too busy looking out of the windows, from side to side like a tennis match observer, to attempt an escape.

I take the route past the old tip. It's now a council truck depot and even though it's not been raining, there's still an awful lot of mud on the road. I drive carefully through it. I know it's not as dangerous as wet mud but my tyres will still lose traction. I'm nothing if not cautious. I should have been a girl guide.

Considering how much my mum loves clubs these days, I'm surprised she's not an owl, or whatever they're called. A thought to google it flashes through my brain but that's all it is. It's not important enough to find out. Should my mum ever get the urge to join the… club, clan, or whatever a group of guides, or owls is. Now I'm curious about that and wish that Amazon made an Alexa for the car. It's only a matter of time.

Ten minutes later and we're parked up at the reservoir. Elliott's going nuts in the back because he recognises where we are. I turn round and the harness connection to the seatbelt is bouncing. He's still securely fastened, not that it matters as we're stationary, or at least the car and I are, but Elliott and his immediately surrounding area are a bit of a blur.

He's very good off the lead when we're where he can run around but this is a car park so I swap the harness for the lead. We walk sedately… okay, I walk sedately, he's still a mad thing until we get to the bottom of the crazy-steep steps with a buoyancy aid at the top. I wonder if it works on dogs.

"Three... two... one..." I say and unclip his lead. Lightning hasn't bolted faster than this mad mutt. He's from bottom to top in warp speed. Lewis Hamilton couldn't have been prouder and nor could I. He's adorable... Elliott, not Lewis, though Lewis isn't bad either. Although I'm four, maybe five, years younger than him, the thought of going so fast, quickly, makes me feel old and so does climbing the steps. I need more exercise and taking more mornings off to come here would certainly help. It's all too easy to work, eat, watch TV during the week. Duncan and I are active at the weekends but it's often sedentary like the cinema or shopping. Shopping with Duncan is browsing in half a dozen shops, not a full day wandering around the town, not unless we go somewhere new – to us, the older the better in terms of architecture. I'm not a huge history fan, all those dates to remember, but I can appreciate curves.

Speaking of which, Elliott's a dot in the distance. I'm not worried as he panics if he can't see me, he just forgets to look too often. The main reservoir is blocked at the end so even if I don't get that far, Elliott will have to come back. And he'll have covered umpteen times the distance I will have from all the zigzagging he's doing. Bless him.

I've remembered my iPod so pop the earphones into my ears and click on the remote's play button. *Gnoissienne number one* by Eric Satie plays. It reflects the mood, not mine particularly but the gathering clouds above me. Almost clear blue sky a few miles away but here it always seems to be melancholy. I wonder if something happened years ago here and Mother Nature is still mourning.

I stop to look around. It's actually a great place to hide a body. Probably not the place to kill someone, this bit certainly, as it's so open, but there are plenty of bushes and, of course, the water. I have no clue how deep it is but there are a couple of fishermen on the opposite side so clearly enough for some kind of life. The main reservoir is high up, hence the steep steps. A light bulb goes off in my head. If the bottom of the water is level with the car park... But there's a bit of a hill to the canal so that blows that theory out of the... er, water.

My heart thumps as Elliott's dangerously close to the edge, head hanging over. We've been here dozens of times, with and without my aunt and uncle, and a few times with my mum, and Elliott's been fine but I'm too far away to do much.

I run and scream like a banshee, arms flailing, scaring a couple walking towards me with Elliott in between. Elliott looks over to me, the other way to the couple, then at me. He wags his tail then looks back over the edge. The wind's picking up and he's not a particularly skinny thing, weighing a bit less than Buddy the Beagle but still, it wouldn't take much for everything to go south... literally.

I'm still running and screaming but the couple now seem unfazed, as does Elliott who's ignoring me completely. Seeing as my actions are having no effect, I slow, bring my arms down and stop screaming. I turn as if walking away and this works much better as Elliott speeds towards me and leaps up, almost knocking me over. There's a steep drop both sides of the grass verge and had I not anticipated him, we would have ended up careering into a wooden fence separating the reservoir with parked cars and the road. That would have hurt.

As it is, I stiffen myself against the barrage and make a fuss. He doesn't know he's done anything wrong, which actually he hasn't. The couple has caught up with us and give me a simple uniformed smile. I smile and say, "Nice day." It's cooled down quite considerably so they probably think I'm mad, as if the wailing banshee act hadn't given them that clue already.

I let them pass as I continue to make a fuss of Elliott who seems keen to get away and keep going. I whisper a 'be careful' to him as I let him go and thankfully he trots along in the middle of the grass rather than near either side.

My heart's still thumping and I wonder if I'm ready to be a mother.

Would it be like this every second of every day?

Probably.

Chapter 37 – The Bluebells And Carrot Cake

Still dry, Elliott and I enter the Bluebells Tearooms… not Café as I'd previously thought. 'Tearooms' sounds much more charming, quaint, British, and the atmosphere of a friend's conservatory hits me as soon as we pass the entrance. Except this conservatory is packed.

I look around very unsubtly and thankfully there's no sign of the couple we'd passed up on the hill. Elliott had bolted down the steps even quicker than he'd sprinted up, and I cursed myself as I clung onto the rail that I'd not put him on his lead as he could have gone straight into the car park. The risk of him pulling me over was one I would have taken but I'd not needed it as there, good as the proverbial precious gem, he was sitting – yes, sitting, at the bottom of the steps, head tilted as if exposing his collar and tag for my taking. I'd often love to know what goes through his head.

It's probably cake. It's what's going through mine as I look at the array. There's no queue but plenty of chat going on behind me. There's a party of cyclists who have pushed some of the tables together and are catching up like they've not seen each other for years. The noise blurs and there's nothing that can really be distinguished but I'm more of a people watcher than listener but if I *am* actually going to write a novel…

"The carrot cake please. And do you do flavoured teas?"

The jolly middle-aged-looking lady behind the counter smiles and points to a white wooden unit with shelves of glass containers packed with curious-looking teabags, each container with the name of the blend on the front. I get as far as gingerbread and stop. "The gingerbread one please."

I pay with a fiver and say to keep the change. I feel a bit silly as it's only a few pence so won't make anyone rich but I'll leave a tip on my table when I've finished. The tea will be almost calorieless but the carrot cake with its thick fondant and cute tiny carrot top certainly won't be, and it's not practical to count as my 'dish'. On reflection, this cake wasn't the smartest of moves. I'd gone for it as a belated breakfast but it'll fill me up too much to enjoy something that's less than 500 calories but healthier. Carrots are one of the five a day but I don't think this is what the nutritionists had in mind.

The slice is sitting on top of a napkin so I can wrap it up. I'm not sure why cafés do that because it makes the napkin grubby, albeit with food. Nothing against this café, sorry tearooms, but a general moan. Not like me, I know. I laugh then look up. Nope, no one's paying me any attention.

Izzy was under instruction, from herself probably rather than William – I don't think he would have been bothered – not to reveal who she was but I think I'm okay doing that with this project if I need to. I did with Bhu in the K2 and he was only happy to help. Eateries tend to want to bend over backwards like a Chinese contortionist, especially if they know they're under review. It's not like that now really, it's about what you can get for your calories, but positive commentary – it's not fair to pick – about the place makes it more interesting, like a three-dimensional Trip Advisor rating, and certainly won't hurt the establishments.

I head back to the counter after tying Elliott to the table leg with strict instructions not to move – I hope so or it'll cause a scene like a tablecloth / laid table scenario magic trick gone wrong disaster.

"Is everything all right?" the same lady asks.

"Oh yes. Thank you. Delicious," I say but feel a fraud as I've not taken a bite yet, only a sip at the too-hot tea that smells divine. "I'm doing a project at work and wondered what you could recommend as a main dish that's less than 500 calories. I don't suppose you have a list."

She frowns. I'm not sure whether it's the mention of a project or the list. "Not really but our chef could tell you. I can send her over, if you don't mind waiting, only she's a bit busy at the moment with a party…" The lady points to the conjoined tables and the rabble in full flow.

"That would be great. Thank you so much."

"What is it exactly that you want to know?"

"Just what I could eat that could be classed as a main dish, one course is fine, not a whole meal, for under 500 calories."

The woman nods, makes a note, and takes it out to the kitchen. I hear murmurings behind me as I walk back to my table.

I decide it could be a while so I make do with my tea, which is scrummy if not a little too hot still, and tiny bites of carrot cake. I want to devour the whole thing but do get more of a flavour when eating smaller portions – a not-so-well-known fact when it comes to feeling fuller quicker. We should chew our food at least a dozen times and take twenty minutes minimum for each meal. I've said that a few times in my columns but it's been a while so worth mentioning again, perhaps in the article I do for my visit here. I dig out my notebook and am jotting when I feel someone looming.

A younger lady – I'm rubbish at ages but nearer mine – is standing a couple of feet away wearing all whites and an expectant smile. "My colleague," she says without turning or pointing, "said you'd like some advice."

"Please," I say and open my notebook. I repeat my request and this lady sits opposite me.

"An open sandwich is probably your best bet." She offers me a small plate with a single sausage and points towards Elliott.

"Ooh, thank you. That's brilliant. Isn't it, Elliott?" I look down and he's drooling. Ordinarily, I'd have broken up the sausage into pieces, either with my fingers or my mouth, but I'm here for a reason and the lady's waiting so give it to him whole. Ordinarily, he would have eaten it whole... and he does. I shake my head and return my attention to the 'chef' waiting patiently.

She then goes on to describe the most popular version of the open sandwich and I jot all the ingredients onto my pad. She had me at salmon, and the array of seafood she lists makes my stomach growl. "Could I have one of those?" I ask and she smiles.

"Of course," she says and returns to the kitchen.

With Elliott still attached to the table, the sausage a distant memory, I go to the counter, explain what I've ordered and pay. It doesn't matter that I still have most of the carrot cake as that'll do for afternoon tea, that's cake and a cup of tea, not lunch, dinner or supper-type tea. I, as a journalist, appreciate how confusing the English language can be, not only in my country but especially overseas. Dinner, tea, supper. Decisions, decisions.

I take my change, not wishing to offend with what would be an even smaller tip, say 'Thank you', and return to my table. Elliott, good as the proverbial pot at the end of a rainbow, is simultaneously sitting, wagging his tail and licking his lips. "If you're good," I say as I sit, "you'll get a bit of fish."

He barks.

"Shhh!"

He barks again.

I scan the room but no one is looking at us. I suppose with so many visiting dogs, they get their fair share of barking.

Elliott opens his mouth to bark again but I do an 'uh uh', replicating Cesar Milan's instructions that always work for the dogs he's in charge of training. The dog whisperer I am not... as Elliott barks again. I look at my carrot cake and give in. I lean forward in Elliott's direction and he leans back. "You are very naughty." Thankfully he doesn't bark again but wags his tail and licks his lips, far enough away from my face to not make contact.

"You..." He puffs. "Can have a tiny bit of cake." I emphasise the tiny. "But no barking." He sort of nods and I turn back to my table. I trim off the smaller end of the cake with the fork, pick half the piece with my fingers and rotate back to Elliott, feeling like a crane driver on a building site.

I've just returned my attention back to my table when my open sandwich appears. It's every bit as lovely as its description. I can feel my eyes widen. "That looks *delicious*." I instinctively wipe the sides of my mouth, hoping that I'm not drooling like Elliott. If I were, at least I'd be less obvious but I can't feel anything.

"Thank you," the original lady says. "Enjoy."

I know I will and I do. After me taking a discreet photograph so I don't forget what it looks like, Elliott gets his promised bit of salmon, there's plenty to go around, and I'm stuffed by the time I've finished, the tea being the perfect temperature by the time that too disappears. I go to leave a two-pound coin on the small plate that had housed the sausage but millimetres away from making contact, I retract it, realising that it would then be covered in sausage matter, or the liquid from the skin at the very least. So I leave the coin on the table where it will be perfectly clean, the whole tearooms themselves pristine.

I didn't ask which one of the three ladies – the third I'd not spoken to but would at least smile at and mouth a 'thank you' on the way out – was the owner, and on reflection I don't know whether I should have done, not to ask permission to write my article but at least to explain but hopefully what I said to the first lady about the 'project' will suffice. I'll bring them a copy, I decide as I release Elliott from the table's grip.

I don't get to do the smile and 'thank you' at the third lady as she's busy with the cyclists so I look around for her other two colleagues. Sadly, they're equally engrossed and I decide that standing there like the proverbial lemon, waiting for one of them, would not only make me feel daft but look daft too so I make a quiet but hasty escape.

Chapter 38 – Two And The Same

Elliott hops into the car with no hesitation. I realise that we'll be too early for my aunt and uncle if we return to their house now. There's plenty of time left on the parking ticket so we could do another round of the reservoir and the weather's improved but I decide we'll find somewhere else. I'm fairly familiar with the area. The options are turn left for Mead's Farm (more tea and cake) or right for Ivinghoe and its common. Ooh, there's the Beacon. A perfect hike to walk off my lunch. Brunch. Sigh.

So right it is and I wave at Brookmead School as we come into Ivinghoe village. I didn't go there, to Brookmead, but they hold a yearly 'BeaconLit' literary festival on the middle Saturday of every July and it's one of my favourite events. I make a mental note to see who's on this year but I'll go regardless. Izzy's a big reader and I remember that we've never been together. I don't know why but she always seems to be doing something else. With ten weeks' notice, or thereabouts, she might just be free.

I get a whiff of spices from the Haldi Indian restaurant opposite the school but choose to ignore it as I'm not hungry enough to be tempted although it reminds me to pop in sometime, if I get the opportunity over the four weeks I'm staying here, to see if they could do anything that fits the clichéd under-500-calorie bill.

My car complains partway up the hill so I go down a gear. It's not that steep but with my attention elsewhere, bad girl, I've let the revs drop. Or I assume that's what I've done. Cars get me from A to B, are warm, play good music – Heart FM usually – and look nice; that's as technical as I get with them.

I pay more attention as we climb, in the car rather than on foot, the road alongside Ivinghoe Beacon and nip into a space near the entrance of the car park. It's only the second of May so the schools aren't off until the end of the month, although everyone has next Monday off for May Day bank holiday, just as well we're not here then. That makes me wonder what I will be doing. Not as many places will be open and the ones that are will be busier. Never mind, it's a few days away. Anyway, I'll hopefully be at Duncan's.

There's an ice cream van between the Beacon and the car park and even if I hadn't eaten I don't think I would have had one. For water and milk, they're surprisingly calorific so I tend to avoid them unless it's really warm. Which today it is not. It's still not as overcast as earlier but being that much higher, it's particularly windy and I wonder how much business the man in the van is getting.

There's no queue and I can see through the hatch that he's sitting on top of the fridge tapping on his mobile and laughing. As I go to open the back door of my car, I imagine the man sharing an animal video on Facebook or reacting to a really bad joke. That thought reminds me of Alexa which in turn reminds me of Duncan and I feel a little sad. Only a little as I'll see him in… I look at my watch… forty-eight, fifty-three hours or thereabouts.

I decide to give him a call but there's barely any signal. I shouldn't be surprised but I am. And disappointed. To take my mind off everything, I whistle for Elliott to jump out of the car but he's already done so, lead still attached which is half strangling him. "Sorry, mate." After checking there are no other cars nearby, I lean down to release him. He seems to know better than to run off so stops at my feet. "Good boy." I clip on his expandable lead. He can be let loose completely once we're out of the car park and onto the grass but at least he has semi-freedom before then.

It turns out to be a fairly solitary walk, only a Dalmatian and Yorkshire Terrier and their respective owners to nod to (in my case) and sniff (in Elliott's) on the way out and no one on the way back. We both seem a little despondent when we reach my car and Elliott makes a very half-hearted leap onto the back seat and doesn't complain at me switching leads.

The ice cream man is still on his mobile as I take to my seat, and turn on the engine and heater. The wind has got to me a little and I don't feel like driving until my feet are warmer.

While it's still fresh in my brain, I call Duncan but it goes through to answerphone. *You know what to do*, is his simple directive and I do, so leave a chirpy message, helped by a semi-forced smile on my face. He has a longer, much more professional, message on his work phone but I don't like to disturb him on that. If he were free, he'd answer his mobile and I know he'll get back to me when he has time. Still feeling in the need to speak to someone, I ring Izzy.

"Hey, you. How's Hemel?"

"Hi. Good thanks." Then a thought dawns. "Are you free on… two seconds."

"O… kay."

I check the date of the middle Saturday in July on my phone's calendar then put the phone back to my ear. "The thirteenth of July?" I hear a few clicks as she looks something up on her phone, the calendar too presumably. I'm tempted to tell her why but decide not to in case she'd not want to go, but why wouldn't she? She loves books.

"Yep. Anything special?"

"Yes," I say then change the subject. "Have you heard from Duncan today?" I'm not sure why I asked that because if he'd not contacted me then there'd be no reason for him to contact her, unless it was to speak to William and then Duncan would call directly. It was the only alternative I could think of. "A literary festival," I blurt.

"Oh, okay. That's the July thing?"

I nod.

"Donna?"

"Sorry, yes." I nod again albeit pointlessly as we're only on a voice call and not FaceTiming.

"You okay? Everything there okay?"

"Yes, good thanks. Just been for a walk. Elliott's here."

Izzy squeals and I hold the phone away for a second, allowing my ear to regain its senses. She's even more mad about my aunt and uncle's dog than I am, and that's saying something. She's always said how much she'd love a dog of her own and dotes on Buddy, Duncan's beagle. Buddy's far more sensible than Elliott but that's not saying much at all. Like me, as I realise Izzy's spoken again.

"Sorry?"

"What's going on, Donna?"

"What do you mean?"

"You're away with the fairies."

I realise I am. I'd been trying to think about Duncan all the way round, over, the Beacon but my brain kept coming back to James. Or more accurately, James's almond eyes. I turn round in my seat and there they are. Not James's almond eyes but Elliott's. I'd not realised they were that colour before, they'd always seemed darker but sure enough, they are one and the same. Two and the same. Four and the same. It's scary. No, they're not scary but what is, is me thinking of James so much.

"Donna!"

My phone's away from my head as I'm still looking at Elliott but I return it to my ear and apologise. "Late night," I say.

"Okay."

Neither of us seems convinced.

"Why did you ask about Duncan?" Izzy asks me and I shake my head.

"I've just left a message." It doesn't really answer the question but I figure it'll do. It'll have to as I have no other explanation.

"Going to have to go. Sorry, Donna." Izzy sounds flustered as if someone's beckoning her. William probably. Izzy, the ever professional. And I have to be.

"Thanks, Izzy."

"For…"

"Everything."

Izzy laughs, blows me a kiss and hangs up. I put my phone into a holder above the dashboard's air vent, put on my seatbelt and head out of the car park. The car's beyond toasty so I turn down the heater as I wait for a passing car. I look in the rear view mirror, having to crane my neck a little and smile at the sleeping – or pretending to be asleep – Elliott. Having Buddy is lovely. I do know how lucky I am to have him and Duncan, and wouldn't do anything to ruin it but there's a niggle at the back of my brain.

I shake it away as we descend the hill and think to anyone looking, it must appear that I'm fighting off a wasp. Okay, perhaps not as dramatic as that but there's no other human in the car with me. I could be head banging to some music except I'm going side to side rather than back and forth. Yes, I'm weird. I'm okay with that.

Chapter 39 – Returning The Beast

It's not long before we're back in Tring, me having made another mental note to pop into the Tring Garden Centre café we passed on the way. It used to be a Wyvale but a year or three ago it simplified, became part of 'the British Garden Centres family', their Facebook page said. Sometimes I'm too curious for my own good.

My uncle's car is outside their house which isn't unusual as they often walk into town but I take it as a good sign nonetheless.

My aunt opens the door and I smile at a splodge of blue paint on her nose. I can't imagine which part of the painting, other than the sky, would have blue but I simply tap my own nose which prompts her to rub hers and the splodge is successfully transferred onto her right hand. Her left would have been a better choice, especially as it's holding a tissue…

She looks down at Elliott, or where he should be except he's already gone into the house. We were too busy with the splodge to have noticed. I hear my uncle coming down the stairs, accompanied by a less elegant scurry of furrier feet and Elliott bounds back into the lounge, as we've come in and closed the front door. He jumps up at my aunt and licks her hands. The blue splodge, like the Bluebells' sausage, is history and he looks particularly pleased with himself… until he starts coughing.

"Oh dear," my aunt says.

I didn't think there was enough paint to have tasted anything let alone cause a problem but it turns out, as Elliott regurgitates it, that the offending article was a Cadbury's éclair sweet I'd lost in the back of my car a few weeks earlier, wrapper still intact. I pick it up by its end and don't think about what it's covered in. The sweet itself is mostly toffee but it does have a chocolate centre so just as well it hadn't disintegrated as chocolate's notoriously poisonous to dogs.

A light bulb goes off in my head as I think it would make a great article. Not everyone will know that fact and healthy doesn't just apply to humans. I could do a week-long animal special. When I get back to Northampton.

An image of the Tring Garden Centre red poppy logo flashes into my brain, pushing aside the thought of the non-human articles, for the time being at least.

"Do you fancy afternoon tea a bit later?" I ask my aunt as we trudge through to the kitchen and I deposit the sweet in the bin. My aunt looks at my uncle who looks back at her.

"At the garden centre?" I add.

My aunt looks at the clock then back at my uncle. "Shall we?"

My uncle nods.

"I have to pop back to my mum's," I say, "to do a bit of work but could collect you en route. We could take Elliott and sit outside."

My aunt and uncle are still looking at each other. "Shall we?" my aunt repeats.

My uncle nods again.

"Great," I say. "See you at two thirty?"

They both nod. I smile, make a final fuss of Elliott who's recovered from the regurgitated sweet, and let myself out.

There's no sign of my mum or her car as I get back to hers. She's usually home for lunch on a Wednesday, the only weekday she is, but no, something, or someone, has lured her away. It does make it easier though for me to write up my report on the Bluebells and email it to the Williams. My William, he of the 'never call me Billy', is copied in for info but I'm sure he'd like to know how I'm getting on.

Mum's still not back by gone two. I give her mobile a call but it goes straight through to answerphone. It's only a five-minute drive from here to my uncle's so I'm okay to wait a few minutes but I like to be prompt, especially as it sometimes takes time to round up Elliott from the garden… until we say the word 'car' then he's at the front door faster than Mo Farah, pawing to get out.

I've also just remembered to make a note about the dog chocolate article so open up a new Word document and save it as 'animal week'. I do have a pretty good memory but things have to be saved to it in order for me to remember and sometimes I forget to get to that first stage. I have so much buzzing around my brain.

My handbag's packed and ready to go when I hear my phone buzz. It's been on silent since the Bluebells but the vibrate's on twenty-four-seven.

"Hey darling," I say as I hit the green phone icon.

"Hey you," Duncan says and I can almost hear his smile. "Sorry I missed you earlier. I was removing a staple from a cat's tongue."

Little surprises me about what Duncan's confronted with but this does. "A staple? What was a cat doing eating a staple?"

"Oh, it wasn't the cat but its owner."

"What?"

"Not its adult owner. His three-year-old granddaughter. She was supposed to be drawing but went into her granddad's office to get some more paper and took the stapler from his desk, via his chair, apparently, and thought it would be fun to staple everything in sight. He's not sure how the cat got its tongue in the way – you'd think it wouldn't have been that compliant. The chap heard the clicking but thought it was his fax machine until the scream. Not sure if cat or child, but the end result was the same."

"Fax machine? I didn't know people still had faxes."

"Me neither. Our office one went years ago."

I look at my watch. Two twenty-five. "Can I put you on hands free? I'm off to Uncle Pat's, taking them to the garden centre, you know, the one that used to be Wyvale."

"Nice. I'm going to have to go actually – next patient – but chat later?"

"Absolutely. I miss you, you know."

Duncan blows me a kiss and my heart swells. "Miss you too."

I can't help Cheshire catting as I put my phone back into my bag, double-lock myself out of Mum's house, and make my way up the road.

Chapter 40 – Afternoon Tea For Three... Five

So we head off to the garden centre between Tring and Bulbourne. There's a pub on the left if we keep going into Bulbourne and I've passed it a hundred times as it's the way I come into Tring whenever I visit but I've never noticed its name, or it doesn't register. I still don't get to find out this time as we turn right into the garden centre car park a hundred yards or so early.

I pull into an end space four rows from the front, and my uncle remarks at how busy the car park is for a Wednesday.

"Maybe it's OAPs' day," my aunt suggests. I'm surprised she doesn't know, being one herself.

As we're walking towards the café between the pet store and main outside plant areas, I do a quick search on Google but it only mentions pensioner discount on a Tuesday and their rewards card giving five points per pound spent, entitling the holder to £2.50 per 250 rewards. My brain almost whirrs as it calculates a fifty-pound outlay for that recompense. Compared with a pound back for every hundred spent on most other reward cards, that's pretty good. Not that it's going to change the world but for some my aunt and uncle's age, every penny counts. And many of them are here.

We get the last spare table outside, and my uncle and I go inside to get the food. My aunt and uncle usually insist on paying but he and I agree to go halves as he won't let me pay for it all. It's only when we get to the till to order the hot drinks and pay that my eye's caught by a flash of orange on a distant table. I recognise the scarf and look to its owner.

Sure enough, there's my mother sitting opposite a very distinguished-looking man. Charles. It has to be. He must have collected her or I would have spotted her car in the car park but it wasn't at her house so I'm a tad baffled. I'm sure it wasn't intentional, for her not to drive here, as there would have been no way of me knowing they were going to be here, or them us, but it explains why Mum wasn't answering her phone. I debate going over but know they'll have to come out past us so leave them to it. They're engrossed in a conversation so I'm not spotted, which is just as well.

My uncle and I pay without him having noticed my mum and I'm relieved for that too.

We return to my aunt and a very waggy Elliott. It always makes me laugh at how his whole body moves when his tail does and I wish Buddy were as enthusiastic to see me. He's very sweet but he's a one-person dog: Duncan, which is understandable. I smile again as I think of Duncan's call and I sit with a sigh.

We've just struck up a conversation about our lack of summer holidays when a too-young-looking-to-be-working boy comes out with a tray of our hot drinks. I look at his badge. Rather than the standard printed, his is handwritten, as if he's only temporary. A school exchange, I wonder as the scrawl identifies him as 'Laurence'.

He looks at the number on our table and only says, "I think these are yours?" but it's enough for me to detect a French accent.

"Merci," I say as he distributes the drinks, me pointing at the relevant person each time. He smiles and says something very quickly in his mother tongue. Too quick for me to catch.

"Je parle un peu Français," I mumble and struggle to think of how to say 'sorry' in French. I can only think of 'Lo siento' which is Spanish and 'Das tut mir leid' and 'Entschuldigung', both German, and I don't know why I know those when I did Spanish and French at school, but he smiles nonetheless.

"Very good. Your accent. It is very good." Although I'm old enough to be his mother, I blush like a school… well, a girl his age.

I know from experience (Google told me) that the average calories in a cheese scone are one hundred and forty-five but these are whoppers so I can easily double it. I put on a scraping of butter and equally sparse jam so they not only save calories but don't hide the scrummy cheese flavour. There's melted cheese on the top and it looks like Red Leicester. I have a neighbour who doesn't like cheese and although she's lovely, I've never understood why.

I sneak a two-pound tip under my plate. The single coin doesn't seem much but it's a chain so feels less of a local business, although these days everything's franchised so how could one tell. I wonder if that's something I could cover in an article, or another week's worth, and dig out a notebook to jot it down.

They don't ask me what I'm doing but I sense my aunt and uncle's eyes looking at me.

I look up and sure enough, they are. "Something I need to remember for work," I say and they nod.

All the way through our conversation about my project, Elliott's recent visit to the vet (his yearly booster) and my uncle's latest photography client, I've been willing the door into the café to open and my orange-scarfed mother and her companion to come out but no such luck.

We've finished our drinks and food, and unless anyone wants a refill, there's no reason to stay. Plus I have to drop everyone off before getting back to work to meet up with Greta for yet more food and drink. Although this is supposed to be a healthy eating project, I feel I've done little else.

We all stand, much to Elliott's delight as it means we're going somewhere exclusively for him (of course!), just as the door does open. I'm side on to it but get a gust of warm air, even warmer than the tepid exterior. I will it to be my mother and although it's not, it's Charles. Minus my mother. Unless my mother's shown him a photograph of me, he doesn't know who I am, nor my aunt and uncle. And I'm not supposed to know who he is so I have a dilemma: I could engage him in small talk but what excuse would I have? Or do I let him go but delay our exit as my mother can't be far behind; in the ladies presumably. Would she want us to know she's here?

I opt for letting fate decide so I ignore Charles and we casually follow him out into the car park, me holding on to Elliott. Charles heads in the same direction as us so I pick up speed, pretending to trot with Elliott like one of those Austrian Spanish Slovenian Lipizzaner horses. I know, it's always confused me too.

Charles appears to be oblivious as we scoot past then I realise he's looking at his phone screen. I can't see what and I'm not going to peer. I don't want our first meeting, unofficial or otherwise, to be of me perving.

Elliott obligingly hops up into the car, panting away at his little burst of exercise. A Lipizzaner he is not. My aunt and uncle have caught up, and I see that Charles is standing beside a car two spaces away. Between us is a hulk of a Range Rover so I can't see what car he's actually driving but he's super tall, William tall, and I recognise his (Charles's, not William's) greying hair. Considering he's in his sixties, he's still got a fair amount of brown. And hair. Many men I know, other than my uncle, and Duncan, and William, have started thinning in their thirties.

My car refuses to start. It never not starts. I try again. Nothing.

"Maybe it's the battery," my aunt suggests.

"I'm in the AA," my uncle says, "personal cover, if you need it."

"Thank you," I say and hope I *won't* need it.

"There's your mum," my aunt points out as the orange scarf dazzles us from a few feet away.

"Oh," I respond, trying to sound surprised. "What's *she* doing here?" Although I know full well.

Thankfully she's not looking in our direction, despite my aunt waving through the gap between my seat and my uncle's, cooing a 'Woo hoo!'. She much prefers the back, not only having a clear view either side but of us too.

Unsure what to do, I sit and wait. My mum's still oblivious of us and I wouldn't put it past my aunt to stretch even further and honk the horn would she be able to reach it. As it turns out, we all sit and wait, my aunt's retracted arm is, I notice, rested on the top of my uncle's seat. We watch as my mum heads for, and gets into, Charles's car and a few seconds later, it – another Range Rover – emerges and they leave the car park.

"Get the gossip later, yes?" my aunt says and I know she means from me but I say nothing.

The car starts perfectly and I drive us back to their house, a silence descending over us like an autumn mist.

Chapter 41 – Pause And Think, Think And Pause

With a promise to get as much 'dirt' as possible from my mother, I drop my aunt, uncle and a tired – though no reason to be – Elliott at their house, and make my way to work to meet up with Greta. With a desktop and matching network at the office, there's no need to collect my laptop from my mum's however tempting it might be to see if she's gone back there or to Charles's. I'm assuming from them taking his car that they'd have gone to his to collect hers so the chances of her being home are tiny, and time negates curiosity, therefore Hemel Hempstead it is.

Despite it only being just gone five, the office is fairly sparse. Owen's on reception, like the captain of a ship; the last to leave, other than Billy who is actually the captain. I don't disturb Owen so head through the double doors and down the corridor into the open-plan area. The individual offices leading up to it are empty, even Hazel's conspicuous by her absence, as is Leah, her assistant.

Greta and Frank make up the sole entity of the left side of the office with no one on the right. I'm grateful that James isn't there and think of him playing happy families with his however-many-point-four children and beautiful wife. Nathan and Billy are also missing so it's just the three of us. I head for Greta first. Head down, she's engrossed in some kind of paperwork.

"Hi," I say, hovering between her and Frank's desk.

With no reply, I turn to Frank but he too is engrossed. Not in Greta's paperwork obviously but in something on his screen. I can't see what it is and like Charles's smaller version earlier, I'm not going to gawk.

There's a chair between the two desks but facing them so I turn it more towards Greta. I want to sit but think I'm being a nuisance. I want her to know that I'm here, or for Frank to know so he can pass on the message but neither is paying me any attention. I'm not normally needy but it feels quite disconcerting.

I cough. Not as a distraction but because a tickle has launched itself and I need to. Either way, it does the trick and Greta looks up.

"Ooh hello. Sorry. Have you been there long?"

I shake my head.

She looks behind her, at a clock on the wall and gasps. "Sorry," she repeats. "Didn't realise it was so late."

The trouble with it being May is the long hours of daylight. Not that people usually complain but it doesn't give any sense of being past work and into play. At five thirty, it's somewhere in between.

"Are you okay to still go out for something to eat?" I ask and hope she says 'yes'. We've not really spent any time together and while I'm more than capable of going out on my own, I was looking forward to the company, not that I haven't had much of that today. Restaurants are made for two, as the saying doesn't really go.

I realise she's spoken but I missed it. Her face isn't portraying a negative or positive so I wait.

"Anywhere in mind?" she asks and I'm relieved.

"I don't really know..." And I don't. I have a list but it's on my desk.

"Let's just grab our stuff then and head into town."

That sounds like a great plan. And we do.

"Do you like Italian?" Greta asks me as we head down the stairs and towards the main road. I wonder if she's going to suggest Ristorante Alberto. It would be nice, having been there twice, to actually go inside. But we don't get that far. We're standing outside Papa John's and although I've seen adverts for them on the television, and those only relatively recently, I've never been in one. I envisaged a takeaway but we can eat in too. It's rather chainy, as I'd expect, but Greta must like it to bring me here. I go to open the door but she speaks. "Actually..." I let go of the door handle and follow her away.

We then end up outside Pizza Express. "Sorry," she says for the third time. "Nothing wrong with Papa John's, I just felt..."

"No apology needed," I say although I must admit to being a little confused. While I'm more than happy with the change, it felt like her mind has been elsewhere.

"Had a bit of a day."

I feel sorry for her and bad that I was confused. "Oh dear. Anything you want to share?"

She perks up. "No, it's okay, but thank you."

We go inside and are shown to a table for two about halfway into the restaurant and I'm pleased it's not near the toilets or front door. Even though it's not cold outside, tables nearby tend to get wafts of air, and not so pleasant wafts near the toilets.

Our server is a young man who doesn't look too dissimilar to Laurence, hasn't been supplied with a name badge and doesn't offer that information but is very pleasant and prompt. After agreeing that neither of us is hungry for anything other than a main course, I order a 'grand chicken Caesar salad' with no dressing, at 477 calories, and Greta does the same. We both order diet Cokes and I wonder if she's only being polite or whether she would have gone for those anyway.

She seems happier and less distracted than earlier so I start with mutual ground. "So, how are you getting on with the guitar lessons?"

She shrugs. "Not bad, thank you. Early days but yes, not bad."

"And my mum?"

Greta snorts then apologises.

I laugh. "Drowned cat or…"

"Oh no, I didn't mean…"

"It's okay. She does this, has these fads. She will last the ten weeks but she tends to move on to something else. One thing she isn't is a quitter but a mover, yes."

Greta smiles and thanks our nameless waiter as he returns with our drinks.

I'm then regaling my life in Northampton when the food turns up. We tuck in.

"Mmm… this is really nice," Greta says, her face matching her sentiment, and so does mine. With the lowest calorie 'Al Forno' pasta dish being the Peperonata at five hundred and forty-two calories and lowest pizza at eight hundred and thirty-four unless I'd gone for a base only, I'd had to go for the salad but I realise that Greta's really slim so salads are perhaps quite normal for her.

As if she's read my mind, she says, "I love pizza and pasta but come May, I go with the salads. Couldn't tell you why. Must be a summer thing but I love chicken and Caesar sauce."

I'd ordered first so I'm still not convinced she wasn't just being polite. She knows I'm on this project so I think she was probably prepared to match me. I respect her all the more if this is the case. We have no calories left for the dessert but as it turns out, we have no 'space' either, the chicken and large glasses of diet Coke being filling enough.

We haven't talked very much, partly because I'm conscious that she's using her free time to be with me, and she's also a really fast eater. I know I'm slower than most; I like the twenty-minute chew-a-dozen-times rule, but I barely get to double figures. I could have sat there chewing but salad doesn't last long and she would have thought I either had really tough bits of chicken or that I was mad, or both. It certainly wasn't the chicken; that was really tender, melting almost. Delicious.

Greta pays the bill and I insist on leaving a tip. As Nathan had said previously, Greta confirmed that Billy would have paid but I already feel like I'm on a free ride, even if I'm giving up my time for this, and like to play fair.

Our nameless waiter nods his thanks and shows us to the door.

Greta and I chat more about my life in Northampton and I'm pleased that in less than forty-eight hours I'll be picking up where I left off, with Duncan on Friday evening then him and Izzy at some point over the weekend. I'll have washing to do but it wouldn't be the worst thing in the world to do it at Duncan's, or not do it and take a new set of clothes with me when I return to Mum's Sunday evening. I wonder whether I could push the 'flexible office' a little and head down on the Monday but tell myself that I need to take the whole matter that much more seriously.

As we get back to the office building, we aim for the car park. Greta's on the ground floor, I'm one up, so we swap thanks and a hug, and head for our respective vehicles.

As I drive home, I think about Greta; how chatty she'd been previously in the office but less so at the restaurant. A bit of a day, she had said, and we do all get those, so I hope she's fared better when we go out next Wednesday. Not that having a quieter evening did me any harm; I am conscious that I talk too much – Duncan's told me on numerous occasions, light-heartedly of course – so it's good practice.

I tend to either fill in spaces for those who don't say very much or for anyone like my mum, try to get a word in when they breathe! No, I need to pause and think, think and pause.

I do a little 'yay' as I spot my mum's car in the driveway and no sign of the Range Rover. She rarely goes to bed early so I'll get my chance to grill.

Chapter 42 – More Than That, Much More

"Hello, darling," Mum says as I walk into her long kitchen diner.

I can't speak but have a silly grin on my face.

"What?"

I sit opposite her at the dining table. "Nothing."

She knows me too well. "What have you been up to?"

"Me? Oh, nothing. You, on the other hand…"

Her forehead creases as if she can't possibly know what I'm talking about.

"I took Uncle Pat and Aunt Jan to the garden centre this afternoon."

Her forehead decreases… uncreases. Darned English language.

"That was nice."

"It was very nice." I grin again.

We both know what happened or I wouldn't have mentioned it so she spills. "Yes, I was there with Charles."

I wait.

"We had afternoon tea, a lovely chat. The mini scones were still warm."

I wait again.

"What?"

"Oh, nothing," I repeat. "Go on. Afternoon tea, lovely chat, scones."

"Yes. That's all."

"And Charles?"

"He had the same as me."

"Mum."

"What?"

"Come on. The whole story."

She sighs. "Tea?"

I shake my head and wait.

She sighs again. "Okay. We bumped into each other while out shopping in Wendover. Sort of. He was at the Tesco on the hill, back from walking his dog Olly up at Wendover Woods, not really back as it's the opposite direction but he said he only needed milk and bread so didn't need to go to the big Tesco in Tring and we both live the Wendover side of Tring anyway so…"

"You bumped into each other while out shopping in Wendover but he was in Tesco…"

"I'd been shopping in Wendover town – you know how much I like the charity shops…"

I let her continue.

"I was driving back up the hill and spotted his car. The last three digits are OLL and it's a fairly distinctive car."

I recall the black Land Rover, albeit a twin of its neighbour. She's not wrong.

"So I stopped and popped in, on the pretence of needing…" She frowns as if trying to recall what she'd been imaginary buying. "Crisps."

"Oh." I don't feel it warrants any more than that.

"Which I did get. A multi-pack of Discos if you fancy some." She points to a cupboard above the built-in freezer. "So there he was, by the refrigerators, picking a couple of the small milks. What are they…? Half litres?"

I shrug. They're something like that.

"I think they are. He gets the green ones as I do. And he's going to save the lids for Jan. I asked. Something to say when I approached him."

'Hello' probably would have done.

"I can't remember why she collects them now. Guide dogs or a neighbour's school or some such. So he's already got his bread and has the milk. I have my crisps. I don't like the prawn cocktail ones so help yourself to those."

Now she's mentioned it, I do fancy a pack and rarely have prawn cocktail so go to where she pointed earlier. In the cupboard, sure enough, there's the six-pack unopened so I pull the seal apart and remove one of two pink packs.

She continues as I sit. "He suggested a coffee somewhere. I said the garden centre so we dropped off my car and Olly at his – Charles's ex is away at a conference or something – and we continued on in the Range Rover. It's very luxurious by the way. Only a year and a bit old. Bought it ahead of selling the house, which I thought was a bit risky but he said he's on a good company pension so that's okay. Anyway, it's not my business. So there you have it. That's why we were at the garden centre. How come we didn't see you?"

"Charles did."

"Did he? He didn't say anything."

"How would he know?"

She frowns as she thinks. "Oh yes. You've not met yet."

I shake my head. "We were sitting outside, literally the first table, but by the time you came out we were in my car. We watched you but you were away with the fairies."

She blushes. I smile.

Neither of us says anything until she offers again to make a cup of tea. I've not opened the crisp packet yet and am not sure whether they'd make great companions but this time I won't say 'no'.

"So, how's your diet project going?" she asks as she part-fills the kettle with bottled water. She's got it into her head that it tastes better than tap but once it's boiled and a tea bag or coffee granules added, I can't taste any difference though less chalky I suppose. We are in the Chilterns.

"Not bad, thanks. I went out with Greta tonight."

Mum smiles at the mention of her guitar companion's name. "She's really good. We've got our next session tomorrow night but she's miles better than us already."

Mum's said that before but I smile as if it's the first time I've heard it.

"Did she talk about it?"

"She was pretty quiet actually."

"She is in class."

"Oh? But I suppose everyone is if they're trying to concentrate, letting Bernard teach."

Mum sniggers, I guess at 'Bernard'. "Except me."

Shocker. Mum's usually more talkative than me, and that's saying something.

"But you let him speak."

"Of course." She looks wounded as she makes the tea but I know she's only joking. My mum's a hoot and I adore her. She'd make a good actress, although her memory's not what it used to be. We have that in common too. "What did you have?" she asks as she returns to the table with our two mugs.

"When?"

"Tonight with Greta."

"Oh, chicken Caesar salad and diet Coke."

"And Greta?"

"The same."

"Yes."

"Yes?"

"She's a diet Coke girl, brings along a big… two-litre bottle to each session. Offers it around but only brings one cup so unless anyone brings their own..."

"It's not like she needs to be on a diet. She's pretty tiny."

Mum nods. We've both had to watch our weight. Too many afternoon teas and we'd balloon. I'd had issues growing up, nothing to do with my parents but more at school, and that was how I got to be a health and beauty columnist, learning to slim and keep it off to avoid being bullied, not that Mum ever knew; she just thought it was puppy fat. I never cried in front of her or Dad. I sniff as I feel tears welling. "Think I'm getting a cold."

She offers me a box of tissues and I take one even though I'm sure I won't need one. I put it next to the crisps which remain unopened. They've lost their appeal but can come to work with me tomorrow. I've decided I'll be more productive if I stick to office hours. Having the day out and about today was lovely, and I wouldn't have seen Mum and Charles had I not been there but no, I should be a proper worker. How else am I going to fit in if I'm never there?

"So, things going well with Charles then."

Mum takes a sip of tea but winces as it's clearly still too hot. I've not started mine for that reason. "Yes, really well. Early days but..."

I grin. I know all about early days; getting to know each other, the fun part. Should be the fun part. Not that everything thereafter isn't but you settle into a routine. I miss Duncan. He should be here or I should be there. I'm pleased Mum has someone, even if it's complicated.

"I'm pleased for you, Mum. I really am."

She smiles. "Thank you. I know it's not easy for you but..."

While my mum's had 'friendships' since my dad died, I get the impression that Charles could be more than that, much more. She's too young not to have a significant other. We all need one if we're honest. Most of us are happy with our own company, some more than others in their own skin – that's one thing I try to help with in my column, the beauty bit mostly, but there's nothing quite like having someone to look after us, and vice versa. Most definitely a two-way street.

We finish our teas and head to bed, neither of us needing a hot water bottle. Even if it hadn't been late spring, thinking about our respective other halves seems to be keeping us warm, it is me anyway.

We stop on the landing, our bedrooms opposite each other.

"Night, Mum."

"Night, Don Dons."

I drop my head and smile. She's not called me that for years and all of a sudden I'm a little girl again. I shudder at how strange it feels; not bad but strange. Non-funny peculiar instead of non-funny ha ha.

I hear her bedroom door click shut and do the same to mine then lean against the back of the door and burst into tears.

Chapter 43 – Oh Congratulations... Oh No

Thursday 3rd May

I feel much better when I wake. I don't know what got into me last night but whatever it was has gone. I feel resolute, determined, and am looking forward to going to work and writing up last night's dinner with Greta. If James or Leah don't mind, I'm going to invite Greta instead for lunch.

Even if she's brought something, we can sit together and chat. Fingers crossed she'll be having a better day by then but if not, I'm hoping my broad shoulders will help, not that they are actually broad, in keeping with my five-foot-two-and-a-half frame, but you know.

I get to work just before nine and the office is packed. Owen's on the phone but looks up as I walk into the reception foyer and we exchange smiles.

Hazel's also on the phone as is her assistant Leah in the opposite office, and I wonder if it's to each other, although Leah's shaking her head whereas Hazel's nodding so I'm not so sure.

I get to my desk via a quick "Good morning" exchange with Frank. I wanted to speak to Greta but she looked too absorbed in something, and was scowling, so I thought best leave her to it. We're not bosom buddies, as the saying goes, but I'd like to think she could confide in me. She probably does that already with Frank, seeing as they're neighbours, but different genders and generations don't allow for full and er... Frank discussions.

Cracking on with last night's report, it's eleven before I know it. I eat my crisps then go to the ladies to brush my teeth, having forgotten how pungent prawn cocktail flavouring can be. Delicious though. I keep a travel teeth-cleaning set in my handbag as I never know when I need a fresh breath but we should always brush, even just brush without the toothpaste, between meals, not that a bag of crisps can be classed as a meal.

Then it dawns on me. I didn't end up weighing myself before starting this project. I should have used my mum's scales on Tuesday morning to make it official, but am I doing the weight thing officially? Will my readers want to know if I've lost (or gained) x pounds? I suppose some will. It's a calorie-counting exercise after all. Okay, I'll weigh myself tomorrow. I didn't eat loads last night and will be good today so... I shake my head. What started as something simple... Isn't that often the way in life?

With lovely clean teeth and minty breath, I head back to my desk. All my project companions are in but look super busy. I want to talk to someone, it's my favourite thing to do, but equally don't like disturbing anyone. The food van will have been and gone, probably when I was in the toilet, so I'll have to go out to get something. I'm hoping Greta will need to as well and want a walk.

I spend the next hour faffing with my emails, Veronica's being zero other than office round robins, which is a little disappointing seeing as I've been her for two and a bit days. I have two from new suppliers offering me a choice of their wares and I send a very polite and flattering reply back – without being too smarmy! I've had plenty of practice at that… to my suppliers anyway.

"Hi Greta."

Greta looks up and smiles, a semi-sincere smile, and I can tell something's still troubling her.

"I wondered if you'd like to accompany me for lunch." That makes me feel so old, like I should be wearing a hat I can doff. The fact that I even know that word makes me feel even older.

"Love to but can you wait a minute while I finish off something?"

I go to speak but she points to the chair between her desk and Frank's. He's not there so I sit.

"My best friend's just got engaged," Greta blurts while typing something and looking at her screen.

"Oh congratulations." I said it as a natural reaction but I can tell by her face it's not as good news as it should be.

"It's such bad timing," she continues. "I'm happy for her, really I am." She tries a smile but neither of us is convinced. "I… I did have someone…" She looks at the empty desk next to her, James's, and sighs.

Oh no. I'm hoping that doesn't mean what I think it means but suspect it does. "I'm sorry," is all I can muster. I feel doubly determined to avoid him now. Greta's so lovely that I wouldn't want to hurt her more than he's clearly done. I want to be angry with him, and believe me I am but… I shake my head.

"Oh, it's not your fault. It's…" She's still looking at his desk.

I clap my hands and she looks back at me. "Lunch." I give her an air hostess's smile, no, a synchronised swimmer's, and it seems to do the trick.

Greta's younger than me, early twenties, mid at the most, and I'm tempted to say she's got plenty of time but I don't think whatever I say will help so I say nothing as we head along the corridor and out to reception.

Owen, miraculously, isn't on the phone and gives us a cheesy grin. He's a similar age to Greta, and hasn't come across as gay, so I wonder if he's single.

"Owen…" No, I can't do it. *Go on, Donna*, my brain eggs me on but I can't. Izzy might, she's the forthright one of the two of us but I can't do it to Greta. I can't be that obvious. So I resolve to speak to him later. In the meantime I go with the simple, "How are things with you?"

"Good, thanks. And you?"

On a scale of happy, Owen would definitely be at the top, Greta somewhere near the bottom with me in the middle but I don't go into specifics. I just say, "Good, thank you. Taking my new friend here for lunch."

Owen looks at Greta and blushes. Ding! I wonder if they have a history, especially as she doesn't react other than a part-smile, less than I got, but think that her mind's still on her friend. Was life this complicated when I started at the Northampton office? I suppose it must have been.

"See you upon our return," I say, again feeling beyond my years, and usher Greta down the stairs and out into the fresh air. I neglected to see whether Phil was in his box – and whether that's where James was; they seem to be friends, unlike James and Gavin the Gerbil, but I'll have a better view 'upon our return'.

I shake my head but Greta's still in a world of her own so doesn't notice. I've never done an article about the benefits, or otherwise, of shaking our heads and wonder if anyone would be interested. Maybe only heavy metal fans… or their mothers. I smile at that thought and look round at Greta but no, still away with the Tinkerbells.

It doesn't surprise me at all when Greta suggests Subway and I'm pretty sure she's going to go for a salad tub. I'm somewhat familiar with the town centre by now so lead the way. She'll know it far better, of course, but she's lost any enthusiasm she might have had and is traipsing. I'm not the quickest of walkers by any means but even I'm finding the pace a little too slow. I'm tempted to suggest stopping at a bench and talking away her troubles but think we're best keeping going. It's always easier to talk in between bites than with no official reason for pauses, pregnant or otherwise.

The thought of that being Greta's actual issue makes me shudder.

"Are you cold?" a little voice squeaks beside me.

We stop and I say that I'm fine. 'Just someone going over my grave,' I'm tempted to add but think better of it. Anything negative is best avoided in situations like these.

We eventually get to Subway. I remember from my previous visit that the chicken tikka and Italian B.M.T. (R), still not forgetting the (R) trademark, are only 141 and 245 calories respectively. I'm not overly hungry, even only having had a small bowl of Asda's Right Balance before I left my mum's and the prawn cocktail crisps mid-morning, but I could have both salads and still be under the 500 calories. It would also mean two potential reviews in one as I went for the TBG (turkey, bacon and guacamole) wrap last time.

Greta goes for the tikka and diet coke so probably 142 calories all told. I'm tempted to buy her a Mars bar to add to the count but she's unlikely to eat it. The only meal deal this branch does is a sub roll and drink so we'd be little better off even if she went for that. I'm not her mother, legally or otherwise, so what can I do? My shoulders and brain are about all I can offer her.

We find a bench on the way back to the office. It's near the river and although it's lunchtime and the weather's improved, it's fairly quiet. Perfect for a heart to heart. If Greta's feeling up to it. I don't waste any time in coming back to the topic. "Has your friend been dating long?"

I'm hoping Greta says 'no' to show how quickly life can change... after all, mine has in the past year.

"Five years, met at uni."

"Wow." That blows that theory out of the water. Darn it. "Did you go to university?" I ask for want of anything better to say.

She shakes her head. I only know this, as I'm not looking at her face because we're sitting side by side, from the fact that her body, and therefore her salad tub, move left to right and back again. "My dad had a shop so I went to work there."

"Oh?" Mine had too, years ago, so I'm especially interested.

"A fish and chip shop."

"Yum." I love fish and chips.

She gives me a weak smile. "Gets a bit much after a while."

"I suppose it does." I don't think I would have minded, although batter's incredibly bad for the skin. It needs fat but even so. I don't want to harp on about her friend but I like helping and feel Greta needs cheering up, although even I'm struggling. Should I be direct and ask her about James, or would his name, or Owen's, tip her over the edge? I risk the latter.

"Owen seems nice."

Greta's salad bowl quivers. I turn to look at her. She's still smiling. A breakthrough.

"Really nice," I add.

She's grinning. A double breakthrough. James, if he were in her thoughts, seems long distance. "I think he likes you," I venture and wonder if I've been too bold. If I'd misread his blush, I would be leading Greta up for more heartache, but…

"He is," she says and looks down at her part-eaten salad. She stabs at a lettuce leaf with her provided plastic fork and stuffs it into her mouth.

I wonder whether to offer to put in a good word for her but decide to be more candid. A second after that decision though I think that candidity… if that's even a word, never got anyone anywhere. "Would you like me to fish?"

She looks at the river then at me. "Huh?"

"With Owen."

"Oh. Erm…"

"Only if you want me to."

She nods briefly and smiles. Her cheeks even look less pallid, rounder almost, and I know a simple lettuce leaf wouldn't have done that. I'm coming to the conclusion that I wasn't sent to Hemel Hempstead to do a diet project but to mend some hearts. I have my soulmate and want everyone else to be happy. Is that too much to ask?

Chapter 44 – Too Much Of A Good Thing

Tonight is my final first-week dinner out. It's been an interesting time all told and it'll be lovely getting to know my temporary colleagues better as time goes on, although of course I'm looking forward to seeing Duncan more. I'll give him a ring later. The advantage of having dinner straight after work is getting back to my mum's at a reasonable time, not that she'll always be there but I can relax regardless.

So yes, tonight is with Billy. That should be a hoot. I'm hoping he's not forgotten or proxies Nathan in his place but either way, a hoot. After lunch, I type up my salad. I'm conscious of not making too many of the reports about salad as that's the easy, and therefore very clichéd, option for dieters but there's much more choice these days than when I first started at the paper.

I see that Nathan's in with Billy when I approach his office so pop down to see Phil to ask if he'd mind not doing Friday nights so I can head back home before the London traffic gets too bad, not that there's a good time on a Friday other than really late and that's not my idea of how to spend a Friday night.

He's staring at his screen when I reach his box of an office. I don't like interrupting but tap lightly on the door. Without looking away, he raises his hand and beckons me in.

"Yes?" he snaps. Oh dear.

"Sorry, Phil. It's Donna. I wanted a quick word about dinner tomorrow night."

"Huh?"

"Dinner tomorrow night?"

"Oh… yeah… that."

Oh, yes, that. Clearly not keen, which makes my question easier to ask. "Would you mind if we don't, only–"

"Nope. Not at all."

It's difficult to tell for sure as he's still staring at the screens but he looks a little relieved. I don't know whether it's because I've done something to offend him or he'd rather be doing something else tomorrow night, or both. I'm hoping it's the idea and not me, but I'd never be bold enough to ask, or want to know. I bid him a quiet, 'Thank you. See you later' and get the merest of nods in return.

I head back upstairs. Owen's off the phone. Peering through the non-bulletproof plastic sheeting that separates us, I look down at his hands. They're looping a beige rubber band round an impressively large ball of bands. The advantage of dealing with the post is that he's probably amassed those in a fairly short space of time. Duncan has a less impressive one at his house from all the bands he brings back from walking Buddy, courtesy of our local, and not-so-local as they seem to be wherever we go, posties. It's no wonder Royal Mail struggles to make a profit. I'm joking of course but it would go some way.

Owen looks up. "Oh hi."

I smile. "Hi, Owen." *Greta! Greta!* my brain shouts at me. "I know," I whisper.

Leaning towards me, toned chest hanging over his desk, squishing the band ball, Owen whispers back, "You do?"

"Oh no, I mean…" What do I mean? *Greta! Greta!* "I was wondering… It's none of my business but…"

Eyebrows raised, head tilted to one side, Owen resembles a curious dog.

"It's not for me but I get the impression…"

He's still waiting for me to get to the point. So am I.

"I think we have a colleague who really likes you."

He leans back and I think I've offended him but he smiles. "Is it who I think it is?"

I have no clue who he thinks it is but I'm hoping it's the same person. "Greta!" I blurt, just as she comes out through the double doors.

"Yes?" She has the same curious expression on her face as Owen does on his.

They look at each other and blush. It's sweet. I decide to bite the bullet, grab the bull, and any other cliché that comes to mind. I figure that if I've got it all wrong then what's the worst that could happen. I'm only temporary anyway. "Greta. Owen likes you. Owen, Greta likes you too." There, said it. I can scuttle away now.

And I do, but not before Owen's come out of his cubicle, crossed the foyer, and is holding Greta's right hand in his. He almost looks like he's going to get down on one knee and propose but all he does is raise her hand and kiss the back. She and I are speechless, and I decide to do the decent thing and leave them to it. I'm sure one or other of them will tell me all later. Just call me Cupid.

As I walk down the corridor, I'm buzzing that I've coupled a… er… couple. Work relationships are often frowned upon but how else are you supposed to meet anyone? I met Duncan courtesy of Izzy and that was because of work and she met William that way, being our editor and boss. As she'd proven, dating sites are hard work and I'm so glad (and hopeful) that I'll never need to go down that route. Mike, before Duncan, was a work colleague so proves my point yet again, although that was always doomed and he's moved on to Frosty, another work relationship.

I'm glad that Duncan and I don't work together. You can have too much of a good thing, can't you? We're both animal lovers so him telling me all about his patients – the happy endings – gives me goosebumps, plus I love listening to his voice. He says I talk too much but we give as good as we get, no pauses, pregnant, thankfully.

I get back to my desk and realise I've forgotten to see whether Billy's in his office so I stand up almost too quickly for my bum to make contact with my seat, Veronica's seat.

There's no sign of Billy but Nathan's at his desk, audio headphones on. Again, I don't like to interrupt but do need to know what I'm doing, so I hover. I hear a click of the audio machine and assume it's Nathan releasing the pedal. It's the same tape type that Janice uses for William's dictations and I'm surprised that Billy's still using old-school technology rather than everything digital. Now is not the time though to ask. "Sorry, Nathan. I was wondering whether Billy's still okay to come out for something to eat."

Nathan's face drops, as does my stomach, which is pretty empty at the moment. "So sorry, Donna. Forgot all about it. I thought I had a rem–" He looks at his screen as it pings. "Yep, there it is. Donna and Billy dinner. Unfortunately he's been called away. Some family emergency up in Scotland. Will be away until Monday. I'd love to help but I've already–"

"Oh, no. It's absolutely fine." And although it's disappointing, it *is* fine. A night off won't kill me. Maybe Mum. Ah, no. Guitar with Greta. Of course. So dinner for one. In Tring. It'll make a change. "Thank you anyway."

Nathan nods politely, puts his headphones back on, and I hear the click as the tape restarts.

Chapter 45 – Dinner For One Non-singleton

Even though I prefer company, I don't mind the thought of having dinner on my own. I rarely do; I'm usually eating at home or out with Duncan or Izzy, so this will be a novelty. And I've always fancied Black Goo. Tring has a large retired population, especially with money to spend, but eyebrows were raised when Black Goo opened. More the name than its contents, I suspect. It makes me wonder whether Veronica have reviewed or mentioned it so I dig around the archives, those fortunately are digitised rather than tape, microfiche, paper, whatever it was before digital. I should know but my brain's too used to Google-type online searches, internet and intranet.

It brings up all the reviews and articles, and I filter by food rather than music, books etc. but there's no sign of Black Goo. I spot one for Lussmans, a 'fish and grill' restaurant which used to be one of the banks on the high street, HSBC I think, and that certainly appeals. I'm surprised to see it's actually Greta who did the review, but pleased that it appealed to her too.

A quick Google search tells me it was originally built as a bank in 1922 but doesn't tell me what it was when it closed. I don't feel particularly inclined to look further until I go to leave the internet but curiosity gets the better of me. I think I've killed quite a few proverbial cats in that respect in my time. I can only apologise. Enhancing a search from 'lussmanns tring bank', which told me the building's name was 'The Old Bank', to 'lussmanns tring was which bank before it closed' tells me, courtesy of tringtoday.co.uk, it was indeed the HSBC. I congratulate my little grey cells.

So, Lussmanns it is. I double check, again courtesy of my friend that is Google, whether I need to make a booking. I'm not told I have to but am invited to do so by several of the links so decide to. That way I don't have to go in on my own and announce the fact that I'm only looking for a table for one.

The default on the Open Table website is for two, of course it is, and I click the down arrow and go up one for '1'. Despite the website defaulting twice to two people, I finally get it to accept that it will only be me then I'm told they'll hold my reservation for 5:00 minutes, 4:59, 4:58 and counting, allowing me plenty of time to Sign in or Sign up. I need to do the latter and quicker than the clock and ignoring the three 'send you offers' tick boxes, my reservation is confirmed.

Thursdays are tricky days when it comes to restaurants. It's often a friends' night out night, the lads together, the girls-only parties, and I could have run the risk of having an available table for one but having never been there and got the place in my heart as well as my mind, I now have something concrete to look forward to.

I'm also impressed by the fact that they support Herts Young Homeless. I click on the link to hyh.org.uk. Websites like this one make me realise how lucky I am, not that I didn't know that already. Even if I lost my flat, if Duncan and I broke up, my mum would always have me back. Actually, she'd have me back even if none of that happened. She has got me back, albeit for a month. I click on the 'donate' button and PayPal thirty pounds, leaving a brief message, using a nickname.

After popping back to my mum's, I'm glowing a little as I walk down into Tring's town centre which takes me past Black Goo. Even if I'd wanted to go there, I couldn't have done. It closes at four every day except Sunday and then it's two pm. If I spend a weekend here, which I'm sure I will this month, I'll pop in and see if they can accommodate my temporary diet.

I continue along the high street, cross the road at the zebra crossing, then back track slightly and push open the heavy door into Lussmanns. I'd only ever been in there once when it was a bank and it's changed out of all recognition, unsurprisingly. It's spacious, as to be expected, but much brighter than before. It's still daylight outside so that helps but the walls are a pale blue with white wooden lower halves, pale wooden hatched flooring, wooden or grey marbled tables and wicker cane chairs or salmon pink sofas. It reminds me of a scene from Raffles. I wasn't born when it came out but remember my mum loving the reruns on UK Gold and the likes, so I can recall snatches.

An enthusiastic waitress comes up to me and I nod when she asks if I have a booking. I tell her my name and she smiles and guides me to a table at the far end of the main area. I have the choice of a wicker chair or sofa and go for the latter as it looks far more comfortable, enough to make me nod off if I'm not careful. I'm pleased I've not been led to the middle as I'd have felt like the solitary goldfish with everyone at the fair peering in.

I don't know why singletons are so hard done by, not that I am one of those, and maybe it's just singletons who feel hard done by, or me thinking they are. I did cover being single briefly, when I was single, and what the stigma from the press can do to our mental health, and think a revisit of that topic is probably overdue.

The same waitress asks if I'd like something to drink and seeing as I've walked, I ask for a vodka and lemonade. It's light and refreshing to start and I'll be eating soon, hopefully, it is quite quiet so far.

I spot on the menu a 'Hunter's linguine wild rabbit and free-range pancetta, oyster mushrooms and garlic (may contain shot)' on the menu and while I've only had rabbit once years ago, the idea of biting into a piece of lead doesn't appeal. Fair enough they have to be cautious but thank you but no. That's just a starter and it's sounds quite a lot. Billy's budget will easily accommodate whatever I want as it's only me but I decide to stick to a main.

I fancy fish and although I know it's going to be far superior to any of the fish and chip shops in a gazillion-mile radius, I can't help but go for the cod. I don't usually opt for dishes I could get anywhere else, or at home, frozen or otherwise, but like my drink, I fancy something light.

My waitress takes my order, my menu, then almost immediately returns with my vodka. Thankfully, it's quite a large glass so plenty of lemonade to keep a clear head. I'm only little so it doesn't take much to make me a bit woozy. Woozy. I love that word. I jot it down in my notebook so I don't forget to use it sometime. With my menu gone, there's not a lot to read. I like to keep occupied before and while I'm eating but without people watching – because there aren't many people to watch and it would be rude, I know I'm going to get bored. I flick through my notebook but that doesn't help. I don't want to make notes of the evening until I get home or I'll look like a food critic which technically I am but don't want to make it obvious.

Thankfully, my food arrives really quickly and it looks and smells divine. Ten out of ten for presentation at least. When I was googling earlier, I did spot some rather derogatory reviews but the place passes with flying colours so far. I tuck in.

The cod is the softest I've ever tasted. How they get it to melt without making it dry, I really don't know but that's why I'm a journalist, columnist, not a chef. There's a peperonata sauce which looks lovely but without running the risk of going over my allowance – there are no calorie counts on the menu, I have a tiny taste of it. It's delicious and while I could have it but not include it in my report, I feel that would be cheating so leave it be. I've also swapped the pommes frites for salad which is a shame because, looking over at two tables down, they're just how I like them but no, they would have pushed me over the limit for sure.

I'm grateful now that I don't have to live on a five-hundred-a-day diet as some with metabolic issues have to. I had a colleague, in a former life, who lived in 'tent' dresses, usually plain black, and was on that limit a day and people were horrible to her. They didn't know. How could they? But there was no excuse. Things have changed but I certainly feel sorry when I'm out and see how the larger in society can be treated. Some don't help themselves, of course, but many… It all goes to keeping me in a job. How boring would life be if we were all the same? Sometimes I think it would be easier if there weren't so many extremes but still. I like the way life is... mine anyway.

I finish my food and almost Mr Benn like, the waitress appears. She'd come round as I was eating to ask if everything was okay, as restaurant staff usually do, but I had a mouthful so could only nod and give a tight-lipped smile.

"Was everything to your satisfaction?" she asks with more than a hint of an eastern European accent.

"It was lovely, thank you."

"Would you like to see the menu again for desserts?"

Although I would, I decline. I had taken a look earlier but was spoilt for choice so am glad I don't have to choose. I don't need to include it in my report and I know Billy's allowance would stretch but I settle for a cup of something warm at my mum's and maybe whatever she's got in her freezer to go with it.

"Just the bill, thank you," I end with and it's presented to me. It's spot on; not difficult with only two items on it, three including a 'discretionary' 12.5% tip. I have no cause to complain because although I was no trouble, 100% goes to the staff so I'm all for that. I don't know about here specifically but most restaurant staff are on minimum wage or thereabouts so every little helps, as the local big-boy supermarket says.

Chapter 46 – Feels Like Christmas Morning

I'm not surprised when I get back to my mum's and she's not there. I'd forgotten to leave a light on so the house is in darkness. She usually puts a lamp on in the hall, on top of what by rights should be a plant stand but I'd switched it off when I came home and forgot to switch it back on again when I went out. She's not the type to tell me off but just as well I'm back first.

Mothers, even if they don't mean it, have the habit of treating their offspring like four-year-olds and in this case, I feel better for switching the lamp back on, even though I then switch on all the kitchen then dining end lights. With a chessboard effect of lights, courtesy of the dinky GU10s (I only know because I've changed them a few times, and been sent to Tesco to replenish her stocks; my mother is even less technology minded than I am), she'll probably tell me off for being wasteful but while I'm making a drink, getting a snack, and reading her Bunte magazine (a German 'Hello' equivalent that her friend Ursel sends over), needs must.

Neither of us speaks German, by the way, so all we ever do is look at the pictures, my mum at least refers to her rather battered leather-look dictionary – I suspect left over from school – to pick out the important words. Germans love our royal family and America's equivalent; whichever president's in at the time. I'd love to know what they think of Donald Trump and Melania (born 'Melanija') but as I said, I don't speak German. Izzy did it at school so maybe I should ask her but my mum's dictionary can attest that school was a long time ago. I did French and Spanish and as we know from my encounter with Laurence yesterday – was it really only yesterday? – most of that eludes me.

I look at the kettle, a plastic jar of mint Options hot chocolate sitting next to it and the freezer door and decide that actually, I'm neither hungry nor thirsty. It's Friday tomorrow and the sooner I go to bed, the sooner it'll be Friday, a step nearer going home to Duncan. I smile at the thought, leave a note for my mum, and trudge upstairs.

I'd already put the light out when I hear Mum come home. I debate getting up and going down to see her but having got all cosy and really quite sleepy, I decide to stay put. With my door closed and the note saying I'll see her in the morning, she won't disturb me. At least she's not done that since I was a lot older than four. Not that I'd know if I were asleep.

I'm so excited when I wake up. It feels like Christmas morning and I'm going to get my present tonight… which I know I will. I can't help smiling as I brush my teeth which makes a blob of toothpaste drop onto my pyjama top. It doesn't matter; it's going in the wash tonight anyway. I scoop up the blob with my toothbrush and splat it into a small open-top bin between the sink and toilet. It'll make the bin liner sticky so I apologise in advance to my mum, in my head anyway, and squeeze another blob onto the toothbrush. I do my twenty-four times up and down; the lower number quoted as Harold Crick brushing his in one of my favourite movies, *Stranger than Fiction*.

Izzy thinks she's a nerd but we're a pretty close match, probably why we get on so well. Thinking about the film reminds me to check whether Duncan's ever seen it. He likes reading, though not as much as Izzy and me, which isn't difficult, given the time, and it's all about reading, sort of, so I'm sure he'll like it. I'm surprised we've not watched it together before. I would have thought that Izzy buying it would have reminded me, or reminded me enough to ask Duncan. Never mind. I'm overthinking again, as I do.

Ooh… it's Friday. I've said that already, haven't I.

Teeth brushed, mouth gargled, face rinsed, I get dressed and head downstairs. It's only just gone eight but Mum's already dressed and at the dining table.

"Hello, love," she says, flicking over the last page of the Bunte. She's been there a while if she's gone through the whole magazine.

"Hi, Mum." I'm tempted to say 'Been here long?' but that feels like a question to ask a date rather than my own mother. I can see by steam rising from a mug in front of her that maybe she hasn't.

"The kettle's not long boiled if you'd like something." She returns the magazine to its front page and flicks it over. The dictionary's nowhere in sight so she's still at the pictures stage. She usually goes through it a couple of times before 'reading' any of it. I'm guessing this is the start of phase two.

I'm not sure what I fancy so just sit. "How was guitar last night?"

Mum snorts. I don't think I've ever heard her snort before and it's a strange noise. Maybe she's picked it up from Greta. I wait for Mum to say something.

"Don't think I'll ever get the hang of it. It's all fingers and thumbs."

Yes, that's exactly what playing the guitar is. "It's only practice. What are we now… week three?"

She nods.

"You've got seven more to go then."

She snorts again.

"Is Greta putting you off?"

Mum tilts her head.

"Because she's so good."

Mum's shoulders slump. "I wish I had her natural ability."

"She's probably played before whereas you haven't, have you?"

Mum smiles a little. "True."

"There we go then. My English teacher told me once that no one would put me in front of a canvas and expect me to play a concerto." I think about what I've said when my mum frowns. "No, I mean my English teacher told me that no one would put me in front of a canvas and expect me to paint a Dali. No one would put me in front of a piano and expect me to play a concerto. That's better."

"True," she repeats and smiles a little more.

"Why did your English teacher tell you that? She wasn't teaching painting or music, was she?"

"No. She was comparing it to creative writing. That no one would give me a pen and a blank piece of paper and expect me to write a masterpiece."

"Couldn't she have just said that?"

"I don't know, Mum." I do but I'm not going through it all again.

I decide to skip a hot drink and have a bowl of Tesco's four-nut and maple cereal. I've never wondered what the four nuts are until now so study the pack. Almonds, hazelnuts, brazils and pecans. For some reason I'd always just thought it was maple and pecan, pecan and maple. As I said, I think too much. Or too little about that until now. Something else that isn't going to change the world.

"So how come you're up so early?" I ask between mouthfuls as my earlier curiosity returns.

"We're off to Dunsley Farm this morning."

"At ten thirty. And you mean with Aunt Jan and Uncle Pat."

Mum nods then grins.

"Mum..."

Looking like a caught-out schoolgirl behind the bike sheds – snogging or smoking, either or both, I can almost hear her brain whirring. I know she's trying to think of an excuse, one I'll believe. This can only mean one thing. I look around the room and it's spotless, other than the magazine and my breakfast things.

"Is Charles coming over?"

She licks her lips. I'm hoping that was sub-conscious but from one's mother, it's too much information.

"For breakfast or before you head out?"

"Yes."

"Oh okay. Do you want me to go or be here when he gets here?"

More brain whirring.

I make it simple. "Would you like me to meet him?"

She purses her lips. I wait. "That would be nice."

I assume she's answering the latter two parts of the three choices but I need the clarification. "Stay here?"

She nods.
"Okay. I can do that. What time's he due?"
She looks over at the microwave clock. 8:17. "In about thirteen minutes."
I ought to be going to work but wouldn't miss this for the world. Thirteen minutes gives me time to finish my cereal, put the dish and spoon in the dishwasher, and get ready for work. That way, I can be polite enough for a couple of minutes' overlap but make a retreat so I'm not a gooseberry.
As if she's read my mind she says, "You won't be in the way, you know."
Thanks. "Thanks."
"I mean you have Duncan."
I do but he's not here.
"I'm not sure why I said that."
Nor am I but I do and smile. She's flustered. She's in love.
"What?"
I shake my head. "Nothing."
She squints. "You're looking at me in that funny way."
Now I do the behind the bike shed caught thing. "No."
"What?"
I feel like we're going round in circles so finish my cereal, deposit the aforementioned items in the dishwasher and do indeed get ready for work. I'm coming back down the stairs when the front door opens. Not on its own of course but not by my mum either. He has a key. I look at my mum through the open kitchen door and she knows what I'm thinking. She's pursing her lips again. I turn round and go back up the stairs before he spots me so hope I've been quick enough. I wait round the corner on the landing and hear him shut the front door and go through to the kitchen. I come back downstairs again and feign surprise at his arrival.
My mum's on her feet with her arms outstretched as if to give him a hug. Timing's never been my strong point. He's not seen me yet so I usher my mum to continue. She does but it looks lack lustre and Charles obviously thinks the same.
"Are you okay?"
My mum pulls back and looks in my direction.
Charles turns round. "Ooh, hello. You must be Donna." He holds out his right hand and I shake it. He's wearing the same Barbour-style jacket as the one at the garden centre but the sweater underneath is salmon rather than blue. I'm not the most observant person who walks the planet but sometimes there are things you just have to remember. He looks like Jack Reacher, not Tom Cruise but the person I pictured Jack to resemble when I read the books, or rather when Duncan read them to me. We're both fans.

He, Charles not Duncan, nor Jack, sadly on both counts, towers over me and I almost feel cold in his shadow. Not that he's not a warm-looking person but I get a chill from somewhere, then I realise that the fridge door's open and the milk is sitting on the work surface above it so his arrival must have interrupted Mum retrieving the bottle and she panicked and sat at the table as she heard me coming down the stairs. Something like that. My mum's normally pretty cool, more so than me, but Charles definitely has her on edge. Or I do. Or the combination of us both.

"Lovely to meet you," I say and shake his hand again, not that either of us let go. "I'd love to stay and chat but I'm afraid I have to get to work. I'm only here temporarily and can't go skiving."

"Oh yes, your mother told me about that. It sounds really interesting."

I'm not sure anyone else would think so but smile and appreciate the gesture. We part hands and company and I wish them both a lovely day. I'm sure I'll get the run down from either my mum or aunt and uncle so I don't regret going to work but would love to be a fly on the wall after I've left.

Chapter 47 – Catching Up

Friday 4th May

Being that much nearer nine, my drive to work takes a little longer than normal but is uneventful. Thankfully Charles had parked the hulk that is his car in front of my mum's so I didn't have to ask him to move. I'm not sure I could have faced whatever sight greeted me had I to go back in the house.

Phil's on the phone in his box when I arrive and he nods at the screen. I don't know whether it's because I appeared on his monitor or he's agreeing with something the person he's talking to said. It doesn't really matter as he's not looking in my direction so I head up the stairs towards reception.

Owen too is on the phone, to be expected, but smiles as he hears the door go. I smile back, of course. I want to mouth something like 'I'll see you later' but think better of it as he's frowning at whoever he's talking to. I wonder if it's Phil.

Not having had a lunch break with Leah this week, I pop to the kitchen for a squash then next door to her office. I wonder, I think for the first time, why she has an office whereas the journalists, Frank the accounts chap, and even Nathan have desks within the main open-plan area but personnel, human resources, offices contain such sensitive information that it all has to be locked away. Simple really.

I knock on her closed door.

She looks up, holds her left palm flat to me, clears aside some paperwork. "Sorry about that," she says when I enter.

"No problem at all." I sit as she invites me to do so with the same hand. "I was wondering if you were free to go to lunch today."

She ponders the question then smiles. "Love to. I do remember Hazel arranging this and I'm sorry I've not really been around much this week, or rather not available." She taps the turned-over pile of papers. "With Veronica on maternity leave, interviewing for a new agony aunt, things like that."

I smile. "No problem." I'm curious about the agony aunt but figure Leah will tell me when we're out and about, if she's going to tell me at all, which she shouldn't really, being the human resources assistant. "Do you have lunch at a set time or…?"

"Not really. Shall we say one so I get ahead with this little lot?"

"One sounds great. Thank you. I appreciate it."

"No problem at all."

"And I'm happy to pay." Not sure why I felt the need to add that but I would be.

Leah smiles. "Billy's told me what's what. It's fine. I have a company card. It'll go on there."

"Thank you." This is so kind of everyone. I'm rather stoked. 'Overwhelmed' as my mum would say, and often does, and it doesn't take much to overwhelm either of us.

As I come out of Leah's office, James is inconspicuous by his absence. I know it should be conspicuous however, no one but me seems to notice he's not there. No one's said anything and I'm certainly not going to ask. Not yet, anyway. Leah will know and ooh, we're having lunch. Ding.

I go to my desk and type up last night's Lussmanns' experience. There's not much to tell as the only interaction I had was with the waitress and I don't even know her name.

The rest of the morning flies as I log into my own emails and deal with those. It's gone half past twelve when I look at the clock so do a quick check of Veronica's emails and answer a couple from readers. They say they're enjoying the new project and are looking forward to whatever I eat thereafter. One is replicating my experiences so I'm pleased that I'm bringing local businesses new er… business. That takes me to 12.56 so I log off, grab my bag and head to Leah's office.

There's still no sign of James as I walk past his desk. Greta's on the phone and I don't like to disturb Frank who does look rather swamped with paperwork but that's accounts for you. Leah's on the phone but beckons me in when I hover outside her shut door. There's no shuffling of papers but I'm going to keep my eyes level with her so it doesn't look like I'm prying, even though I'm dying to. I'm rubbish at keeping secrets so it's probably just as well.

Although I'd love to know all the gossip, I'm going to have to tell Leah that she's not to confide in me… unless it relates to James. I wonder if he's had a family crisis like Billy has but it might mean one of James's 'howevermany' children being ill and I wouldn't want that.

Agreeing on a walk to the town centre, Leah and I seem to be heading for Marlowes and I'm hoping not for Subway. I *could* eat there every day but it would be nice to have some variety. I didn't eat a huge amount yesterday, and the cereal I had this morning wasn't particularly filling, so I am quite hungry.

We have the choice of a few places but some, like The Dragon Garden and Banana Leaf, which both look hugely appealing are only open in the evenings. They're proper sit down places anyway so too much for lunch. Roastino, I recall from a review when I was researching, does 'the best fish and chips' in Hemel but having effectively had that last night, or fish and salad, I wouldn't go for that anyway.

"The Marlowes Café okay?" Leah asks and as another reviewer called it the best café in Hemel, I agree. It has some outside seating but we go inside, Leah first so I'm following her. It's quite simply decorated with salmon pink – clearly a popular colour locally – chairs and white melamine tables. Above the serving area is a large blue illuminated sign in the form of the café's name, and that of the nearby shopping centre.

Looking at a plated chicken salad on the neighbouring table, I'm tempted to go for the same but take a look at the menu. There's almost too much choice and a variety including snacks to full Sunday roasts but somewhere in between will do me, so I go for what my neighbour had. Leah has the same and we both have diet Cokes.

"I'm sorry," she said after we've ordered. "You must think I'm such a copycat but it looks so lovely."

"It does. We didn't really need the menu, did we."

"No, although they do pancakes so that was good to know." Leah's not like Greta then.

The chicken dish does look filling but thankfully most likely less than 500 calories. It depends on what sauce they use and I'm kicking myself for not mentioning it when we ordered but I can always discretely scrape it away, but it only looked a drizzle so I should be okay.

"How long have you worked at the paper?" I ask, hoping that eventually I can wheedle the conversation more specifically to James. I'm itching to know why he's not been around.

"A couple of years. Hazel, our matriarch, had managed for years on her own but we got too big so they brought me in."

I'm about to say something but Leah continues. A girl after my own heart.

"I know what you're thinking…"

James. James. I bet, no hope, you don't. *James. James.*

"…there aren't that many people in the office. They've downsized permanent but brought in a lot of freelancers."

I nod, knowing only too well how things have changed. I'm surprised really, given that Izzy and I are so specialised: technology and health and beauty respectively, that we've not been downsized but we do our near-daily column and the readers seem to love us so long may it continue. "I don't think I'd be any good working from home," I say at the thought of having to go freelance. "I'd get nothing done."

"Me neither. I love daytime TV. Live and catch-up. Jeremy Kyle, Jeremy Vine, all the other Jeremys."

I laugh. "Beadle."

Leah, who like Greta is younger than me, frowns.

"Someone my mum liked," I explain, although *we* used to watch *Beadle's About* and *Game for a Laugh* together. I do love a catch-up channel.

"Oh. So yes, a couple of years. It's really interesting, especially taking on new people. I don't always get to do the interviewing; it depends on the level we're recruiting, but I see all the CVs, put the best ones on the top. Hazel insists on reading them all but usually agrees with me."

"You're quite a team," I gush and see the perfect shoo-in. "James is convinced you have ESP because you and Hazel seem to communicate without speaking to each other."

"The joy of email."

"No, literally. He says…" I try to recall what he'd said. "He said, 'they have some kind of code. Not exactly lip reading but they can communicate just by looking at each other. Not ESP because their lips do actually move…', something like that."

"And you have a photographic memory."

I blush. "It's not bad. Not quite Carrie Wells but…"

Leah frowns again.

"She's a character in *Unforgettable*, an American TV series that Duncan, my boyfriend…" I'll never tire of saying that, although fiancé would sound even better. "…likes. He says because we both have good memories, Carrie and I, but she's always wearing skin-tight clothes." I laugh, as does Leah.

"So, James…" I say before we go too far off. "Is he…?"

Leah says nothing, clearly waiting for me to elaborate.

"He hasn't been in for a couple of days. Is everything all right?" There, I've said it, stuck my nose in, not the worst offence surely.

"I'm not sure. Something family related, I think. James did say but…" She takes a sip of drink but doesn't continue.

Not to me. Someone has to be doing his work while he's away and his equivalent, like a role reversal of Veronica and me, is Izzy. I don't know how asking Leah directly would go down but I don't know how else to, although I phrase it as if I'm being helpful. "Is someone covering his work while he's away? Anything I can do?"

Leah swallows. "Thanks but Simon's picked up some of the things. He used to do James's role before becoming a manager. James has set his email to forward so that's covered. I think he was pretty much up to date though and he's due back on Monday."

I'd already been told that somewhere else in the building are Simon, Hemel's sales and marketing manager, and his two assistants, Steph and Zoe, so plenty of spare 'arms'. Heads? Some kind of anatomy.

The conversation pauses while our food and drinks are brought over. They look every bit as delicious as our neighbour had, with even less of a drizzle on mine for which I'm grateful, and Leah and I devour without another word uttered.

We finish at the same time and lean back like twins, dabbing the edges of our (own!) mouths with our restaurant-quality paper napkins and laugh.

"It's a shame you're not staying," Leah says, "you fit right in."

"It is but, and please don't take this the wrong way, I'm missing home already and I'm only a quarter of the way through."

"It's gone quickly," she says but I don't agree… not really. I've been looking forward to tonight since I got to my mum's on Sunday which is bad because it's wishing my time away which she never approves of. My mum, that is. I don't know if Leah approves or not and it would be too weird to ask her.

"I bet it'll be lovely to get back to Duncan tonight."

I can't help smiling as she speaks. "It will," is all I can manage without drooling. I dab at my mouth again, this time with my right thumb and I'm pleased that I'm not actually drooling.

With heartfelt thanks, I leave Leah at her office and return to my desk. It's gone two o'clock already and I plan to leave at four so the next two hours are a blur. With Veronica's emails and my own up to date, I don't feel at all guilty, and remember what Billy said about flexible hours so sneak away at three forty-five. Owen's not on the phone for a change so a chance to speak with him before leaving entirely.

"Hello, Miss," he says as I approach his cube-like reception.

"Hello, Mister," I reply and feel a little foolish but he doesn't seem to notice.

"How's your first week been?"

I glow and before I can say anything, he continues.

"That good. I'm pleased, really pleased."

He has somewhat of a glow about him too if I'm not mistaken.

"And your week?" I feel that's general enough to not be prying but I'm dying for him to mention Greta.

"It's been grand, thank you, just grand."

I'd not detected any hint of Irishism before now but the way he says it does have a certain twang, but it probably would even if I'd said it. I'm about to speak when the reception phone dashboard lights up with, I look over, four lines incoming.

"Never rains," he says, mouths a 'have a good weekend' and takes the first call.

Without going round to the side of the cubicle, leaning over and attracting his attention while he's speaking, there's no point in saying or mouthing anything so I leave.

Phil's staring at his screens as I get to the bottom of the stairs. I debate whether to interrupt him and decide it's worth it. Had it been any other day, I wouldn't have, but not being back until Monday and it being the first Friday, it's the first time we should have been going out.

I tap on the door and wait. He doesn't move. I tap a little louder. Again he doesn't move. His cameras cover the stairs, right up to the top, so I'm sure he would have seen me. Third time proves to be unlucky and again, he doesn't move. I'm about to turn when I see him jolt.

I smile as I realise he'd fallen asleep. Maybe he has more in common with Mike than I thought.

Chapter 48 – Welcome Home

I squeal as I open Duncan's front door. I'm still squealing as I hang up my jacket… or I would have hung up my jacket; I actually threw it on the floor along with my bag and kicked the door shut. Duncan's usually in his kitchen diner so that's where I go first but it's empty. The light's on but he's not there. There's no music either. I go through to the lounge diner but no, light on but a distinct lack of Duncan and music. "Hello?" I call but no reply. I go to the bottom of the stairs. "Duncan?" Nothing. A fine welcome home this is.

I slump down on one of two stools at a breakfast bar in the kitchen then scream as I feel something touch the back of my neck. I'm about to swat it away when Duncan's face appears as I turn round. I realise the touch was a kiss. "Where were you?" I ask a little hysterically.

"In the downstairs loo."

"Why?"

"What do you mean why?"

"Why didn't you answer when I called you?"

"I was hiding."

"Why?"

"Because I wanted to surprise you."

"By frightening me to death."

"That was the plan. No, that wasn't supposed to happen but, okay it sort of was but it was more romantic in my head."

With that, and the puppy-dog expression on his face, I can't be angry but a little part of me is.

"I saw your headlights as you pulled up so I got Alexa to turn off the music. I knew you'd know I was here if the music was playing."

"But you were here."

"Yes, but I didn't want you to know that."

I sniff.

"You okay?"

"Yes. I wondered whether you'd planned anything for dinner." It's traditional for Duncan to cook on a Friday night, regardless of how his day's gone.

"Chicken salad. They're plated all ready in the fridge."

Oh great, another chicken salad. I can tell by Duncan's face that he knows I'm disappointed. He then smiles and pulls out two takeaway menus from one of his back pockets. "Chinese or Indian?"

I smile. "That's more like it." I shake my head. "I don't mind which, you choose." I secretly hope for Chinese.

"Chinese it is."

I clap, lean over and give him a kiss. "Don't order too much though. You always order too much."

"Saves us cooking Saturday lunchtime."

While that is true, Saturday mornings are our weekly fry-up so three such meals in a row would certainly be too much. It never is because there's so little left after we're done on a Friday night that it ends up being breakfast on Sunday. I know; unhealthy and unhygienic. Microwaved meat thirty-six or so hours later. Asking for trouble.

It turns out we eat very little. A bowl of cereal each. We get a little… erm… way laid, as the saying goes. The takeaway's not ordered so no Sunday morning salmonella or botulism either. Okay, slightly over dramatic. Campylobacter bacteria and Clostridium perfringens. Lovely.

And it was; getting way… erm, yes.

Chapter 49 – A Bolder Donna

Saturday 5th May

There's nothing quite like waking up in the arms of someone you love. In my case it's Duncan's arms; we're spooning but quite disturbingly, as I turn to face him, there's a paw over his shoulder so he too is in the arms, legs, of someone he loves. His five-year-old beagle.

"Buddy!" I say not too loudly but not quietly either, and the paw retracts to be replaced by a head, a canine one. He's smiling and licking his lips. He always goes out in the garden first thing but for micro seconds, doing the bare minimum of necessity, before his lord and master gives him his breakfast.

Buddy likes me, I know he does, but whenever I feed him he just looks at me, his bowl, then back at me. Duncan then has to swoop in, remove the bowl, stir it round with the dog fork (one that doesn't match any others) and return the bowl to the mat. Buddy bolts the food down quicker than… oh, I don't know, a starving animal – which he's not, he's got a bit of a tum – as if Duncan fed him in the first place.

I've bought him toys – Buddy loves anything that squeaks, which he demolishes in about thirty seconds flat so it's Poundland almost all the way. Rubber toys are pointless because they don't even get to double-figure seconds or they're ignored. No fun out of that for either of us. I love dogs, especially Elliott, and I'm sure Charles's Olly is also very sweet, but not on the bed. Duncan's softer than I am in that respect but I've never owned one personally. We had them growing up but they were either Mum or Dad's, usually Mum's because she spent more time with them, so they never really attached themselves to me that closely.

When Duncan and I are… let's say, having 'quality time', the bedroom door is most firmly closed with Buddy on his bed, normally at the end of ours, on the landing. He whines to start with but gets the hint. Occasionally we'll hear squeaking but even that dies down after a while, usually because he's forgotten he has any toys that do still squeak so de-squeaks them. Bless him.

Duncan must have caved during the night and opened the bedroom door because we had quality time last night. I'm still grinning. Absence most definitely made the heart grow fonder for both of us.

Duncan has to go into work today so I'm meeting Izzy for lunch. It seems like ages since we saw each other but it's only been a week. We'll probably meet in town and hit the charity shops. We both love them and a lot can change in a week, two weeks actually for some of them.

"Morning." A sleepy Duncan realises I'm awake.

"Good morning." I, on the other hand, am more wide awake than… what's wide? The Forth Bridge? It takes forever to paint so it must be big.

I hear Buddy thump down onto the floor and sigh as Duncan nuzzles into my neck. I don't think I can love him any more than I do right at this moment. He groans. "I have to go to work."

"Uh huh." I want to tell him he really doesn't have to but that's one thing I love about him: his work ethic. He puts the animals, and their owners, above almost everything else. I am number one in his life, he's told me often, but this is more than a job to him, more than his business, it truly is a vocation. I love my job but it's not the same. If it all ended tomorrow, and I sometimes wonder if it will, especially with technology moving on, I'd find something else I enjoyed.

I can be insecure. Some previous relationships have set me up to be that way, not that I haven't always been to some extent, but that's what makeup does. It sounds silly; put on a bit of colour, whether it's makeup or clothes, and you immediately feel better. Hazel has the right idea and I need to be braver. Bolder. And it starts today.

Duncan and I get up at the same time. I put on a dressing gown and head to the kitchen to get the kettle on and toast done. I don't know why but as soon as the clocks go forward in March, we have cereal for breakfast during the week and toast or leftovers at the weekends. Not that we don't have toast or leftovers at the weekends all year but thinking the days are going to be warmer when they're longer just meant us having cereal. I can't even remember whose idea it was, it sort of happened.

I smile as Duncan plods through in his dressing gown, a darker blue version of mine… and about a foot longer. I think mine's a fat child's version as it's the perfect length, although for me that's not far off my ankles whereas his is by his knees but hey, I'm a child in almost every other respect.

We have toast and the last of my mum's St Leonard's marmalade. It's supposed to be St Clements' as it's orange and lemon but St Leonards-on-Sea, East Sussex, is one of her favourite places on the south coast. I never know why but she can spend hours walking around Hastings Castle, a former eleventh-century Norman fortress, which would take most people a fraction of the time because there's so little left. I think she likes the romance of the Battle of Hastings, not that Harold losing an eye is romantic but it's one of the few dates she can recall when asked. 1066 and all that.

Duncan and I have a long romantic snog, much to Buddy's annoyance as he's raring to go. Duncan takes him to work every weekday so the dog's not to know today's any different. It does mean I don't have to rush back from meeting up with Izzy and it's a nice day so I'm going to walk into town. That way, I don't have to get back to the car or pay a silly price for leaving it more than the free two hours. Oh, it's Saturday. It's two pounds all day. I'll still walk. I've not done a huge amount of that this week; the Hemel office to town centre and back isn't exactly pushing things.

Having been distracted last night, I've just put my phone on charge, when the screen lights up with Izzy's picture and name. I put the phone to my ear, tricky as the charge cable's not very long but the battery's almost dead so I have no choice. "Hi," I say, half leaning on the kitchen work surface.

"Hi. You okay?"

"Oh yes, just charging."

"Charging? Around or someone?"

"My phone."

"Ah. You still up for meeting in a while?"

"Sure thing, crocodile." It's not come out how I meant it but she gets the idea.

"Starbucks at noon?"

"Ooh good plan, Batwoman."

Izzy laughs. "We've got so much to catch up on."

"We do."

"I've got four Starbucks cards and I don't know if there's anything on them but if there is it's my treat."

To be fair, it *is* Izzy's turn – I paid for Costa last Saturday, we alternate venues – but I know she'd pay regardless of whether there was any credit on the cards. She keeps forgetting them when we go so buys a new one and puts a tenner on each one then spends almost that with our drinks and snacks. We only ever have one round as we rarely have much spare time to stay very long. It's the lure of the charity shops.

I look over to a bowl below the double three-pin and USB power socket. Duncan loves his technology. The bowl is where we dump our coins when we get too much and there's plenty so I get my purse and tip most of the coins into it. I tuck the purse back into my bag and hang it above the radiator in the hall. That went off ages ago so no chance of my bag getting too hot, not that we need the heating on at all as it's been so mild recently but when the sun goes in it gets a bit chilly so an hour or two last thing and first thing and we're good to go.

Speaking of which, it's gone ten so I need to get a move on. I have a lovely warm shower – my showers have to be warm regardless of the time of year; it's good for the skin. Not too hot, not too cold. Just right. Like Goldilocks's porridge. Ooh... I really fancy some now. Well, not right now as I'm not that hungry but I wonder if it's something Starbucks does. Probably only in the winter and by the time I meet Izzy and we order, I'll likely fancy something else anyway.

Standing in front of the wardrobe's full-length mirror, I turn from side to side. I'm not skinny but am pretty happy with what I've been given, and work relatively hard for. I could have a better diet so pot kettle black given my job but when I have a splurge, I cut back to make up for it. It's not easy being in a relationship because who wants to date someone who's constantly on a diet. Life shouldn't be like that anyway. Yes, don't go mad but equally don't calorie count everything that goes into your mouth.

I blush, thinking about last night. I'm glad I'm not drinking something as I can't help laughing. Izzy would be so proud.

Chapter 50 – Ravishing And Ravenous

Izzy's standing outside the Market Square Starbucks when I get there. It's one on the dot and it's not like her to be early.

"Hey, Izzy. Sorry, have you been waiting long?"

"Literally just got here." So on time too. Yay.

"Hungry?"

"Ravishing." She always says that instead of ravenous but it makes me giggle every time. "We've so much to catch up on."

"We do."

Instead of standing outside, starting what we know is going to be a long conversation, we go in. It's been a couple of weeks, no three, four? – I didn't see her the Saturday before last, but things can change so we look at the board. She usually goes for chai tea latté and something gooey, and I have a skinny Caffè Misto, more milk, steamed, than a regular coffee but all the better for it, and a cookie of some description. It's the bits of chocolate I love. I often have hazelnut in my coffee but today I fancy it plain. Hopefully not losing my sweet tooth.

Sometimes I feel a fraud, doing what I do but eating and drinking rubbish. I have no dietary qualifications but I did do media at school and always knew I wanted to be a writer of some kind. I was also plump back then, more than the teachers' lessons learned.

"So..." Izzy says as we take our goodies to a spare table near the back of the restaurant. We're usually not bothered where we sit but we've got loads to catch up on so it's easier if we're away from everyone. That suits me fine.

Bold Donna. Bold Donna. Oh well, too late. Next time for sure.

I am being bolder with my colours and Izzy comments on it. "Have I seen that top before?"

I shake my head. "I got it a few years ago and it still fits."

"I can see that, Miss Curves." She wolf whistles and I look around to see if anyone heard. If they did, they're being polite. No, this is the twenty-first century. No one pays attention anymore.

"So..." Izzy repeats. "Tell me what's been happening down in Hemel."

So I tell her everything, warts and all, James and all, and she wolf whistles again.

"But nothing happened."

Izzy looks shocked as if the thought hadn't crossed her mind. Knowing how much I love Duncan, she knows I'd never cheat on him. I can window shop, sure, we all can, but never cheat.

"And how are things going with William?" I ask. "Moved in yet?"

"Give me a chance. He's only just asked."

"A couple of weeks ago. Three. The evening before we were here last if I recall. Plenty of time."

"I've moved a few bits over but there's no hurry. It's not like I'm giving up my place."

"And the lodgers?"

"They're fab. And they're getting on really well together. Shame Tom's married. I think Amanda thinks so too, although St Andrew's is bound to have hot male nurses or doctors."

"Or patients."

Izzy gives me that look. "Anyway."

"Yes, anyway. So we're caught up, are we?" I suggest, itching to go and buy some bargains. I realised how dowdy my wardrobe, or the clothes I have at Duncan's anyway, has become when looking for this. And I hadn't had this for years. I popped into a charity shop on the outskirts of town, one I knew we wouldn't be going in so wouldn't be recognised, and found the top I'm wearing. I purposely wore something I wanted to get rid of so left that for them to sell. It was fresh on other than me walking into town and we all know I don't walk quickly enough to get sweaty.

Other than teeny white lies – you know, 'Oh yes, that absolutely suits you', that kind of thing, I don't think I've ever lied to Izzy before and I feel bad, but not that bad. Oh, Donna, you tyke! I can't help smiling at feeling a little more confident. Too much coffee? No, less than normal. Something in the Hemel Hempstead air, possibly. Whatever it is, I feel good. Life is good.

We get some fabulous things, mostly clothes, from the charity shops along Gold Street (British Red Cross and Salvation Army), St Giles Street (Age Concern and Save the Children), even before we've gone back to the Market Square (RSPCA and two Cancer Researches).

Izzy and I say our farewells outside the Cancer Research at the top of The Drapery. I really fancy a McDonalds strawberry milkshake, just a small one, but it's the bottom of The Drapery and I'm losing the will to live. I think I'm going to be naughty anyway and get a bus as the plastic bags are digging into my palms. I usually bring cotton ones, big ones, but in my hurry to leave Duncan's I forgot to get them from the boot of my car. I always keep them in the lower half of the split boot just in case but now when I need them… brain like a sieve, that's me.

She's disappeared, cutting down the top of College Street, when it dawns on me that Duncan suggested going out as a foursome this evening. I don't know why I didn't remember. Izzy and I talked about everything else. Subconsciously I think I want Duncan all to myself. Maybe I thought he'd be tired. Or I'd be tired. Maybe… I don't know. I'm losing it. I have had a lot on my mind recently.

I can't ring her, she'll have her hands full so it'll go through to answerphone. Maybe that'll be better. It'll give her time to ask William. Where did she say he was right now? Work? No. Golf? Does he even play golf? I can't remember. I shake my head in an attempt to latch the right information to the right memory cells but all it does is give me a headache. Oh great. Now I'll definitely have to get a bus. I decide to do that so I'm not worn out by the time I get home then ring Izzy when I get there.

I still feel frazzled when I arrive at Duncan's. He's not here yet which means no Buddy either so a quiet haven until their return. Knowing they won't be long, I sit on the sofa and get Alexa to play some 'nice classical music'; *Classical for a Relaxing Bath*, she tells me. What I would give for one of those.

It's only when I feel a tongue licking me that I realise they're home. I'd like it to have been Duncan's tongue of course but sadly Buddy was quicker to greet me. I've fallen asleep on the sofa and my neck aches. I sit up and it clicks. Ow.

Duncan looks at the bags then at me and smiles. "Exhausting shopping trip?"

I laugh. "Someone kept me up late last night."

We laugh at the memory. Yep, no relationship issues for sure. Then I think of James. *Get out!*

"Huh?" Duncan's in the doorway, having turned to go into the kitchen, probably to make a drink.

Did I say that aloud? "About going out. I forgot to ask Izzy and William to join us."

"Let me guess: you forgot when you met then planned to when you got home but fell asleep." He knows me so well.

"I'll ring her now." Not that I know what time it is. It's still daylight but early May and it doesn't get dark until nine. I look at my watch. Just gone five. That's okay. It's early enough for her not to have made any plans. If she has, I'm sure she won't mind us gatecrashing unless it's a loved-up meal for two at home or something equally mushy but William doesn't really do mush… not that I know anyway.

"Something to drink?" Duncan asks, pointing towards the kitchen.

"Please. Anything, I don't mind."

He nods and disappears.

I phone Izzy and she answers so quickly it's like she's been expecting my call.

"Hey, Donna."

"Hi. Erm..."

"You okay?"

"Sorry, yes, just woken but... I... no, it's okay. I'm okay, yes, thanks." I'm not making any sense.

"Okay..."

"Are you and William busy tonight? It's short notice, I know, and feel free to say no, but Duncan and I were wondering if you'd like to join us."

"There? At his?"

"Not thought that far yet."

Izzy laughs. "I'm sure we would. William's out at the moment but I can check when he returns."

I don't pry so just say, "Fabulous. Whatever you fancy doing will be fine by us. Maybe a movie and food, or more likely food then a movie otherwise it would be really late by the time we eat. Or maybe we'll just go out for a meal, or we could cook here, we've always got something in." I'm hoping... and freewheeling.

"I don't mind. I'll text William actually rather than wait until he gets back. I'm not totally sure where he is but he knows we'll be doing something so..."

"Fab," I repeat.

Though Izzy and I spent the whole afternoon together, it still felt like we hadn't properly caught up. We had an overview of our week apart but there's always more detail to come out when you really think about it. What we can say in front of our respective halves will be different to what we'd say if it were just the two of us... because we always talk about them, but there'll be plenty to share.

Duncan comes through with a couple of halves of cider, I'm guessing; they're in Rekorderlig glasses. Buddy follows behind with what looks like a frozen filled cow hoof in his mouth, his favourite. Duncan plonks the glasses onto the coffee table in front of me. I take one and he holds the other out in front of me as if to toast. That's exactly what we do.

"To..." I can't think of to what. To us? To dinner as a foursome? To health, wealth and happiness.

"To being in love."

My mouth instinctively drops open. Duncan is a romantic but I hadn't expected that. I know he means it though.

He puts his glass down, takes mine, adds it to his then leans forward, closes my mouth and kisses it. He turns my wrist and the digital display on my watch comes on. "Yep, plenty of time."

"Time?"

He looks up to the ceiling. "A repeat of last night."

I blush. "And this morning."

He smiles, kisses me again, and leads me upstairs.

Chapter 51 – Dinner At The Very Least

Izzy's left a message when we resurface. I'm semi dressed when I return to the lounge and am grateful that we have the blinds shut so Buddy doesn't go nuts at anything walking past. While Duncan had given him the cow hoof, the dog's distributed bits all around the floor, like he'd been chasing it rather than doing the sensible thing and sitting or lying in one place and digging out the filling. He's done that all right but hasn't gone after it, licking or eating it all up.

"I thought you were supposed to be a canine hoover," I say to him and instead of looking sorry, he grins and wags his tail. "At least you won't get any fatter." Although he won't have understood a word, he doesn't look impressed. About as much as I am with what he's done.

Duncan's still upstairs so hasn't seen the mild carnage yet. We both know that dogs aren't the tidiest of creatures but Buddy's excelled himself this time and Duncan likes a neat house, Buddy allowing.

"Clean all this up," I instruct the dog, waggling my finger around to indicate what I mean. Buddy tilts his head from one side to another. "Hoover," I say as if that's going to help. I point from him to the mess and back to him again but it only garners another head tilting. "I give up." Buddy goes to his bed, most of which has the filling spread around it, and curls up. "Great. Thanks for your help." He wags his tail and closes his eyes.

From the bottom of the stairs, I call up, "Izzy's texted!"

I get a distant, "Oh good."

"She and William had no plans and said yes to dinner. Said the cinema would be too much of a rush but food for sure."

I get a distant, "Great."

"Sixfields – so there's plenty of choice?"

I get a slightly less distant, "Sure," which means he's on his way out of the bedroom, except he takes a few seconds to appear. He's brushing his teeth.

"Oh sorry."

He stops and swallows. "No, it's okay. Nearly done."

I don't like to tell him that you shouldn't swallow toothpaste but I can't think of anyone who died from it so I think he'll live, until dinner at the very least.

We meet Izzy and William outside Frankie & Benny's and like earlier, we arrive at almost the same time, them a few seconds before us. More William's influence I think than Izzy's.

"Nice dress, Donna," William says and I look down at myself. It's one I bought earlier from the charity shop. It's a Kaffe burnt orange floral wrap, RRP £79.99 but the previous owner had bought it from TK Maxx at a mere £24.99. A fiver to me. An absolute bargain, a 'steal' as Jason Flemyng so eloquently put it in *Lock Stock and Two Smoking Barrels*, one of my top… twenty at least films.

We're quickly shown to our table. William, it turns out, had booked ahead of us turning up and it was just as well as the place is really busy, to be expected on a bright, quite warm, Saturday night. Izzy and I sit next to each other, facing into the restaurant so we can people watch. Clothes watch. Anything watch. Izzy's writing a novel, or planning it at least, but won't tell me what about until it's finished and she promises to send it to me. We've had this seating arrangement for a while so she can see if anything, or rather anyone, grabs her as 'fiction fodder'.

Anja, our waitress, takes our drinks order and brings them to us a few minutes later, putting them in exactly the right places. The guys are on beer, Izzy and I on soft drinks as we're driving back, the guys having driven us here. We alternate; the other times we drive in, the guys drive back. It's only fair.

Anja pulls out a notepad and writes down our order: a house special burger for Duncan, a Nashville hot chicken for William, a BBQ cheese chicken wrap for Izzy, New York BBQ chicken grill for me – I really can't get enough of chicken, and sides of calamari and dough balls to share. As her name would suggest, Anja is not a native Englander. My first thought as she took our drinks order was eastern Europe but as she reads back our food, she sounds more Scandinavian.

With her gone, Izzy and I excuse ourselves to go to the ladies. The guys are already deep in conversation about a new car William's thinking of getting. Beyond its colour and interior design, a car is a car to me but boys will be boys.

Inside my cubicle, I do a quick Google search on my phone for 'Anja' and apart from several links to an Australian-Danish singer-songwriter, one for urbandictionary.com peaks my curiosity.

'Anja is the most beautiful and cutest person you'll ever meet,' I read to myself. 'Anja loves noodles and likes to eat sweets, but at the same time she wants to get rid of eating both.' Interesting. 'She likes hanging around guys but she secretly hates all her female friends, even the ones she calls "best friends".' That's not good. I'd never do that to Izzy. 'Anja loves long relationships and enjoys the attention from her boyfriend. She is the most loyal person if you prove that you are worth being trusted. Don't hurt her emotions because that'll be the biggest mistake you'll ever make.' Go, girl. 'She doesn't let anyone in her life that easily. Most of her love goes to animals, especially dogs. She already owns at least one, so if you love her, you must love her dog too and treat him like your best friend because she / he is her best friend. You can get her mad really quick, but be careful, if you go too far with jokes you can end up in bruises.' I smile. 'Pretty much, Anja is everything you need in your life to be happy, so hurry up before there is no single (not in relationship) Anja left on this world. Look at her, she is so adorable and cute. Of course, her name is Anja, what did you expect?'

Wow. The image of a Mr Men 'Little Miss Perfect' comes into my brain, not that I know whether there is actually one so I google that too. The results aren't very forthcoming but without delving further, it looks like there is only a male version. Mmm.

"Are you okay in there?" Izzy.

"Yes, fine, thank you," I say, stand, and flush.

We wash our hands in silence, not because we've nothing to say, we always have, but more that we don't feel we need to; we're enjoying each other's company.

We walk behind Anja as she heads in the direction of our table. She's carrying a huge tray in one hand and a folded tray support in the other. Superwoman, she certainly is, but all the other waitresses and waiters do exactly the same. I bet they're not called Anja though. *Of course the waiters aren't called Anja*. I shake my head. Our Anja stops at a table short of ours. I would have been surprised if our food had been ready in the time it took Izzy and me to visit the ladies, even with the extended Google searches.

It's not long though, the length of the recap of my week, mostly for William's benefit, before Anja reappears, in Superwoman mode, with our food. She snaps open the tray support and plonks down the tray. It's a replica of how our table will look in a few seconds. My food in the nearest corner, Izzy's to its left, William's to its right and Duncan's in the opposite corner. Anja distributes the plates perfectly with the sides in the middle, and extra forks should we need them. She thinks of everything, but it's her job and I'm sure she's well practised.

"Can I get you anything else?" We look around the table and shake our heads. All the sauces we could want have either come with our dishes or were there already. None of us are having pasta or pizza so we don't need the usual addition of parmesan, although I love it so much I'd have it on anything. She smiles and is about to leave when I ask her a question.

"How do you remember which goes where?" I point at all the plates.

Anja turns the notepad round to me, and I see a column with little numbers one to four on the left-hand side. "I always start with the right, at the back... with you on this occasion." She's still looking at me so means me. "And I work clockwise."

Smart as well as beautiful, cute, loyal, and whatever else the Urban Dictionary claimed her to be. Tall. It didn't say tall but she's really tall. Not William tall but around six foot I'd say. I'm tempted to ask one of the others to stand next to her as Izzy and Duncan are five-ten and William six-four, but that would be silly. And I'm braver bolder Donna not even more silly me.

"Thank you," I say and sit back in my seat.

Izzy's been talking to William but I've not heard a word. They're both laughing though, as is Duncan, so it must have been funny and I'm sorry I've missed it.

It's lovely to see them both so happy. Izzy and William. He's come out of his shell so much since they got together, and I know they'll work. Unlike me, Izzy will never consider straying. I know I won't with James but if the thought was there, what does it say about my relationship with Duncan?

I don't know why I'm feeling so insecure; everything's fine. I just don't feel like me at the moment. I think it's being apart. I don't like it. *Only four more weeks*. Urgh! That sounds like forever. But it'll fly. This first one has. *PMA, Donna, PMA.*

So I put on a broad smile and make myself enjoy the rest of the evening. It's not that difficult as we work so well as a foursome. William hadn't met Duncan until after he and I had started dating but they clicked, like we did.

The rest of the evening flows. We stay for coffees, a Bailey's latté in Izzy's case, of course. Anything Bailey's. I'm more of an almond girl so go for a café Amaretto whereas the guys have black Americanos. I'd spotted something recently on Facebook that said if you drink your coffee black, you're more likely to be a psychopath. Other than Izzy, we all like black coffee but I can't imagine any of us being psychopaths. Threaten us though and I'm sure we could turn, even quiet diminutive me.

We finally spill out of the restaurant, one of the last parties to leave. It's been such fun that I don't want the evening to end, but end it must. We do a round of couple hugs – we're not really a group huggy party – and promise to catch up again next weekend. That only goes to remind me that I'll be the absent one for five days and I get sad but everyone else looks so happy that I keep on my smile.

I drive Duncan back to his and Buddy's ecstatic to see us, Duncan first of course but Buddy then leaps all over me as I fill up and switch on the kettle to make Duncan and me a final coffee to take up to bed. Duncan pops Buddy round the block while I do that and the dog's equally energetic when he rushes back in and paws at my dress. I don't want to discourage him but I have only just bought it so I turn, crouch, and we hug. We've not bonded as well as Elliott and me but we've known each other longer.

Buddy is a very sweet dog. I need to spend more time with him, one on one, buy him toys, take him for more walks, and we'll be fine. He's always been more loyal to Duncan, but a dog can have two masters… can't he?

Chapter 52 – Playing House

Sunday 6th May

Sundays vary in this household. Sometimes we're at my flat, but mostly we're at Duncan's house. There are always chores to do but more so this Sunday because we let them slip last weekend and I'd not been around to help during the week. There's been a mix of rain and sun so the lawn needs mowing, one of Duncan's favourite things so I leave him to it while I de-weed the borders.

We don't say a lot because of the noise of the mower but it's lovely being together. Buddy knows not to get in the way of the machine so he stays over the other side of the garden trying, and failing, to catch butterflies fluttering around one of the huge buddleia plants. He's the same with squirrels although that's much more fun and more of a chase but he's never quick enough with either, which is just as well.

When the front and back gardens are done, I get lunch. It's a fine day but not too hot, always useful when working outdoors. We eat light as neither of us is particularly hungry after last night's dinner out and with no leftovers, a couple of rounds of toast each this morning do nicely. There's tuna, couscous, and most of a washed bag of Sainsbury's mixed salad leaves between us, with some baby tomatoes and sweetcorn thrown in.

After a quick bit of television – the rest of an unfinished episode of *Suits*, we head upstairs for a shower. There's a wet room in the guest room's en-suite and standing up, naked, we're conscious of our size difference; seven and a half inches, but it's never bothered either of us, although we both get neckache we never complain about. Izzy, at Duncan's height, is still six inches shorter than William so not too different from Duncan and me, but they seem better matched, not sure why; I guess they're just tall to me.

There's nothing quite like skin on skin, especially when it's wet and soapy, and without getting all Fifty Shades, I'll just say that we end up in our bedroom. With the door closed. Buddy outside. Whimpering. While I'm inside. Whimpering.

We finally emerge two hours later, mostly so I can take Buddy for a walk while Duncan prepares dinner. Having had a cold lunch, we have lasagne, accompanied by the rest of the salad leaves. Remembering I'm on this project, Duncan gives me a portion that sits comfortably within my 500-calorie limit. He's such a darling. We talk about Izzy and William, and I shudder slightly at the thought of how perfect my life is.

Duncan frowns and looks at the fireplace below the television. "You cold? Would you like me to put that on?"

I shake my head. "But thank you. No, just happy."

"Ah, okay. Good. Great." He smiles and my heart swells.

"Mind if I carry on with my book?" he asks when we've finished eating, tidied away, and we're sitting side by side on the sofa.

"Ooh, good idea. I've been meaning to get back to Robert."

"Robert?"

I pop upstairs and return with a rather battered copy of Robert Galbraith's *The Cuckoo's Calling*.

"Oh, isn't that JK Rowling in a suit?"

I laugh. "I have the series, charity shops of course, but only just started this one." I point to a bookmark about a dozen pages in. I open it and it's page thirteen. Unlucky for some.

Duncan smiles and shows me his book. I'd forgotten what he'd been on last weekend and am reminded that it's Richard Branson's autobiography, *Losing my Virginity*. It always makes me smile and see from Duncan's bookmark, a bright orange post-it note, that he looks no further forward.

As if reading my mind, he says, "I did pick it up a couple of nights this week and got on to the next chapter but both times was woken up by the book hitting my nose." The same thing happens with me. We're usually so tired that we don't get very far. It's just as well we prefer paperbacks to Kindles or iPads as they're more solid, although a bit of a brick, Duncan's book would hurt more than mine.

Having had a fair amount of adult fun over the weekend, we settle for some simple skin on skin, and soon fall asleep, despite the sound of a police helicopter flying overhead.

Chapter 53 – Imagine All Sorts

Bank Holiday Monday 7th May

Although it's a bank holiday Monday, Duncan has to pop into work. It's his practice so it's to be expected and thankfully he's not there long. It gives me time to pop back to my flat, swap a few things over, go through any post (bills, a bank statement and takeaway leaflets). Buddy's gone with Duncan so I don't even have him as company. My flat feels eerie and I'm hoping I don't have to spend more time in it in future than I am now.

Duncan and I should have the 'what next' conversation, meaning me moving in with him, especially as he owns his house, but I've put it off for as long as possible in case the answer's not something I'd like.

I figure I'm going to be here for an hour so do a load of washing. Even though Duncan's happy for me to do it at his (for him to do it, more accurately) – and I do love the feeling of him being all domesticated there, I pick things that will stay here so they can hang on the airer before I leave.

After closing the washing machine door, I shiver as I stand. I'm sure I heard a scratching sound but then remember next door's teenage son is home and his bedroom's behind this end of my kitchen so it must be him.

I wonder what he's doing and imagine all sorts including him lying on his bed, looking at a particularly racy magazine and I shiver again. I'm thinking of teenage boys now? Having spent more time than for a while with Duncan, I guess I have sex on the brain. No, not sex, making love. And I love when I do so with Duncan. I'll spare you the details but he's very… generous.

I set the washing going and flush as I picture a scene from a movie where a woman sits on the counter above a moving washing machine, let's just say to 'enjoy' the vibrations. I can't remember the movie and it's not something I've ever done. I'm tempted but then I have the real thing later, may well have as I'm off in the morning, back to Hemel until Duncan joins me at my mum's Saturday morning. Can't wait… then I realise how silly that sounds as I'll be seeing him in… I look at the washing machine's countdown timer… fifty-seven minutes and hanging / driving time. The clothes hanging, not me. My brain's like the washer, going round in circles, although I'm not sure mine ever returns to the same place.

The scratching sound's back so I head to my bedroom to sort out some clothes. Despite only being a health and beauty columnist, some clothes do come my way, usually from Karen. Izzy and I often get second (after Karen) dibs before other girls in the office are given the choice and any that aren't snapped up (not many) are given to charity.

With clothes packed (dry) and hung (damp), the scratching noise ignored – I *really* don't want to know what Mason's doing behind our shared wall, I'm ready for the off. I won't be home, here, for at least a fortnight so I make sure everything's switched off that should be, and shut and double lock the front, pausing to stroke the front door as I remove my key. I don't know why, some affinity to somewhere I've cherished because it's kept me safe when I've been having a tough time yet I know, hope, I'll be deserting it at some point in the future.

Buddy's unusually enthusiastic when I get back and open Duncan's front door. He, the dog, usually comes to greet me but then realises it's only me (as if it's likely to be Duncan when he's already there) plods back to wherever he was sitting, lying or whatevering. Even if I bring a treat or toy, it's a short-lived enthusiasm but today he's especially cheery even though I have nothing for him.

"He's just back in from the garden," Duncan explains, "and chased a squirrel," he concludes as he pulls me into a clinch for a long lingering kiss then tips me back as he leans in towards me.

I squeal and 'kiss him right back', as Julia Roberts said in… in… *Pretty Woman*. Yes, when she's describing Edward, a.k.a. Richard Gere to her friend, the diminutive Spaniard. No, that wasn't it. It was Julia and Richard on the fire escape for their weird kiss. It was all kind of… lippy. I shiver and that reminds me of the scratching sound. "You'll never guess what I heard Mason, my next-door neighbour's son, doing…" I tell Duncan 'all' as I follow him into his kitchen. It's a little late for lunch yet he's made a full Sunday roast. He's even made it being careful of calories in case I want to include it as one of my thirty-one 'dishes'. He's amazing. He's so capable and I sometimes wonder what I bring to the relationship. Of course I say nothing.

We take Buddy to Harlestone Firs to walk off our lunch. For a nice day, especially a bank holiday one, and given there's a garden centre opposite, it's surprisingly quiet. We only meet two other couples, with their dogs, Giles a cockerpoo very similar to Elliott, although darker in colour and far less springy – not difficult, and Dante a springy springer spaniel whose on an expandable lead 'because he can't be trusted'.

Although he's suitably sociable, Buddy's more interested in squirrels so runs off as soon as pleasantries (sniffing bums and doing their circular dances) are completed. He finally finds one and although he has no chance of getting anywhere near it, he's in his element, barking at the tree it shot up.

"Of course it's going to come down for you," Duncan says and squeezes my hand.

I smile, squeeze his hand back and nuzzle into his shoulder. Being seven and a half inches shorter than him, that's more or less where I come up, down, to anyway. He's often said how he loves me being 'pocket sized' and he doesn't mean it in any derogatory way. I always thought, or rather Izzy told me from experience, that most tall men liked tall women but Duncan's ex, Daff – her real name was Daffodil rather than Daphne. Daffodil! As if I wasn't jealous enough of her already. Duncan's ex was six foot tall and half an inch so he had to stoop, he said. He still has to when kissing me, especially when he does his gallant sweeping swooning kisses. I like that: sweeping swooning. I'd love to get that into one of my articles but unless it's for a particularly sexy dessert, I can't see that happening. Just like keeping Buddy clean on this walk.

It's not been raining for a few days but if there's a muddy ditch to be found, Buddy finds it and true to form, his white bits are now darker brown than his brown bits. He's having such a fun time though so I can't complain and, of course, Duncan's not going to tell him off. Buddy's like the child Duncan doesn't…

"You know what," I say to change the topic we weren't on, although I'm not sure what topic I'm changing it to.

He stops and turns to look at me, still keeping hold of one of my hands. "Ooh, what?" He's got such a childlike expression that I sometimes wonder whether he's the child he doesn't…

"We should come here more often," I blurt.

"We should," he says, and leans forward to kiss me, before we continue walking.

"Oh by the way," he says, "the helicopter last night…"

I'd forgotten but glad he reminded me.

"Turns out to be a boar loose on Bradlaugh Fields."

I stop and turn to face him, still holding his hand of course. "A boar? As in a pig-type boar?"

He laughs. "One of the bigger houses along Kettering Road has one in its garden."

"As you do."

"Yes, Donna, my queen," he raises my hand, kisses it and looks at me with a devilish smile, "as you do."

"And…?"

He shrugs. "It's fine. Tranquiliser dart, shipped it back to its owner who penned it again, left it to wake up."

"Oh…" I say and we walk on.

"I think I should have been something to do with wood," Duncan says as we approach the timber yard at the top end of the road that splits the mass of trees.

"Pinocchio?" I ask and burst out laughing. I look at him and realise he's serious. "Really?" I look up at him.

"I've always fancied being a… oh, what do they call them. Arbor…"

"Arborist. Tree surgeon?"

He nods.

It's something he's never mentioned before and we've talked a *lot.* I recall a conversation where he said he loved swimming and used to dive off a one-metre board but anything above that scared him. He's okay in a plane, much more so than me, but because he's inside and someone else is doing the flying. "But you don't like heights," I remind him.

"That's true," he says casually and walks on, pulling me slightly as he still has hold of my hand. And the topic's forgotten as quickly as it was raised.

He'll never cease to amaze me and the thought again pops into my head of us spending the rest of our lives together.

As I look at the trees either side as we walk back towards the main road, I think how lovely a place this would be, albeit away from the concrete straight, for me to propose, to get down on one knee so I'm even tinier than him, and I want to blurt it out but of course I don't. And he doesn't. Of course.

Our evening meal is simply a mix of crackers, cheese and fruit: grapes and strawberries. Neither of us wants to eat too much as we're still full from lunch and given that this is our last night together until Saturday, we both know some 'fooling around' is on the cards.

After our longer-than-usual lunchtime walk, Buddy's asleep in his bed, one leg twitching as he probably recalls chasing the squirrel.

"He's such a baby," Duncan says innocently as he turns the page on his Sunday Times once we've finished our meal, cleared up and set the dishwasher going. I have the Times' supplement, ingeniously called 'The Sunday Times Magazine', and am looking at all the tall skinny girls in their weird outfits.

Karen, my fashion colleague, and I have had countless conversations about 'haute couture' and while she's not quite… oh, what was the Vogue lady called? Something de Winter. No that was Daphne du Maurier character Rebecca. Anna Wintour. That's her. Scary. I shiver again, for no apparent reason, although scary women do intimidate me.

"You cold?" Duncan asks and I shake my head.

He blows me a kiss and I blush. "Are you concentrating on that?" he asks and points at my magazine. I shake my head. He raises an eyebrow and looks at the ceiling then back at me.

I look at the ceiling but keep my gaze there. "You've got cobwebs."

"I do?" he asks, looking where I'm looking.

I playfully throw the magazine at him but it's only when it leaves my hands do I realise how heavy it is and it whacks Duncan on the side of his face. He was still looking up so wasn't expecting it and understandably shrieks. And not a Donna shriek but a Duncan shriek which is far louder.

I leap out of my seat and rush towards him. "Oh my god, I'm so sorry!" I burst into tears as I see that one of the pages has also sliced a thin cut in his cheek and I see that actually paper cuts can do some damage so I owe Gavin an apology for even thinking I'd do that too him.

Buddy, by this time, has joined in the fray and is barking and leaping at me, clearly thinking I'm doing some harm to his master, which is totally true.

I slump to the floor and sob, almost wailing like the proverbial banshee. This month has become too much already and although the magazine was an innocent throw, it's sparked something much deeper.

As I tremble on the floor, Duncan's enveloping me and now Buddy's leaping all over him as if to join in with a group hug.

"It's okay, it's okay," Duncan soothes while trying to push Buddy away, gently but masterfully. And boy, is Duncan masterful.

The next thing I know, Duncan's picked me up and is carrying, yes, carrying me upstairs and into his, our, bedroom. We can hear Buddy following us so Duncan kicks the door behind us and it's only when we hear the dog scratching at the door a couple of hours later that we resurface; Duncan to take him for a walk and me to brush my teeth before Duncan returns, does the same, and we pick up where we left off.

Chapter 54 – Nicer To Have A Routine

Tuesday 8th May

With a mother who's rarely at home, and a boyfriend I'd rather spend the night with – sorry, Mother – I'd already decided to head down to Hemel Hempstead after rush hour on the Tuesday morning. I don't feel overly cheerful when I arrive at the office. Thankfully, Phil appears to be and gives me a very warm welcome.

"Sorry I didn't get to say 'goodbye' on Friday. Was remiss of me, Donna." He says 'remiss of me' in a very British way and I think about asking him how long he's lived here except he continues. "But I wanted to make sure I said 'hi' this morning." The American twang's back. "I've been looking out for ya. Billy did say you may not be in every day but here you are."

"I am indeed. It's very kind of him to say I could be flexible but I think it's nicer to have a routine."

Phil doesn't reply, just nods.

"I'd better get on," I say and point upstairs.

"Sure thing. You have a good week and we'll chat at some stage, for sure."

"Oh, absolutely."

"Let me know if I can help with anything. There's not a lot that passes me by."

Apart from me on Friday afternoon. I smile at the irony and mouth a 'thank you'.

I do indeed settle back in and the day flies. James is still away, despite Leah saying he'd be back after the bank holiday but then 'after' doesn't have to mean the next day. I don't like to ask but I will if he's not returned by the time she accompanies me to lunch tomorrow. I'm looking forward to it as we've said very little after our lunch last week but then she's always so busy, and I'm surprisingly so despite having this new(ish) project and my old job, oh, and dealing with anything that comes in for Veronica, not that I'm qualified to do that… literally. Knowing Veronica she probably does have qualifications.

I look around and above her desk. There's nothing to indicate any but despite her photo with Beyoncé, I've got the impression that Veronica's actually quite private. Other than the celeb pic and the one of her and her children, there's nothing else personal. I go on the company's website and while there is a biography of her, it's very short and simple, surprisingly close to mine, but then we do the same job…

It makes me think of James again and I admit that it does make my life easier without him around. Part of me feels guilty, as if I gave him the wrong impression, but that's so easily done, especially in texts, not that we've done anything other than speak to one another. We've not even swapped phone numbers, why would we? We're only colleagues. I have all of Izzy's numbers, of course, including her family's, but that's to be expected. I have William's mobile but only as an extension of her. I'd have no other reason to call him. He's my boss. I'd speak to him at work or pass on a message via Janine.

Speaking of which, I go to speak to Hemel's equivalent, Nathan, but he's on the phone so I veer away and go to the kitchen to get a drink. I have tea, for a change, and by the time I get back, Nathan's finished the call.

"Hi, sweets!" he says and jumps up from his chair, pushing it back with his foot and rushes round his desk.

I look behind me to check he means me and there's no one else in spitting, or throwing, distance. My first thought is to put my tea down but there's little clear space on his desk and what there is isn't big enough even for a mug, plus it's a really sexy glass and chrome desk, like from Ikea but probably way more expensive, and I wouldn't want to leave a ring mark. So I clasp the mug and hope that his eagerness doesn't mean a full-on hug. Normally, of course, I'd be only too delighted but we have only known each other just over a week and I'd rather not get scolded. No, scalded. Either. Both.

Thankfully, he spots the mug – surprising it took so long as it has a bright red KitKat emblem on both sides – and retreats but only enough to give me air kisses instead. I reciprocate and we laugh. I feel silly for being so serious and immediately apologise. "And I'm sorry we didn't get to have dinner last night."

He waves his hand and says "Pish" then I remember he would have been otherwise engaged anyway.

"Ooh… you had a date last night."

He blushes brighter than my mug and that's saying something. Pointing towards the kitchen, he says, "Shall we?"

I never need asking twice if I want to hear some gossip. Plus someone had brought in some cookies so the kitchen smells gorgeous. I had to restrain myself the first time. Okay, I didn't exactly restrain myself; I had one but ate it while I made a drink then redistributed the others around the plate so it didn't look as if there was one missing.

As I already have a drink, I take a seat at the table furthest from the cookies but that doesn't stop Nathan bringing two over on a simple white plate while holding his mug of something that looks like dishwater, probably weak tea – Izzy would approve, in his other hand. I don't really hope he's going to eat both cookies, I should resist, and he does indeed offer one to me. I don't like to offend so I take one, that's my excuse.

"So, spill," I say, meaning his date last night and not his mug of whateveritis. He catches the side of the table as he puts down his mug but thankfully the entire swamp-looking contents stays inside the porcelain. Or is it ceramic? While it's not something I've ever thought of covering in my column, I do wonder the difference and make a mental note to google it.

"Well…" Nathan starts and wiggles into his chair which isn't design for comfort but hey. "His name's Brad."

The image of Mr Pitt springs to mind but I doubt it's one and the same, although Nathan does say his name with a hint of an American accent.

"He's from Chicago."

Definitely not our Mr Pitt then as I know he was from Oklahoma. I'm not sure why I know that but it's something that stuck. Something to do with the annual Big Foot festival, voicemail, cow chips (another story), mistletoe, and the shopping cart, trolley, being invented there, I think. Sylvia something, owner of the Piggly Wiggly supermarket chain, conceived of a 'folding basket carrier' in nineteen thirty…

"Sorry, Nathan. Yes, I'm still with you. What's Brad doing over here?" It reminded me of asking Phil the same thing so thought I'd get that out of the way.

Nathan grins. "He's working for Kodak up on the hill." He waves the same hand in the general direction.

I know where he means. It's somewhere between us and the M1 motorway.

"'Cept he was given the old address so came to town…"

As a cowboy would. I'm not sure how 'west' Oklahoma is but fairly sure it's a cowboy movie, musical, both. Richard Rogers and Oscar Hammerstein. Yes, Curly McLain and Will Parker. My mum's a Howard Keel fan. Oh no, that was Annie Get Your–

"…and knew it couldn't be the apartments next door so came here. I was coming back from lunch and we met at the front downstairs. It was quite Wuthering Heights as we approached each other except we weren't running, jogging, whatever they were doing."

"Running, I think." It's one of my favourite books; it sooo romantic. I think of Duncan as my Heathcliff and me as his very short and very unbrunette Cathy. "How romantic. Where did you go?"

A smile lights his face, not that it isn't positively floodlit already. Like me in the early days with… no, that's not fair. I still am. We still are.

Nathan's about to answer when Billy walks past the kitchen and out into the open-plan office. "Ooh, gotta go. Tell us later," Nathan chirps, pops the final bit of cookie in his mouth and leaves.

My cookie's uneaten, and certainly untouched by me, and I debate whether to drop it back onto the original pile but know that Nathan will have to have picked it up so I leave it where it is. If someone wants to help themselves to a not-quite-second-hand cookie then they can, er, help themselves.

When I get back to my desk, I do indeed google (other search engines are available) 'what are mugs made of' and the second YouTube video offered catches my eye. 'What's the difference between porcelain and ceramic mugs?' is a one minute and twenty-six second documentary by a very helpful company 'Quality Logo Products' and their cheerful narrator. The artistry is a little rudimentary but I like it and play it again, at a low volume so as not to disturb my colleagues.

I could live on YouTube as I love finding out everything about everything but I have work to do. Frank's already said I can choose the venue for tonight, 'not that you couldn't anyway' he'd said but we both know he's the native and will have better insight. I don't fancy anything too… foreign but not sure what counts as English. A Nando's perhaps? More chicken. Never a bad thing. Before I'd ever been in one, I imagined it to be a posh KFC and don't suppose Phil or Brad would mind either, although I don't know what nationality Nando's is.

Back to Google and I'm way off. There was I thinking they were both American but Nando's, Wikipedia tells me is a 'South African restaurant chain that specialises in Portuguese-African food, such as peri-peri style chicken dishes. Founded in Johannesburg in 1987, Nando's operates over 1000 outlets in 35 countries.' Wow. Nando's it is.

Chapter 55 – Not Been There For Yonks

Before I know it, it's gone five thirty and Frank rings me. "Sorry, I'm being lazy," he says. I can't see his desk from where I sit but I assume he's there.

"No problem," I reply. "Shall I collect you?"

"Erm…"

"Oh."

"I'm really sorry but I'm going to have to cancel tonight."

"No problem. I'll pop round. Give me two seconds."

"Okay."

Considering we're only a few feet away from each other, it's easier to speak face to face and within a few seconds, more than the proffered two, understandably, we are.

"I'm so sorry," Frank says and indicates a spare chair. I sit.

"Really, it's fine."

"Had you chosen somewhere?"

"I thought Nando's at… actually I'm not sure where at."

Frank's face crumples even more. "Oh that's a shame. I've not been there for yonks."

I smile. Another word I love. Yonks. Yanks.

"It's up by the cinema." Like Nathan, Frank points in the same general direction.

"Jarman Park?"

Frank nods. "Can't remember the address but you can park anywhere."

I nod, though not as enthusiastically. It reminds me of James and our climbing wall. I hope he comes back tomorrow but then I don't. Mass of contradictions.

"Is everything okay?" I ask, knowing that Frank wouldn't have cancelled unless it was important.

He shrugs. "Our next-door neighbour's broken her hip."

"Oh no."

"She's fine but I promised I'd visit her at Watford General, seeing as Frankie's at chess."

"Of course." I know there's a hospital at Hemel, in a lovely late nineteenth century building – which probably means everything needs fixing, but Watford's bigger, so not surprised she's been taken there. I feel like asking Frank to pass on my love but then feel daft as I've never met her so I leave it at that and return to my desk to collect my bag.

Frank and I have a quick chat on my way out – he's going straight to hospital rather than home first and it's a good excuse to get some work done while the office is quiet, he says, like it's normally a madhouse.

I get a parking spot next to one of the end disableds and feel bad. Not because I'm doing anything wrong but because someone might think the space I've used has a yellow or blue figure painted on it. Even though I know it's okay, I check when I'm out of the car that it doesn't, and someone walking by frowns at me. It could be because they think it is but equally I do look as if I'm checking as if someone's strapped a bomb to my undercarriage. I smirk at the thought, not a real bomb, you understand.

A lovely young man opens the door for me as I head inside Nando's. I thank him and he smiles. Even though he's wearing a suit, it turns out he doesn't work there but it's too late to swap my 'it was your job' thanks to 'you're a customer, how kind' thanks. Someone behind me coughs and I realise I'm blocking the doorway. I apologise and go further inside. I've not booked but fortunately Tuesdays aren't busy so I'm shown to a really nice table about halfway through the restaurant to one side.

I'm given a couple of menus but don't say I'm not waiting for someone which, on reflection, was silly as I'll probably be ignored until it's clear that the 'someone' isn't turning up. I try to catch the eye of passing waitresses but they're like homing pigeons; fixed on their destinations. Not that I actually mind. The place is amazing.

The ceiling is strip upon strip of wood hanging by thin straps of presumably wire that looks straight out of a Tate Modern exhibition. The wooden planks continue down both side walls, with pictures of, presumably, South Africa in front of them one side and some kind of mesh weavings the other. My description doesn't do the place justice and despite being hungry, I'm happy to simply sit and take in my surroundings.

I'm soon joined though by Arya, who informs me she'll be my waitress. She doesn't refer to me being alone, doesn't ask whether I need more time, but takes up position, finger poised over handset, ready to take my order. Because of the aforementioned view-taking, I've not looked at the menu but don't want to say so, or ask for extra time unless it's more than I need and I'm left long enough to start gathering dust, not that there looks like even a speck here. It's impeccable. As is Arya.

"I'm on a… bit of a diet. Do you have anything that…?"

She grins, a very broad, very white smile against her dark skin. Her teeth are so bright that they could easily compete against the spotlights set into any of the beams. "No problem," she says in an accent so rich it could outdo Charles on a generous day. She returns less than a minute later with a 'Healthy-ish' menu.

The passion fruit and mango supergreen pitta, as it stands would have been 477 calories, thirteen calories more than the lemon and herb version but when in Jamaica… South Africa. Stuffed with broccoli, edamame beans (I make a mental note to wikipedia it) and kale, it sounds lovely… for a low-calorie restaurant offering. I'm about to opt for that pitta but spot the sweet potato and butternut above it so go for that until I see that it's 501 calories. Darn. The lemon and herb is only 488 so I compromise and order that. "And a diet something please."

"We have Diet Coke, Coke Zero, or Sprite Zero."

"Ooh, Sprite Zero please."

"Any sides?" she asks, yet is shaking her head so I decline. I shouldn't anyway if I'm to stick to below the five hundred calorie limit but then it's thirty-one dishes in thirty-one days rather than meals. Or at least I think so. I thank her as I hand back the menu and the first thing I do while I'm waiting is to google 'edamame beans'.

As expected, Wiki's not far away in the search results and it tells me that 'Edamame is a preparation of immature soybeans in the pod, found in cuisines with origins in East Asia. The pods are boiled or steamed and may be served with salt or other condiments. In Japan, they are usually blanched in 4% salt water and not served with salt.' They look very much like broad beans, and while they wouldn't be my first choice, they are nice mixed in with other things.

Arya returns really quickly with my drink and amazingly, with my food. I guess it's not that big a deal for someone to have put it together that quickly and I'm sure it wasn't already sitting under a heat lamp for someone to order it. Not that it needs a heat lamp but that's the picture that sprung to mind.

The pitta is scrummy. It is actually slightly warm and the bread tastes as if it's only just been baked and the insides are an interesting combination. There's a nearby stand with a variety of sauces but I've stuck with the accompanying lemon and herb. I'll have the peri-peri next time because it's Nando's specialty. If there's going to be a next time. Perhaps next week with Frank.

I pay my bill, thank Arya for a VAT receipt and leave her a two-pound tip. I feel a little mean but for an £11.70 meal it's more than the usual ten percent.

Before returning to my car, I look across the 'park' and see the climbing centre, XC, and can't help thinking of James. I don't feel the same as before and absence isn't making my heart fonder in his direction. If anything, it's helping my bond with Duncan.

Yes, Donna, you tell yourself that.

Chapter 56 – The Inside Does Match

I'm not ready to go back to my mum's and feel I've not explored Tring enough yet. There's a pub, The Anchor, I think, opposite the end of Miswell Lane. I often take Elliott to the park by the school off Goldfield Road so have seen it many times but not been in there since a pub crawl back in my early twenties… maybe even late teens. Was I driving? Not that night for sure. Anyway. I decide to go there for half a cider. My mum's isn't far away so I drop my car at hers – she's not there (shocker!), and walk down so I can 'drink'.

As it's been so long since I've been inside, I'm expecting it to have changed, not that I really remember what it was like the last time. It looks rustic from the outside and the inside does match, although there's a contemporary old feel to it, if that makes sense. I wait to order my drink and take a look around. The walls are brick but they've been sandblasted (as if I know what I'm talking about) to reveal the 'exposed brick' (just paler versions of brick brick). At the far end there's a feature wall with a huge TV in front of some fascinating posters and Chesterfield-type seating the entire length.

Part of me hopes there's a space so I can kneel on the seat and read the posters but I feel that would be rude, but then who am I being rude to? An incredibly tall (even more so than William, definitely basketball tall) barman smiles at me and nods as an unsaid request for my order.

"Hi," I say.

He nods again.

"Do you have any flavoured ciders, please?"

He nods a third time. "We have Rekorderlig," he says the name with a hint of a Scandinavian accent even though the little he's said so far sounds English, "in strawberry and lime… we have that in Kopparberg too, wild berries, rhubarb… that's Rosie's pig–"

As he says it, in a very English accent, I snort like Rosie's pig. "Sorry."

"Elderflower and Lime…"

"Mmm…"

"Passionfruit and Apple, that's Old Mout."

Having missed out on the passion fruit and mango pitta earlier, I snap a "Perfect" at that one before he says any more that might dissuade me. "Thank you," I add and he goes to one of the fridges behind him then pours the drink into a matching 'OLD MOUT CIDER' glass with what looks like a kiwi sitting on the 'T' and a row of arrows that could be swallows underneath the writing. He goes to throw the bottle in the bin and I don't stop him but have spotted some yellow writing on the label under the flavour.

I'm curious about everything so after paying for my drink but before heading for the postered wall, I google the drink and smile at the 'You Old Romantic'. Sweet.

As I approach what I *thought* were posters, I realise the wall's actually covered in wood rather than paper and, more specifically, sides of wine crates. Not as much writing as I'd anticipated but a really clever touch. The football's on the TV, a replay of an earlier match, so few are taking an interest and being a Tuesday night, the pub's not heaving as it might be at the weekend which means plenty of space on the Chesterfield sofa-cum-bench. Rather than kneel and read, I sit.

My face lights up as a message comes in from Duncan. He's already in bed and is cosy after a lovely hot bath. He has a modern version of a rolltop bath which is bigger than the 1930s one Izzy has in her house and has the taps on one side rather than at one end which means we can lie face to face and chat (or anything else!) without either of us having stainless steel digging into our skin.

We have a tennis match of messages until I say I'll text when I'm in bed. He says he can't guarantee he'll still be awake but he'll try really hard. I have no doubt. Then I look around the pub some more. On one of the pillars in the pub there are some framed photographs and illustrations. Ever curious, I wander over and take a look. They cover the life of the pub's centenary, although most are from the first couple of decades and one looks like instruments of torture but I'm assured they're farming implements.

After finishing my really-lovely-definitely-have-it-again cider, I put my empty glass on the bar, and thank 'Stretch' for his hospitality, to which I get a polite nod as he's busy drying an engraved pint glass with a very traditional white and blue striped tea towel.

I take in more of Western Road as I walk back to my mum's. The road turns into the high street, via a roundabout at the top of… my mind's gone blank… Christchurch Road, and while businesses come and go, especially one next to the church opposite the library's car park, possibly because it sells designer clothes next to a charity shop that often has super-cut-price designer clothes, the town's still retained its English charm.

I remember Mum mentioning something about someone, probably council-related jobsworths, wanting to make Tring be in Buckinghamshire rather than Hertfordshire but everyone (presumably those who live here) have fought against it. Aylesbury's only at the end of the A41 and Aston Clinton, the nearest town (village?) to Tring, is Bucks too, I think, so it's creeping like a… creepy vine thing.

As far as I know, the bulk of Hertfordshire is the other side of the M1 so most people think of St Albans, Watford and the likes, Hertford too, I suppose.

I soon reach my mum's and I'm pleasantly surprised when I see her car. It doesn't guarantee she'll be there but I'm hopeful, despite only the hall light being on at first sight.

In case she's asleep, it is gone eleven, I don't call for her, and after getting a glass of water, switching off the hall light and using my phone's torch to see my way upstairs, I see her bedroom door's shut. Not knowing whether she's alone, or even there, I don't knock.

I've just brushed my teeth and am making my way to my bedroom when I hear a giggle come from my mum's. I'm hoping she's reading a funny text, seeing something cute, if not adorable, on Facebook, but have my suspicions that she has company.

With my mind reverting to *my* beau, I snuggle under my duvet and text Duncan. I wait a couple of minutes but there's no reply. I can't help feeling sad, even more so when I hear another giggle as I switch off my light. I bury myself deeper under my duvet. I'm sure I'll find out the cause of her merriment in the morning.

As Scarlett O'Hara said, "Tomorrow is another day." And it certainly is.

Chapter 57 – Not Only My Comfort

Wednesday 9th May

It's no surprise when I come downstairs that there's Mum and Charles at the breakfast table. I had expected love's young dream but they're acting their age. But then by me not wanting them to be all over each other, I feel I'm acting their age too, older. I'm the disapproving old spinster great aunt who tuts every time there's something jolly going on.

"Morning," I say breezily as I remove a bowl from a cupboard and the familiar packet of Tesco's four-nut and maple cereal from another. I tip a small amount as I'm not terribly hungry.

I've missed two 'morning's in return but smile as I return the packet with one hand and pour on some milk from a bottle my mum must have left out, figuring I wouldn't be long coming down. I wasn't paying attention and have tipped in too much and now have to carry the almost-full bowl from one end of the kitchen to the other, the dining area, without spilling a drop. I could do a Will Ferrell in *Stranger than Fiction* and 'curse the heavens in futility', when he's soaking wet outside Maggie Gyllenhaal's bakery, except there's no need and it's not fate, just me being careless.

Mum moves along one chair as I approach so she's sitting diagonally opposite Charles. She tucks a strand of my hair behind my nearest ear which almost wants to make me cry. I'm usually a strong independent woman, as Beyoncé and Destiny's other children, Kelly something and I can't remember the other one's name, would say, but today I'm feeling vulnerable. I only hope James isn't back today.

"So everything okay?" my mum asks. I'm eating to hide my blushing face. I look over at Charles and give a non-toothy smile because I'm sure I'll have something stuck in one of them. I nod and take another mouthful of cereal. "Great," my mum says and switches on the television, although she immediately stabs at the mute button and Philip Scofield is silenced while trying to persuade us to sell our cars because it's so much easier than trading them in. I love my Swift and while it's running well, I have no wish to do either.

Charles is also eating but toast, and for a big man, he's being incredibly graceful. Not even the toast is making a sound and I really don't know how he's doing that. Maybe it too is intimidated. I cock my head. Is that what I am? I look down at the tablecloth and imagine the ladybird fluttering its wings and flying off, I hope to somewhere nicer than a suburban kitchen.

"I like your top," Charles says. It's one of my favourites, a simple blue and white striped affair with a red fake bow, giving it a nautical look.

"Ah, thank you." I know I was hesitant, and then some, at first, but I'm really warming to the man. He'll never take my dad's place, of course, but it's been so long that my mum deserves to be happy. I look at her and I can tell she is.

She looks from me to Charles and back again. I'm willing her not to say my dad's last words: 'You are a lovely lot' but then he was saying that to my mum, Izzy and me, and Charles and I aren't exactly a 'lot'. Instead she says, "How lucky am I?" We know she's not expecting a reply and it's not forthcoming. Charles and I just look at each other and smile.

"Right, I'd better get to work," I say and add, "Lovely to see you again, Charles," as I'm putting my plate and spoon in the dishwasher. And I mean it. "See you later maybe, or sometime." He nods. I turn to my mum, who's sitting on the side of her chair with her legs between it and the one I'd been sitting on. "See *you* later maybe, or sometime."

She laughs and they both wish me a good day. Not knowing yet whether James will have returned, I hope it's going to be.

My stomach's in knots as I walk down the corridor towards the open-plan office. I feel sick as I see James at his desk but he's chatting to Frank. They're both laughing, which is a good sign. Frank's such a positive person, as is James really, sometimes a little too positive, and I feel rather a dread at speaking to James rather than a longing feeling. I love Duncan. I will always love Duncan. I don't love James. I don't, of course. How could I after ten days and some of that with him not being here? *Because he's all you can think of.* No, that's not true. It isn't.

And it really isn't. The men turn as I approach their desks, not actually with the intention of saying more than a 'hello' or 'good morning'. And I don't get the 'pang' of longing for James. The fact that he clearly caught himself shaving as he still has a tiny square of tissue on one side of his chin that has a red splodge dead centre, does help. I smile a nonchalant smile at James then Frank, only because James's desk is first and say a sprightly 'morning'. They repeat the greeting in unison and laugh, only at that, I think, not at me. I continue walking so there's no opportunity for 'how was your long weekend's or anything else and head to my desk.

It's only when sitting that I realise I don't have a drink. I hang my head over my desk and sigh. Although it means a trek back past 'the' desks, I am thirsty, only having had milk with my cereal this morning. I sit for a few seconds, open hands either side of my face, index fingers touching my forehead, thumbs on my cheeks, elbows on my desk. My arms and hands look like two swans coming together, except I don't feel that graceful.

The sick feeling's returning again. I know I have to face him so I make the epic journey back through the office. Nathan's there but on the phone. We do jazz hands at each other and smile. He smiles. I laugh. Which is good. Very good.

James and Frank are still chatting but no sooner have I gone past, not looking or speaking, than I hear someone walking behind me. I refuse to turn but whoever it is (James) follows me into the kitchen.

"Donna," he says before I can even reach for a mug. He puts a hand on my hip and I swing round. I want to slap him but he's already too close for comfort. Not only my comfort but that of any non-dating colleague.

"No," I say and push him back.

"I'm sorry, I was just getting past to grab a mug. I'm expecting a call."

Likely story. "Mmm."

"But seeing as we're here." His eyes are doing that annoying sparkly thing but I'm strong. I can resist. I *shall* resist.

"No, James, I won't do that to Veronica… or more importantly to Duncan."

James frowns. "Veronica? What's Veronica got to do with it?"

"Your wife."

James puts down his mug and bursts out laughing. "I'm sorry. You thought…" He points his finger at me which I don't take kindly and go to bat it away except it's already gone in the direction of his mug and I'm batting air. "Veronica's not my wife. She's my sister."

And now it makes sense. All the 'James and Veronica' mentions because they're related but only by blood rather than marriage. And of course he'd take time off because his new nephew's poorly, very poorly, which reminds me. "How's Ethan?"

"To change the subject."

I think I've done that rather well, although it wasn't my intention. It doesn't alter the fact that he's married. To someone other than Veronica.

"He's on the mend. Thanks." James takes a sip of his drink.

"So who *are* you married to?" I blurt. I don't see the harm now of asking.

"Callie. Veronica's soon-to-be ex-husband's sister. All very incestuous."

"Mmm." That doesn't give him the right though to hit on me. Just because things aren't going well in that direction, and presumably not well between him and Callie…

"True."

"Huh?"

"Things aren't going well between me and Callie."

Oh bugger. I thought I'd only said that in my head. Still, it had to be said, thought, said.

"Of course I'm going to take Veronica's side."

Of course. You only have howevermany-never-been-confirmed children with Callie. I feel the slightest bit of empathy though for him being stuck in the middle until he badmouths the mother of his howevermany children.

"Right, well," I say. "I'm terribly busy so I'll see you later... or not."

I feel like Bridget Jones when she confronts Daniel Cleaver. She does so with her head held aloft so I do the same, turn and high tail my way out of the office. Or I would, had James not reminded me that I'd forgotten my drink.

Chapter 58 – Lots Of Maybes Flying Around

After blanking James all morning, not difficult when tucked round my corner of the office, I think I might get away with not seeing him when who should loom over my desk… And he's looking very pleased with himself.

"Now we've established I'm not married to your temporary predecessor," he says, "will you accompany me for lunch?"

Oh.

Erm.

"I'm sorry, James, but I have plans." Of course I don't, because in the process of avoiding James, I've also been avoiding Leah. "Yes, my mum has made plans for me."

"Oh. Okay then. Maybe tomorrow."

"Maybe." Ooh, I like this new forthright Donna. "But maybe not," I say a little too quietly as he leaves for his desk, or to go to lunch. I'm starving. I have to hope he's gone out out so I can go… out out.

Actually, why not go back to Tring? Ooh… Black Goo. Yes, let's frequent Black Goo. Good plan, Donna. "See, James, I have a plan." I even stick out my tongue. Not that anyone can see or hear but it makes me feel good. So there. I can't help chuckling and it feels good. I should do it more often.

I'm pleased to see no James when I go back through the office. Greta's at her desk so I go to speak to her about tonight.

"Oh gosh. I'm really sorry," she says. "I hadn't forgotten as such but…"

I'm hoping it's something to do with Owen and she does blush when our thoughts transmute. Not transmute. What's a clever word for collide? That doesn't happen, obviously, but she does blush.

"I was actually going to say that I can't so that's worked out well." I'd been looking forward to chatting to her, and of course getting the gossip, had there been any to have, on Owen but I'm pleased for her.

"I'm off out for lunch so maybe see you later." There are lots of maybes flying around today.

The drive to Black Goo is fine, although it seemed to take almost as long to get out of work's car park than it did to get three junctions on the A41. There are two for Tring, and Black Goo is sort of nearer (quicker probably at least) the second but I decide to pop to Tesco on the way – in theory just for a magazine but spend over twenty pounds including ice cream and snacks because Duncan's coming at the weekend and it's not fair to eat all my mum's, even though I suspect some were bought for us (me).

Ice cream means popping to my mum's, a good excuse to leave my car at hers and walk, not that I have any intention of 'drinking' because I have to drive to work thereafter but figure the exercise – because I've not exactly stuck to only the five hundred calorie dishes, will do me good.

She's not there so she'll be out somewhere enjoying Charles's company and retirement. I'm not going to go all cynical and add 'money' because although he'll undoubtedly insist on paying for everything, Mum has her own little pot of gold and is as strong willed as they come…

I'd googled (of course) Black Goo before I left the office and they promise to 'bring a taste of London café society to Tring and Berkhamsted'. I'd forgotten there was one there too. Maybe I'll do that one lunchtime, seeing as it's between work and my mum's. Or I could go there now. No, I'd have to drive and parking's tricky on the high street and… *Decisive Donna*. Mmm…

I'd called in to the Tring branch once before, to ask if they knew when the pet shop on the same strip of shops might be open then felt foolish because they didn't know and when I'd got back to Gosford Pets, I'd missed a post-it note that had said 'back in ten minutes'. Which I'd been reading, blocking the path of the owner, manager maybe, who'd been waiting behind me to reopen her shop. I was only going to buy a bag of treats for Elliott but ended up spending over twenty pounds. I have a habit of doing that, on squeaky toys and rawhide chews, at the time debating which would last longer; the squeaks or the chews. The chews won.

Thankfully no one at Black Goo recognises me, why would they, and I'm shown to the only free table, to the left of the main door. They take bookings, which I'd not been fortuitous enough to consider although I had noticed it on their website, but I'm grateful they don't ask so they clearly weren't expecting anyone else. I'd also spotted the 'dirty' afternoon tea of which I'd be 'treated to the most generous, sumptuously delicious homemade savoury and sweet treats. From chunky sausage rolls to scones, clotted cream and jam, washed down with your choice of *unlimited refreshment... be it Tea, Prosecco or G&T's (in high summer pimms!)' with a small 'p'. The asterisk limiting the unlimited to ninety minutes. I can imagine most people could drink their way through quite a lot in an hour and a half. 'We also cater veggie and vegan' (with a little cress picture) 'options,' it said. I may be hungry but not *that* hungry which is a shame as I don't have company.

The room is lovely. Not too big, not squished. It's airy despite its size, probably helped by the cream interior and the hanging trendy light bulbs. There's a bench, an actual wooden bench rather than a Chesterfield version, but a more comfy seating area to the right of the door, or it would have been had I come in and gone that way. It's currently opposite.

I look back at the menu and am still deliberating when a shadow looms over my table. For a fleeting second, I think it might be James, it's so large, but it's 'Stretch' from the Anchor.

"Hi," he says.

"Hi," I say, hesitant that he's saying 'hi' because he recognises me. We're almost at as many words as exchanged between us last night.

"Do you mind…" he continues then looks around at the packed café, "if I join you?"

I shake my head. "No, not at all." And I don't. I really don't. He's too young for me but I certainly don't think he's asking to join me for any other reason than the chair opposite is the only one free.

He sits and thanks the waitress who gives him a menu and asks if we'd like any drinks. I've had my fill of Coke, lemonade and the likes already this month so I fancy something different. Orangey perhaps. So I ask for exactly that, which makes them both laugh.

"We do," she says with a hint of an Australian accent that's probably New Zealand or even South African. "There's an orange juice and lemonade to play safe or we could do you a non-alcoholic cocktail."

"Ooh yes, that sounds nice. Thank you."

Rather than making a note, she keeps it in her head then turns to my new companion.

"Double-shot espresso please."

"Great. I'll be back to take your orders." Before she leaves, he speaks again.

"Could you do separate bills please."

She nods and returns to behind the counter.

"I'm sorry," he says, facing me. "I'd offer to pay but…"

"You're on a barman's wages."

He frowns then the penny drops. "Right! Last night. Yes, Miss Half a Cider."

I cluck. (I cluck!? Where did *that* come from?) "That's me." Mother Hen.

He holds out his left arm and it almost reaches my elbow. He draws it back until our hands are level. "I'm sorry."

I'm not used to left-hand shaking, most people are right handed (ninety percent of the population, I believe… I wonder why I've never done an article on left-handed cosmetics) so it's a little awkward but he doesn't seem to notice. "No problem."

I hadn't noticed him being left handed last night and he coughs as it's clear I'm staring at his left hand… which I'm still holding so now

it becomes very awkward. I apologise, release his hand, and he laughs then apologises.
"Why?" I blurt. I seem to blurt a lot. I need to learn restraint. What did I say about being thirty-one going on twelve? No, I didn't because I'm thirty not thirty-one. Wishing my time away.
"I do most things right handed other than eat and shake hands. Don't know why." He shrugs.
"I think it's sweet. Sorry, I didn't mean that to sound condescending."
"Not at all. I'm... flattered."
Again, I don't think he's taking this as anything more than the compliment it was.
"Shall we..." He points to the menu then blows out at the description of the Afternoon Tea. "I think that would be too much even to fill my long legs."
"How...?"
He raises his eyebrows. "How?"
"I was going to ask how long your legs actually are but that's silly."
He laughs. "They're rather out of proportion."
"They are?"
"I have a short body but stupidly long legs, like a spider."
"But thankfully only two."
He laughs again. "He's a lucky chap, your..."
"Duncan."
"He's a lucky chap, your Duncan."
"Thank you." Good, I'm glad we've got that sorted. "Right, food. Not the Afternoon Tea."
"No," Stretch says and shakes his head in a very serious Winston Churchill manner. I can't keep thinking of the man sitting opposite as Stretch. "I'm Donna, by the way."
Stretch goes to move his hand as if for us to shake again but changes his mind. "Finn. Two 'n's. After Finnegans Wake. My mum was a James Joyce fan."
"Oh."
"Oh? Not a fan yourself?"
"It's not that... not that I've read much, any, if I'm honest. No, you said 'was'."
I can tell the conversation's going to get morbid and we're thankfully interrupted by the waitress bringing our drinks. Finn and I sit back, giving the nameless waitress space to place our drinks. While she does so, I take a quick look at the menu.
I like that the prices are in whole digits, no ninety-five or ninety-nine so we think it's cheaper than it is. For a place as nice as this, it's really not that bad. I'm not sure yet whether this is going to be a

'project' meal but it'll be well within budget regardless and I'll ask for a receipt just in case.

The budget would stretch to er… Stretch, Finn, too but I don't think Frank would accept a receipt for two 'covers' as they call a customer… or is that the table. I should know but then I'm not a restaurant critic, as such.

I look up and see Finn's not looking at the menu. Either that or he's superpeeked and chosen already.

"I'm a regular," he says.

Ah. I waft my hand to indicate for him to go first. He smiles and looks up. Even though he's so tall, he's average body height, the rest of him casting long shadows under the table no doubt.

"Could I have the Veggie Goo, please."

I wouldn't have had him down as a vegetarian. Not sure why though.

Again, as if reading my mind, he explains. "I eat meat, lots of it actually, but you don't get bubble and squeak with the meat version."

I'm glad he's said that as I was going to change my Eggs Benedict for the Eggs Royale so he didn't feel bad but revert to my original choice and hand back my menu.

"Thanks, Sandy," Finn says and returns his menu.

"No probs, Finn… ma'am."

I can't remember the last time I've been called 'ma'am'. My mum loves it, thinks it's respectful but it just makes me feel old.

Finn and I, thankfully, don't pick up where we left off; his mother.

"So you're a regular here," I say to make sure we don't.

He nods. "I eat at The Anchor most of the time but I love it here. Have you seen the sofa's at the end?"

I know there is another seating area past the counter but have never been that far. Instead of moving, he googles the place and shows me. "Oh wow." There, in all its fabulous glory, are two non-button Chesterfield-type (which probably means without the buttons that they're not Chesterfield at all) brown sofas adorned with black and white leopard print cushions.

After our meal, which was dee-lish-us, we retire to the aforementioned comfy area where we have cappuccino coffees and talk about everything and something. We do have separate bills although I insist on paying for the two cappuccinos because he's such enjoyable company. Given his knowledge of Duncan there was awkwardness – unless you count the sofa farting when I went to stand. "Does that to me all the time!" Finn says and we laugh.

We're kicked out, not literally, when the place closes at four. I'd already decided not to go back to work. Suspecting that my Eggs Benedict was way over the five hundred calories (nutritionix.com confirmed it was 733, more generous than foodnetwork.com's 1,020), I knew I wouldn't be including it as one of my thirty-one dishes. Even the Eggs Royale would have been 600 or I don't know how many as I couldn't find that on the foodnetwork site. Although their Canadian site did have a recipe for a 328-calorie version, I don't suppose it was one that Black Goo had used.

"So..." I say as we stand outside. "It's been lovely seeing you again." I make sure I don't include a 'really' in case it comes across as... you know.

"And you. I'm at The Anchor all evening if you're at a loose end." Like me, he says it in a friendly but not friennndly way.

Knowing my mum, she'll be at her needlework class, needling who knows what (I must ask her as I'm curious), I know my end will be 'loose'. I've never been one to stay in and watch television, unless I have someone (Duncan) to snuggle up to. Even so I say a non-committal, "I probably will be."

"Great. Maybe see you later."

"Yes, maybe."

I think of James as I walk back to my mum's. The charity shops would have still been open but I feel like going back and slobbing, if not for the whole evening, for at least an hour or two. If Mum's not at Charles's, she'll hopefully be there. With or without him.

She's not, although I think she is but it's only her car. He must have picked her up and gone wherever it is they've gone. It's too early for her class but he might drop her off there. I wouldn't put it past him to join her – they are cemented at the hip – as he constantly surprises me, and her, I'm sure.

And she's still not back by the time the class would have started; they're usually seven until nine, so The Anchor it is. I think I would have gone anyway, having an evening off, but dragged my mum along with me – not that I'd have to do much dragging, she's always loved going to pubs with anyone who asks.

Chapter 59 – Not So Little When You're Missing Duncan

The Anchor's surprisingly busy. What a difference a day makes, twenty-four little hours. Little when you're having fun. Not so little when you're missing Duncan. Although I do know someone (Finn), it's not the same being in a pub on your own, especially when the 'someone' is working. Better though than home alone, even if no one but you would know you were.

Seeing as I wasn't having a low-calorie dish, I'd not mentioned the 'project' to Finn so I'd forgotten to ask what they might have that would fit the bill. Unlike Izzy's one man a day (sort of), I could have a work work lunch and dinner on the same day, tomorrow, but I'll try tonight if I can in case it doesn't work out. Plus I have to have something to talk about. I don't want to get behind.

"Hi." Finn grins at me as I walk through the door that someone, having a conversation with himself, is holding open, not for me I don't think. As I walk past, I see a white 'bud' in his ear so he's obviously on the phone, not with himself. Izzy, being the techie, would have likely spotted it earlier.

"Hello." I grin back and laugh as Finn's holding up a cider glass. "You know me so well." Although it's a repeat of yesterday, it's exactly what I fancy. "And a menu please."

"Ooh... okay. That I can do."

He pours me the cider and gives me the menu. I'm about to tell him about my 'requirement' when he points to someone waiting to be served.

"No problem," I say and am happy to peruse the menu. I don't fancy salad or a pitta-type and spot a delicious looking veggie ensemble which has to fit the bill as it's only the cheese that can do any damage. It looks like the old 'Mac and cheese' except it's vegetables instead of macaroni pasta. Offer anyone a plate of vegetables, even with melted cheese, and they'd probably say 'fine' as a side dish, but whatever they've done to this, in the picture, at least, makes it look divine.

"Hi, sorry about that," Finn says when he comes back to me.

"No problem," I repeat.

He looks at the menu, at my finger on the description of the 'Anchor's Away Veggie Cheese Bake'. "Good choice. A popular dish." He nods sagely, making me laugh. "No, honestly. It tastes as good as the picture. I don't know what Wally, he's our chef, does to it but..." Finn forms a circle with his right (I note) thumb and forefinger, which he puts to his lips and smacks them away. "Bellissimo. Or is that bellissima. I think food is feminine."

"Oh. I should know."

"Oh? Do tell..."

"Oh yes." The everything and something we talked about earlier was not only lacking my project but also my job, so I fill him in.

"Int'resting," he says, with the first 'e' missing in very much a Nathan manner, before going to the till and processing my order, having accepted my ten pound note. Other than the fact that Finn is English rather than American, isn't called Brad, and is a barman rather than… I'm not sure I ever found out what Brad did other than work for Kodak, formerly The Eastman Kodak Company, and nothing to do with the 'often-repeated urban legend (that) recounts that photographer and musician Linda McCartney (née Eastman, first wife of Beatle Sir Paul McCartney) was related to the George Eastman family. Her father was of Russian Jewish ancestry and changed his surname to Eastman before becoming known as an attorney.' Thank you, Wikipedia. Other than all that, I think the two of them would get on well. Finn and Nathan. Except that… looking at Finn interacting with a barmaid who's been out collecting glasses, they wouldn't get on *that* well.

Finn was right. The cheese bake was awesome. The veg, although I love cauliflower cheese, broccoli and the likes, didn't taste like vegetables. Knowing how tricky some children are about eating their greens, their parents should bring them here. He, Finn, was also busy almost all evening so I didn't get to chat much, though I did make sure I got to say a proper 'goodbye'. Other than that, I sat in a corner so I didn't get in his, or anyone else's way. It was also just as well because I was rather busy sending, and receiving, rather raunchy text messages from a certain Northampton-based vet who, he says, is missing me like crazy.

So all in all, I was alone yet not alone, and although I was only there a couple of hours (enough though for three glasses of cider), the 'little' hours flew.

Chapter 60 – Not Quite The Same

Thursday 10th May

Thursday morning comes and there's no sign of James. Other than him being one of my lunch accompaniments, it's not my business to ask anyone of his whereabouts and I'm sure I'd have heard on the grapevine if something awful had happened to him, or Ethan… or wonderful; I know James does the Euro Millions. With the exception of Hazel and Leah, both being human resources, and perhaps Nathan, there's one other person who knows everything that goes on and I'm having dinner with him this evening. Billy returned on Monday so his family emergency was thankfully short lived. Nathan had held the fort majestically.

I've brought in lunches or gone into town, mostly to charity shops, when on my own since I arrived last week. Today however, I fancy getting something from the van. On other days I've looked out of my window when they've blasted the horn but either been too slow, had something that needed using up, or forgotten my purse, fortunately on the same day as I'd brought the something that needed eating. Today though I'm ready with my purse, at the bottom of the stairs, and see the van before I hear it. I'm therefore not only first in the queue but the only one.

"Ooh, hello. You're new." The lady with 'Val' embroidered on her blue and white striped candy-style top smiles.

I blush. "I am. Only temporary though. Just for the month."

"Welcome. Everything's labelled and priced but let me know if I can help."

"Thank you." I take a look and am grateful that there's not yet anyone behind me. I turn to check and they are actually all piling towards the van so I need to hurry.

"I'm sorry to be a pain, and I don't want to hold you up, but do you know which of these are less than five hundred calories?"

With no rolling of eyes, as if she's been asked hundreds of times, she smiles and points to a chart on the wall behind her. There listed are the items split into sandwiches, rolls, wraps, baguettes and ciabattas. Underneath each option, just like drinks at Starbucks, are the calories, with a disclaimer at the bottom which states that they are a guide only, I assume because the size of the bread can vary, but they're very specific. My first choice is a tuna melt ciabatta but that's way over so I opt for the wrap as that squeezes under my limit. I resist the crisps but buy a couple of bottles of Sprite Zero to support this local business, ingeniously called 'Val's Lunches'.

I'm contemplating inviting her to keep the change but I don't think that's really done with sandwich vans, even one that has such an impressive array, so I take my thirty-seven pence and drop it into my top's one and only pocket.

I smile at Frank and Greta who are next to each other in the queue. There are a couple of other people I recognise from the first day's group huddle but have never spoken to. I'm tempted to hover but that would be weird so will make sure I do introduce myself after lunch. After Billy's welcome, they'll probably know who I am, just not the other way round. I think one of them will be the fashion columnist, mainly because of what she's wearing, the other one maybe… I don't know who. I thought I'd met everyone other than fashion and that's only because we've not been introduced. She's not on the rota Hazel set up, nor is the guy, so I presume they didn't want to do it or Hazel thought they wouldn't. The girl's very young, late teens, early twenties at the most, and wearing a stunning dress that hugs her amazing curves. Lara Croft eat your heart out. And I bet it's not from TK Maxx.

I take my wrap and one of the Sprites, popping the other in the fridge, back to my desk then get going with my reports.

Typing up my visit to Black Goo and The Anchor are fun as I relive sharing both venues with Finn. Although I didn't eat a relevant low-fat option at the former, I include it in my article and recommend it to my (Veronica's) readers, especially for their vegetarian and vegan dishes, and fans of an all-day breakfast. My stomach rumbles at the thought of a full 'English' so I tuck into my wrap. Not quite the same but I have a good imagination. Maybe I should write that novel. Izzy said once, I think it was Izzy anyway, that some writers don't think JK Rowling or Dan Brown, he of *The Da Vinci Code*, are particularly good writers but they tell a good story and that's the important thing. I like words so would want it to be well written too. I'll leave the novel writing to Izzy, I think.

Chapter 61 – Finally Billy's Turn

Five thirty is finally here. I've already checked with Nathan that Billy's still okay for dinner and he says 'with bells on' which is lovely. I'm not entirely sure that's true but it's flattering nonetheless; from Billy if it is true or Nathan for making it up.

I'm debating whether to collect Billy, and if so what time, when I hear a voice. "Ready?"

I look up. "As I'll ever be." I cringe. How silly do I feel?

But Billy smiles and yee haws. I feel my shoulders relax and realise how tense I've been. It's been a tough almost couple of weeks and I think, with the extra knowledge I'm armed with, that I can handle the next three a lot better. There'll be no 'feelings' between James and me, if and when he does finally reappear. No. Professional all the way. And I shall tell him so if need be.

"Anywhere in mind?" Billy asks as we walk through the relatively quiet office and out towards reception.

I shake my head then realise that Billy doesn't have eyes in the side of his.

Before I speak, he says, "Shall we go up to Jarman Park and see what takes our fancy?"

This immediately reminds me of James but that's not a bad thing as it's a way I can raise the topic.

"Absolutely."

"One car or two?"

"Erm… I don't mind."

"You're in Tring, right?"

"My mum is, yes."

"We'll take mine then. We'll have to come back this way so…"

"If you don't mind."

"Not at all. Be my pleasure."

And it turned out to be mine. Billy's ride is a blue Jaguar XF something or other. Beyond the James Bond-type silver and the gorgeous smell inside, I don't pay much attention to specifics but I can tell Billy loves it. From what I caught of William and Duncan's conversation about William buying a car, it certainly wasn't a Jaguar. Ford and Vauxhall were two of the models mentioned so unless they were a Mustang and… whatever a flash Vauxhall would be, there's no comparison. What the two Williams spend their money on is their business but buying something like this wouldn't leave much for anything else if what Izzy tells me of their frugal lifestyle is true.

We settle on Chiquito and I can feel another wrap or grill coming up but I'm easily swayed by something a little different and go for the

Jambalaya. I'm hoping it's not too spicy, not that I can't handle it but I do have to share a very lovely smelling car back to my very ordinary smelling one and I wouldn't want any of the 'tang' to transfer. I needn't have worried as Billy goes for the same. I have a large lemonade, in anticipation of my mouth being on fire, whereas Billy goes for a small beer, having 'just the one'. I get squiffy on half a cider so I never drink when I'm driving but knowing how much Billy loves his car, he wouldn't risk anything happening to it, or me, I'm sure.

I don't ask Billy why James is still away but when we talk about Veronica, Billy opens up.

"Little Ethan's very poorly. It's all very sad. There's a problem with his heart but they hope he'll make a full recovery, albeit slowly apparently. Lots of tests, some surgery expected."

"That's terrible." It's not the sort of thing you would wish on anyone, and I wonder if James declaring his feelings for me was a distraction. "Simply terrible," I repeat.

Our food arrives and we eat at similar speeds, slowly so we can enjoy it but also so I can drink plenty of lemonade per mouthful.

"And you had some trouble yourself the tail end of last week," I say. "I understand. I'm sorry to hear that."

Billy sighs and puts down his fork. "Yes, my wife's nephew. Silly lad. Bought a bike that was way too powerful for him. Hannah, that's my sister-in-law, lets him do what he likes, no expense spared, then wonders why he comes off the thing two days later. No one else involved and he's only broken an arm and leg, landed on his side, but worrying nonetheless. Imagine how she felt when she got the call. She'll have a tighter rein on him from now on hopefully. I took the Friday off to go up and see them. Hannah doesn't drive and her husband died Christmas Eve last year so it's been tough for her. I suppose she thought it would give the lad some independence seeing how she can't ferry him around." Billy shakes his head.

I nod mine. And there was I thinking that tonight would be a barrel of laughs. My fault really for bringing up the whole James thing, indirectly, and the wife's nephew directly. When will I learn? So I try something else. "I love your car."

Billy smiles. "Thank you. It's an extravagance but I promised that when I reached fifty, I'd treat myself."

I'm surprised he's that old. I would have said a decade less tops.

"I'm not quite there yet," he admits, "but couldn't wait."

I laugh. "It suits you."

Billy blushes. "So tell me more about this man of yours."

And I do. Almost everything there is to know and we're on to coffees by the time I'm finished. Billy settles the bill, leaving a fair tip, refusing my offer to do so.

"It's been a really lovely evening, thank you," I say as Billy pulls up beside my Suzuki in our offices' car park.

"It has. We should go out for dinner more often, my wife and I. Sorry, I didn't mean..."

I laugh. "It's okay. You should. They don't have to..." I was going to say 'cost the earth' but he's driving a ridiculously expensive car. "Thank you again. And I'll see you tomorrow?"

"You will indeed," he says and I get out of the car, taking one final silent inhale of the opulent aroma.

Mum's not back as I return home. Thursdays are guitar with Bernard, Greta and co. so I slob in her lounge with back-to-back *Big Bang Theory* episodes and the remainder of a tub of Halo Top Sea Salt Caramel. I'd never heard of it but I'm a convert. It's a mere 320 calories per tub so the thought hits me for a micro second that I could use it as one of my meals but laugh it off as ridiculous. Some people would have a tub as a 'meal' but I wouldn't be setting a good example, would I... even if it is high in protein (according to the label).

I'm still peckish as I scrape the last of the golden nectar. I know there's an unopened tub of Peanut Butter Cup, another mere 320 calories, but I resist. I'm better when something's sealed, like a box of chocolates. Ooh, there's a bar of Galaxy, my favourite, in the fridge.

The fourth episode's just finishing when I hear a key in the door. I look around, making sure there's no incriminating evidence of anything untoward lying around but one look in the freezer at the space left by the now-empty Sea Salt Caramel tub (that's in the paper recycling bin) would be enough to know I'd not been angelic. I had taken Mum at her word when she'd told me on day one to help myself to anything I fancied. I don't think she meant tall dark and handsome with almond eyes. Almond flavoured Häagen-Dazs maybe.

I get up and go to greet her. "Hi. How was guitar?"

She smiles and props her guitar-shaped case against the hall wall. "Really good. It was 'John' night."

I picture a street full of prostitutes and their pimps. Again, I don't think this is what my mum meant.

She reels off the list. "John Denver, Williams, Lennon..."

I struggle to think of any more Johns. "Travolta?"

Mum laughs. "Cuppa?"

"Please. Lewis? Malkovich?"

Mum keeps laughing as we walk through into the kitchen. I plonk myself on one of the dining room chairs as Mum makes the tea.

"Bon Jovi?"

"Yes! We did *Wanted Dead or Alive*. A fabulous song. When I say 'we', I mean Bernard of course. I struggled, even Greta did with a couple of them so it's good that she's learning too."

"She'll want to, having spent the money."

"She didn't pay for the course."

"She didn't?"

"No, she got a grant."

"She did?"

"Yes, a hardship allowance or something. I shouldn't know but Bernard let it slip over coffee during the mid-session breaks in the first or second lesson. I can't remember which. First, I think. She wasn't there, it was just Bernard and I… me thankfully. Big mouth has Bernard."

Big mouth Bernard. Love it. "I didn't know. I assume because she works…"

"Something to do with her living arrangements, parents' debts before they died."

"Her parents died?"

"Early last year. Car crash. Intentional apparently so no insurance payout. Her dad had his own business, owed a lot, remortgaged the house a couple of times." My mum takes a sip of her tea.

It doesn't surprise me that she knows so much. She could wheedle information out of a stone. If it had a mouth. It does surprise me that Bernard knows so much but I don't say anything. "So you had a good evening. Do you think you're improving? You weren't so sure last week."

She shrugs and moves her head side to side in a 'comme ci, comme ça' fashion, not a shake exactly but somewhere in between that and a nod.

"Early days," I say encouragingly.

We finish our teas and yawn at the same time.

"Bed?" she says and I repeat the word.

We go up together, I go to the bathroom, her to her en-suite, and we say 'goodnight'.

Chapter 62 – In Luck

Friday 11th May

My mum's still sleeping when I leave for work, after a quick bowl of four-nut and maple cereal. She and my aunt and uncle go to Dunsley Farm near Tesco on a Friday morning at ten thirty so she has plenty of time.

Duncan's coming to Tring for the weekend but not until tomorrow morning so I get an evening with my mum… or I would if it weren't her night with Charles. She's going over to his so at least I won't be gooseberry. No, I'll just play solitaire instead. The Carpenters song pops into my head. One of my dad's favourites.

I could always pop to The Anchor again or see if Phil's up for going out. He seemed keen to start with and we're back on good terms. It'll make a change for him too I'm guessing.

He is friendly when I walk up to his booth. "Good morning, Donna. How're you keeping?"

"Morning, Phil." I cut to the proverbial chase. "Are you free tonight?"

"Er…"

"Only I'm not going home this weekend. Duncan's coming here instead but not until the morning so I wondered…"

"Er…"

"Don't worry. It was just a thought."

Phil winces. "I'm sorry. I'd love to but I've made other plans, what with you saying you were going home each weekend. I could see if I could rearrange it but I've sort of promised this friend that–"

"Oh, no. It's absolutely fine. I'm sorry for messing you about."

"No worries. No messing."

I smile and I think we're okay. We'd never be besties but I like to get on with everyone. So unless anyone wants to come out to play tonight, I will be solo but that's fine. Maybe I'll see what's in the freezer… other than the Peanut Butter Cup. I think Mum has some Weight Watchers ready meals. They do a mean risotto. Knowing my luck there'll be everything else but that would be a great excuse to walk down to Tesco. It's the other end of town but it'll work off some calories before Mr Three Hundred and Twenty Calories puts them back on, not that I'd eat the whole tub. Ooh, I wonder if Tesco stocks them.

I'm not a very good advertisement for a health and beauty columnist, am I. I don't wear much makeup, but less is most definitely more; subtlety the name of the game in beauty. In life really. Donald Trump… suntan, Fifty Shades of Grey… everything.

No, that's mean. It changed a lot of women's lives, mostly for the better, but I'm a tough crowd, being a wordie. That said, I actually prefer the numbers round in Countdown. One from the top, five from the bottom. One large: fifty, five small: one, two, three, four, five. Pick a random number… four hundred and twelve.

Oh bum. Now I've got to work it out. The thirty-second clock jingles in my brain as I grab a piece of paper and pen from my bag and sit halfway up the stairs. If Phil's been keeping an eye on the monitors, he might wonder why I've not appeared in reception yet, although he'll also see me sitting on the stairs. I think he thinks I'm pretty weird anyway. In keeping, even.

Ooh easy. Three plus five equals eight, times the fifty is four hundred. Times the three by… oh no, I've already used the three. Okay… one plus two is three, times the four. Twelve. Do I get any bonus points for using all the numbers? No, I didn't think so. My mum makes her own rules in Scrabble so I probably would, even though this is a different game.

I stand and head for reception. Apart from killing a few minutes as it's not yet nine, it's woken up my brain if not the rest of my body.

The day goes soooo slowly. I'm counting the hours before I see Duncan but don't have much work to do. I've brought in a sandwich so no van Val and I resist eating my BT (the lettuce in my mum's fridge was black and wet… ew) on granary until one o'clock, although a larger than before bowl of four nuts helped.

James still isn't around and everyone else looks like they're busy. I do finally get to speak to the fashion girl, Amber, who is sitting at one of the freelancer desks and is as gorgeous up close as she looked passing by on my exit from Val's van that first time.

"Are you busy?" I ask, hoping she'll say no. I'm in luck.

"Oh hey, Donna." American. She sounds American, the deep south, if I'm not mistaken. I wonder if she's related to Phil. Not that that's likely; America's a biiiig place. "Mississippi. In case you were guessing."

I'd not quite got there but it was my next move. "M… i… double s… i… double s… i… double p… i," I sing and she laughs.

"The one and the same."

"I'm sorry. I'm keeping you from…" I look at her desk which is covered in magazines. Thick ones. Like Vogue. She's wearing another gorgeous outfit.

"I've been meaning to come find you actually."

I'm stunned. "You have?"

"Sure. I thought we should do a project together. I suggested it to…" She turns to the next desk but it's empty, or rather the chair behind it is. "Oh, he's not there."

No. He's not. I presume she means the guy she'd been in the snack van queue with, whose name I still don't know.

"I've not met him yet," I say. "Can you tell me something about him so when I do…?"

"Oh sure. His name's Calvin, like Klein, the boxers."

"What does he…?"

"Do?"

"Press."

"Press?"

"Handles the press. Enquiries from other media."

"Oh." We don't have anyone who does that at Northampton. I'm not sure why because they'd need someone like him.

"Covers your patch too."

"He does?" First I've heard of it. And there was I thinking I had my finger on the pulse… as my mum would put it, but I can't have if I'm quoting my mother.

"Ah ha. Liaises with someone at your office. Not sure who, sorry. You'd think I'd know, given that I sit next to him but I'm only part time and he's out a lot."

"You're part time?"

"Newly. A couple of weeks ago. Had a baby and agreed to come back sixteen hours a week. Billy's been very good."

Everyone's having babies. May. Nine months. May is five, December, November, October, September. September babies or thereabouts. End of the summer holidays, weather changing, three maybe four weeks before the clock changes, more nights staying in. September's the ninth month. I wonder how many babies are born on the twenty-fifth of September. What else is there to do on Christmas Day? Not that…

"Donna?"

Amber's caught me grinning. "Sorry. Just thinking."

"Something fun, judging by your expression."

"Fun, yes, definitely."

"Care to share."

Oops. "Erm, just a joke I heard on the radio on the way in."

"I love jokes. Do tell."

"Sorry, forgotten the punchline but I remember it being funny."

"Okay."

"I'd better get back to my desk and leave you to your…"

Without turning to her magazines, she explains. "What's the hot colour gonna be for this fall… sorry, autumn. I think burnt orange but not many others do. They're all going for safe: beige, pink, bland."

I think of the dress I wore to Frankie and Benny's last Friday, of my mother's scarf at the garden centre, and smile. "I think it's the perfect colour."

"Yeah, exactly. Huh. What do the experts know?"

"Nothing."

"Nothing, right?"

"Right. Well, lovely to finally speak to you," I say. "Sorry it took half my time here. I don't suppose… No, it's okay."

"You don't suppose what?"

"I'm at a bit of a loose end tonight…"

"Loose end?"

"On my own."

"Oh I'm sorry. I'd invite you to where I'm going but it's a dinner party and it's strictly couples." She grimaces, showing off beautifully white teeth. "I'm sorry."

"No, no, it's fine. I have a boyfriend." *Overcompensating.* "He's up in Northampton, coming down in the morning but tonight…"

"I get it. I totally get it. You don't want to be on your own. Who does Friday night, right?"

Absolutely. Who would? "Right."

I'm about to leave when Amber's next-door neighbour returns to his desk.

"Hey Calvin. Meet Donna. Donna's here covering Valerie."

"Veronica," I whisper.

"Veronica, of course. Sorry. Baby brain." Amber looks up to the ceiling then back at me. "Just as well I'm only part time."

I'm not sure what that has to do with the price of… What was it I had at Lussmanns? Cod? Now my brain's failing me.

I turn to Calvin and I almost curtsey but thankfully don't. He's a little older than Amber, but not by much, and the duo make me feel old. "Lovely to meet you, Calvin. I'd love to find out more about what you do sometime."

"Nothing to tell," he says and I'm disappointed. I don't think he meant it the way it came out but it did feel as if he wasn't interested in telling me. I'm here for a couple more weeks so plenty of time to speak to him again, although Amber did say he was 'out a lot'.

I while away the afternoon getting my emails up to date. It makes a change from trying to make my dishes reports sound more interesting than they are. I'm not the best person to have done this – you can probably tell – as I'm not the strictest at sticking with the rules. My mum used to call me her 'little rebel' when I was younger and it got me into trouble sometimes, not illegal or anything, just naughty, pushed more boundaries than… Donald Trump?

Sometimes I wonder where these thoughts come from. I know he won on state rather than individual votes and he'd been harping on about building a Mexican wall before, during and after his campaign but even so. There's Donna logic somewhere.

And so I have my Friday night in for one. I've struck lucky with a Weight Watchers chicken and lemon risotto in mum's freezer which means I don't have to trek to Tesco, although I'm then a little disappointed that I don't actually have to trek to Tesco so tell myself that I still can but don't want to.

You can probably tell that I adore chicken. I could literally have it every meal. At a mere 342 calories, I have a hundred and fifty-eight to spare and am tempted by half a tub of Peanut Butter Cup – two calories less than half a tub… half a tub minus a teaspoon?

The television's not bad but my mum has Freeview and Sky, although I don't know why as she's rarely home. She did tell me once, to get Sky Atlantic I think, but I can't remember the show that she couldn't live without. Probably *Grey's Anatomy* or something similar. We're alike in fancying men in scrubs. The thought of that makes me miss Duncan all the more and I give him a call but it goes through to answerphone. Strange. I hang up as I'd expected him to answer.

He did say he was probably going to have to work late but it's gone nine.

I call again and leave a soppy, yet professional, message. "Can't wait to see you. Miss you. Love you." Okay so much more soppy than professional. Totally soppy.

I settle back to another *Big Bang Theory*. I've seen them all at least twice but not all in the same order, thanks to being on different networks across different channels. Duncan got me hooked on it, although I'd seen a few and had loved it anyway, especially Amy, the nerdy brunette, and of course Sheldon. Who wouldn't love Sheldon the most?

Chapter 63 – Couldn't Wait Any Longer

Saturday 12th May

I wake up super early because Duncan's coming at ten. Mum's house is spotless, not that it never is – unless I clutter it, so there's nothing to do in that respect, not that Duncan minds. Living in clutter is one thing, staying in clutter for thirty… something hours.

I stay in bed until half seven but I'm wide awake and have exhausted my personal Twitter and Facebook's notifications, shares of cute animals doing crazy things. (I'm not quite up to sharing babies with my 537 followers and 142 'friends'.) So I get up. I can have a shower nearer Duncan's arrival but having had one last night, I don't feel too sweaty. The thought of that reminds me that it's been too long since I've done a hot vs. cold shower skincare article for a while. It also reminds me of the last time Duncan and I were together and the shower we had. Feeling definitely more hot than cold, I now need a shower.

A tiny bowl of four nuts later – tiny because I don't know whether Duncan will have eaten and will want to go out for something, I'm sitting in front of the television watching more *Big Bang Theory*. I thought I'd seen them all, twice, but don't remember this episode where Penny meets Leonard's mother for the first time. She, Beverly Hofstadter, aka Christine Baranski, is one of my favourite characters. She's so dry, something I aspire to be but could never carry off, and Christine does so well.

I need to watch this on repeat as research so pause it, bring up the 'i' information, noting the series (two) and episode (fifteen) numbers then search for the series. It's on another channel later today so set it to record. I'll only be able to watch it while I'm at my mum's so must jot it down somewhere so I search for it when I get back here… or I could just YouTube it, assuming there's an official version or a pirate one that's not been removed yet.

I'm engrossed in the first viewing when the doorbell rings. I look at the clock on the mantelpiece. Just gone ten past nine. Too early for Duncan. And there's no sign of my mum yet. Maybe the postman but even so, it's the weekend.

I'm in my pyjamas and dressing gown, decent enough to answer.

The front door's glass is frosted so I can't see who it is exactly, just an outline. He's tall though not tall enough to be Charles, but then he has a key. He, it's stocky like a 'he', is the perfect height to be Duncan and I squeal as I open the door to him.

He lunges forward and envelopes me, and Buddy rushes past. I hear him clatter around the kitchen as if searching for anything edible that someone might have dropped just for him.

As Duncan and I are hugging, I notice that my mum's car's not there. That's why she's not come down yet. Dirty stop-out. I'd gone to bed relatively early considering it wasn't a school night and unsurprised, given it was her one weekday evening with Charles, that she'd not come back by then.

"I know I'm early," Duncan says as we release our hold and step inside so I can shut the door – he closes it actually as he's nearer. "But I couldn't wait any longer."

We kiss and I so want to take him to my bedroom but I don't know what my mum's doing. Her reappearing, with or without Charles, during a moment of passion isn't something I want to think about so instead of leading Duncan upstairs, we go to the kitchen. "Cuppa or did you want to go out for something?" I ask.

"I fancy going out. I'd love you to myself but plenty of time tonight." He winks and I blush.

I feel warm again yet goosepimply like I'm cold. I'm nothing if not a whole little bundle of contradictions. Okay the aforementioned 'mass'.

A thought strikes me. "You've never been to the museum, have you?"

Duncan frowns. "The one in the market square?"

Tring has two museums. The most recent one, a local history, houses almost everything you can think of that's Tring-related. The other is the world-famous natural history, with close links to the Rothschilds, über fans of zebras, I think they even had them as pets. Now that would have been fun; taking Elliott to Tring Park and seeing how he'd react to black and white stripy horses. He's the world's biggest wuss and pretty much scared of anything that moves if it's bigger than him: horses, cows… probably very wise. He'll gladly chase anything that's smaller, although he tends to avoid cats. I think there's history there. A swipe or two.

"The zoological one near the park."

Duncan shakes his head.

Saturday's probably not the best time to go but it's not yet half term, we have two clear weeks until that so parents would probably wait until then to amaze, or horrify, their offspring.

"Does that appeal?"

Being a vet, it's a given that Duncan loves animals and although there's a slight hesitation, he grins, much like Elliott when confronted with a new squeaky toy. I've lost count of how many times I've been to the museum but not for a few years, since I took Izzy not long after we started working together. I don't know why it had never occurred to me to take Duncan. Maybe because the animals are dead? As it's near the town centre, we went to the local history museum as part of the 'never been here' before tour but the natural one is a bit outside, albeit only at the end of one of the roads, Akeman Street, that feeds off the high street.

"And," I add, "they have a café so we could go there first."

To this suggestion, he doesn't look so sure. "Could we do Costa?" I know exactly why. He loves children but not ones who have spent the past hour or two looking at magnificent exhibits and want to talk about them, at full volume because that's all children know, or run around pretending to be them. Costa is also opposite the bottom end of Akeman Street so an easy walk.

I smile. "Absolutely. And Buddy?"

We look at Buddy who's sniffing around the dining table, wagging his tail furiously as if he's on to something juicy. Hoovering is pretty much the only thing that my mum is religious about so I can't see there being anything to interest him but it keeps him busy.

"He'll be fine. We went to Bradlaugh Fields first thing and he watered one of your mum's roses when we got here."

Bradlaugh Fields, back in Northampton, is a huge former golf course, and Duncan always does the whole thing. What time he would have had to get up to do that and still get here for nine-ten doesn't bear thinking about. "I'll be quick then and get changed."

Duncan follows me upstairs and my smile broadens as he places one of his hands on my right bottom cheek. I sashay a little more pronounced as I climb each step. Buddy, thankfully, is still downstairs, oblivious, as I close the bedroom door.

Chapter 64 – Peace Disturbed

Despite my earlier reservations, Duncan and I surface from my bedroom an hour later, our peace undisturbed.

Buddy's lying on the landing, looking very neglected, but perks up when Duncan comes out.

I go along the landing into the bathroom and have a quick shower while, he tells me later, Duncan and Buddy go into the garden. Although close to Tring town centre, my mum has a proliferation of squirrels in her garden and Buddy would stay out there all day if he could but we bring him in and give him some long-lasting, even at Buddy's destruction, chews and toys to keep him occupied while we're out.

Costa is busy, as to be expected on a Saturday morning, but more adults than children and thankfully just chat rather than screaming. I'd love children of my own but, like Duncan, I feel other people's can be a handful. I figure it's why grandparents always seem happier than parents; because they get to give them back.

We have black coffees and a chocolate twist and almond croissant to share. Thanks to previous research, and www.9to5strength.com, I know the calorie content of almost everything (nearly four hundred and just over three fifty in today's choices) at Costa before we get there although each option has it conveniently on all the cards, as if treble figures starting with anything but a one wouldn't be scary, and am glad to have saved some calories on the milk, as if adding fifteen calories to a two-calorie drink really makes that much difference. Sometimes, doing what I do makes for a cluttered brain.

When we get to a table, away from the front door, and chatter, I cut the pastries in two; purposely smaller pieces for me and redistribute them on the two plates. Duncan looks at them then at me.

"What?" I say. "You have longer legs to fill." It's the first thing I think of to say. Half a twist and croissant in no way constitutes a meal so I don't need to be bothered calorie counting but I do have to weigh myself on Monday so I'll try to be good(ish) until then. From the next meal until then. I tend to wear leggings or tights so not so easy to judge when I've put on weight, but I can usually tell roughly.

When we're Costad out, we head up the road to the museum. Despite not having been there for ages, I don't expect it to have changed all that much and am astounded when, while the exhibits haven't, the building itself, inside anyway, feels very different. I don't remember it needing anything doing when I was there last, but it feels bigger, brighter, even more welcoming.

The lady greeting us as we enter is delightful. We buy a catalogue, mainly because we want to support the place as there's no admission charge, but also because Duncan doesn't have a copy and the one I have (probably in my mum's garage) is years old… although not that much, as I've said, changes.

I show Duncan my favourites: the huge and somewhat intimidating, especially to anyone young, polar bear, the baboon and his brightly coloured backside, and my absolute all-time, why I'd go there just for them: the Mexican dressed-up fleas.

"No!" Duncan exclaims while looking through the first of the two magnifying glasses, the 'man' in his white suit and hat carrying his bundle of twigs. "No! How can they…?" Duncan moves on to the 'woman' in her white and red dress and white pinny, carrying whatever it is she's carrying in her hands. "And they're from when?" He looks away and reads the accompanying narration. "1905. That's amazing."

"I know. Gives me goosebumps every time." I've not seen them yet but even knowing them as well as I do, I know they still will.

"How do they…?" Duncan repeats, going back to the 'man'. "It's… I'm…"

"I know," I say and smile. Right in front of my eyes, my thirty-two-year-old boyfriend is now seven. "There's nothing to top that, sadly, but further on are the animals you'll be more used to: the dogs, cats, horses, whales and so on."

"Oh yes, I often get whales brought in with poorly fins," he says, back to looking at the wife so he can't see me smiling.

We live in almost the furthest point away from the sea so the only time we get to see any kind of fish is in batter or breadcrumbs from our local chippy. Of course I know that whales are mammals rather than fish but the only water-based life we get near Northampton are ducks. "Do you ever get ducks brought in?"

He looks up. I repeat my question.

"Yes, occasionally. Not wild ones though. I go out to those. You know about Animals in Need and their swans." I nod. "They look after ducks and geese too. Anything that moves actually." He goes back to looking at the woman. "These are simply…"

"I know," I say and feel like I'm stuck on repeat mode.

We've realised that we should have come here earlier. They're open for three hours on a Sunday afternoon so we could do the whole thing again tomorrow but I'm sure, fabulous as this place is, that Duncan wouldn't want to spend his whole weekend here. For another weekend. I'm going home next weekend then Izzy's coming down for my final weekend so another time.

Duncan eventually tears himself away from the fleas and we move on, coming out into a corridor with a side room to our left.

The last time I visited, there was a photography exhibition. I remember being impressed rather than astounded but having a photographer for an uncle, I've seen some fabulous photographs. This time there's a craft exhibition, all still to do with the natural world, and I'm more impressed, the fabrics used in most cases incredibly ingeniously. There are patchwork frogs, mostly green but surprisingly some pink ones too, hedgehogs made of old pencils, and foxes made from what look like old hunting jackets. I love the irony. I don't realise until I read a notice on the way out of the dedicated room that none of the creators were older than fourteen. I'm as speechless as Duncan was with the fleas and want to have another look around but see that Duncan's already outside 'hunting' whales.

The domesticated animal area holds more sentiment for him and he looks almost choked.

We're both emotional as we go to leave… but not before he takes one more look at the fleas.

We get back to my mum's and there's a scene of carnage, with the only suspect looking very pleased with himself… and panting way too much. As soon as I see a ripped-up oblong of cellophane, I know what's happened.

"No!" I chase Buddy out the kitchen's rear door and into the garden, something he finds hilarious, then rush into the lounge. Sure enough, there's a gap on a shelf where a box of chocolates that Charles had given my mum earlier in the week had sat. She'd been saving it, she said, for the weekend but must have forgotten to take it with her as her car's not back yet. I look down and there's a trail of black and purple shredded cardboard from my feet to the sofa, and the only other evidence remaining of the chocolates is the plastic tray they came on. The saving grace is that it was a single layer rather than double. Not the whole hog that I would imagine Charles normally goes for.

Speaking of hogs, I look out the lounge patio door and there's Buddy, on the previously immaculate beige paving, trying, ultimately successfully, to regurgitate the aforementioned chocolates, although not as beautifully presented as Cadbury's would have liked. It's almost enough to put me off my tea.

Thanks to Buddy's indulgence, our planned evening of going out for a romantic dinner becomes another evening in front of the television. Neither Duncan nor I are hungry but instead snack on

Pringles, Doritos, cider and toasted teacakes. Needless to say, nothing that's been anywhere near a cocoa bean.

Other than the cereal, I've not eaten anything today that can be classed as a meal, especially at less than the requisite five hundred calories. I'm three articles ahead – all safely stored on the work server for Nathan to pick up whenever suits him, the tuning and retuning taking much of the week – so even if I don't eat anything sensible tomorrow, I'll still have a day in hand.

Our initial worry about the chocolate being so poisonous to Buddy proved to be unfounded. His artwork on the paving slabs – which Duncan cleared up, Buddy being his dog; I did offer, and think Duncan believed that I was sincere, I can be a great actress when I need to be – thankfully purging Buddy's system enough for him not to suffer any obvious lasting consequences. Duncan, at least, best placed to look after him.

We ensured Buddy had plenty of water and kept an eye on him. The panting soon dissipated, although he too had lost his appetite. Until the waft of the laden toaster persuades him otherwise but we didn't risk a repetition of earlier by giving him any human food.

When we're ready to go to bed, we bring Buddy's bed upstairs, together with his water bowl, a smaller bowl with a couple of dried biscuits and some newspaper laid underneath it, just in case.

When I've brushed my teeth, I pop downstairs for a final check of the doors and windows. I feel safer with Duncan staying but I'm still a little OCD like that. Having a dog, even though he's not technically mine, is another reassurance when I'm at Duncan's and it's good having them both here.

There's still no sign of Mum so I send her a quick message on WhatsApp and she replies almost immediately.

Yes fine thank you darling Charles is looking after me dont worry hes not an ex murderer

My mum text speaks as quickly as she sometimes in-person speaks, no pausing for punctuation. I'm hoping she means axe instead of ex because if he's not a former murderer it means he either wasn't or he still is. The fact that it's gone eleven and she's still alive is a good sign. The moon's a few days away so he's not a werewolf either… yet.

Chapter 65 – Somewhere In The Middle

Sunday 13th May

We're woken by a scratching at my bedroom door. "That'll be Buddy," Duncan mumbles, yawning and rubbing his eyes. He does know that you shouldn't do that – rub your eyes, not yawn; yawning is actively encouraged as it circulates blood around your body. Most people think it's air, and of course it is, but when we yawn, 'powerful stretching of the jaw increases blood flow in the neck, face, and head. The deep intake of breath during a yawn forces downward flow of spinal fluid and blood from the brain. Cool air breathed into the mouth cools these fluids.' I have webmd.com to thank for that little nugget.

If the scratching isn't Buddy I'd be worried but I don't say this either.

"I'll go," I say and feel like I'm a parent of a newborn baby whose crying has woken up both parents in the middle of the night. Not that it's the middle of the night as it's daylight outside so any time after five. I snatch a glance at my watch as I head for the door. 9:52. No wonder Buddy's scratching.

Buddy rushes in as I open the door and leaps on the bed. I'm not a huge fan of dogs on beds, especially ones who've been sick in the past few hours, but it's so cute seeing my two boys together. Buddy can't be that desperate as he's snuggled up next to Duncan and looks as if he's falling asleep. Duncan, on the other hand, was never really awake. Feeling a little like a green prickly fruit, I leave the pair alone and head downstairs to make some breakfast.

Although we vegged out on stodge last night, I'm surprisingly hungry. All the teacakes have gone, sorry Mother, but there are a couple of cinnamon and raisin bagels. Yum. I've not asked Duncan if he's hungry but we did work up a bit of an appetite. It would have been foolish not to, knowing my mother wasn't coming home.

I still have a silly grin on my face when Buddy comes padding through into the kitchen and whimpers by the back door. I'm torn between buttering bagels while they're still warm or risking a puddle, or worse, on the coir 'Hi. I'm Mat' mat. Although neither my mum nor I knows anyone called Mat, we thought it hilarious when we'd spotted it online when searching for some very elusive gin… as you do. Mat one, bagels zero.

I keep the door open and it's surprisingly warm for… I look at the microwave. 11:01. "Huh?" I look at my watch. 10:01. "Huh?" Then it dawns on me. My mum's lack of technology. The hour changed weeks ago so she must just leave it to be the same all year round, although when the hour goes back in October, it'll be two hours out, which doesn't make sense.

Buddy bounds in, looking the picture of health. He sniffs the air.

"Oh no." I turn to the toaster and there are two perfectly toasted but nearly cold bagels. The last two bagels. I've tried to reheat bagels before but they only go hard. I could try in the microwave but they go soft. "Someone invent a machine for somewhere in the middle," I say in Buddy's direction and he tilts his head.

I take coffee and the bagels upstairs. Hopefully if Duncan's still sleepy and eats while drinking his coffee, he won't notice the difference in temperature. The butter hasn't melted but hopefully he won't mind that either. I was tempted to add jam but that would just be weird, given that they've already been flavoured with the cinnamon and raisins. And no, of course, nothing about me is weird.

We have a relaxing what's left of the morning and decide, when he appears to be fully recovered, to take Buddy for a long walk.

"Tring reservoir or…" Somewhere else of that magnitude escapes me. It shouldn't as I know the area well enough to string off a load of different places but it's my favourite, especially as the Bluebells Tearooms (I remembered it's not just a café) welcomes dogs. Considering we're a dog-loving nation, supposedly, so many places don't. If this café, sorry… tearooms, can welcome dogs, why can't everywhere? Because people are irresponsible. My brain whirrs, wondering how I could get an article on this matter into my column. Because dog walking is healthy. Ding.

"Hello?"

I've been staring at the dining table, at the ladybird not going anywhere. "Sorry."

"You're away with Tinkerbell again."

I do that a lot. Walter Donna Mitty. "Yes?"

"Tring reservoir or… you said. That sounds fine by me. There's a café there, isn't there?"

I'm tempted to say tearooms but just nod.

"Excellent." Duncan pushes back his chair and stands. I look up as my favourite man in the world looks down at me and blows me a kiss. "I do love you, Donna Dawn Diana Evans DDDE."

I'd forgotten that in a moment of cider-fuelled craziness, I'd blurted out my whole name, complete with the royally bestowed acronym. My paternal grandmother was Dawn, and very much a morning person.

I can't help laughing. I stand and give him a really tight, really warm hug.

The weather's kind to us as we walk round, or half round, the reservoir. Being a Sunday, it's quite busy and Buddy's in his element as he meets other dogs. There's one in particular, a black long-haired something or other – Duncan suggested a schnauzer of some kind – that does a western-type standoff. Buddy, the supposedly white (and tan) good guy – we know otherwise – at one end with the black baddie at the other, neither budging until the baddie's owner claps her hands and her dog's brought out of its trance.

They make a run for each other, almost skidding to a halt as their noses nearly meet, then do their rotational dance, sniffing wherever they feel the need to sniff. We do the equivalent; a polite nod, smile, and 'Hello' before going on our way, leaving Buddy to follow when he's done.

The next dog we meet needs no introduction. He sees me before I see him and I prepare myself for attack.

"Elliott!" I squeak as I'm pushed slightly backwards by his over-eager welcome. My aunt and uncle are still dots in the distance. After I've made a fuss, Elliott finally realises I have company and goes to greet Duncan who he's met several times but his welcome is naturally less enthusiastic though still double figures on the Elliott scale.

"Hello, boy. How are you?" Elliott's tail wags furiously but more for spotting Buddy, who I see is finally catching up with us as I turn round. I'm hoping he hasn't 'done' anything as we've not been paying attention but as he's a few feet away, he does the honours, seemingly undistracted by Elliott sniffing around. Duncan trudges forwards, green biodegradable bag at the ready.

My aunt and uncle have almost caught up by the time we're back on our way and we're all reunited as we meet. I've resisted the urge to do the usual 'Cathy and Heathcliff' with my uncle and he doesn't seem to have missed it, engrossed in a 'lively' conversation with my aunt all the way along.

After exchanged 'Hello's, I continue. "I should have called, or called in, to see if you wanted to join us, or to offer to take Elliott at least."

"Oh, don't worry," my aunt says. "We wouldn't have been there. We left early this morning to go and photograph a chicken."

"As you do," Duncan says and smiles.

"And how are you?" my uncle asks Duncan.

"Really good, thank you. I'm enjoying being somewhere else at the weekend." He looks at me with the kind of expression that he's said something wrong but relaxes when I blow him a kiss. I feel reassured that I'm not the only one to be insecure at times.

"We're just off to the Bluebells if you fancy joining us," I suggest, looking at my uncle then Duncan who winks, then back to my uncle.

"Great idea," he says, "but we've only just got here and we don't want to gatecrash your party."

Duncan and I laugh. "No problem," Duncan says. "The more the merrier."

The dogs in the meantime seem to have had enough of each other and are looking up at their respective owners as if to ask 'Can we go now?'

"We'll be there a while, I think," I say, looking at Duncan again who nods. "Join us when you're done, if you have time."

My uncle smiles, my aunt nods, and we go our separate ways.

"Did they seem okay to you?" I ask Duncan as we venture on.

"Erm… yes."

"Oh okay."

He stops and turns to face me. "Did they not to you?"

I shrug. "I suppose. A little distracted."

"Maybe they were deep in a really interesting conversation."

"Mmm…" It looked more than that but I remain silent, not something I'm used to.

We've almost finished our open sandwiches, two different variants so we have half each, when my aunt and uncle, and mad thing, join us. While my uncle orders, my aunt comes over with Elliott and sits at the neighbouring table, allowing Elliott enough room on his expandable lead to make a fuss of me, or more accurately vice versa. It's as if we've not seen each other for years. "Hello, long lost dog," I say as he rolls onto his back and kicks one of his hind legs as if I haven't got the hint quickly enough for a tummy rub. His, not mine, sadly.

I can't resist asking the question that's been bugging me. "Is everything all right?"

My aunt brightens a little. "Oh, fine, you know."

I don't really until she tells me but don't say so. I do a lot of not saying sos.

"Pat, your uncle…" As if I need that explaining. "…wants to get another dog. One of his clients is emigrating and needs a new home but I've pointed out that Elliott's enough of a handful."

My aunt and uncle have had two dogs at the same time before and while they've worked from home for almost as long as I can remember, and there are two of them so one dog each when they're out, they've decided since hitting sixty that one is enough. Although Elliott is smashing, I'm inclined to agree.

"They *do* get on really well though," my aunt continues as if persuading herself. "And we can afford to have two." Yep, she's going to say 'yes'. "But getting on well for an hour or two doesn't necessarily mean getting on well living together."

I look at Duncan who smiles but I wonder if the same can be said about us.

"How long have you got to decide?"

"They're not moving for a couple of months but they obviously want to know the dog's going to be happy before they go."

I frown but don't know why. "What kind of dog is it?"

"A very small, very scruffy Yorkie."

My frown lifts. "Oh, that's okay. Not a proper dog." I clamp my hand to my mouth. I really should engage brain before opening mouth.

My aunt laughs so heartily that Buddy and Elliott look at her and tilt their heads. "That's what Pat said."

As if on cue, he joins us. "Is she telling you about our dilemma?"

"She is. I wasn't sure but it doesn't sound as if it wouldn't be too bad. And if they know each other already and get on well…"

"I know, right."

Duncan goes to order some more coffees for us and the conversation's changed to holidays by the time he returns.

"We've not planned anything yet," I explain as Duncan sits.

"No. We should though. Once you're back in situ."

"We should. I've got a fair chunk of days to use before the end of the year, most of the five weeks actually."

"Ooh…" Duncan looks at his watch, points it at me and taps it.

"It's a watch."

He sticks out his tongue. "Tesco shuts at four."

"Ooh, yes. I forgot." I turn to my aunt and uncle. "Sorry but we need to buy food. We're eating my mum out of hers, and Duncan's cooking."

"No problem," my aunt says while my uncle's taking a sip of his Earl Grey.

The rest of the day passes off uneventfully. We do pop into Tesco on the way back to my mum's to buy food for supper. Despite my job, Duncan's a far better cook than me and he's intrigued by my mum's high-tech cooker, bought because it was pretty. It's certainly impressive with all its chrome buttons and dials. I've never used it either so I'm no help other than knowing where all the dishes and implements are, and getting the table ready.

Buddy, in the meantime, is happy with a new Kong that Duncan brought with him – the black less-destructible version – and hasn't worked out that his chances of getting the treats would be greatly improved if he tried to get them out of the bigger end. Beagles, unlike border collies, aren't known for their intelligence. It keeps me amused while Duncan's busy. We talk while he cooks, before, during and after actually, and never seem to run out of things to say.

"So you're all for them getting that dog," he says as he offers me a spoonful of homemade carbonara sauce to taste.

"Gorgeous. My favourite."

"I know." He smiles.

Forget the pasta and garlic bread, I could eat him right here and now. I blush.

"What?"

"Nothing. Just silly thoughts."

"Donna Dawn Diana Evans. Queen of the silly thoughts."

Yes, that's me.

"And I wouldn't change a thing."

No, nor would I… apart from living with him, marrying him, having his two-point-four children.

Chapter 66 – Detail Schmeetail

It's Sunday evening and Duncan's been gone less than ten minutes when the front door opens and Mum appears, grinning so widely that it probably hurts. It certainly hurts to see, despite her having fabulous teeth.

"Oh… kay. What's up?" I ask as she takes off her jacket.

The grin lessens, but only to allow her to speak. "What do you mean?"

"You're unusually… weird."

"Me?" she asks, fluttering her eyelashes. Yes, something's definitely up.

It's then I get a flash of something on her left hand as she hangs her jacket on the first of five hooks in the hall.

"Oh my god! Mum!"

The grin's back. "I know!" She thrusts her hand out towards me and waggles her ring finger. It's an impressive rock. Diamond solitaire, very traditional, on a plain silver band. Not that it'll be silver, more platinum or white gold at least if Charles has anything to do with it – and I'm hoping he had everything, or almost everything, to do with it. I hardly know him but he seems nice. Not sure yet if he's 'dad' material but as long as Mum's happy and judging by her grin… It wouldn't have been a decision she'd taken lightly and it's not like they're getting married tomorrow, given that there's still a wife in the picture.

"But isn't he still married?"

"Pfff…" She swipes her unringed hand as if it's a mere detail. "Detail schmeetail."

"Uh huh. That would explain why you've been away the whole weekend."

Everyone's getting married, moving in, having babies. Not my mum for the latter obviously. I'm not normally a person for self-pity but for some reason I have been lately. I seem to have lost my 'bounce', as Izzy would put it.

"We thought you'd like the space."

"Thank you." I'm grateful yet jealous at the same time. Duncan and I have talked about having a life together and it's only been a year, but here's my mum, having met Charles relatively recently, way way ahead of us. Too soon? Is she more fearless because she's older? I must admit I've worried about when she gets to the point that she needs help. Not for me, of course I'd do more, but for the day-to-day things that I can't do an hour, forty-five minutes on a good day, away.

Listen to me, she's only sixty-six, not eighty-six. It's something to worry about twenty years away.

Even though I don't feel like it, I put on a broad smile. "I'm thrilled for you. Really I am." I feel like Judi Dench in *Jack and Sarah*, another of my top-twenty films except that it's daughter disapproving of mother rather than mother disapproving of son. It all comes good in the end so I needn't worry. So why am I? Because I'm Donna and it's what I do. "As long as he makes you happy." As soon as I've said it I realise it's a stupid thing to say because she's been the Tigger of the family for the past few weeks. That's *my* job.

"So... you've eaten?" she asks, being the eternal nurturer.

"Yes, thanks. Duncan did spaghetti carbonara."

"Ooh, your favourite."

"It is."

"He's a good 'un."

"He is."

Mum puts her hand out and touches my arm. "A keeper."

"I plan to."

"Good. Great. Isn't it wonderful that we've both found someone to be happy with?"

It is. It really is so what's stopping me being happy?

You, Donna, you.

It's late so we don't stay up long but I get the full rundown of the proposal at the truly romantic setting of Tring Park's summerhouse, which I'd forgotten existed and would certainly have picked for my leap year proposal had I not forgotten and Charles not beaten me to it so couldn't copycat.

"Charles dropped his handkerchief and while going to pick it up, went down on one knee, his right, as is tradition. I thought he was having a stroke or heart attack or something so I knelt too to see if he was all right. He then got up so I'd get up but had to drop the handkerchief again to get down on one knee... again. Then I knew something was up but never thought for a second that he'd be doing what he was trying to do." Mum takes a mouthful of tea but winces as it's still too hot. She spits most of it back. Very ladylike.

"I thought maybe he wears contact lenses, even though he'd told me he has forty-forty vision, even better than twenty-twenty, he said but I think he was joking. So he's on his knee because I thought one of his contact lenses had fallen out and I offer to find it for him when he puts his hand in his right pocket and pulls out a little red velvet box." She points to her handbag as if to indicate that that's where it is now. "And of course I go nuts. Good nuts but he doesn't know it's good nuts and looks gutted but I'm squealing a 'Yes! Yes!' before he's even asked the question. Then I realise he's not asked the question so I go quiet and he asks the question and I say yes again and he gets up and we hug and I hold out my hand to look at the ring. I'd only just taken off your dad's wedding ring – I'm sorry but I didn't think you'd mind seeing as I'm dating again."

I shake my head. It's hard to hear but it's been so long.

She continues. "So I guess that told Charles that I was free again."

"Except he's not."

She bats her hand. "It's a formality. We're in no hurry. Next year, the year after, it doesn't matter when. These things take time to organise anyway. Tring Mansion's probably booked up for months."

"Tring Park Mansion?"

"Yes, you know, on the hill."

"The ballet school."

"Yes, but Charles knows the principal. Stephan something."

Of course he does. "They do weddings there?"

"Not officially, I don't think, but Charles reckons they could get a licence, just for the day. It'll have to be outside term time, in the summer holiday probably."

"It is a lovely setting, not that I've been to the school, but it's in the grounds of the park, isn't it?"

Mum nods.

"So when did he propose?"

"Yesterday morning. Today would have been better, weather wise, but it wasn't that cold at least."

"Yesterday? You should have messaged me."

"It's not something you message. I had to tell you face to face."

"Or let me find out when you're hanging up your coat."

Mum blushes. "Yes, sorry about that but I couldn't just come in, flashing the ring, and say 'Hey, darling. Look what I've got.'"

I wouldn't have put it past her.

"He won't let me take it off so you would have seen it sooner or later." Later would have been fine.

Now I feel guilty. At least they're taking their time. They have to; he's not divorced yet. "But he's applied for a divorce, hasn't he?"

When she doesn't reply, I continue. "Isn't it a bit weird, to even give you a ring when someone else is wearing one too?"

"Oh I don't think she'd be wearing a ring. They're separated."

Of course she wouldn't. Of course they are. Still living under the same roof.

"Have they sold the house yet?"

"Erm… I don't know. I didn't ask."

"And will Charles move in here?"

"Erm… I don't know. I presume so in the meantime. Or we'll buy somewhere together."

That does hurt. My dad lived here. My dad was happy here. Now someone else is going to be happy here. I have to let go, make space for a new… not dad, Charles can never be 'dad' but he can be Charles, my mum's husband.

"I'm tired." And defeated. "I'm off to bed." To think. No, I need to stop thinking. Everything's going to be wonderful. It is. It really is.

Chapter 67 – PMA

Monday 14th May

I feel so much better when I wake the next morning. I slept surprisingly well, even though I'm sure my brain would have been doing overtime. My doubts and self-pity seem to have vanished and I'm all together feeling much more positive. I have someone who loves, no, adores me, as does my mum because I don't think Charles would have jumped from one ship to another without giving it, me, a lot of thought because he'd be taking me on too. Now I have the image of someone walking the plank in a *Pirates of the Caribbean* movie.

I already miss having Duncan and even Buddy to wake up to but we're almost halfway through the month and the first two weeks have gone incredibly quickly so there's no reason why the next three wouldn't.

I throw myself into my work especially with my mother being even more busy squeezing Charles into her already-packed schedule, which I hope she keeps up as she loves the clubs she belongs to. Have him join her, probably. I can imagine them side by side, learning to play the guitar together with Bernard and Greta bemused by their 'talent'.

It's funny seeing my articles surrounded by Hemel news. Even though I have two reports in hand, I'm going to take my third week more seriously; have healthier, less carb-heavy, lunches. I'm back home this weekend so it'll be lovely not having to think about what I'm going to eat. But then remind myself that I'm still supposed to have a low-calorie meal each day so would use those two reports in one go, one weekend.

After last Wednesday, I don't mind at all being on my own during the day. Here, I love wandering around the town, along by the river, being in the fresh air so it doesn't matter if someone (James) isn't free – Leah has said she'd always be happy to escape. It's too wet to go out today though – it's like a whole week's worth has fallen in a few hours.

It's my evening with Nathan and we head to The Paper Mill at Apsley. The website said it is a 'great modern pub' and while it's an old:new conversion, it does have a contemporary feel to it. We pass outside tables, typical brown wood slatted square tables and chairs, but it's not quite warm enough so we head inside.

We're right by the canal. I love anything watery but then that reminds me of Duncan's bath and I get nostalgic. Four days' time and I'll, we'll be *right* there.

Inside is deceptively massive with high seating in the main open-plan area and lower tables and standard chairs at the sides with a rustic black and wood staircase leading upstairs, presumably to the function room mentioned on their website. It's busy but there are plenty of seats so we go to the bar to order drinks before deciding what we want to eat.

Being a Fuller's pub, Nathan's in his element with the choice of ales, and wiggles his whole body, Elliott-like, as he flits his pointed finger between London Pride, Frontier and Cornish Orchards. Although he's not from London, I have a sneaking suspicion I know which one he'll plump for.

"This goes perfectly with steak," the barman, Matt with two 't's, says, tapping the London Pride. That seals the deal, I feel. I used to be a poet… No, never written any poetry. It scares me.

One of Matt's colleagues, and as it turns out, our waitress, Dawn – great name – is lovely and couldn't do enough for us. With her guidance, and a dietary version of their main menu, I choose the pan-fried chicken breast, parsley potatoes, and spinach, sadly minus the chorizo butter, all of which, the menu explains, contains lupin, milk and mustard, none of which I'm allergic to. Not that I'm actually allergic to anything. Lucky me.

Nathan does indeed opt for the steak and all the trimmings. Dawn asks where we'll be sitting and we point at a free table. She nods as if she knows what table number it is and Nathan gets out the company credit card from his wallet to pay what we've ordered so far. It's under £30 so he waves his card, the card, over the swivel handset and it beeps.

"That's all done for you," Dawn says, smiling, and we thank her and head for the table we'd chosen which, fortunately, is still available so we avoid an awkward 'we saw this first' situation or asking Dawn to change the number because we were too slow.

"She's nice," Nathan says as we sit.

I look at Dawn then at our surroundings. It's ironic, given where we work, that the mill is (was) the oldest mill in the UK, something I have to get into my report… article. Ooh, I must also mention, not that I don't always say where the restaurants are so my (Veronica's) readers can look them up, that it's on Stationers Place (no apostrophe I note so stationers, the people, plural).

"Earth calling Donna…"

I look back at Nathan. "Sorry. Just curious."

"Mental notes for your article?" He taps his head. "I get it." He does. "So tell me about the past week," he says, his eyes wide, and he's wiggling again.

So I do, and as I've got to the weekend (some details more salacious than others, which he L… O… V… E… S-es! – his enunciation) when our food arrives. It looks dee-licious – my enunciation this time. Some places you go, although not this month, have these staged shots of the dishes on their brochures but when it arrives it looks smaller, flatter, something else 'er', but these look even nice… er.

We're part way through when the manager, Rob, comes over. I know his name, and what he does, from his badge but he introduces himself anyway. He asks if everything's okay. We're both eating but I swallow and say a hearty, "Yes, thank you. This…" I point to my plate, "is gorgeous." Rob laughs so we laugh, Nathan's even more raucous than Rob's or mine but then Nathan's the more wildly spirited of the two of us. I don't know how spirited Rob is, of course.

"Can I get you any more drinks?" Rob asks, pointing at Nathan's almost-empty glass.

"Go on then," he says, swallowing, "I'll have another half of London Pride."

Rob looks at me and I still have most of my pineapple juice and lemonade so wave a hand at the offer of a replacement. "Thanks anyway."

Rob nods, leaves and returns a few minutes later with Nathan's drink.

After a couple of coffees, Nathan pays for the extra drinks with the company credit card and I leave a five-pound tip, more the 'norm' with two of us eating and Dawn's worth every penny. The whole place is worth every penny.

We go to stand when Nathan suggests a stroll along the river. I squeal. He laughs and suggests we pop to the loos first. "Great idea," I say and we go arm in arm, like a scene from *The Wizard of Oz*, although we're a couple of people missing. And I wonder if Rob and Dawn would like to join us but that makes me laugh so Nathan laughs, even though he doesn't really know why, just that we're acting like children, which is wonderful.

As I do what needs to be done, I wonder our roles. Dorothy (Gale, I remember for some reason) wasn't overly tall but then she was only sixteen, or rather Judy Garland was only sixteen, at the time, half my age so had some growing to do.

Anyway, so I'm Dorothy, Nathan has to be… My first thought is the lion but there's nothing cowardly about Nathan. Plus he already has the biggest of hearts. I recall the tin man crying and while Nathan may be soft, he doesn't strike me as an easy cryer. The scarecrow wants a brain so I'm really torn as Nathan's clever.

We emerge at the same time and link arms again as we leave the premises, saying a rather loud "bye!" to Matt who's oblivious as he's serving a rather irate-looking female customer. Poor him.

It's cooler than when we arrived, but our stroll by the river is calming, although in Nathan's company, I'm pretty much there already. We talk about life within the commuter belt, how house prices in our two areas are staggeringly different yet food (and other essentials from major supermarkets isn't) isn't, something that mystifies us both.

Nathan and I hug by our cars – we'd driven in convoy as it's an eight-minute drive from work. He's already told me he lives in Nash Mills, the next town (it might even be a village) on in Watford's direction and the M25 side of where we are. My mum and I used to go to car boot sales in a field at Nash Mills and I paid for my first car from the proceeds of selling some of my stuff. It wasn't much more than three hundred pounds (three twenty-five, I think) which I made in two sales, back in the days where people would pay way more than they do now. The likes of Poundland and 99p stores haven't helped. Not that I sell at car boot sales anymore. Haven't done for years. It's much easier to give things to charity shops. Take a bag of things in, come out with two. The ultimate recycling.

"It's been fun," Nathan says.

"It has." It feels like we won't be seeing each other again, like Rhett and Scarlett, not that we know whether they did ever see each other again. Unless Nathan knows something I don't though, it'll be business as usual tomorrow.

I head back towards Hemel but turn left and pop on the A41 bypass. It's then a fifteen-minute max easy peazy to my mum's and the car's barely warm when I pull it onto her deserted, of course, driveway.

It's book club night tonight; a Stephen King, apparently, which seemed like an odd choice but being a fan of his short story collections, his appeal is wide.

With everything that's been going on, I head straight to bed. The hall light's usually on when Mum's out but she'd obviously gone before it got dark, not difficult being mid-May, and forgotten to switch it on for when she, or I, got home. So I do that and plod upstairs. With fourteen days down, seventeen to go, I wonder when I'm past the mid-point, whether I'll get ploddier or have more of a spring in my step. I smile as I think of Elliott. While it has been known for me to body-wiggle, he's the master.

Knowing there'll be an easy article to write after tonight, I decide on taking tomorrow morning off and collecting a certain hound. With influences like Nathan and my aunt and uncle's dog, I'm going to view the rest of the month with renewed optimism. PMA. Positive Mental Attitude. The Paper Mill at Apsley.

As my head touches the pillow and I pull the duvet up to my neck, I smile, and my thoughts drift between the wiggling pair, Duncan and his bath, and it's microseconds before sleep takes over.

Chapter 68 – Delighted To Be Going Somewhere

Tuesday 15th May

Elliott is available for (free) 'hire' and is, of course, delighted to be going somewhere. Having enjoyed the walk at Apsley, I decide to return, although we only get as far as Berkhamsted as I remember there's a lovely walk along the canal there, behind Waitrose and a small-but-usually-space-available car park.

It's a risk bringing Elliott somewhere like this because there are so many distractions but I keep him on his expandable lead and while there are moments of frustration, for both of us, we have a whale of a time. I frown at the thought and google the expression while Elliott takes a particularly long sniff at a very ordinary-looking bush.

I scroll down past some 'Whale of a Time' clothing and the next few entries are for the meaning rather than origination so I add 'origin' to my search. Varsity.co.uk tells me that: a dictionary of American student slang by Willard C. Gore records 'whale' in 1895 as "a person who is a prodigy either physically or intellectually", or "something exceptionally large", giving the example "a whale of a time" to demonstrate the phrase's "jolly" connotations.

The lead's tugging, or rather Elliott at the end of it is, and I look up to see he's spotted something moving. There are no ducks, thankfully, but there's another dog, a shih tzu, coming over one of the bridges. Although I work full time, I'd love to have a dog because there's no doubt it makes us all more sociable but remind myself that should I move in with Duncan, Buddy would be mine too.

I should offer to have him one day when I'm not working and Duncan has to. Some Donna:dog bonding.

Elliott and I walk towards the bridge and the two dogs do their dog:dog bonding sniff twirl, during which time the shih tzu's owner and I do our own little dance, trying not to get the leads entangled.

"Sorry," the woman, a lady in her seventies I'd guess, a little older than my mum, says despite her dog, Priscilla, being the less enthusiastic one of the two. I can't say I blame her.

"Not a problem at all," I say as I weave the blue plastic end of Elliott's lead through Priscilla's cord.

The woman and Priscilla continue behind us as we walk in the opposite direction, far easier to go our separate ways, even if we'd not wanted to. Me not wanting to. Elliott would go anywhere anytime, just like the Milk Tray advert. Or was it Cinzano. Anyway…

We do a huge loop and end up back at the car, a mere five minutes before our ticket runs out. I read somewhere that you're allowed ten minutes' grace but I'm grateful I didn't need it.

I pop Elliott back to my aunt and uncle's, decline the tempting offer of a cup of tea as I have to be getting back to work but do accept a brownie wrapped in a Christmas red, white and green napkin. They have the same set every year and I imagine a big box of them up in the loft, from which they remove a handful every now and then. It would make a perfect nest for mice, I think as I make a fuss of Elliott and say a final, for now, adieu.

What's left of the afternoon goes quickly, with my articles and emails up to date.

Tuesdays are dinner with Frank, and boy is he on form. His wife, Frankie, it turns out, has won a trip to the Bahamas and they've already booked to go mid-June. Not being very good at geography at school, I asked him whether it's going to be warm there.

"Thirty-two during the day, twenty at night." Yes, very nice.

They're both sun worshippers, which I would never have guessed as he doesn't look like he picks up a tan but what he overproduces in melanin, apparently, Frankie makes up for though she has to be careful.

"She has this huge…" Frank spread his arms, nearly knocking into a waiter walking by, "sun hat. Takes almost the entire suitcase." That's our Frank, the quiet dramatist.

Despite Frank's comment about Nando's last week, The Plough at Leverstock Green is our chosen destination, a Great British Inn chain this time so assured of quality and it doesn't disappoint. Google described it as 'spacious venue with a light modern interior serving a range of drinks and British pub grub' and Messrs Page, Brin and co. aren't wrong.

With a choice of 'balanced, nutritious and tasty traditional British food', we both go for their carvery's Tuesday Sunday roast: lamb for me (which they only do on Tuesdays for some reason so I'm especially lucky), and too-red-for-my-liking twenty-one day aged mature British beef for Frank. I could almost imagine the meat twitch. Ew.

Even though it's not supposed to go on lamb, I avoid the horseradish, which is gutting as I love it. That's more for face than calories as it only has twenty-one per tablespoon (nutrionix.com). calorieking.com disputes this and suggests twenty-five pre *tea*spoon, although it uses Heinz's as an example. Either way, I'd use a ladle which would be half my calories for the whole dish. I do however have a smidge of mint sauce which nutrionix says seventeen for a tablespoon. Calorieking agrees, albeit at sixteen. I only know all this because I've done more than one article on sauces, them being a largely unknown factor in some diets going wrong. Sauces are just flavoured water, right? <Cue Family Fortunes 'uh uh' buzzer>

"So why did you… or was it Frankie who chose the Bahamas?"

Frank swallows his mouthful of Yorkshire Pudding, probably not Aunt Bessie's but home (Plough) made. He blushes and I don't think it's because of the savoury 'pudding'. "We went there on our honeymoon."

"Sweet." And it is. They've only been together five years so presumably married a year or two after that but as I'm thinking it, Frank answers my unasked question.

"This time last year."

"Oh really?"

"It took a while for Frankie to go out with me," he explains. "She'd not long lost Wyatt, her husband, and really wasn't looking for anyone else, she said. Dancing though brings you close and well, we did." He blushes again and points at his food as if there's something spicy on it as an excuse. "It took another couple of years before she'd move in with me, a year after that for her to wear my ring…"

As he's talking, I'm thinking how romantic it is, yet it reminds me of a song about unrequited love. I can't remember the title or who sung it but remember a reference to Johnny wearing her ring. Or her wearing his. Or someone else wearing it. No, it's a blank.

Frank stopped to eat so I've not missed anything he's said. "So," he continues, "we're going back to where we got married, the beach. Our witnesses were a couple we'd met the day before. It wasn't spur of the moment but neither of us have children or parents or siblings so…"

"No one important to share the day." As I say it, it sounds really sad but it doesn't seem to bother him. He's still smiling. And clearly in love. I naturally think of Duncan and I do honestly feel for him what Frank must feel for Frankie. Duncan's my world.

As I drive home, I think about that. We've not messaged for a few hours, not since I got to work, so it's long overdue. Absence is definitely making my heart grow fonder.

For all the thought that the distraction of James isn't helping, I think it is because I'm resisting. Have resisted. Will resist. How many days down with how many to go? Oh boy.

Chapter 69 – The Us That Isn't Us

Wednesday 16th May

I make my lazy way into work (mid-morning) but no one seems to bat their proverbial eyelids at my lateness except for James. Of course. Not that he remarks at it but he does notice me walking in his direction (I have to, to get to my desk) and goes to stand. I don't know whether he was going to anyway but I shake my head so he sits. After thinking about him and Duncan last night, or rather him vs Duncan, it's made me even more resolute to hold my ground.

Regardless of whether he's having trouble at home, that's no excuse for him hitting on me, especially when he knew I was living, practically living with someone else. Someone I adore and who adores me; Duncan told me so during a rather heated… in a good way… FaceTime last night. Needless to say my mum wasn't there so we had free reign. I'm blushing now just thinking about it. Him. Not James. No, definitely not…

"Oh. Hi, James." He's walking towards my desk, looking all sexy and… ugly, he looks ugly with those shimmering almond eyes and – *Married, Donna, he's M… A… R… R…*

"Donna…" He's looking serious as he sits in my, Veronica's, his sister's not wife's, visitor chair. "I was wondering if you'd like to come out to lunch with me. No strings. Just friends. Colleagues." His eyes tell a different story. They're saying 'more strings than a harp', 'as just friends as all those movies about friends who end up together… *When Harry Met Sally* just friends'.

I take a sip of my coffee and almost choke as I recall the scene in the café where Meg Ryan has a fake orgasm and the woman near her says 'I'll have whatever she's having', or something like that.

"Just colleagues," I confirm as I ignore whatever his eyes are saying about those.

He smiles a Colgate toothpaste smile. No, it's a whatever's classier than Colgate. Arm and Hammer. Sorry, Colgate. There's nothing wrong with you it's just that– "Do you have somewhere in mind?" I ask so I can prepare, google it, to have something to talk about; the building's or company's history for instance, instead of about 'us' that isn't 'us'.

He sticks out his chiselled chin in thought. "Nando's?"

I'm due to go out with Greta tonight and providing she chooses, we choose, somewhere that can cater for my 'project', I can let all hell go loose, so to speak, this lunchtime. I recall passing Haldi a couple of weeks ago – it seems sooo much longer than that, but think an Indian would be too much for lunch, which is a shame because it looks really nice.

I nod pathetically then cough, straighten more in my seat, which seems to surprise him as he's backed off a little. *Great work, Donna*! "That would be nice." There, just a 'nice'. An insipid non-committal, other than lunch, 'nice'. Poor 'nice'. What did it ever do to the world to be labelled as insipid?

"Great," he says, standing. "See you in a few minutes."

Huh?

When he and his Levi 501s have 'left the building' (the area around my desk), I look at my watch. 12:13. How did that happen? I arrived mid-morning. No later than eleven… Okay, maybe a little later than eleven, and now it's already 12:13.

At twelve thirty on the dot, so he doesn't have to come looking for me and make it obvious, I slink my way to his desk. He's ready and oh too eager to go to lunch. He resembles the Duracell bunny and it makes me nervous. The coughing and standing straighter worked last time so I do it again.

"You getting another cold?" he asks as he joins me.

"Erm, no. Not that I know of," I whimper and feel my shoulders constrict.

"After you," he says and waves his hand in that annoyingly gallant way he has. I'm not wearing jeans, I have a pretty floral dress on – it's the middle of May after all, so he wouldn't be looking at my bum but my dress would still sashay. I therefore walk down the aisle, taking small steps but only end up feeling like a Mummy… and not the Yummy type but more the Egyptian type.

"You okay?" he asks from too close a distance behind me.

"Yep." I half expect him to touch me but he at least is savvy enough to know that would constitute as sexual harassment in the workplace. Even so, I can almost feel his hot sexy breath on my neck.

There are double doors in front of us and I don't want to slow down and certainly not stop in case the gap between us gets any closer so I swerve instead and turn, only to find he stopped a while ago. Him and his hot sexy imagined breath.

"Sorry," he says. "Forgot the credit card. I'll meet you downstairs."

"Okay," I whimper and leave him to it.

Owen's not on the phone so we chat. I've not got as far as downstairs when James reappears and although I've enjoyed Owen talking about everything other than Greta but seeing a Greta-shaped twinkle in his eyes, I wish I had, otherwise James and I would have a nearly-conjoined-at-the-back foray to the front door.

He stops to drop off some post so I use that as an excuse to make a bolt for it but feel rather foolish as it highlights the fact that I don't want to be near him. Yet we're going to lunch together and

James knows that, of course, as does Owen because it was the first thing I said to him while (not) waiting for James.

When will this month end? *Two weeks and two days, Donna.* Gulp.

James is a perfect gentleman (or has taken my hints) and is companionably distant. It's still work hours so there are no come-ons, no innuendos, no pretty much anything other than politeness. We don't quite talk about the weather but it would be next on the agenda. We don't talk about Callie, although Veronica's mentioned but only in relation to me covering her.

"I'm enjoying it all, yes, thank you," I say as if I'm being interviewed for a job between bites of chicken, dipped in the peri-peri sauce I missed last time. Unwisely or not, we're sharing half a chicken but that's all we're sharing, other than a bench seat, but we're managing not to get close to each other. Despite having held the door for me, he went to the table first and took the bench. I deliberated whether to sit opposite, ideal except I'd then have to look at him, and decided not as the long seat did look more comfortable. Risking him edging closer, I opted for that and so far he's behaved.

Sometimes I wonder if I'm imagining all this attention but then he does indeed move closer.

"I've… I'm er, going to have a look at the sauces," I blurt and get up, taking my bag with me. Of course he's not going to steal it and I *could* walk back to the office should he abandon me.

Seeing as I have my bag with me and it doesn't matter if the chicken cools any, I go to the ladies. That way it looks like it was an intended visit with the sauce happening to be on the route back. Had I not mentioned the sauces.

I pick up a coconut and lemon sauce bottle from the selection and take it back to the table. Needless to say I sit opposite. I'm sure his arms are long enough to reach my knees but we're on a runway from the front to the sauces and cutlery so I wouldn't be able to push my chair back.

"You okay?" he asks, putting a slab of chicken in his mouth. Even doing that looks sexy, although there's a globule of sauce – he's on XX Hot Peri-Peri, of course. Everything about him is extra hot – threatening to drop and I thank Mr Newton for discovering gravity except it doesn't and the whole thing disappears between his luscious lips. James's, not Isaac's.

"Yes, thanks." I try to make it sound breezy but it comes out as a croak. I clear my throat and he removes a tissue from his jeans front pocket. Not a hint of blue fluff. He offers me the tissue but I shake my head. "I'm good, thanks."

Without agreeing or otherwise, he returns the tissue and takes another perfect mouthful of chicken.

"We should be heading back," I say when it's clear we're done. And we are done. We're more than done. We're overcooked in a dad's barbeque kind of way… except my dad. He was the only person I knew who could get everything just right, all at the same time. He was a legend. A legend who wouldn't have approved of James. But that was because Dad adored my mum, adored me, and that's what I want. I want Duncan.

"Okay." James stands and he looks defeated. Nothing's been said between us about 'us' but he knows. We are the us that isn't us. Finally.

Chapter 70 – Beyond Happy Might Be A Stretch

Come Wednesday evening, it's a welcome return to the old town, Greta seems even more quiet than usual but after one drink, just a lemonade, I can see her relax. "Owen and I are dating, officially," she whispers from behind her Mogul menu.

I lean forward to pull it away from her. "Really?"

She smiles shyly. Having skipped starters because we're not terribly hungry, we're waiting for our mains: tandoori lamb shashlik in my case, partly because it was less saucy and I love the name, Mogul's special biryani in Greta's. We've already ordered yet she's still holding her menu. It's a defence mechanism I know well, although not usually with menus.

"That's great," I say to the back of it.

She finally lowers it, folds it, and puts it to one side. "He's lovely."

He is. The little I've had to do with him, mostly because he's usually on the phone, has told me that. He seems genuine, as does Greta. I think they would have got together anyway but I'm proud I sped that up. I'm certainly no cupid but I did hint at how much William liked Izzy and hey presto, they got together. Again, that probably would have happened anyway.

Until the food arrives, we continue talking about our respective halves, Greta blushing at every mention of Owen's name, which is sweet. I don't know why I don't blush, perhaps because Duncan and I have been together longer. Not that that should make any difference. Frank and Frankie have been together five years and they're having a second honeymoon only a year after their first one. Charles and my mum have a wonderful connection. He makes her happy, beyond happy it seems, so I'm happy for her. Beyond happy might be a stretch but I hardly know the man.

Greta pops to the ladies so I take the opportunity to look around. The Mogul isn't much from the outside during the day but at night it's much more inviting. Come inside and it's warm and cosy. The decoration is simple, very much less is more without the 'fuss' of some other Indian restaurants I've been to.

Our food arrives as Greta's sitting back down. The waiter, Amir, looking more like a manager in a very smart dark grey suit, white shirt and matching grey tie, bows and puts our napkins on our laps, nice touch.

"Can I get you another drink?" he asks with a hint of an accent, pointing to our nearly-full glasses. We decline but thank him nonetheless. He bows again and leaves.

Our food smells amazing. I've had lamb two days straight yet they look, and smell, totally different. The menu had said 'marinated lamb skewered between chunks of capsicum, onions and tomatoes, grilled in the clay oven' and while that could have meant they were rather dry, they're far from it. I know from the tandoori that there's going to be a kick, but remember that capsicum is a pepper but want to investigate.

"Do you mind if I look something up really quickly?" I ask Greta but she looks like she's away with the fairies. Owen, I suspect. I google 'capsicum' and am told, by my friend that is Wikipedia that 'Capsicum, the pepper, is a genus of flowering plants in the nightshade family Solanaceae. Its species are native to the Americas, where they have been cultivated for thousands of years.' "Nightshade?" I whisper and get a 'huh?' from Greta.

I don't suppose there's anything poisonous about either of our dishes so I point to the window and say a feeble, "The nights are drawing out." It's still early, barely six thirty, so it's going to be light for a couple more hours at least being mid-May.

She nods and seems to return to 'us' rather than 'them'. The Pink Floyd song starts up in my head. My dad was a big fan, me almost as much, although I couldn't say which song was from which album, or even decade. I like their slow stuff rather than the weirder experimentals. Then I remember Greta plays the guitar, very well, apparently. "What kind of music do you like? Do you play, not in class?"

She smiles sweetly. "Anything really. We do all sorts at school." Although she's not that much younger than me, she seems so innocent and I hope Owen isn't going to break her heart. "My favourite at the moment is Lana Del Rey's 'Video Games'."

"Oh I love that!"

The smile broadens. "It does help that it's slow."

Life really *is* worth living if somebody's loving you. "Moody but in a good way."

We talk more about music, how, as Lana said, the world really is built for two, then our fathers' passion for photography – hers a Nikon fan, mine Canon. There always seems to be a friendly rivalry between the two camps, with the others: Olympus, Pentax, Kodak, of course, Minolta, erm… the others, not getting much of a look in. Sony, Fuji, other 'e' brands, not that any others spring to mind.

Our drinks – my lemonade, Greta's slimline tonic, have gone before we've finished eating, Amir brings us refills, bows, and goes again, only returning when Greta signals for our bill which she pays there and then with the company credit card.

We've left our cars at work so chat on the walk back. I've been dying to talk about Owen all evening but have waited for her to bring the topic up again which I'm delighted she does.

"He's said he's always wanted to learn the guitar."

"Oh really? I played a bit on the piano when I was younger but never learned properly."

"You should do a course."

"I should." Getting back to Owen… "Is he going to join you on Thursday evenings?" I'd love that because then my mum could spy on them.

Greta sighs. "Sadly not. He has football training."

I stop walking so Greta stops. "Really?" Owen has a slim build but I'd not thought of him as a 'player' but then I didn't really think of him doing any kind of sport. Watching, of course, all men his age do. God, I sound sooo old.

"Been doing it for years. I think his dad was a professional. He still lives down in London but I think the guy who runs the squad, team, they're amateurs not… is a friend."

"I suppose it's like most industries; everyone knows someone everywhere." As I say it, I'm not sure that makes total sense but it seems to to Greta.

"Owen loves it. And keeps him fit, of course." Greta blushes and I giggle. We carry on walking. "So," she continues, "we have… er, private lessons at his house. I'm in a flat so don't play often."

That surprises me, not that she lives in a flat; I remember what my mum said about Greta's finances, but how good Mum said Greta was at the guitar. But then had she been *that* good, she'd not need to go for lessons.

We're at our cars, both on the second floor with a space between us so we get to chat leaning against our vehicles, me on my driver's door, hers on her passenger's… It's then I notice the steering wheel on that side. "Is your car foreign?"

"It is. I brought it over from Austria."

That answers the question I'd never asked. Not that far from Switzerland.

Even though we'd parked almost side by side, and her car, a generic white VW Polo, had been there first, I'd not noticed it being a left-hand drive, or the foreign plate. I walk a few steps and take a peek. There's a solo letter W followed by a red shield with a white cross, a tiny Wien (which I know is Vienna so the W totally makes sense) then 26285 and a solo T. Izzy drives a Polo so I'd noticed that much, and that it was white; the colour of a car being one of the first things we girls ask when someone buys a new one.

"I'm waiting for the paperwork to transfer it to a UK plate. Held out for as long as I could. Not that I don't like living here…"

"You could put it," I point to her existing number, "on your wall. At home."

She smiles. "I could."

We have a brief hug and say goodnight then drive to our respective homes, a temporary one in my case.

My mum's car is there so I slot mine in beside it. I don't expect her to be there as the hall light's on but, for a change, she is.

"Hi, darling!" she calls from the bowels of the kitchen as I open the front door.

"Hi, Mum!" I call back, hanging my coat on a hook and popping my bag beside the bottom of the stairs to take up. It's still quite early but I want to chat with Duncan, tell him how much I'm missing him and how I can't wait to get home the day after tomorrow. Mum adores him so she won't mind me cutting my evening short with her for his sake.

She's all ready for me, holding out a mug of tea. It's my normal; a bigger than usual china, rather than porcelain or ceramic, with dogs running all over it. One's the spit of Elliott, probably why my aunt bought it for me for no reason. She wanted to, of course, but not for a birthday or Christmas. The best kind of present; someone's been thinking about you, and not because they have to.

Before I have any of my tea, I ask, "How are things with Charles?"

Her face flushes like a pyrotechnic firework. "He's lovely," she coos. We squeal, put down our mugs – hers has yellow and black cartoony smiley faces all over it, and I give her a hug.

"Lovely to see you though it is," I say, "do you mind if I take my tea upstairs?"

"Not at all. If you have work you need to do, I can clear the table."

It is rather a mess. It looks like she's doing accounts. There are small receipts in neat(ish) piles, I'm guessing by month; invoices, printed and handwritten; but what look like brochures in the far corner. She sees me looking puzzled. "I'm helping Charles. He still does a bit of… oh, no, I can't really say." I can see she's itching to tell me as she's fidgeting in her seat so she reclaims her mug, as if that's going to help any. It doesn't and some of the tea plops over the side so she puts the mug down again.

"You can't tell anyone," she says.

I burst out laughing. She, of all people, knows how hopeless I am at keeping secrets.

"But you'll find out eventually," she says before taking a steadier sip of tea.

"Not if it's a state secret. If he's signed the Official Act 19-something-or-other. It's probably 20-something-or-other by now."

"1989," she says with an unusual air of authority.

I grin and she caves, eyes rolling towards the ceiling then back at me.

"He's a…" She leans towards me as if there are bugs hidden around the room. "He's a…" She looks left, right then at me again. "He's a…" She whispers even quieter. "Private investigator."

I laugh, a hearty belly laugh, and it feels good. Really good. My mum though looks a little put out. "I'm sorry, Mum. I don't mean that as a joke." Although I respected Charles, something about him had felt a little distant on the few (two) occasions we've met. I can see why my mum's still acted naturally around me, until tonight, when I'd sort of caught her out, albeit doing something totally innocent, and nice. She'd help my dad with his taxes so she probably offered here.

While I do want to find out more, I make my excuses and take my lukewarm-won't-drink-it-like-that-but-can't-throw-it-away-in-front-of-my-mum tea, and bag, upstairs, and shut myself in my room.

"Hi, honey!" Duncan says as he fiddles with his phone because we're facetiming. Having realised it was upside down but had corrected itself, he turned it sideways, not realising that would make him on his side so he turned it again, only for him to be upside down because the phone *hadn't* corrected itself in time for him to twist it again.

It made me laugh so I said a 'hi' until he was how he should have been and we could talk without distractions… other than something smashing and swearing downstairs before Mum shouts up an 'It's okay! No harm done!'.

"Your mum?" Duncan asks snuggling down a little in his, our, bed.

"Uh huh. Full of surprises."

"Oh yes?"

"Can't tell. State secret."

Duncan frowns. "What's going on."

"I can't tell you."

Uh oh. Puppy-dog Duncan; lower lip protruding, head tilted, wide eyes.

"I…" Sigh. I lean in and whisper. "Charles is a P.I."

Duncan squeals, making me tap the 'down' volume a few times but then have to tap the 'up' volume as I realise I won't be able to hear him.

"Does Lesley know?"

"She's just told me."

"And…"

"And?"

"What else did she say?"

"I can't tell you."

"Donna…"

"I don't know. I came here after that. There was paperwork all over the dining, kitchen, table so she *had* to explain."

"I bet she did. I know what you two are like."

I smirk. "So everything okay with you?"

Duncan knows to only tell me the good stuff. He learned after telling me about a hit and run dog he couldn't save that I can't hear anything sad. It's bad enough in a movie but to know it's real is unbearable. "We had a baby hedgehog in today."

"Oooh…" I purr.

"A six-year-old girl found it yesterday morning in her garden. They put some dog food out for it last night, and a bowl of water but it didn't have either. So nothing major, just lost its appetite."

"What did you do?"

"I'm *glad* you asked me that, Donna." Duncan smirks and wiggles his glasses in Eric Morecambe fashion as if he's the mad professor. "We put him on a drip."

"Oh that's sooo cute." I'm going to melt into a puddle.

"And how's it all going down there?" We spoke last night but not much about my week so far so I recount as best I can. Duncan laughs at my description of Stretch aka Finn. "He sounds nice," Duncan says without a hint of jealousy that Mike would have displayed. He seems happy with Marion but they are an odd pairing. Not that Duncan and I aren't, to look at, but we gel. Everything about Duncan feels so natural, so right.

"I love you, Double Dee," he says with a yawn.

"Love you more, my supervet."

"Not possible," he says and blows me a kiss.

I put my right index finger up to my lips then put it on my screen. Part of me would think of the smudge it would leave but I dismiss it as soon as I think of it. I don't care. Duncan, my mum and Izzy are my world, my little bubble, and nothing, no one (James) is going to burst that.

Chapter 71 – Unfinished Business

Thursday 17th May

"James!" I blurt as I wake. No. No, no, no, no, no. I *cannot* wake thinking about him let alone saying, blurting his name. What if… oh my god, what if I'd been home, lying next to Duncan and I shout out another man's name. And not just any man. A man I've been spending time with over the past almost three weeks.

It's clear there's unfinished business, in my head at least, and until I leave for good, two weeks tomorrow… can't wait… I have to be in the same office as him, breathing the same air. Help.

I decide the only thing to do is face the bull head on, take it by the horns… or whatever the expressions are. My head's such a mess. As is my hair, I see, as I'm brushing my teeth in the bathroom. I take a quick shower and the world feels a little better. Showers have the same effect as taking Elliott out for a walk; invigorating. He's such a live wire, unlike the very sweet but ploddy Buddy. I think if I didn't have Elliott as a comparison, I'd feel more empathy with Duncan's 'beagle child'. To be fair, I've only known Buddy the past year and I've tried. Not that I'll stop trying. I really will but dogs are supposed to love everyone. I wonder if he was a cat in a past life. No, because Duncan can do no wrong in Buddy's eyes, or mine.

My mum's still asleep, or out; her car's there but who can tell these days? So I head to work after a quick bowl of cereal and the remains of a dodgy-tasting probably-been-open-in-the-fridge-for-too-many-days orange juice.

Seeing as I have to work with, for the same company at least, James for two and a bit more weeks, I decide in the car on the way over to do the noble, but possibly stupid, thing and invite him out for lunch. I toy with the idea of asking Leah to join us, as a chaperone, but realise I wouldn't be able to say the things I feel need to be said to finally draw a line under the James:Donna debacle.

"Good morning." I smile as I hover outside Owen's booth. "Everything good with you?" I'm almost Joker-like in my false happiness, trying to psych myself up for the main office.

Owen hesitates so I tone down my smile. "I'm good, thanks. We're good, thanks." So he knows what I'm *really* asking.

"Good. Great! See you later." I don't wait for Owen's reply but make my way, before I bottle out, down the corridor. The orange juice, I feel, has already made its way through my system, along with the milk from my cereal, meaning I need to go to the loo. I debate whether to pop there or do the James thing but that would mean I'd only have to go back to the ladies and past his desk again which wouldn't do my street cred any good at all, not that I really have any.

At least the ladies gives me a few seconds to compose myself, and spot a speck of some kind of grain on my cheek. Why I didn't feel it, I don't know, but I can see why Owen hesitated. He was far too polite to point it out.

Passable, I leave the cocoon and adopt a semi-Joker-like smile. It's all been pointless as James isn't there anyway. Frank is so I tone down the smile further and say 'good morning'. He seems engrossed in something on his screen but looks up, smiles, and returns my greeting. He's a really nice guy. I've not met Frankie but I can see why she'd want to marry him, not that I would because he's old enough to be my–

"You looking for me?" a familiar oh-so-masculine voice pretending to be Robert De Niro voice says behind me.

I turn and want to say 'no' but I was. "Hi, James." It's not ideal that Frank's so nearby but relying on whatever's been captivating him to continue doing so, I continue. "Just wondered if you wanted lunch today. To go out for lunch today." *Cool, Donna, ice cool.*

He looks a little wary, and I don't blame him. I wasn't exactly nice the last time but still feel I had good reason not to be. Besides, he's not been fair but bygones should be bygones so…

"That would be nice." Good, the old insipid 'nice'. I can handle 'nice'.

"Nice. I'll collect you later."

"Right."

"Right," I repeat and strut to my desk, only realising, not for the first time, that I didn't get something to drink on the way because I was too intent on disposing of the previous one. Which *still* means I have to go back past James's desk. When I'm, we're, out at lunchtime, I'll get some supplies, a six pack of Diet Coke or anything, water, whatever. It'll spare me from myself. *Nope, Donna, that's never going to happen.* Thanks, voice.

After two coffees, an hour and a half apart with no looking at James or his desk on the way through or back, I return to him at twelve thirty-five. I know I'm a few minutes late, not that we're timing, but I do it to prove a point; that I'm in charge. *Yeah, right.*

"Ready?" I ask, all masterful.

"I am," he replies, just as much. Darn it.

"Great. Any idea where you want to go?"

He shrugs. "Lead on, Macduff." It's lay on but I'm certainly not going to suggest he does that. Apart from the obvious, he'd squash me.

So I do 'lead' and we head for Papa John's. I have no fond memories of the place and, although it's a bit of a way down Waterhouse Street, it's a lovely walk along the river. And it's given us time to talk. No face to face – not that we could as I barely come up to his hulk of a chest, certainly not close enough to touch, just plain old simple honesty. His feelings for me (plenty, he said), my feelings for him (none, I said).

He stops and turns to look at me. Down, way down, at me. "None?"

"I didn't mean it to sound so brutal but I have to be honest. You know I'm with someone, with Duncan, you've known that since day one, day two, whenever. I should have been clearer from the start but we're just colleagues. You and I."

"And you invited me out to lunch to spurn me?"

Spurn. A word of confliction. I love it as a *word* but it can wound and I don't like that. I stay strong. "I shouldn't have needed to. If you hadn't kept coming on to me, declaring your undying whatever to m–"

"My undying whatever?" He's smiling.

"That's not fair."

"Come on, Donna. You know you like me."

Now I do look up to the heavens in futility although I don't curse. He gently lowers my chin with a finger. A finger that smells of Diesel. The aftershave rather than petrol substitute. Now that's got me thing of whether it is actually–

"Come on," he says, taking his finger away. "Let's go eat."

Although I don't think the topic of 'us' is closed for good, I know we're a step nearer in the right direction. Whether it's a Donna- or James-sized step, I don't know.

Billy insists on taking me out in his Jag even though we're only going to the Boxmoor Steakhouse, a few yards from the office. Despite the lure of venison, kangaroo, ostrich and zebra – I know! – being 'healthier, leaner and flavourful', we both go for the high-quality graded Pavé Angus rump steaks, 180gm in my case, 230gm in Billy's, and well done to his rare. Yuk.

Whether they taste all the better for being 'carefully dry-aged in a temperature-controlled environment with a balanced grain diet for a high-marble score, tender and succulent texture', I can't tell you but they're absolutely delicious. Mine is perfection, as is Billy's, this he tells me while I look at him rather than it as he cuts into it.

Neither James nor Veronica appear in our conversation but Billy and I hardly talk about work, what with everything that's going on in the world: America vs. Korea vs. Russia rattling on, stabbings on

London streets, enough to make you appreciate how simple your life actually is. It does me.

"So, Donna."

Uh oh. This makes me sit up straighter. He smiles so I relax.

"How are you finding everything?"

I assume he means generally rather than geographically.

He continues. "I'm sorry I've not been around much but you seem very self-sufficient."

I appreciate the compliment and the fact he has more confidence in me than me. I.

"Thank you. Yes, everyone's been very kind." I was going to say 'lovely' but veered to the more generic 'very kind' instead. Billy's more relaxed than many bosses, not that I've had that many, but even so, he's still my boss.

"I've enjoyed your articles. I like the subtle humour you weave through them. Not too much description of the venues, a bit about the staff you met, nameless of course. Wouldn't want you getting into trouble now, would we."

I shake my head. "I hadn't planned that but some names I hadn't known and once I'd started the articles like that, I decided it was the way to go. Otherwise the relevant people might get asked for, picked on even. I don't know. Besides, I'd not told many what I was doing there so didn't exactly ask their permission."

Billy nods sagely. "Less is more."

That's exactly what Duncan says when the issue of my height arises, and it makes me warm to Billy all the more, even if he didn't mean it in relation to me.

We don't quite talk for England while we finish our steaks then desserts (seasonal berries Eton Mess for Billy, chocolate fudge brownie with marinated cherries coulis and cherry ice cream, hazelnut tuile and salted caramel for me!) but for at least half of Hertfordshire, this half (probably more a quarter) this side of the M1 anyway. I learn more about Cassandra (never Cassie or Cass), Leo and Milo, their sons from the fourth round of IVF. Wow.

"We were going to have triplets but..." Billy doesn't need to say anymore. It's clear from his expression and the fact that only two sons are ever mentioned that the third child didn't make it. Respectful Donna doesn't ask whether it would have been a boy or girl but Billy adds, "Poor Cassandra's outnumbered as it is."

I can't imagine losing a child. I thought I was going to have one but I was wrong. It's not the same at all. I wonder how Billy always remains so cheerful but it's clear they're used to their situation and incredibly grateful for the two they do have.

And that's the biggest lesson, to be grateful. We're alive. We're healthy (although slightly less in my case after such an extravagant dessert). And while some might be wealthier than others, my life's been nowhere near as tough as Billy and Cassandra's. I hope I'll have a child, more than one, whenever it's meant to be. With Duncan. I can already see what a wonderful father he'd make, is to Buddy.

And as I drive home, I give them a call, handsfree, and leave a message when it goes to answerphone, noting that Duncan's probably having a bath, with Buddy chewing one of his many semi-abandoned rawhides.

I'll call Duncan later, have our usually catch up and he'll tell me how much he loves me. I'll say I love him more. "Not possible," he'll reply and blow me a kiss, making me want to cry because I'm that happy.

And so life goes on.

Chapter 72 – Become Quite Formidable

Friday 18th May

It's Duncan and my one-year anniversary today so we chat on the phone, albeit quietly as Mum's still in bed, alone I think but there's no noise so for that I'm grateful, until it's time for me to get up and go to work. I had a lovely bath when I got back (Mum's car was here but no sign of her) so no need for a shower. I have visions of a lovely romantic dinner followed by a soak for two tonight.

Although I've enjoyed my outings this week, and caught up with Mum's antics (by text): still engaged, still blissfully happy, and yes, Charles is going to join her on the next course of guitar lessons, Friday afternoon can't come soon enough. I've been up to date with my articles, reader and other external and internal emails, helped by Veronica being on top of hers remotely – which I take as a sign of Ethan being on the mend, either that or working was taking her mind off things – so very little for me to do when it comes to my project.

Considering I've been Veronica all month, we seem to have had less contact than normal. That's actually not true but it feels like it. We've been aloof, certainly intentionally on my side, especially because of what she's been going through; respectfully on both sides I think.

My journey up the M1 is slower than normal but after a day solely in the office with a mum-made cheese and apricot jam (in the same) sandwich (because I asked for cheese and jam, meaning separate but she knows I like weird stuff) for lunch, and only nods between James and me, I'm so thrilled at going home, that it doesn't frustrate me. By 'home' I mean Duncan's, although I will pop back to mine at some stage as I've worn everything I have with me and at Mum's.

I'm past halfway through the month so on the home stretch, literally and figuratively. Duncan texted me to say he was already home and is 'getting the place nice'. I love that he'd do that for me. As I sit in a seemingly never-ending stream of stationary traffic – there's a bend ahead so I'm hoping it doesn't go too far past that, I picture his lounge, main light off, the room lit only by a gazillion nightlights and candles. But I think of it as a fire hazard. I'm such a romantic.

The traffic eventually moves and I get going. As with most holdups, there seems to be very little reason for it, just the usual Friday afternoon 'weight'. The radio, Heart FM as normal, has already livened up in preparation for everyone going out on the town. Duncan and I are usually too tired but often make up for it on a Saturday evening, with or without Izzy and William. We've become quite a formidable… I struggle to think of the four equivalent for trio, quad? Quartet? Must be the latter, and another great film. I get sad whenever I think of Billy Connolly. Such a funny man.

I finally pull onto Duncan's two-car driveway, or at least try to, but it's already full. And I recognise both cars. Duncan's, obviously, and a familiar hulking black Range Rover.

"Charles? What's Charles doing here?" I ask my car as if she can answer me. I leave her on the road and head inside. I assume my mum's here too and am pleased when she's the first person I see.

"Mum? What…?"

She waits as if for me to continue as I shut the front door but I don't feel I need to say anything else. We usually know each other so well that we finish each other's sentences anyway.

"I've asked Duncan to give me away," she blurts before I've had time to take off my jacket. It's just as well I've already lain my bag on the floor as I would have surely dropped it.

How I don't burst into tears, I really don't know. I also hadn't realised her plans were so advanced. "You have?"

I look into the kitchen and Duncan appears as stunned as I feel. He's holding a bottle of red wine in his left hand and corkscrew in his right. They're touching but barely, as if he's gone to make the first turn but been interrupted when asked 'the question'. Charles is leaning back against the work surface, a smile planted on his face.

I'm still semi speechless and can only manage, "I…"

"Come, come in. Duncan's pouring wine for us all. Charles is driving obviously so a small one for him please, Duncan."

Duncan nods.

I finally find my voice. "Why didn't you tell me you were coming up?"

"Spur of the moment. I'm sorry," Charles says and holds up a hand, palm out. "When she told me that's what she wanted, I said 'let's ask him'. I meant on the phone but your mother, rightly so, said it could only be asked in person, so here we are."

And here they are indeed. Our romantic evening kyboshed for the second time in less than a week, not that I don't enjoy seeing my mother but I was looking forward to just being Duncan and I. And Buddy.

With no notice, Duncan makes the meal, spaghetti Bolognese, stretch to four by adding more pasta, an extra loaf of garlic bread, and the whole bag of mixed leaf salad rather than half. Just as well he bought a big one.

My mum and Charles, as she explains, were partway here (Dunstable) so thought they may as well carry on up the A5. Dunstable, it turns out, is where Mum's temporarily non-mobile mobile hairdresser lives, being unable to travel to Tring, to drive at all, as she's broken her leg. Not so badly though to not do her clients' hair, providing they're prepared to venture over to her.

"I didn't think you knew where Duncan lived," I say, before tucking into the delicious-smelling meal, then hope it didn't sound like a gripe.

"You listed him as your next of kin."

I swallow then blow out as the hot sauce burns its way down my throat. "I did?" I croak.

"At work." My mum looks horrified, as if she's just let the biggest secret ever out of its padlocked bag.

"Mum..."

"It's my fault," Charles admits. "Don't blame your mother. It's just that I know Leah and–"

"Personnel human resources Leah?" I snap, now not feeling the least bit guilty. Is there anyone Charles doesn't know?

"I'm sorry," he says. "I was just looking out for you."

I'm not sure how to feel about this so turn to my mum. "You could have asked."

She looks down at her feet. "I know."

"Anyway," Duncan says cheerily, "you're here now and it's lovely to see you both, to meet you, Charles. Let's eat."

I've lost my appetite but I love spaghetti Bolognese almost as much as carbonara so tuck in.

With Charles's apology accepted, more by some than others – me – the rest of the evening improves and more red wine flows. It's not my favourite drink; I'm still at the tastes-like-vinegar stage but have a small glass to prove to Duncan that I'm willing to try. After the first one, Charles sticks to sparkling water, which Duncan thankfully stocks as I don't like still. Duncan had mentioned to me, when we were alone in the kitchen between courses, about suggesting Charles and my mum stay over but I didn't want our Saturday morning interrupted.

Buddy's loving the extra attention throughout, having not seen my mum for ages, given she missed him when he and Duncan visited at the weekend. She's dog mad so will make a fuss of any mutt going, and he, being a typical dog, will enjoy it for as long as it lasts.

Finally, after some unsubtle yawns from yours truly, Charles says they should really make a move. I have mellowed, admittedly helped along by the wine, so although not forgiving them completely, and I will certainly have words with Leah on Monday, our wishes of a safe journey are heartily meant. I'd be lost without my mum and I hardly see her so her having Charles in her life probably won't make that much of a difference so as long as he makes her happy.

And if he doesn't, he'll have me to contend with.

Chapter 73 – None Of Us Faultless

Saturday 19th May

It's lovely not having to get up at a certain time. Duncan's been an angel and brought me breakfast in bed before going to work. He's rather behind with paperwork due to a new vet starting and one of two courses, seminars, I can't remember which he's been on and which is outstanding, next week sometime.

I, on the other hand, have a lazy day planned, and I'm starting as I mean to go on. Buddy's gone off with his lord and master, so a lovely quiet house. Or it is until I hear my phone ringing. I remember having removed it from my bag part way through the evening but have no clue where it is now. It's distant enough to be downstairs but when I go downstairs, it's still distant. So I come back upstairs. Thankfully whoever's calling is persistent enough to try again when the answerphone kicks in.

I finally find it on the windowsill in the bathroom. I have no clue why. Even trying to think about it while swiping the green 'slide to answer' bar comes up with nothing.

"Morning, darling."

"Morning, Mum." I'm a little less chirpy than her but I can't help it.

"I wanted to give you a quick call before I head out with Charles… He's in the en-suite getting ready. We're going for a quick coffee somewhere then to the craft exhibition at the museum. Did you see it when you went with Duncan? It's supposed to be really good. I don't know why I haven't been before. It's not on for much longer so this is my last chance really, given how busy I am in the week, and we're off somewhere tomorrow… I can't remember where. Anyway how are you?" Typical Mum, she doesn't pause for breath.

"I'm okay, thank you." I try to sound more chipper but I'm struggling. It doesn't matter that she found out where Duncan lives… I would have told her if she'd asked, it's the way she got Charles to do it. Anyway, I have to let it go. I realise she's said something but I missed it. "Sorry?"

"No, I'm sorry. I should have asked you. Please don't get Leah into trouble. I think Charles said it was an emergency. It really wasn't. Leah's so lovely apparently. He…" Mum pauses for breath so I chip in.

"How does he know her?"

"Erm… he did say. Sister's cousin or sister's niece or niece's sister, but wouldn't that also make her his niece. I can't remember. A relation I'm sure. He said he had to phone her anyway about a job."

"He wants a job at the paper?" I'm thankful now that I'm only there for another few days.

"Not for him, no. For someone he knows." It could be *anyone* as he seems to know *everyone.*

Then the penny drops. "The agony aunt position?"

"Yes! How did you know? Of course you work there, and you go out with Leah sometimes, don't you."

"Yes, sometimes."

"Oh, I'm sorry. I really am. I feel terrible."

The last thing I want to do is make my mum feel bad but sometimes she doesn't help herself, although I can say the same thing about me. We're none of us faultless. "That's okay. I won't say anything. It's not the worst thing in the world."

"We wanted to surprise you."

"You did that."

"We were on the way anyway."

About a quarter of the way. "You were, and it made sense." In her head if not in mine. I shouldn't give her a hard time and I decide not to do so anymore. "Really, it's fine. It's a lovely thing that you did. Duncan's beyond honoured." He's been pretty much speechless on the subject since it was raised. He accepted, was happy to accept, especially knowing it's going to be months off. I make a mental note to google 'how long does a quick divorce take if we both agree?' or something like that, when I come off the phone.

"That's all I was ringing for mostly. Again, I'm sorry. Won't happen again."

I know my mum. While that exact same thing won't happen, there will be something she'll need to apologise for at some stage in the future. Like her daughter, she does have a habit of speaking or doing before truly engaging brain. "It's fine, Mum, really. It's fine. You have a lovely day, weekend, with Charles and I'll see you tomorrow evening or Monday evening, more likely Monday."

"Okay, darling. See you then. Love you."

"Love you too, Mum." And I do. I can't stay mad at her for long. However hard I try.

I google the divorce question and find it can be as little as twelve weeks. Yikes. The way my mum and Charles are going, they'll be married the day after. I shudder at the thought. *PMA, Donna, you were going to have a more positive mental attitude.* I was but I'm not sure what happened to it.

I've just shut the Google app when my phone goes again.

"Hi Izzy."

"Oh dear. Is it that bad?"

"No."

"Donna..."
"Just my mum."
"Oh no. Not split up with Charles."
"I wish. No, I don't wish. That's a horrible thing to say. I retract that."
"You said it like you meant it. What's happened?"
"It's too long to say over the phone. Are you still up for coming out to play?" The thought of that makes me smile.
"You bet ya. Do you want to come to mine or me to yours?"
"'Mine' being William's? And 'yours' being Duncan's?"
"Er, yep. Although I do have to pop over to mine at some stage. Amanda's texted me to say there's some post. Mostly bills I think but I'd better check. I've not transferred my post and don't really see the point. It'll all just be stuff to do with the house anyway."
"The advantage of only renting out rooms."
"Indeed."
"Shall I meet you there then and we can walk to... Romany? White Elephant? Heather's? What do you fancy? Picturedrome?"
"Ooh... how about Heather's for a drink and chat then White Elephant or Picturedrome for lunch."
"Perfect. See you at yours at..." I look at my watch. It's only half past nine so I'm hoping she says no earlier than eleven.
"Eleven for just gone elevensies?"
Great minds. "Perfect."
"S'later."
"S'later." We know the norm is s'la'er but we're both too well brought up to not pronounce our tees, even if we wanted to. It's also the journalists in us. Always the Queen's English.
So I have an hour to have a shower and get ready. Loads of time. Ooh, I've not looked at Facebook yet this morning.

Making it with literally a minute to spare, not that Izzy clock watches that specifically, I pull up outside her house. It's a lovely little detached in a quiet sort of cul-de-sac that no one really knows is there. 'They were using up a piece of land,' she had explained to me once, 'back in 1936.'
My flat's modern and while the rooms in Izzy's house aren't big by any means, mine are tiny. It's why I like the more open plan feel of Duncan's house, and why I don't come home very often. I do have to though this weekend so I'm prepared and have a few bits in my car boot that I won't need for a while, clothes mostly.
Izzy opens the door as I walk up the driveway. Her front door is almost made entirely of lightly frosted glass which would freak me out, the fact that people can see in but also if someone shattered the glass, all they'd need to do is step over the white plastic frame.

I don't suppose the people who design or make these doors think about that but I do almost every time I visit. "Hey, Donna. Nearly ready."

"No problem," I say as I step inside and shut the door behind me. A woman calls Izzy's name from upstairs. I hear, then see, a thud of bright pink Doc Marten-booted feet. In fact the woman, presumably Amanda, is dressed entirely in pink. Even the bow, clips and grips in her hair match, albeit in differing shades. If only I were half my age, as she isn't far off, though probably late teens rather than mid. But I don't remember being that bold when I was whatever age she is.

"Amanda, Donna, Donna, Amanda."

"Hi!" Amanda thrusts out her hand and by the time she's shaken mine, it almost hurts. She's got an army major's grip and as much enthusiasm as… Tigger, I suppose.

I put on my best smile and return her 'Hi'. "Lovely to meet you. Izzy's told me a little about you but more about what you do."

"Yes, St Andrew's. Love it. Not been there long but yes, I love it." Her hair, which is plaited in two, very much like Kim Kardashian's Double Dutch, and almost as long, is bobbing as she nods furiously. "I'm like a floater; different departments, wherever they need me. Only been in adolescence so far though. So much going on there. But it's fab. And I get to go down to Workbridge for lunch, take one or two of the kids there sometimes. It's amazing. Have you ever been?"

Amanda and my mum would get on well, although they'd only get a word in if they spoke over each other. "I have a couple of times. Café, charity shop. It's great."

Amanda smiles. "I love the ethic. Such a great ethic. You know they do printing too. Fabulous. And they involve so many of their guests."

Everything about Amanda is 'fabulous' and I'm sure if I spent much time with her I'd be back to my old self but for the moment, I need Izzy love. She's looking like a spare part, so I conclude proceedings. "It was lovely to meet you, Amanda."

"And you." She gives my hand another firm shake, which is fine as I've not quite got the feeling back from the first time.

Chapter 74 – Some Izzy Love

We're lucky, given it's a Saturday and a nice day, the outside space isn't being used when we get to Heather's. It's a cosy coffee shop and popular with locals and passers-by, and a glance through the window shows the tables inside are full. Just as well it's not raining, although there's a huge red umbrella to protect us had it been.

It's my turn to pay so I go in and there's a buzz, as well as the inevitable warmth, about the place. I know a lot of writers say they go to coffee shops because they like the noise and they'd certainly not be disappointed here.

Heather's husband Bungle is at his computer by the café's right wall and he's half chatting to one of the customers about the local council – often a debate whenever I've been here with Izzy. Bungle's sort-of-Mohican is bright orange today. I think it was blue last time. That in itself is a talking point, that he's 'on trend', not that it would have been his intention.

Izzy and I are not eating until later so I order a chai tea latté and Americano but get lured by the gorgeous cakes and I'm about to order a muffin to share when Bungle switches from the other customer to me.

"I've got a story to tell you about your chai tea latté."

I turn to face him. "Oh?"

"There's a lady came in here a few weeks ago, over from Mumbai, asked if we did chai tea lattés. I said we did and Heather…" He points to his wife, as if there'd be any doubt as to who he was talking about. "…did the honours. The woman tried it and said, 'Oh my god, I've been in Northampton for six months and I've been looking everywhere for a chai tea latté just like we have it at home.'"

"Wow."

"I know."

We look at Heather who blushes.

"And," Bungle continues, "she's been back several times. Each time says 'it's just like we have it at home.'"

"I shall get Izzy to report back to you." I point outside to the only person sitting under the closed red umbrella, as if there'd be any doubt as to who *I* was talking about.

Heather smiles, still looking a little embarrassed. Bungle grins with pride. They've been married a few years and look like they're still very much in love. I can only hope that Duncan and I will be so happy.

I return to Izzy, forgetting about the muffin, and I'm mid-flow telling her all about my mother when Heather comes out with our drinks, which reminds me about the muffin but I remember what

Bungle said to keep that in my mind so it doesn't disappear. "I've not told her yet," I say to Heather, "but will." Heather nods politely and goes back inside.

"What was that?" Izzy asks as the door closes so I tell her everything Bungle told me, almost word for word. "Oh how sweet. I'd better have it while it's hot then." Izzy takes a sip but winces. "Maybe not that hot."

I continue telling her about last night and this morning until we're up to date.

"Wow," is all Izzy can say as she takes a large just-right mouthful of latté.

"I know."

"But why would Leah do that?"

"I don't know."

"I don't know her but you just don't do that."

"I know."

"Even in an emergency, you don't give out personal details. Isn't there a procedure to follow? Wouldn't she at least have given the information to your mum?"

"But how would she know she's my mum? At least she knew Charles, albeit vaguely."

"Because your mum would have given her enough information about you."

"Which she'd probably given Charles."

"Okay, fair point. Strange though, isn't it. Would you trust him with the rest of your mother's life?"

"Mmm..."

"She said they were doing it because they cared, or something like that?"

"Looking out for me, yes." I take a mouthful of my Americano.

"It was a very sweet thing to do; to ask Duncan to give her away."

"But she could have asked me for his address."

"And you would have asked why."

I can feel myself frowning. "Probably."

"But she wanted it to be a surprise."

"So she said."

"Wouldn't you?"

Even more frowning. "What do you mean?"

"If she'd told you ahead of time, you would have blabbed. You couldn't keep something like that a secret. You'd have been straight on the phone to Duncan and blabbed."

My frowning turns into mock shock. "I'm wounded, Isobel MacFarlane, that you would think such a thing."

"It's absolutely true."

I swallow another mouthful of Americano. "And you're *absolutely* right."

And there, my mother is instantly forgiven. Charles a little less so as he did the underhand deed but he did it for her, so yes, maybe he's not that bad after all.

Izzy takes our empty cups inside and reports back to Heather that it is indeed a fabulous chai tea latté. She returns with a square cake-box shaped paper bag.

"Mmm... what have you got there?"

"A couple of slices of self-indulgence for our afternoon tea."

"Ooh... what flavour."

"For me to know and for you to find out."

"Same or different?"

"Different."

"Ooh..."

Resisting the... whatever they are, because I have no choice, until afternoon tea, we hit the three charity shops along the Kingsley Park Terrace. This is Izzy's old stomping ground so she knows, and chats to, each manageress in turn. First up is the bright and airy Extra Care. Nadia's in today and immediately smiles at Izzy.

I'm not sure I know any shop well enough for any of the members of staff to recognise me which makes me feel a little sad but Nadia smiles at me, mouths a 'hello' and I immediately feel welcome. I only know her name, apart from the badge I see she's wearing, because Izzy told me ahead of time.

Nadia knows Izzy loves audiobooks and texted her in the week that she'd put some by so not only a trip to Kingsley to collect the post. It's worth coming just for this as Nadia goes into the back room and comes out with a stack of about a dozen multi-CDs. Izzy's had quite a few previously but only passes on a couple.

She pays for them but I know she'll lend them to me, via a memory stick, when she's recorded them on her computer and brings them back for Nadia to resell – the ultimate recycling. We usually end up buying more of the authors' books so not wholly naughty and I'm sure most writers, while, yes, wanting to sell gazillions of books, write to be read. Izzy's talked for months about writing a novel, and says she's planning it, yet I don't think she's got past writing the title. Not that I can remember what she said it was going to be called.

Laden with several bags of shopping: the audiobooks, clothes (most from the British Red Cross), and a fabulous pair of long black cowboy boots for Izzy (courtesy of Age UK), we head for the White Elephant for lunch. We debate popping to hers to drop off the shopping but agree that we might not walk back again. Plus lovely as she is, we'd end up getting Amanda-d.

"Aren't they men's?" I ask when Izzy tries her boots again. We've sat at a table near one of the doors to the pub's rear garden, an orange juice and lemonade in front of me, diet Coke in front of Izzy.

"They are but they look okay, don't they?"

"They're gorgeous." They'd drown me as Izzy has boats for feet, as the saying sort of goes. We both struggle to get nice shoes, even new in shoe shops, which is a bit ridiculous given that Northampton's known for its shoes, men's mostly, and why the football team is The Cobblers.

"Aren't they a bit big though? Aren't you an eight?"

"Eight and a bit usually so I have to get a nine and these are tens but pretty small so extra thick socks and they'll be fine."

"Cool. Food?"

"Absolutely. Eat, drink and be pretty darned merry."

Being a Greene King pub there's almost too much choice, but we finally settle on a Hunter's chicken for Izzy and chicken and bacon salad (less than 350 calories!) for me, helped by being from the 'two pub classics from £10.99' section. We do love our bargains. And salads vary surprisingly from establishment to establishment so it's good research.

We catch up on Izzy's week and mine minus my mother's is-it-isn't-it-a-faux-pas drama and, clean plates later, we grab our booty and head back to Izzy's house, enjoying the walk along the Kingsley Road with the old racecourse, Kingsley Park, on our left.

Needless to say for mid-afternoon on a Saturday, it's packed with dog walkers, picnickers, cricketers and amateur footballers, some dads and their sons. I picture Duncan being one of them with our son Tyson. Tyson? Where did that come from? I can't imagine calling my son Tyson, especially not after Mike.

"Huh?" Izzy calls back, the pavement's a bit too narrow for us to walk side by side and we'd block the path for anyone coming up behind us, or in front, although we'd be able to see them coming. We're nothing if not considerate.

"Wondering if Amanda's going to be there," I call.

"Don't think so. Said she was going to visit her mum."

"Oh really? Where does she live?"

"Market Harborough."

"Nice."

"I know. I get the impression she's quite well off. They. Amanda talks about her father so I think they're still together. She has some really nice things, not cheap, so unless she's a charity shop hunter too, she has more money than she earns 'floating' at St Andrew's."

With Izzy's back to me, I've caught most of that, filled in one or two words so it makes sense. We spend the last few hundred yards in silence before arriving at Izzy's.

She's right; no sign of Amanda, just Izzy's car in the two-car drive and mine blocking hers only for Amanda to could get out easily.

After going back through our bargains and trying on a couple of outfits, we watch a movie, accompanied by Mr Ben and Jerry with their Pfish Food and Cherry Garcia. It's at times like this that I'm glad my brief was to eat the five-hundred-max dishes and report back on them and wherever I was eating them at the time, instead of losing weight. Just as well as I'd not been weighing myself religiously. (At all.)

We agree on Izzy's recent purchase of *Stranger than Fiction* and I still can't believe she's never seen it, especially as she's the one out of the two of us who's often talked about writing a novel. The title of her book, she reminds me when I less than subtly ask, is going to be *The Luckiest House*, which I'm not convinced sounds like a best seller but I'm sure Mrs James's friends weren't smitten with *Fifty Shades of Grey* either. I'd be only too glad if Izzy proved me wrong by selling gazillions of copies.

"My god. I loved that!" she exclaims as *Stranger than Fiction*'s credits roll and the two slices of cake, chocolate orange beetroot and coconut berry, are long-distant memories.

"I know."

"I'm going to watch it again. You?"

I shake my head. "I need to pop back to my flat. It's been too long and for all I know it could have been burgled or flooded while I've been away."

"Oh, I should have thought. You could have given me a key and I could have popped in from time to time."

She's right. I hadn't thought of it either. "That's kind of you but so could I at the weekends."

After hugs and cheek kisses, and a promise of keeping in touch until she visits me and my mum next weekend – can't wait – I pop home… home home. I know I've not seen Duncan since breakfast but he had a few things planned, including golf, which can take hours, especially when meeting up with some of the regulars (William?) at the nineteenth hole, not that he drink drinks, never does when he's driving, but it doesn't matter.

It's not late, just gone six, so still plenty of time to go out if we want to but I suspect we won't, given we've both been out all day.

Chapter 75 – Home Not Alone

The cold hits me as I open my front door. I'd forgotten that I'd switched off the heating, or rather set the remote to 'off' so it doesn't drop below five degrees. I'm not going to be long but set it to manual so it can have a quick blast of heat, good for the flat, not only for me. I write a note on my notebook to switch the heating back to off, and leave my notebook on the doormat so I can't forget. Only a few months ago, I'd not have to have done things like that but the thought of hitting thirty-one, which is scarily not far away, has turned my brain to mush.

I potter around until I think I've done everything I need to. Left until last because there's nothing I really need from the kitchen, I switch on the light and scream. There's a very small mouse, possibly a dormouse, on my work surface and it appears to be eating, and enjoying, some cheese. I look over to the fridge and the door's open. I'm normally fastidious about ensuring it's shut, especially if I'm going away for a few days, but unless this mouse is as capable as… whatever the rat in *Ratatouille* was called, and able to open heavy fridge doors, then I don't think it was him… her… it.

It takes a moment for the mouse to realise I'm there. It freezes, looks left to right without moving its head then scurries down through a gap between the cooker and work surface, so small that only something tiny like it and crumbs would be able to squeeze through. And it's taken the cheese with it.

I go to the fridge and what little is there feels unsurprisingly warm so I bag it all up, including a bigger piece of the same cheese – I feel mean but I don't want to encourage it, and put the bag by the front door to throw in the communal black bins. Everything in the freezer is thankfully fine, just as well as it's packed with a variety of ready meals (mostly Weight Watchers because, although I'm careful with my weight rather than being on a diet, they're delicious, especially the risotto), bags of different vegetables and yes, in the bottom drawer, an impressive selection of ice creams, no Halo as yet but I will get some when there's space. To help in this endeavour, I remove one of the tubs of Häagen-Dazs Pralines and Cream and pop it in a carrier, an orange Sainsbury's bag… possibly the one it arrived in as I remember me not resisting it being on offer there, and pop it on the front door mat, next to the note about the heating.

One final check of all the doors and windows and I'm good to go. I stare around the lounge as if I've forgotten something. I have enough different clothes for the rest of the month, I've brought in the ones bought today and have popped them in the laundry basket, none being new new so all warranting a quick wash next time I'm home for a while. Everything's already neat and tidy, or as neat and tidy as I get. So what have I forgotten?

I do another three-sixty and shake my head. I'm definitely losing it.

Remy. That was the rat in *Ratatouille*. It finally comes back to me as I close my front door, heating set to off, and I shudder.

I'm not unnerved exactly by the mouse, I've had to deal with worse (famine, flood) living on my own, but it's certainly put me off having cheese for a while, which is a shame because I adore the stuff. Maybe I should get back on the horse, as the saying goes, and have a cheese fest. While not as big a fan as myself, Duncan does like cheese so always has a mixed platter at his house, one of those that has smallish pieces of different types so you can 'try them before you buy' big versions.

Pulling a stack of local takeaway and eat-in restaurant menus from between the cutlery tray and the edge of its drawer, Duncan flicks through them as if inspecting a dodgy pack of playing cards. "We haven't had pizza for a while…" he suggests, waving a Pizza Hut brochure.

All I can think of is the mouse but say, "Sure."

Duncan frowns then unfrowns. "Something else?"

I've had so many different types of food already this month that I really don't know what I fancy. Whatever I have it'll probably have cheese in it if not on it: lasagne, Hunter's chicken – it did look lovely when Izzy had it. "No, that's absolutely fine."

"Fine?"

"Delicious. Whatever you fancy, I'm easy."

Duncan sniggers which sets me off and the mouse is forgotten. I'd have to eat cheese again. Okay so I wouldn't die without it and I'm not at my flat so pizza it is.

"Speaking of which, have we got time for…?" He looks to the ceiling and while it's the guest room above us, I know exactly what he means.

"Not if you order now. They're notoriously quick. But if we worked up an appetite first…" Being away from home, and therefore one's boyfriend, five days a week, certainly builds up an appetite for something.

He puts the menu on the work surface, returns the others, closes the drawer, and we head upstairs.

An hour and showers later, we return. Buddy's sitting in the kitchen, looking up at the menu as if knowing that he's likely to get a piece of whatever we order. In some respects, he's not as stupid as beagles would have us believe but he goes to his water bowl, hits it with one paw, making the not-long-filled water go everywhere.

"Buddy!" Duncan shouts and I grab the bowl while he fetches a tea towel, there being too much water for the usual dishcloth or paper towels. The dog looks up at me, as if butter wouldn't melt. I think I detect a slight grin. "What did you do that for?" Duncan asks as he wipes up.

"It's past his dinner time."

At the word dinner, Buddy tilts his head to one side.

"So why didn't he tap his food bowl? The water one's bigger. It's not like he can't tell the difference."

Being a vet, Duncan should know how clever dogs are or not but I don't say anything.

Duncan orders a medium meat feast pizza with extra pineapple, and we've only just finished talking about our respective days, while feeding the dog and setting the table, when the doorbell goes.

I go to grab my purse from my bag sitting on one of the kitchen table chairs but Duncan raises a hand. "Don't worry. I've got it."

"Ah, thanks." He's such a doll.

"Ooh, hello," I hear from the front door.

I'm intrigued but know that Duncan would call me through if I were needed. *Please call me... please call me.*

The front door shuts and Duncan comes through, putting the pizza box on the work surface.

"Someone you knew?" I asked, hoping that I've asked the most obvious question.

"One of my customers. Her son has a mouse."

Don't we all. Mmm. "A poorly mouse?"

"Was, yes."

"That's good."

"Not really. I couldn't save it."

The image of Duncan doing mouth-to-mouth on a rodent pops into my head, in fact on the mouse I saw earlier. I shudder.

"Want me to turn the heating up? It has turned a bit chilly. It might not actually be on yet."

I hadn't thought about it but now he's mentioned it... "Please. Just for a while."

Duncan gives me a hug, rubs my back, which feels reeeeally good, then goes to sort out the heating while I bring the pizza and warmed plates to the table.

I'm seated with a slice on each of our plates when he returns. Buddy's sitting but looking up at me almost drooling. Him, not me, although the pizza does smell divine. Duncan and I add salad to our plates, together with some requisite garlic bread which adds nicely to the overall aroma.

“Yum,” Duncan says and Buddy licks his lips. I look at the dog then at Duncan. I say nothing but Duncan gets the hint. “Bed… now.”

“Okay,” I say and move my chair back. Duncan howls with laughter which makes Buddy howl and I get a fit of the giggles which gives me hiccups. Oops.

I know I thought this recently but I really couldn’t be any happier, and apart from cementing our relationship, I don’t want anything to change.

Chapter 76 – Beyond Superman Status

Sunday 20th May

We both ate too much last night and are lying in bed, or rather on the bed, the duvet having been kicked onto the floor because we forgot to switch off the heating, which we did as soon as we realised.

"I'm stuffed," Duncan says, pushing out his naturally relatively flat stomach.

I do and say the same which makes him laugh. He rubs my 'bump' and I want to cry, wishing it weren't just food inside it. That said, we have an uncomplicated life as it is now; we can go out when we want without the thought of taking half the house with us or finding someone we can trust to look after mini Donna, even minier than the real Donna, or mini Duncan. Donnetta or Duncanette… Duncette. "Wasn't there a medieval torture implement called the Dunkette?" I ask randomly, knowing he wouldn't know where that thought had come from.

"I don't know. It sounds feasible."

"I'll google it." This is exactly what lazy Sundays are for; googling things you don't actually have to know and would probably never come up in a quiz. "It's a character in Warcraft…"

"Right. Never played it but good to know."

"A TripAdvisor reviewer, a hashtag and member of Twitter… are Twitter profiles members? I suppose they are."

"Uh huh." I think I've lost him as he seems to be peering at his navel. "Go on…" Okay, maybe not.

"Some kind of thoroughbred pedigree horse. Aren't thoroughbred and pedigree the same thing?" Forgetting for a millisecond that Duncan is a vet, albeit of relatively small animals, he's bound to know this so I hold up a hand and continue. "And a chap called Timothy on LinkedIn. Do you have a profile on LinkedIn?"

"I do," Duncan says, still gazing at his stomach which seems flatter than earlier. "But I don't really do anything with it. People ask to connect and if they're animal related or local, I accept. I don't post anything on it, although I do click on the 'new posts' button thing on the app to get rid of the number that appears every few days.

I do the same with most of my apps, especially the ones I never use… except to open then tap random options to get rid of the number.

"Anything else?" he asks.

"Just one on the first page. I don't really go past page one."

"Okay…"

"Someone called Windy has some Dunkettes. Equibase so we're back to the horses." It's interesting but only vaguely, especially to Duncan if he finds his navel more amusing.

"I suppose we'd better get up," he says, finally retrieving the duvet when the room's cooled enough.

"Why?"

"To take Buddy out, for one thing."

"I suppose…" I can't think of anything I'd rather do than be cosy in bed, however nice it is outside. I look over at the clock. "Half nine."

"You've done well to hold it in, mate," Duncan says to Buddy who wags his tail. I'm surprised he didn't hear his name, immediately followed by the word 'out', and go nuts but as I've said before, not the sharpest tool. Bless him.

"Where are you going… with him…?"

"I'd only planned on round the block but if you wanted to go out out."

At the double use of one of his favourite words, Buddy does go mildly nuts, cautious in case he misunderstood.

"Do you mind if I stay here, unless you want to go out out."

At this, Buddy barks. "Okay, wait a minute," Duncan orders a little too sharply and the dog looks dejected and lies down.

"It's just that I've only got two chapters to go then I'm done with this book."

Duncan looks over at my bedside table. "*Elizabeth Goes Missing*. Does it do what it says on the tin?"

"Sort of." I read the back to him. "'Meet Maud. Maud is forgetful. She makes a cup of tea and doesn't remember to drink it. She goes to the shops and forgets why she went. Sometimes her home is unrecognizable' with a zed so I think it's American, 'or her daughter Helen seems a total stranger. But there's one thing Maud is sure of: her friend Elizabeth is missing. The note in her pocket tells her so. And no matter who tells her to stop going on about it, to leave it alone, to shut up, Maud will get to the bottom of it. Because somewhere in Maud's damaged mind lies the answer to an unsolved seventy-year-old mystery. One everyone has forgotten about. Everyone, except Maud…'"

"Sounds a bit… what's the name of that Guy Pearce movie I always forget?"

I laugh. "Memento?"

"That's the one. Also sounds a bit like you lately… Sorry, my love." He blows me a kiss.

"You're not wrong… What was your name again, Daniel?"

He laughs. "And it's good, the book?"

"Really good. 4.3 stars with nearly three and a half thousand reviews on Amazon. Last time I looked. Probably more on their US site."

Duncan whistles, setting Buddy off. "But you've read it before." He points at the battered cover.

"Ah, no, charity shop. A while ago. I was going to buy it for my Kindle then I spotted it for a pound buy-one-get-one-free and thought I'd treat myself. You know, sit and read rather than get Alexa to dictate it to me."

"Good plan, Batman. What else did you get?"

"Huh?"

"For the buy-one-get-one-free. Can you remember?"

"Sadly. The second *Fifty Shades* book, darker or deeper, I can't remember."

"That bad."

"Awful. No, that's not fair, but not my kind of reading."

"Done really well though, hasn't it, for its author. A woman, presumably."

"E.L. James. Yes, very well. Beyond well."

"Do you still have it?" Duncan winks at me and I grin.

"Somewhere at my flat." My flat-that-has-a-mouse flat. "Oh yes, I have a mouse at my flat. I forgot to tell you. Not that I had actually forgotten but I wasn't sure whether to tell you."

"Why?"

"I don't know."

"Do you want me to go over and get rid of it?"

"I don't know. I suppose so. The landlord will want to know." *For when I hand in my notice and move in here.*

"Absolutely he would. He?"

I nod. "My landlord's very sweet but lives miles away. He uses a management company who are useless and probably would either say it's not their problem because they only deal with the flat and not the whole building or take forever. Would you mind?"

Duncan looks mortified that I would even ask, as if he'd do anything I ask. *Marry me*? I need to get this fixation out of my head. It's been a year. Who marries after only… my mum.

"Shall I pop Buddy round the block, let you get dressed and we go over, get Mr or Mrs Mouse rehoused?"

Not how I had envisaged spending this particular Sunday but the thought of not having company next time I go over on my own does appeal. "Thanks, darling."

He blows me a kiss and takes Buddy downstairs. I turn to my book. "Sorry, Elizabeth, Maud, Helen. See you later."

With the mouse sorted (found, humanely captured, then released into a spinney at the back of my block) and Duncan catapulted to beyond Superman status, especially as he'd also fixed a wobbly picture frame – a picture of me and my beloved dad, which made me cry so I got a long and cosy Duncan hug, and fitted a blind that had been waiting weeks to be hung – who knew except Duncan that he had a whole toolkit in the back of his car, we head back to his, have a quick lasagne from the freezer; made and reheated by yours truly, for a change, with the remains of the bagged salad, but no garlic bread as we'd used the final packet last night.

We're both quite exhausted so slob in front of the TV, although flicking through there's nothing that grabs us.

"Elizabeth?" Duncan asks.

"Huh? No, Donna."

Duncan smiles. "Your book."

"Oh yes. Do you want to read?"

"I wouldn't mind. I just fancy a bit of hush."

"All over the world."

"That was a song, wasn't it?"

"Carpenters. One of my dad's favourites, although I think they rerecorded it from someone else." I try to sing but only get as far as the words I know.

"Very nice." Duncan's just being kind. I can't sing. I can but not in tune and don't inflict him any further.

So we have our kind of hush and head to bed.

I'd already decided, especially after Mousegate, to drive down to Hemel after rush hour tomorrow. It'll be my last Monday morning doing this as next week is not only a bank holiday but school break so should be quieter. Famous last words.

Chapter 77 – Groundhog Week

Monday 21st May

My last but one week. In one way, this month seems to be flying – in another, dragging. They are feeling a little groundhoggy, just the weekdays, I've done something different each weekend and the next one will be my last before I go home, back to Duncan's, for good. Izzy's coming down here in between so definitely something to look forward to. Her and my mum adore each other – Mum adores most people who should be adored, so that'll be fun, when she, my mum, can prise herself away from Charles, love potion number two… as The Searchers didn't sing. One of my mum's favourites. Ew, just the thought of my mum and Charles needing to be prised apart. Way too much information.

The A45, M1 and A414 are relatively kind to me, and I'm at work by ten. Everyone's where they should be and it's oh so groundhoggy with a small g. James and I swap 'mornings' and I'm pleased it's all very professional.

With everyone busy, I pop to the sandwich van at lunchtime and have a lovely hoisin duck wrap, at, Val tells me, 413 calories so it could serve as one of my 'dishes', although not technically a dish but Nathan and I have talked about going to The Mazza, an Indian restaurant within the Marlowes Shopping Centre in town where it may be more difficult to get something that suits.

Regardless, I make a note of it and add some nutritional information courtesy of fitbit.com as well as tips for slicing the cucumber thin enough from Moon Cho of Yin & Yang Living on YouTube. As the saying goes, I learned something new today: that what I always thought of as a regular cucumber is an 'English cucumber'. Who knew? Everyone other than me, probably. I love that she used scallions (spring onions here) to give it a kick. And the lime dressing. That and some peri-peri chicken. Yum.

Sundays, Mondays and Tuesdays, it turns out, are The Mazza's Special Banquet Nights. One starter, one main course, one side dish and a pilau rice or nan for £12.95 per person. Pilau's my favourite in either form. The menu tells us that the word Mazza originates from Bangladesh and has a number of meanings such as fun, enjoyment and tasty. I'm hoping for all three tonight.

"You can have whatever you like though, of course," Nathan says but I'm already sold, as I can see he is.

He opts for the Popcorn Chicken Pakora (fresh chicken pakora made from minced chicken with curry leaves and hint of red chillies – brave!) as a starter, and I have the Mass Bora (fish meat coated in homemade breadcrumbs, deep fried – definitely not a dietary dish).

"And for your main course?" our waitress Maali asks, digital handset at the ready.

I'm sticking with the fish. "Hash tikka, please." Duck marinated in mild spice and grilled. Duck twice in one day isn't greedy, right?

"And the butter murgh for me, please," Nathan says and hands back his menu as I'm reading that it's 'a traditional home-cooked butter chicken cooked in garlic, tomatoes and medium spice then topped off with butter homemade butter cream sauce.' A serious amount of butter. Definitely not within my five-hundred calorie limit.

Oh, then I see the Murghi Mo Mo, chicken cocked(!) with honey with mild spice creamy and sweet very tasty dish… also available in lamb. Oh that's not fair. Under that is the Mango Monsoon: a delightful dish which is cooked with mango and cream, making it a very mild and fruitful delight, garnished with ground almonds and coconuts. Available in chicken and lamb. Now I'm *really* torn.

"I'm sorry, can I change my order please."

"Of course." Maali smiles genuinely.

"Could I have the Mango Monsoon please."

"Absolutely." Two taps on the device and it's done. "And sides?"

I look at Nathan. "Shall we have a rice and naan to share?"

He squeals (actually squeals!). "Great idea." It wasn't actually mine as I was led in that direction by the menu, although on the banquet specification it said 'pilau' but I notice under 'accompaniments' that it's called 'pulao', Bangladesh again perhaps. I smile, say nothing, and Maali tap taps.

We have drinks but have already some headway on them. Maali points at mine and raises her eyebrows. "Shall we?" I ask Nathan and he nods. "The same again then please." Maali tap taps again and takes my menu.

She goes behind the bar, normally I'd say to enter our order but the handset is likely linked up with the system so she's probably just… I don't know what she's probably just doing but… checking it maybe. Everything looks fine and she goes to another table to start the process again.

"So," Nathan says, shuffling his seat a little nearer, "our last Monday together."

I hadn't thought of that but next week is another bank holiday so yes, he's right. I'll see him in the office, of course, connected or not to his audio headphones but it won't be the same as quality time like this. "It is," I reply and sigh.

"Ah… that's really sweet," he says and takes my hand.

I'm rather taken aback and jolt a little.

"I'm sorry," he says and lets go.

"No, I'm..." but I feel I've spoiled the moment. I want to take his hand but I can't. And now it feels weird. It seems to pass as he blows a raspberry and chuckles. He has this habit of making light of any situation and I love that. I think we could all do with a Nathan in our lives.

"I play the drums," he says from nowhere.

"You do?"

He shrugs. "Badly, but I play them." And the spoiled moment has most definitely passed.

I tell him all about my mum and the guitar lessons, Bernard, and Charles next term.

"And Greta, of course."

"Greta?"

"She goes too."

"Oh really? The little minx has never mentioned that."

I don't suppose it's something that's ever come up in conversation in exchanges in the kitchen or work parties. They're not exactly close geographically at work although I can't imagine Nathan not getting on with anyone, at work or otherwise.

"And James?" I ask but them remember Nathan calling James 'Jamie poppet' the day I arrived. I can't imagine anything going wrong since then. *Of course not, Donna. It's been an easy breezy three weeks.*

Nathan frowns. "James?"

"Erm..."

"Everything okay in that respect?"

I'm saved by the arrival of our starters.

My Mass Bora is even better than it looks, and that's saying something. Nathan's popcorn chicken does too but I'm glad I've gone for mine. So Nathan doesn't return to the topic of James, I ask Nathan about his weekend. He blushes as he says, "Brad and I went to London."

"I *love* London, especially the South Bank. It's easy enough by train from Northampton so should go more often."

Nathan devours another popcorned chicken.

"But more importantly, how's Braaadd..." I lengthen his name like the woman does with 'Wanna take a baaath?' at the start of Pink Floyd's 'One of My Turns'.

Nathan pops another 'corn' into his mouth then points to it with the end of his fork.

"Good, I take it." This came out dumber than it meant to. "Great." I have another bite of bora bora, and we finish our starters in companionable silence.

No sooner have we finished than our plates are removed and the mains are presented to us. And how well they are presented.

Around the edges are little garnishes of spiralled cucumber, radishes and tomatoes, crinkled like something out of MasterChef. Like those fancy candles, it all looks too good to eat but eat we must and eat we do.

"Nice?" Nathan asks out of one side of his mouth.

"Mmm..." I reply.

Even though the food is plenty hot enough, we keep eating, murmuring every now and then and nodding, pointing to our food like... I don't know what like... children, I suppose.

We skip dessert, not because it's extra but because the portions were really generous and we're full.

Nathan pays with the company credit card and I leave the usual fiver tip.

"You don't have to, you know. You're doing all this in your own time."

I laugh and wave a hand around the room. "*This* is no hardship. I don't know what I would have done without all of you. Stayed home alone at my mum's and moped, probably."

"Could you go home from here, from work, I mean."

"I could but wouldn't want to leave again," I smile but then go serious. "I could, quite easily, but with traffic it would probably take an hour and a half, two hours maybe, to get back then a couple of hours there before bed."

"Ah but sharing that bed..."

"I know. I'm not sure why I haven't gone home. Duncan and I had agreed at the start that we'd see each other at the weekends. Perhaps with things a little uneven, I thought the space would do us good."

Nathan pulls a sad face as we hover by our cars.

I wave a hand. "It's fine. We've talked a lot. Sworn our undying love to each other..." I roll my eyes which makes Nathan giggle. He's so funny. We hug, say our goodbyes and I head home.

Mum's not there, two nights in a row would have been a bit much but she's left a carrot cake in a container at the near end of the dining table with a note to 'help yrslf'. Since when did my mum do text speak? Worse than text speak. To be fair, the pen was fading at the 'p' so maybe she didn't think it would last the whole eight letters. As I think that, I look a few feet away to a pot of pens of various colours and thicknesses. Always in a hurry, my mum.

Chapter 78 – At The Same Places At The Same Time

Tuesday 22nd May

Not wishing to invite James to lunch again… I only have… oof, eight left, I discretely (peering round the corner of my hideout, and really leaning because her office is soooo far way, making Nathan smile) look for Leah but there's no sign of her.

"She's gone away," Nathan whispers but loudly enough for me to hear… plus he's staring straight at me for the whole office (James) to see so I walk, no stride, to his desk, head held Bridget Jones high.

"Gone away? Not gone gone."

Nathan shakes his head making his skinny neck wobble. "With…" He leans forward. "her boyfriend."

Boyfriend? I squeal and clap my hands. If the office (James) hadn't noticed me before now, they (he) certainly do (does) now. As the month's gone on, part of me feels more like a piece of the Hemel Hempstead news office furniture but another part of me is more sensible, logical, detached.

These people, I hope, with maybe one exception, have become my friends and I shall certainly call in whenever I'm visiting my mum during the week… if she can pull herself away from her betrothed. Boy, that feels so weird. I hope I get to see more of him before the month is up. As long as my mum's happy but she has been known to be rather impulsive. Still, she must know what she's doing and he seems good for her so far.

Being chicken, I purchase another lunch from the van, popping downstairs after I'd spotted James walking across the car park and getting in his car as the van pulled up. There are several advantages to having a window-sided desk and watching him get back out, chat to Val – not close enough to see what's said but then I can't lip read. He returns to his car and drives off, which means I can race (*sedately, Donna*) downstairs and get something for my lunch and still have plenty of time to get a drink from the kitchen and return to my hideout.

I successfully do all that and have scored (paid for) a delicious-looking thick ham salad wrap (439 calories, which is fine and will make for another article as I can talk about processed vs thicker more natural protein) with a massive – because it's so cold (not), although because I'm really thirsty (greedy), specialty roasted hazelnut latté at probably not far off the same count!

That's not true as I go for skinny milk but as a favourite, I know if it's anything like Costa's it's around 350. Unlike history dates, I'm quite good with figures when it comes to my job and remember, courtesy of nutracheck.co.uk that my drink, even as a 'Massimo take out' only has 333. The fat content, understandably, is quite high at 15.7g and the protein worse at 13.5 but carbs are good for you in small quantities, and while 34.8g isn't exactly small, I don't have one of these every day so…

Other than trips to the loo (engrossed on my phone – I've got to know the route through the office without having to look up (at James) or bumping into anything (James's desk), I keep myself to myself and five thirty rolls around quickly.

Frank's ready and looks raring to go. With many places yet explored, we return to the Marlowes centre for Turkish, at the Maramis, for a change. At Frank's recommendation, a medium Cop Shish chicken kebab is my weapon of choice – I'm a sucker for anything barbequed and this is 'lean chunks of marinated small cubes of chicken skewered & grilled over a charcoal BBQ grill'. The 'lean' is good too.

Frank opts for the 'Iskender Kebab', sliced lamb doner on a bed of Turkish flat bread topped with chef special tomato sauce and yoghurt. That does sound nice and I'm torn as to whether to stick or twist – my dad and I used to play Pontoon, as it's a couple of minutes before our waiter comes over.

"Hi Karawan," Frank says and I look at the man's name badge. I wonder if it means something, most names do, but then Frank speaks again. "And a Coban salad to share please." Frank looks at me. I don't know what that is but nod.

While the men are talking, I find the salads on the menu. 'Coban Salad' consists of chopped tomato, cucumber, onion, fresh peppers, parsley marinated with sumach, pomegranate sauce, lemon juice and olive oil. It all sounds very healthy, although I don't know what sumach is. It would be too rude to google it and while I'm sure I wouldn't be the first to ask the origin of an ingredient, I feel I should know so keep schtum. The parsley being 'marinated' means it has to be some kind of liquid but Frank fills me in.

"I'm not normally a parsley fan but the berry marinade…"

And when it comes, it does indeed look red, and delicious. It goes perfectly with our kebabs.

I'm reminded by Karawan's badge to ask Frank if he objects to me looking something up on my phone.

"Not at all. Can I help?"

"Karawan. I wondered if it means something."

"It's an expression used to 'avert the Evil Eye'," Frank informs me. "In fact… I'll let you into a little secret." He doesn't get any closer, but as he points at our meals he *does* have a conspiratorial feel about him, something no doubt Charles would be intrigued by, or join in. My mum certainly would. "This is what Frankie and I have every time we come here." He sits straighter and laughs.

I'm more than happy to be Frankie's substitute for the evening. We've never met but Frank has told me so much about her already and he tells me about their hippy days and how they may well have been at the same places at the same time: "And even Woodstock, New York, in August 1969," he says. "It was *the* place to be back then. Frankie and her family had gone especially for it. My parents, on the other hand, had a holiday home in Rochester, rented it out to tourists going to Niagara Falls, but had kept it back for those few days so they could go. Fabulous part of the world. We've not been back, Frankie and me, since then, and the recession hit my dad's business so they had to sell the house. It needed a lot of work doing to but it still got them out of a hole because it was *pretty* massive. But then they are, aren't they over there. I think someone connected to Eric Clapton bought it. That's what my mum told me so I passed on that little nugget to Frankie who has all his albums. CDs, you know."

I do, so I nod. My mum's also a fan, probably just one reason why she and Frankie have bonded.

Frank and I share a portion of Baklava and Häagen Dazs vanilla ice cream for dessert and it's lovely being this up close and personal to someone I know would have got on really well with my dad. I look up to the ceiling to stop threatening tears. A cobweb is dancing to the tune of a nearby air conditioning unit and I'm mesmerised.

"You okay there?" Frank asks and my attention returns to him.

While the fairies and I were away together, Frank's paid the bill and already put a five-pound note on the dish that would have housed the receipt.

I look at the money. "Oh, please let me–"

"Tosh," he says and swipes his hand. "It usually costs me way more and it's been a pleasure."

None so truer words have been spoken. That doesn't sound quite right but I say, "Absolutely. Thank you so much."

We part company at my car with a brief hug and Frank pecks me on my right cheek before returning to his car, a generic Ford Mondeo, a few spaces up.

He would be the person I'd choose as a second dad but of course he's already taken. Although we only met three weeks ago, three weeks and a day, I feel a certain kinship with him. I hope I'll have that with Charles. Frank though is more like my dad, more laid back, more… dad like, I suppose. But I suspect Charles will be good for my mum. She's not exactly been a wallflower this past few years but having someone a little more… dynamic will be good for her.

And what's good for me is bed. So that's exactly what I do in the empty shell of a house that used to be my dad's.

Chapter 79 – Almost A World Tour

Wednesday 23rd May

After a standard day and third visit of the week to the van (a repetition of Monday's lunch, it was so nice), Greta, who's on fine form after her second official date with Owen – how proud am I, joins me for dinner at the wildly named Smoky Boys, a fabulous American restaurant on the Saint Albans Road. I've had so many different dinners this month, I almost feel like I've been on a world tour. Not as exhausting as one of Mr Clapton's but I'm sure as enjoyable nonetheless, although he'll have eaten something akin to what I've been eating in their original locations. Except, it comes back to me, that he's a vegetarian. Oops.

"That sounds nice," I say as Greta orders halloumi skewers for starters and a grilled chicken 'haus' salad.

"What are you having?"

"I was going to choose the chicken barbeque shots followed by a cheese burger but…"

"You could order that and we could share?"

"We could."

"Let's?"

I nod at the waitress: Colleen. I remember there being a Colleen in 'Neighbours', or it might have been 'Home and Away'. She was a very sweet but rather doddery and clueless little lady. The gossip queen, if I recall. She wasn't particularly old but more my mum's age than mine. This one though is tall, skinny and has bright purple hair. I'm rather jealous. I don't have to dye mine yet but I'm sure it's only a matter of time. I get sent dyes which go to Karen, our fashion columnist, or friends and friends of friends who are more than willing to be guinea pigs. None though were this colour. Our Colleen's slightly younger looking than me, early/mid-twenties, I'd say, and is the kind of girl, woman, who would look great wearing the proverbial cloth sack.

Colleen smiles and retrieves our menus after jotting everything down on a jazzy red, white and blue notepad and tucks it into her red, white and blue stars and striped pinny. Everything about the place is traditional American, or certainly what we think it would be, with its Elvis Presley memorabilia, Route 66 metal signs, 'American Graffiti' guitar on the wall (although that looks a little out of place with its black background and yellow ZZ Top-type car), and gazillions of beer bottle stops all across the walls. It's impressive.

As is our food that arrives mid-conversation about Owen, who, Greta tells me, had scored the winning goal at a 'friendly' at the weekend. "Some take it way too seriously," she says… very seriously. “They lost the previous week and Owen moped about for days.” He never struck me as a moper but then people are often different in private as they are in public, at work.

Although I have another week and two days to go, it does feel like I'm nearing the end of this ‘project’. While it's not been easy at times, having such lovely people around me has made it feel less like a job. The statistics, however, are only too keen to remind me that it *is* when it comes to putting my articles together, but I enjoy that side of it.

My mum's still out when I get home; needlework, and possibly Charles thereafter – I can't see him as a needleworker, so I leave her a note. I could text her but think she may not check. She's old fashioned in that she loves to receive letters – I'm under strict instructions to send postcards if I go anywhere. I don't suppose she meant Hemel. *Had a good evening. Hope you did too. :) See you in the morning? D x*

Duncan and I have a catch-up. It's horrible to think I won't see him for another ten days but when I do, that'll be it. No more coming to Hemel, no more staying at my mum's.

“Love you,” he says with a smile as he knows what I'm going to say next.

“Ditto,” I say for a change, all Patrick Swayze-like from *Ghost*.

Duncan pouts.

“Love you more,” I say and his smile returns.

“Not possible.”

And all is right with the world.

Chapter 80 – More Than A Hint Of Recognition

Thursday 24th May

In the middle of a very ordinary day at the 'office', giving only a hint of recognition to James as I walk past his desk, I pop out to Asda for a chicken and bacon tubbed salad, with the mayonnaise scraped off, in case I need to use it as an article.

I decide it wouldn't actually be a bad idea anyway as I can include a recipe for homemade mayo. Not *my* homemade but that courtesy of Gordon Ramsey's Cookalong Life on YouTube.

I remember last time I watched it, I ended up on the site for over an hour, making spurious notes and clicking on so many different recipes then sidetracked by 'I bet you didn't know that…'-type videos. I didn't in most cases: celebrities dying before their time and other cheery stuff.

It's a treat later when I return to Ristorante Alberto but with a somewhat subdued Billy.

"Cassandra's nephew's come off his bike again… when he shouldn't have been back on it as his bones hadn't healed but 'there's no telling the young'." Billy does air quotes then perks up when the head chef, Giuseppe Morello, comes over for a chat. It turns out it's not just Charles who knows everyone who's anyone in the area, but being the editor of the local paper, Billy has all the right connections. Especially when you're writing a column about food.

"I recommend the red snapper," Giuseppe says to me. I've never had it before so why not. "Served with a rice alternative which only has twelve calories per serving."

I look at Billy and he smiles as if they've already had a conversation about who I am and why I'm there. I hadn't thought for a moment that Giuseppe would think it was because I needed to lose weight, although…

"Red snapper for two please," Billy says.

Giuseppe clicks his fingers, does a part twirl and returns to his kitchen.

We're at a table by the window and had we been in a relationship, it would have been the most romantic setting with the restaurant's red centrepiece candles, a yellow glow outside leading the eye to cream-painted picturesque buildings opposite. Duncan would love it so a venue for when we come to my mum's sometime but then Billy drops a minor bombshell.

"Alberto retired last month so they're closing."

"Oh no."

"It's been a long time coming because he loves the place but his health isn't so good these days and with no family to take over..."

"What a shame." I point to the kitchen. "What about Giuseppe?"

"Moving to London. He's been made an offer he can't resist."

"Oh?"

"Michelin-starred. I don't know any more than that."

By the look on Billy's face, he does, but like with my mum and Charles, it's a state secret. Except, although despite knowing Billy for only a short while, I already know it would take a lot, possibly Charles, to make him crack.

"Well, I shall wish him all the best then if he comes out."

Unfortunately that doesn't happen. It's as if word's spread and a coach load of people pile in. An old man, Alberto presumably, hobbles from a back room and seems to know each one.

"This isn't the last night is it?" I ask Billy.

He nods and takes a mouthful of red snapper so he doesn't have to answer.

I feel honoured. The whole month, albeit with its downs and ups, has humbled me somewhat. I certainly feel more relaxed than when I arrived... twenty-five days ago, twenty-six if you include my mum's on the Sunday night.

And as Billy drops me back to collect my car, I tell him how grateful I am.

"My *very* pleasure," he says, the grammar slip I know to be intentional, as if the first thing that sprang to mind.

I blush, do a short curtsey, and click open my car.

It's an enjoyable drive back. Another day is almost over and I've got the red snapper to write up about in the morning, or afternoon, should I fancy the morning off.

Chapter 81 – As Prepared As A Girl Guide

Friday 25th May

I do indeed indulge in a morning off and Elliott gets to chase anything that moves over at Tring reservoir followed by Christmas tea and carrot cake at the Bluebells Tearooms. I'm one of these people who doesn't mind repeating anything nice. Despite knowing the outcome, I almost prefer watching a film the second time because I know the plot so can spot little details missed.

When I drop Elliott back, I collect my aunt's horse painting and go straight to work, taking as much care with the gift as if it were the crown jewels.

Frank is, needless to say, delighted beyond words, although I did get a very heartfelt 'wow' and 'please tell your aunt thank you so much'. She probably gave him a 'friends' discount but I'm sure he would have paid full price. That's between them, and I'm happy to have the involvement I did.

As prepared as a girl guide, not that she ever was one, Izzy comes down straight after work today and gets to my mum's just after I do from work. I'm getting out of my car when I see headlights pull up, foolishly thinking that it's my mum but recognise the VW Polo.

"Hi!" I say, going round to Izzy's driver's side as she zips down the window. "Block me in, it's fine. You can always move if we need to take my car." I wait while she does as suggested.

I go back to her side but give her enough room to get out. "Do you need a hand?"

"I'm good, thanks, only an overnight and handbag."

Having both flitted between our homes and boyfriends' for the past few months, we've learned to pack lightly. "I'll put the kettle on then show you to your room."

Izzy's visited before, travelling down with me when I've come for the day, but never stayed for the weekend. It's so exciting. We've not discussed what we fancy doing and some of it will depend upon what my mum's up to (no, not that image again!), how much she's around. She's promised to be so I hope she hasn't forgotten. I'll send her a text to remind her.

"Can I use the loo?" Izzy asks as soon as we get in the house and shut the door. "Bit of a slow journey, what with the whole of the country going away for the weekend."

"Absolutely. You know where it is." She does.

I take the pause in proceedings to check Izzy's room, tempted to take her overnight bag with me but I resist as I'm unsure whether she'll need it before going upstairs. Her (the guest) room's not been used for a while but it seems fine. I know there's fresh bedding as my mum did that as soon as I asked if Izzy could stay – my mum's face (of happiness) was a picture; like having two daughters come home.

Then when I'm back downstairs, I send my mum a message.

Hi, Mum. Izzy's here for the weekend. I know you won't have forgotten but would be useful… I remove the 'would be useful'… *let me know if there's anything you fancy doing.*

I've not even reached the kettle when there's a quack.

"What's that?" Izzy asks, looking around the room as she returns.

"My phone. WhatsApp. It quacks when the screen's locked, pings when the app's open."

"Sweet. I'll have to see if mine does that."

"What does it say? Can you check for me please, Izz."

Izzy has an iPhone so knows to tap the round bottom home button. It needs my fingerprint to unlock it to open the app to read the whole message but it shows the first couple of lines.

"*Hi, darling. Thank you for the remindr.* Only one e. *Charles and I didn't get to…* That's all I can see. No punctuation. I've added that in when reading it back to you."

I laugh as I make our drinks. "Yep, that's Mum. Okay, I'll take a look in a second. We can plan the weekend and change it if we need to. Is there anything *you* fancy?"

"I'd like to do the charity shops."

"Goes without saying." I know we'd still get on if one loved charity shops and the other didn't but it helps enormously that we do.

"You went to the museum with Duncan, didn't you."

"We did but be more than happy to go again. There's an amazing craft exhibition. The frogs and foxes are amazing. Said amazing twice. Three times."

"Then that's a definite. Big fan of foxes."

"I didn't know that."

"As much as anyone else."

"Oh, okay." That's why I didn't know, I suppose.

"Anything else?"

"Can we get a dog to walk?" Neither William nor Izzy has a dog so it seems a strange request but she continues. "The weather's supposed to be nice."

"We can, absolutely. Elliott's always up for a stroll, or manic rabbit, squirrel, anything he can chase."

Izzy laughs. "That sounds like my kind of walk. Are there any official ones?"

"You mean like a walking group?"

"Not necessarily. Is there a tourist office?"

"On the same road as the museum."

"Great. Let's pick up some maps on the way. Does the museum have a café?"

"It does."

"Perfect. We'll get the maps, do the museum, then sit have a drink while we think about where we're going to go. How fit are you feeling?"

"I don't feel too bad actually, not unless you're talking a half marathon or something."

Izzy laughs again. "Let's just leave it at the maps, I'm sure they're not that epic, and see what your mum wants to do."

"Oh yes, I didn't check." I thumbprint the home button so my phone unlocks. I hit the green and white icon with the red one attached to it. WhatsApp duly opens. "*Hi, darling. Thank you for the remindr.* You're right, only one e. *Charles and I didn't get to the museum so we could do that but not sure if you want him to come along…*" I look at Izzy who shrugs non-committally. I wait so she has to say something.

"I am quite curious to meet him."

And I'd like to spend some time with him. Apart from passing ships, the only quantity has been an evening but that was 'the' evening where things were a bit weird. "Okay. I'll say that's fine. If she doesn't come home tonight though, she may not be that early tomorrow. And if Charles is going too then it's unlikely she'll be back in between."

"Then we get a girlie evening. Movie and ice cream?"

"Ooh… like your thinking."

So we settle in for the evening with *The Hitman's Bodyguard*, one of a selection of DVDs Izzy had brought with her, not knowing what we had – very little; we tend to rely on Sky and Freeview. My mum's sneakily stocked up since I last went to the freezer so we get a choice of Halo Top Birthday Cake (rainbow sprinkles and beetroot juice in the ingredients list, and it being 280 calories per pot, seals the deal), Mint Chip (320), Cinnamon Roll (a vast 360) or Red Velvet (also 360).

Rather than pick a couple, we decide to grab two glass dishes and have a spoonful of each. My mum's dessert spoons are bigger than the average but hey, it's all low calorie. Even if we ate all four pots it would still be 1,320 calories. Okay, that would be too much but who could eat two tubs' worth on their own? Even Izzy, the bigger ice cream lover of the two of us would struggle. I'd have no chance.

We wash it all down with white wine, a New Zealand Tesco Finest North Row Vineyard Sauvignon. It's my mum's but I don't think she's been saving it for a special occasion (the engagement's already official) and it's Tesco. I can always pop out and get another.

With not a bubble in sight, there's no fizz so no bloating stomachs. Plus, we're very good and don't go back for seconds… but we couldn't see any of the dishes when they were so heavily laden the first time. I couldn't count ice cream and white wine as a 'meal' which is just as well as, apart from being over the five hundred limit, I'm ahead and the project finishes next Thursday. Bring it on!

After the movie, we decide we're pooped. There's no sign of Mum as expected so once I've checked all the doors and windows… I had forgotten to lock the porch door when Izzy and I came in, but the front door's a Yale so 'they', whoever they are, would have to break it down, or pick it, to get in.

Our rooms are at right angles so we can hear each other but have to raise our voices which is why we don't chat for long. I've started another book since 'Elizabeth' (which was brilliant), *Eleanor Oliphant is Completely Fine*, a recommended read apparently; I wouldn't mind doing another chapter or two before lights out but my brain has other ideas and I'm only a couple of pages in when the book hits me on the nose.

"Night, Izzy!" I call but get no reply so she's either listening to her iPod or fallen asleep.

It's lovely having her here. William's very lucky, but he knows that. I do feel she's like the sister I never had. I'm one very lucky girl.

Chapter 82 – Some Inexplicable Reason

Saturday 26th May

I wake up quite early and almost scream as I come out of my bedroom. Mum's back. Mum's not only back but she's sitting on the edge of her bed. And Charles is coming out of her en-suite. Naked. I know I said I wanted 'to see more of him' but…

Mum looks up, squeaks, and closes her bedroom door but it's too late. We all know I've seen what can never be taken back. I'm not sure whether that makes us even or if it's two nil. I'm just grateful I wasn't Izzy, but would it have been better? Now I can see though why my mum wants to marry Charles… not just for his money. And because she loves him of course, no question.

I've lost my appetite. I fancied a bagel but no, not even a raisin and cinnamon one would lift my spirits. Would raise… *Donna, stop.*

I go downstairs and open the back door. For some inexplicable reason, I'm boiling. It's not even that warm a day. I put the television on low and half-watch the national then local news. It's all quite depressing other than a delightful story of a hundred and seven-year-old woman who's doing an abseil. She looks about eighty and I can only hope I'm as sprightly as her even at that age.

Izzy's first to come down, dressed and raring to go. We have some toast and cereal, and there's still no sign of my mum and Charles. With the breakfast things in the dishwasher, there's nothing else keeping us so I call up the stairs. "Shall we see you there? At the museum?"

I get a distant, probably because her door's shut, 'okay' back. I won't hold my breath. They've had plenty of time to get ready and the alternative doesn't bear thinking about so I don't.

"Ready?" Izzy asks, shrugging on her jacket and slinging her bag diagonally across her shoulders.

"More than you'll know."

Izzy laughs. "Okay."

We resist the lure of the charity shops we walk past (Save the Children and Emmaus), because we plan to do them on the way back, if we can still walk after our post-museum trek, and we pop into the Tourist Information Office for the maps.

The lovely lady behind the desk can't be more helpful and we come out with what feels like half the display. We'll decide while having a drink at the museum's café, and can leave the other leaflets at my aunt and uncle's when we collect Elliott, but have been recommended Tring Parish Walk number three: 'Tring Park and beyond'.

There's no sign of Mum and Charles when we get to the museum, and I don't know why but I do keep an eye out for them. I check my phone occasionally but there's nothing there. "Should I text her?" I ask Izzy.

"Do you think you need to?"

I shake my head.

Izzy gives me one of her sympathy looks. I put my phone back in my bag, ensuring the volume's on full, just in case.

We've both been here before but are still in awe. I think if we came here every day we'd still spot things we'd missed on previous visits, there's so much surrounding us. We marvel at the polar bear, smirk at the baboon, swap sides several times at the dressed fleas.

"How do they do that?" Izzy asks, not for the first time when we've been where we are.

"I don't know." My standard reply.

My second visit to the exhibition and I spot things I missed with Duncan. I'd not noticed a parade of ants made from bent paperclips. It's quite astounding. "How young minds work," I say to myself, not realising Izzy's standing behind me.

"What's that?"

I point at the ants.

"Amazing isn't it. What do you mean about young minds?"

I look around the room. "These have all been created by children. Fourteen max."

"No way."

"Yes way. With help from their parents though I'm sure."

"Do you think?"

"Have to be."

"Amazing," Izzy repeats and after another glance around, we move to the whales.

We're both standing looking above us when we hear a voice.

"Aren't they beautiful?"

We look to where the words have come from.

"Oh hello," I say. "Weren't you…?"

The woman nods. The Tourist Information Office woman. "I help out for a bit on a Saturday because Rosa has to take her children to various clubs. She's got six."

"Wow," Izzy and I say in unison. One more than a handful.

Mrs TIO continues. "Once she's dropped them off, she relieves me and I come here."

Izzy and I share that 'that could be us' look and we frown. Then laugh then frown.

The woman spots someone scratching their head, excuses herself, and goes to assist. My only thought is of the fleas escaping.

We're done and head to the café for a drink but not before we venture to the gift shop where I buy a postcard of the fleas. Izzy buys a programme, which includes a picture of the fleas but I get the postcard to send to Duncan. I just have to think of something witty to say.

After two teas and shares of flapjack and teacake, we head to my aunt and uncle's to collect Elliott. On the way, along Park Road and down into the top of Langdon Street, Izzy pulls out the walks brochures. "This is perfect for you: Hertfordshire Health Walks. Free and sociable short walks across Hertfordshire."

She opens it up. It's a simple green and white A4 sheet folded in two. "Why walk? Getting active can be difficult… blah blah blah. Walk grading. Walks graded choose suitable… twenty to thirty, thirty, one point five miles, forty-five minutes, an hour, ninety minutes, here we go… longer than ninety minutes."

I gulp. I was picturing the first option.

She continues. "What you need to know… medical advice… trained volunteers, refreshments, dogs welcome… oh great! No special equipment. Getting started. Oh."

We're nearly at my aunt's but Izzy stops. "Find your local walk. We have to go online."

"We can do that. I have my phone." I pat my bag. I've not heard any beeps but could have missed a message from my mum so dig it out as if to offer to go online for Izzy.

"No it's okay. We'll just use one of the other maps, otherwise we have to keep looking at your phone and it'll use your data and battery."

"True." I have almost-endless data but do want to leave the battery for my mum. Who's not going to text.

Izzy starts walking again so I follow and we arrive at my aunt's.

I ring the bell and point to the other brochures Izzy's holding, the HHW returned to her bag. "There'll be something there."

It takes a few moments for the door to open but in the meantime, we can hear scratching.

Izzy bends down to the letterbox. "Hello Elliott!"

"Yes, that's really going to stop him scratching." I laugh. Elliott whines.

Izzy stands. "Sorry."

"It's okay. He'd get excited at a pin dropping." Not sure why that was the first thing that came to mind.

My uncle steps back as he struggles to open the door. "Elliott, get out of the… Oh hello, girls. Lovely to see you again, Izzy." My uncle's lovely, so warm and fuzzy. Not that my aunt isn't but he's a bit younger than her and likes his gadgets so he and Izzy get on particularly well, though Izzy gets on with everyone who gets on with everyone else.

My aunt comes through into the lounge from the neighbouring kitchen. They have two two-up-two-down cottages knocked into one with the door between near the front of the house and a walkway in the middle. "The kettle's boiled if you'd like something."

"Just had one but thanks," I say while Izzy makes a fuss of Elliott, or rather attempts to lessen his licking by distracting him by putting her fingertips together as if she's got something for him.

"Here." My uncle hands her a squeaky ball which surprisingly still squeaks and that's enough for him to transfer his affection.

"Hello, Isobel," my aunt says.

"Hello." Izzy's never known whether to call my aunt by her surname or first name so just says 'hello' then always makes sure my aunt's facing her so she doesn't need to get her attention. It's silly really at our age, especially as she calls my mum Lesley, but one of life's little dilemmas.

"We're heading out for a walk so better not have another drink," I say rather redundantly as they know we're here to take Elliott off their hands for a while.

We all head through to the kitchen where my aunt, it turns out, is at the start of baking some of her almost-world-famous brownies. "They'll be done when you get back, may still be warm depending on how far you go."

That prompts us to spread the maps onto the nearest half of the table. She has all the ingredients ready: some melted butter, sugar, cocoa powder, some eggs, flour, what looks like baking powder and salt, a tiny bowl of something that looks like gravy but I presume is something sweet.

My aunt sees me frowning at the bowl. "Vanilla extract."

"Oh. I thought vanilla was white or a stick." Comments like this remind me how little I know my stuff (the minutiae of food).

She laughs gently.

Izzy coughs and draws my attention back to the job at hand.

On top of the pile there's a coloured A4 sheet of Tring reservoirs. Having been there twice recently, it wouldn't be my first choice and Izzy dismisses it. "We'd either have to drive or it would take so long to walk there that we'd just turn round and come back again." She has a point.

Next up is 'Tring Days Out'. Being a forty-eight page book, it's a bit off-putting to wade through although the crossroads sign on the front with a lovely open-field scene behind it is encouraging. Izzy opens the front cover and we skim the contents page. "Bit too heavy to carry," she says and closes it again. "Grand Union Canal Circular Walk Three," she announces from the next leaflet's heading. "Kings Langley, Hemel Hempstead. Fine if we were at your work but no." I agree. So that's another dismissed.

We're left with five individual numbered Tring Parish Walks. We have one, two, three, five and six. Not sure what happened to number four.

"One," Izzy reads as she opens the sheet. "Little Tring."

"Little Tring's nice," my aunt says, spooning the mixed ingredients into a high-sided rectangular metal tray. "But a bit far again. Not as far as the reservoirs, you'd likely go through Little Tring to get there, but even so."

We could go back to Mum's and get my car but I'm loath to suggest it as I still don't know what she and Charles are up to.

So map number one is also dismissed.

"Map six. Tring Station, Wigginton and Tring Park."

"Tring Park's not far," I say. "We could do it in reverse order."

"I think they're circular walks so you start and end at the same place." Izzy's being gentle with me.

I feel silly.

"Map five. Drayton Beauchamp." Izzy looks at me for guidance. I have no clue where that is so shrug and we look at my aunt who's brushing her hands.

"Little Tring, A41 Wendover way."

"Oh. That's a no then. Two left: two and three."

"Three was the one the Tourist Information lady suggested?"

"Let's have a look at two then first. Save the best till last. Stubbings Wood. That sounds nice." Izzy opens the sheet and looks at the hand-drawn map. Doesn't look too bad. Car park, past the museum… not sure if that's the…" She moves to the central strip of text. "Yes, the natural history one where we've been."

Elliott nudges her arm. "Hello, boy. Won't be long." She continues reading. "You can see from left to right: Aston Hill, The Vale of Aylesbury, Mentmore Towers, Ivinghoe Beacon, Pitstone Hill, Aldbury Nowers, whatever nowers are, The Bridgewater Monument and below you to the right Tring Park. That sounds lovely." She closes the front. "An hour and a half. Mmm, bit short."

Elliott nudges her arm as if to agree. "Nearly done. Last one," she says as she puts map number two on the 'no' pile. So it's map three or go back through them again.

She looks at the front. "Tring Park and beyond. It's three hours and fifteen minutes. Seven miles. Is that okay?" Elliott's looking over at me as if to say 'please say yes!'

"Sure," I say a little less enthusiastically than Elliott's eyes.

Chapter 83 – In Mind If Not In Body

"Okay then," Izzy says when we're by the front door. She bends down, takes Elliott's lead and hands it towards me.

"Oh no, it's okay, you carry on."

Izzy looks down at the map's front. "A circular walk starting from Tring town centre and exploring the historic parkland. Sounds lovely." She opens the map. "Looks simple enough. And presumably we get to see an owl." She shows me the illustration of a barn owl.

"Nice. It's daylight though so…"

"True. Right. Frogmore Street East car park, behind Dolphin Square and the Church of St Peter and St Paul. Do you know where that is?"

"I do. Seeing you've got Trouble, shall I take the map?"

"Trouble?"

I look down at Elliott who's sitting patiently, wagging his tail. "Not that you ever are of course, are you?" He barks his innocence, making us laugh. I don't know how I feel about the fact that the walk is going to take us through Tring Park, and possibly the summerhouse where Charles proposed to my mum. I'm happy as long as she's happy and she seems tremendously happy. Perhaps a little cautious because I've not exactly been jumping for joy. I need to, for her. Be there for her, whatever happens.

"Does it take us to the summerhouse?"

"Summerhouse?"

"Tring Park, where Charles–"

Izzy silently skim reads the main page. "Mmm… doesn't say so specifically." She turns the map over to the first third of the back which is headed 'Tring Park'. "Nope. Just about the animals, slops and valley bottoms." She pulls Elliott's lead slightly and talks to him. "You have a valley bottom, don't you, boy." Elliott barks in agreement.

We do the seven miles and it takes us nearly four hours rather than the 'approximate time' of three and a quarter hours but we probably meander more than the author anticipated. We don't see any owls but plenty of other animals, including squirrels. Elliott's in his element, especially when we're clear of any roads – he has no road sense whatsoever – and he can be off lead. While he never catches anything, he certainly gives them a run for their pocket money.

We do very little of the park itself so don't see the summerhouse, which is fine. On leaving my aunt's, I'd sent my mum a message to let her know what Izzy and I were doing, knowing full well that any walk over an hour, especially one that doesn't involve shopping, isn't going to be Mum's thing. There's no reply by the time we get to the park so I put my phone in my bag to listen out for the buzz or to check later.

Although we had some bottled water, thanks to my aunt, two thirds of us are exhausted by the time we return to my aunt's. Elliott could do it all again. I've taken him on some long walks, not quite as long as this one but hillier, and accompanied my uncle a few times, aunt and uncle a couple of times, and have never seen him – Elliott, not my uncle – tired. Whatever batteries Elliott uses, he should donate them to science. Every time I'm with Elliott, I wish Buddy was more outgoing. He's very sweet, when not being naughty, but Elliott has way more personality. Poor Buddy.

"The kettle's on," my uncle announces as he opens the door.

"Lovely," Izzy says as she bounces into the long lounge.

I'm too tired to think, let alone speak. I can't even nod. Removing my not-really-muddy-but-not-clean-enough-to-keep-on boots is an effort. My head's thumping as I bend down to loosen the laces.

Izzy's already removed hers and realised that I'm struggling so is a pal and undoes my laces for me. "Sit," she orders and I hobble round to one of a pair of chairs facing the television at the end of the room.

I sit and she removes my boots. "I don't think I can ever get up again," I squeak.

Izzy smiles and goes through to the kitchen where my uncle's already gone and I hear a clinking of cups.

Izzy returns almost immediately with a tray and some goodies. She likes her tea really weak so there's a pot but the tea bags have been left to one side. I'm proud of my aunt for remembering. Izzy puts the tray on a small table between the chairs and offers to be 'mum', pouring the tea and distributing two brownies to two side plates.

That reminds me of my phone, unchecked for quite a while. With some effort, I lean round the corner of my chair and pull my bag towards me. There's a green notification.

All good Charles and I will go tomrrow sorry for being lazy see your both latr lve you

My mother speaks really good English, she picked me up on it often enough when I was younger, but when it comes to messaging, she seems all fingers and thumbs and never corrects, or probably even reads, what she's written. I had hoped she'd be around for some of the time while Izzy's staying but at least she was spared naked Charles this morning. The thought of that doesn't help my head.

I blow on the tea and take a sip. My aunt and uncle use Fairtrade tea and it tastes really nice, which gives me an idea for an article I've never done. I finally get out of the chair and shuffle through to the kitchen, to ask my aunt a question before it leaves my brain. "Hi."

"Hello." She's plating up what looks like a second batch of brownies which she covers with a glass dome. The wooden knob on top of it reminds me to get Duncan to fix a chest of drawers where one of the knobs seems too big for its screw. Now I've forgotten what I came through for.

"Oh yes. Could I have one of the teabags please?"

"Certainly." She turns round and pulls forward a container marked 'Tea'. "Not strong enough?"

"It's to remind me to do an article on different types of tea. What brand is this?"

My aunt frowns. "Tesco, I think, or it might be Twinings." She goes to the bottom of the stairs and shouts up to my uncle. "Pat!"

I hear a distant, "Yes?"

"The tea bags. Are these Tesco or Twinings?"

Again a distant, "Are they plain or in bags?"

"They are bags, dear."

I hear a thump of feet down the narrow staircase that adjoins the two halves of the house, and my uncle appears. "Hello, Donna."

"Hi, Uncle Pat."

My aunt's holding up one of the corners of the teabags between two of her fingers as if it's contaminated with something.

"Those will be Tesco. Twinings come individually wrapped."

"Thank you," I say and my uncle nods and disappears back upstairs.

"There we go, dear." My aunt goes to move the domed brownies when she points them at me. "Would you like another?"

I shake my head. "But thank you." I'm not sure I'll even eat the first. I'm way too tired. By the time I've got back to my chair – with Izzy still there but engrossed in what's probably a text message from William, I'm hungry again. My aunt's brownies have that effect.

Elliott's been asleep in his bed the whole time, oblivious of me moving around, which usually garners him following, oblivious to the second batch of brownies, the smell of which reached us soon after we arrived but presumably after he'd gone to his bed, and now oblivious of me eating one of the first batch. It's not warm anymore but it's lovely and soft, sticky almost. Elliott's missing a treat but I remember it's got cocoa powder in it and don't want a repeat of Buddy on my mum's patio so am grateful Elliott's elsewhere, in mind if not in body.

Izzy and I finally make our way back to my mum's. Her car's gone so I know she won't be there, which means Charles, naked or otherwise, won't be either. I didn't notice his car when Izzy and I left this morning so I assume Mum had driven them back late last night or first thing. The Range Rover is so huge it would have stuck out like the proverbial sore thumb; a very big, very black sore thumb.

After such an extensive walk, we have another evening vegging out. It's a bank holiday on Monday and with neither of us working, Izzy's in no hurry to leave Sunday though she and William have plans, and of course want to spend some of the long weekend together.

We choose two more DVDs she's brought with her, a fabulous romantic double bill of *Notting Hill* then *Love Actually*. I don't think it matters in which order they're watched but we agree it feels natural to watch the earlier released first and we're puddles of mush by the end of each one, more so the second because we were semi-mush when that started. But most of all, we're missing our men. Izzy goes into the kitchen and I stay in the lounge and we're each on the phone to our respective halves for at least half an hour.

There's been no sign of my mum but she did message to say she'd be around tomorrow, before she and Charles went to the museum, for the last day of the exhibition.

The museum's not open until two and then only for three hours so I send her a quick message back.

I don't know what we're doing tomorrow, Mum, so please come early in case we go out for a coffee. If not, I can let you know where we go if we do, and you and Charles can join us.

I take the *Gret* reply to be 'Great' rather than 'Greta' and send her a solitary x.

It's nice she's found someone to be with but I'm a little annoyed that she's been so elusive since Izzy arrived. It's the first time she's stayed over and while I'm more than happy to play host, they're like sisters so they're both missing out. "Priorities," I mumble and click my phone to sleep.

It's nearly eleven so I think that's a great thing to do, and am thinking that when Izzy comes back into the lounge.

"You'll be pleased to know that Northampton's still there for us to return back to, some sooner than others. I bet you can't wait."

She's right, especially me having chatted to Duncan and both of us being on the verge of tears. Izzy's face looks a little red. "You okay?"

She sniffs. "Bit emotional. Silly really. I'm seeing him tomorrow night."

"No, that's sweet."

"Don't know how you manage a couple of weeks."

"I managed before I met him," I say sagely. "Can't imagine being without him now."

"Hopefully you'll never have to be. Have you talked about…? Do you think he might…?"

I'm surprised Izzy asks because she knows pretty much everything Duncan and I have ever discussed, the important stuff anyway.

I deflect, reflect, the question. "Will William?"

She blushes. "Sometime, I'm sure. When the time's right. You know him."

"It's the next natural step after moving in, isn't it. And none of us are getting any younger."

Izzy's not long turned thirty-one and I'm hanging on to thirty by too thin a thread. Not something I'm looking forward to.

"We should think about what to do for your thirty-first."

"No," I say a little too sternly, "we shouldn't," but laugh.

Chapter 84 – Tender Bones

Sunday 27th May

We both oversleep, gone eleven, and it's just as well we don't have a dog as it would have seriously been crossing its legs by now. I think yesterday's walk has caught up with us as everything aches. My head feels okay on the inside but everywhere else complains when I move.

There's no sign of Izzy when I get downstairs but the noise of the kettle seems to do the trick and I hear a thump, plod, thump, plod and her socked feet appear, followed by her pyjamas and finally a scowling face.

"Did we drink last night?"

I know she means alcohol.

I shake my head. Neither of us fancied it despite thinking it might help the post-walk fatigue.

"It feels like we drank last night."

She plonks herself, albeit gently, at the table.

I've just put our mugs down when I hear a key in the door.

"Sorry! Sorry!" my mum pants as she opens the front door, wiggling her key loose. "I know you said to be here… Oh, you're not dressed yet. That's good. Has it just boiled?" she asks, pointing to the kettle.

"Want me to–"

"No, you're fine. You have yours. I've not decided yet."

I ask the obvious question. "No Charles?"

She picks up the kettle and wiggles that as if to see if there's enough water, the transparent strip in the side clearly lying. She adds a few millilitres, puts the kettle back on its stand, and flicks the button so it turns blue. "He'll be along in a bit. Got something to sort out first."

A wife? I'm tempted to say but resist.

As if she's only just realised we have a guest, my mum turns to Izzy, rushes over and gives her a big hug. She's too quick for Izzy to stand straight so she's at an awkward forty-five degree angle and winces as her already tender bones are semi-crushed.

"So how are you?" Mum asks, finally letting go and returning to reboil the kettle for her drink before awaiting the reply. She thumps a mug on the work surface, making Izzy wince, and spoons in some coffee and a sweetener. She turns and looks at Izzy for her answer.

"Not bad, thank you," she lies but my mum doesn't seem to twig.

"Great," she chirps, turning back to pour on the water and stirring the drink far too loudly. She then taps the spoon on the edge of the mug with enough ferocity to chip the enamel, except it doesn't. Joining us at the table, she thumps the mug onto her mat, making the coffee slop over the side slightly. "Oh darn."

Darn? Whenever does my mum say 'darn'? In Izzy's company.

"Would you…?" Mum points to a box of paper tissues on a windowsill behind Izzy's right shoulder.

She turns carefully and retrieves the box which she equally carefully puts on the middle of the table as if placing such a weighty object would be tornado-loud.

"So, Izzy. How are things with you? William?"

Izzy nods gently. "Very good, thank you. We've just moved in together. I've… moved in with him."

My mum goes to clap but looks at our faces and clearly thinks better of it. Rather than ask us what's wrong she remains upbeat. "Oh great. That's lovely. Did Donna tell you about Charles and I?"

Me, Mum, Charles and me. It wouldn't be 'Did Donna tell you about I?' now would it.

I gently throw Izzy's earlier question back at her with as much gusto as a toddler throwing a ten-pin bowling ball. "Are you sure we didn't have alcohol last night?"

We look around the room as if there might be evidence of empties. Apart from a half-opened, lid on, prawn cocktail Pringles tub and two empty Asda bolognaise pasta bake ready meal card outers and black plastic trays, there's nothing. No empty bottles of even fizzy water.

"So you girls had fun last night?" Mum asks, trying to surmise the morning after the night before. So are we.

"Watching a couple of movies and eating…" I look over again at the Pringles. "…things we shouldn't have been."

Mum blows a raspberry. "It's the weekend. Izzy's a guest. It's obligatory to have fun."

Izzy's about to speak when the front door opens.

"Hello, ladies." Charles is grinning and I notice he's carrying a Harrods woven bag. Not a bag for life as much as one for a millennium. He puts the bag down on the work surface and pulls out a white box with gold ribbon around it. There's a label of some kind on the top but it's too far away for me to see. It looks expensive. He carries it over and places it on the table as if the item were made of gold.

I look at Izzy and she's almost drooling. She sits up straighter, furrow on her forehead gone, and she's smiling, no beaming. I look again at the box. "How did you know?" I ask him.

He doesn't answer but looks at my mum then back at me. Of course. Everyone who knows Izzy knows how much she loves banoffee pie and now he knows her. She wouldn't kill for it because she's too much of a goodie two-shoes and certainly wouldn't die for it because I know she loves her life, but...

"And in case it wasn't your favourite, Donna..." Charles returns to the Harrods bag and brings over another box of a similar size. The label on this one lists three items instead of one: 'Double Caramel Millionaire's Shortbread, Tiffin, Florentine'. I never knew Millionaire's shortbread was anything but single caramel. So the kind man had been to the bakery before coming over. "Your mother gave me some clues for you too."

I look at Mum who's smiling.

"They're probably still warm."

I struggle to think of a bakery that would be open on a Sunday morning. It certainly doesn't have a Tesco feel about it.

"It took a bit longer than I expected because I couldn't remember where I'd put the ribbons."

That's sweet. He added the bows afterwards.

"He made them." My mum's almost glowing with pride.

"Sorry?" I say to her.

"Charles, he made the cakes. This morning actually. I said he could have done it yesterday but no, he wanted them to be as fresh as possible. I put the boxes together. He had them from... Where were they from?"

"A friend's wedding. I helped with the catering. It was only a small affair. A hundred or so."

I'm struggling to think of fifty people I'd know, let alone like enough, to invite to my wedding... if and when I have one.

"You..."

Charles blushes. "Right, shall we have a bit now or pop out for lunch and come back and have some."

I can tell we're all tempted to go for the first option but reality and sanity rule so we 'plan b'.

"What choices do we have?" Charles asks and I list some of the places I'd researched for all these evenings I was going to go out for dinner with my mum, none of which have happened yet.

We decide on a Sunday roast, given that it is actually Sunday, so head over to the Crow's Nest across the local dual carriageway, the A41 that takes its quarry from the M25 to Aylesbury and beyond.

Being a Beefeater, I suspect it's going to be popular and wondered whether we should have booked but yet again, Charles knows the manager so we have a lovely quiet table near the fire. It's been strategically placed to get maximum heat although it's simmering gently rather than roaring, being a nice day.

"I'm paying," Charles announces as we sit.

Izzy and I go to protest but he insists.

"Please. It's a... an engagement celebration."

My mum blushes but nods.

Izzy and I order the Beefeater share platter, at a mere 2,147 calories between us. We love everything listed: 'buttermilk chicken wings, slices of breaded crispy flat cap mushroom, lamb kofta, spicy potato dippers and grilled flatbread pieces. Accompanied by ranch, piri piri (aka peri-peri at Nando's) and smoky BBQ dips with, at Charles's instance, the spare ribs added, so the best of both worlds. So much for our Sunday roasts.

Mum and Charles though do go for the roast and have 'rump of lamb' and 'slow-cooked beef' and they swap pieces. They're just like Izzy and me. Actually a great pairing. I decide I've been far too judgemental of him. He's really nice, thoughtful, and generous. Almost the perfect guy in every respect. I blush as I think of seeing him yesterday morning but take a sip of my lemonade, pretending that my spicy potato dipper is hot, which it actually is. I take an extra sip.

Although the desserts look and sound divine, but don't they always on a menu, we agree to skip them and coffees and go back to Mum's. It's lovely chatting at the pub but it's been rather overtaken by families, as you would expect for a Sunday lunchtime, so Charles pays the bill and thanks Jodie our waitress for stellar service. She is lovely, and particularly attentive, probably having been told the identity of her guest of honour, and we leave.

Mum puts on the kettle as Charles deboxes the cakes and puts them onto platters Mum got out before we left.

"Are you retired then, Charles?" I ask, despite knowing about his P.I. work but am über nosey, as he cuts the cakes into too-generous portions.

He avoids answering the question directly, I note, as he replies, "I was..." He seems shy or reluctant but I can't work out which. "I was er... in the police."

Izzy's eyes light up. "Really? I'm thinking of writing a crime novel."

"You are?" I ask, once I've pulled my jaw off the table.

"Yes. I've told you loads of times."

"Not that it was a *crime* novel."

"Yes."

Now *The Luckiest House* definitely doesn't sound like a winner if it's supposed to be a crime novel. Oh well, at least she's made a new research buddy.

Charles retrieves his bulging (I smirk) wallet from his trouser back pocket, opens the wallet and pulls out a gold-embossed business card which he hands over to Izzy. "Anything you need."

She blushes and almost gushes. "Thank you. That's very kind."

My mum isn't the only one glowing with pride and it feels good.

Chapter 85 – A Little Cold But Familiar

Monday 28th May

Being school bank holidays this week, the traffic's going to be really light. Most people would have gone away for the weekend. Izzy and I both have the day off but she wanted to spend some time with William, as to be expected. I'd suggested she come down a different weekend but workaholic William said there were things he needed to do in the office Saturday / Sunday. I guess a paper doesn't run itself.

So indulgently, I spend the entire day in my pyjamas. I'm tempted to collect Elliott again but I fancy vegging so that's exactly what I do. I am however very restrained and not a mouthful of ice cream passes my lips. I do make up for it with crisps, finger pizza and a mini Twix, but the rest of the time, I'm an angel personified with salad, pasta and spring water.

Yesterday, after we got back from the Crow's Nest, Charles delighted and entertained, and I could really see what had attracted Mum to him, apart from the obvious. He had the perfect attributes any woman would want in a man, while he did have flaws. Yes, even Charles. It turned out, when one walked up the kitchen door, that he's scared of spiders. Fair enough he had been bitten by a tarantula while working in Egypt, as you do, but this was only a money spider. You'd think, out of us all, before his confession, that Charles would have been the first to pick it up and throw it outside but no, Izzy did that. Another tick in the Izzy:Charles log book.

He didn't outstay his welcome, nor stay over, and left before eight last night.

"He's amazing, Lesley!" Izzy gushed before she too headed away.

It was Mum's turn to blush but I still felt proud.

"Feeling better about him now?" Mum asked me, when Izzy had gone, and I could honestly say I did.

"Love him. Not love-him love-him but you know."

"Yes, I do."

Being a four-day week, I'm hoping the next few days will fly. The project officially finishes on Thursday, leaving Friday simply to write up the final article should I have my 'last' meal on Thursday, and answer any related emails.

Come Monday I'll be back in Northampton, at my gone-a-little-cold but familiar desk and all will be well with the world again. I shall throw myself, be myself, back into Donnaland… and now I feel like a Dolly-type theme park.

I'm not a natural exhibitionist but wonder if I would have done, will do something, one day so that people would know my name. Local people do, back in Northampton, they only know Veronica's here, but it's not the same. I'm sure if you stopped a thousand people on the street back home, no, the tens of thousands who buy the paper on a regular or semi-regular basis, only a fraction, fewer than ten, five percent, one more likely, would be able to say who writes the health and beauty column.

I may not change lives but I know I make a lot of people feel better about themselves. I imagine it's like people who read books; out of every hundred who read a book, I guess only one leaves a review. I might be wrong but how dispiriting must it be for authors when they've put however many hours in it takes to write a book – a year? – and struggle to get it published then when it is and they check their reviews for there to only be a new one every full moon.

But what do I know? I'm a journalist, not even that, a columnist, not an author. I don't know what it takes to write a book of what, seventy, eighty thousand words, more if you're the likes of J.R.R.R. Tolkien, or however many Rs he has after the J, or erm… the Games of the Thrones guy. Martin something with a lot of initials. G.R.R.R.?

Being a bank holiday, I'll miss out on my final Nathan tonight, which is really sad. Billy had told me last Thursday of Nathan's plans with a mystery man (still Brad, I'm hoping) so I wasn't going to interrupt that. Instead, I do go to Hemel's Wetherspoon, The Full House, the other nearest 'spoon' being The Bell in Aylesbury so I thought I'd stick with Hemel as it would have felt a little traitory.

I'm glad I went for the one I did as it had an amazing mural behind the bar, very Romeo and Juliet, the perfect thing to remind me that I'm going home to Duncan on Friday.

Chapter 86 – And Splurge

Tuesday 29th May

Leah, it turns out, has extended her holiday with her boyfriend. Like a scene from the 'warts and all' (not that any of them would have had any) television series 'Selling Sunset', Leah's landed herself a rich boyfriend and they decided, with no days off taken since Christmas, to holiday wherever the fancy takes them.

I don't mind at all having the days to myself. After hitting the charity shops with Izzy on Saturday, I plan to resist the urge to hit the ones here. I've got more emails in than normal because of the day off so the morning's gone just going through those. I can also get my articles ready for the last three days of the month, this project, even if they don't have all the details… like the venues or food! A minor… er, detail.

Speaking of which, I didn't bring any lunch with me, and having been in the ladies when the snack van arrived I didn't hear the claxon – I really must be getting deaf in my 'old' age. Oh gosh. Thirty-one nearly. So I head to the town centre, grab a turkey and stuffing (it's only May!) sandwich and do indeed hit the charity shops.

Duncan loves his bargains as much as I do so will be delighted with the remote-control Ferrari for a fiver! The box is a bit tatty but that doesn't matter. It's not like we have a child to sit in it. Had Buddy been a cat… or a child… although Duncan would dispute that.

Frank and I head to The Olive Indian Restaurant on Lawn Lane, on sort of a triangle with the Boxmoor Steakhouse and K2, with the River Gade running along two sides, for the final Indian of the week. I think.

"I'm under instructions," he tells me as we walk to the front door, having driven in convoy and parked next to each other, "for 'the works' so, my dear, you have a night off from 'the project'. So I hope that's okay."

That sound more than okay as Indian is one of the most difficult, with all its lovely sauces, to get a healthy version thereof. We therefore take, presumably Billy's, word for it and splurge on a buffet of starters as mains: bhajis, poppadoms, tikka potato cakes, samosas, duck Nizami rolls, Konkani crab, Chatpata crispy calamari, chicken pakora, a portion of pilau and lemon cashew rices, not forgetting the obligatory aloo gobi and saag aloo.
Even though I'm not working, I take in the array before me and try to memorise them, like a contestant at the end of the Generation

Game. All that's missing is the cuddly toy, and it probably would have been easier to name the things we weren't going to have. Oh, and our waitress, Avani, is bringing something else.

"Lamb keema tawa tak-a-tak," she announces and moves one of the other dishes over to make room on our table for four for two.

"The restaurant's 'street food'," Frank informs me as if he's a regular here too. It wouldn't surprise me but I hold in the 'do you come here often' question.

We look at the food then at each other. "How can we resist?" he asks.

We don't, and end up waddling to our cars, having even had ice cream and indulgent liqueur coffees at the end.

As I was with Nathan, I'm rather sad that this is my final evening with Frank. I'll see him in the office over the next three days but it won't be the same. I'm sure, given how friendly my mum is with his wife, that I'll see him again.

I soon cheer up though at the thought that it's now only three days until I see Duncan. We have a long chat on the phone and end with our usual greeting. I wonder if things will be any different when I get home. In a way, I don't want them to be but I do feel that there does need to be a next step. I'm not going to be the one to say anything though. It's not that I'm old fashioned. It's just not a boat I want a rockin'.

Chapter 87 – Coming Back To Stay

Wednesday 30th May

There are a couple of venues on my list I've not been to. Although Frank and I went to The Plough at Leverstock Green and had a Tuesday Sunday roast mid-month, I still have the Toby Carvery outstanding. "Do you mind?" I ask Greta.

"Not at all. I've never had a carvery."

"Never?"

She shakes her head. "Had Sunday roasts of course but not a proper carvery. I've been there but only for a drink, which was a bit of a waste but the guy I was with was… a bit of a waste." We laugh.

Being a carvery, I can skip on the fattening; like Yorkshire puds, but make up on the protein; the meat. Greta goes all out and has something of everything. "I'm not supposed to do that," the man, Elvis, says. He's big like his namesake in his later years though wearing a white apron over black and white check workwear, rather than a rhinestone-encrusted jumpsuit.

When Greta looks at her heaving plate and my rather bare one, she looks back at him. He sighs, flaps his hand like someone indicating the forward movement of traffic so I return to stand opposite him and he gives me more meat with the instruction, 'Don't tell anyone'. I look at the snake of a queue but say nothing.

Greta's and my entire conversation revolves around music until we finally get to Owen. At the mention of his name, Greta blushes.

"Still going strong?" I ask but then feel bad because it's none of my business so I add a swift, "You do seem really happy."

She nods and I ask the ultimate hairdresser question, "Are you going on holiday this year?" but frown as it feels a silly thing to ask with someone so new in a relationship, unless of course she's already booked to go somewhere.

"Erm…"

I wait. She nods again. "Oh really?" I want to ask 'anywhere nice?' but remain patient. It's never been a trait of mine so there are a few seconds' silence.

"Owen's parents have a villa in Portugal."

I still say nothing but smile a Tigger-D smile.

Two days to go before I get to go home and feel her, Tigger D, coming back to stay.

Chapter 88 – Thursday 31st May

There's no sign of James (or Leah – I'm hoping that's purely a coincidence) as I head into the office. Although part of me would be glad if he doesn't reappear, the rest of me hopes he's back tomorrow as it would be nice to at least say 'goodbye' and draw a line underneath this month. With lots to tie up on my final day, I decide to do some of it today and keep an ear out for the food van.

Val, or someone more holy, must have read my mind as I've only just sat at my desk with a bottle of sparkling water when the claxon goes. Unsure what I'll be doing for lunch on my last day, I go for another thick ham salad wrap although I forgo the hazelnut latté and immediately regret it as I watch the van pull away from my office (desk) window.

I decide to opt for the kitchen's version (Americano no flavourings) but get so engrossed in work that I go the whole day without another drink or even going to the ladies, only being roused by Nathan at gone five when he scuttles to my desk.

"Hiiiii, Donna." He's almost doing jazz hands.

"Helloooo, Nathan," I chirp back.

"Sorreee…" Nathan tilts his head as if delivering bad news, which presumably he is, given the elongated word 'sorry'. "Billy's running a tincy bit late." As Nathan says the word 'tincy', he holds up his right hand with his index finger and thumb almost touching.

Relieved Billy's not cancelling, I blow a breath to which Nathan gets into agony aunt mode – a position which I believe is still vacant and he'd be perfect for. "Tell Uncle Nathan."

"Seeing as we have a few minutes," I say, but then don't know what it is I want to impart. He leans forward, as if anticipating my woes. "Erm…"

He tilts his head to one side. "Oh dear."

Now I feel as if I have to come up with something but again I'm saved from the moment by Billy who, I'm hoping, has come to collect me.

"Ready?"

"As I'll ever…" but he's already turned and is heading round the corner towards Nathan's then his own desk. So Nathan and I follow, me a couple of seconds later, having sent my computer to sleep and retrieved my bag.

The other restaurant on my wish list is back at The Marlowes, the Opuz Kitchen with an average 4.6 rating from 145 reviews on Google. Fortunately for me, Billy loves Turkish as much as Frank loves Indian and Billy actually mentions the Opuz as one of his favourites before asking me if there was anywhere I wanted to go, as if I could have said anything else.

It could be another night ‘off’, because all my articles are done but to end with another wrap does feel a little weak so I make mental – and if Billy goes to the gents, not that he’d mind, paper notes as we go along. I start with Sigara Boregi, a ‘cigar shaped crisp filo pastry filled with halloumi cheese, spinach and fresh herbs’, because I love halloumi. Billy goes for the other one I fancy, though not quite as much, but how I keep a straight face at its name; Sucuk, a grilled lightly spiced Turkish beef sausage, I really don’t know.

Although I love my choice, I must admit that Billy’s sausage does look inviting. The thought of it however reminds me of Charles so I’m glad I went with the Boregi.

Mains were a meat moussaka for me (I didn’t need to look any further down the menu) and an Iskender, a house special of lamb or chicken doner on a bed of bread, layered with a topping of fresh tomato and butter sauce, served with creamy yogurt and rice, for Billy. And yes, he went for the optional ‘spicy hot’.

I’m sad, again, as the evening draws to a close.

“I can’t thank you enough, Billy, for not only making me feel welcome but also so special.”

I timed that with him taking a large mouthful of food so he can’t reply. Although Billy strikes me as someone who can be rough and tough, I know there’s a softer side.

“Even if Hazel,” I continue, who’s been out of the office more than she’s been around, “had organised the rota, I know it would have only happened with your approval, and I can’t imagine every boss, or personnel human resources manager, for that matter, going to that much trouble.”

Billy finally swallows and takes a sip of water. I can’t tell whether he’s going red through embarrassment or whether he can’t actually handle the level of ‘spicy hot’ he’s been given. A little cough before he speaks doesn’t give me an answer. “You’re very welcome, Donna. William did say to look after you.”

I tilt my head in Nathan fashion. “He did?”

Billy grimaces as if it’s a secret he shouldn’t have shared. Maybe he’s not so special agent after all. He shrugs as if it’s no big thing and he’d help anyone.

I am, however, honoured. William’s dating my best friend but even so, this was work. He and Izzy are perfect for each other: both marshmallow on the inside.

As I tuck into my food, I think that saying ‘goodbye’ to Billy and his underlings will be harder than I thought. They’re all, almost all, lovely and have been so kind. I feel special. Yes, so so special.

Chapter 89 – Mission Accomplished

Friday 1st June

My last day is here. I know being the beginning of the month that some people are going to be crazy busy, others catching up from the end of the month if they didn't get everything finished off yesterday. It's like that in our office. It's not like everyone's in accounts so you wouldn't think there would be that cut-off but I guess it's a mental thing.

I feel a little sad when I drive into the car park for the last time, walk past Phil's box for the second from last time, or fourth if I go out for lunch, the last morning anyway. Then the same for Owen who's on the phone but looks up and smiles. The office is as busy as I had anticipated so I go straight to my desk, via the kitchen for a glass of squash.

I've got a few loose ends to tie up so I'll be busy too but will definitely make sure that I get to speak to everyone, thank them for how helpful they've been, especially my lunchtime and evening companions.

James. I must sort things out with James. There's been an 'air' all month and while it's not got worse since our trip to Jarman Park, it's not really got better either, when he's been around. It's a shame because we could have had some lovely lunchtimes but at least when I've gone that'll be it. I don't like leaving things unresolved though so I'll make the first move, so to speak, apologise and everything will be fine.

Now, I'll do it now.

I head for his desk and am just as pleased to see he's there, not on the phone, and doesn't look particularly busy. "Morning, James," I say with my biggest genuine smile.

"Morning, Donna." He's smiling too and not in any kind of 'way'.

Would you… no, don't give him a choice. "I'd very much like to take you out for lunch today, as a 'thank you' for how kind you've been this month." I'm hoping that comes across how it's meant and it won't read anything more into it. Nothing will, can, happen after today. He may well never see me again.

It seems to be taken as I intended, judging by his reaction. He bows slightly, his right shoulder dipping towards his desk before he rights it. "I would equally like that."

I spend the morning tying most of the loose ends so I'll have little to do after lunch, which may mean I can escape early.

James comes to collect me at twelve thirty. It seems that something's shifted. There's an ease I'd not felt before and I don't know how he feels but he looks comfortable in my company. We're back to where we were at the start, just colleagues with no added pressure.

"Ready, madam?" he asks and sways the air to his right in a gesture that I should go first.

"I am, my lord," I reply and after grabbing my bag, I walk past him and through the office. No one's paying us any attention, for which I'm grateful, and Owen's on the phone again, to be expected, but gives us a cursory nod. Everything feels really normal which is lovely.

"Anywhere in particular for your last lunch?" James asks, pointing in the general direction of the town centre.

"Finish where we started?"

His smile turns into a grin and we head for The Marlowes shopping centre and the venue we had our first lunch in: Subway. Not the most salubrious but it's lunch not supper, dinner, tea, evening whatever, and I'm going to have something special. No salad for this girl, oh no. I might even go for something hot. No, not James. Hash browns or nachos or maybe both. I'm no longer on the 500 max so I can splash out all round.

According to Subway's website, a portion of six hash browns are 169 calories but the intro says, 'Default nutritional values are based on the standard six-inch sub recipe' so I'm taking it at face value. They're probably 169 calories per piece. An average sweet is fifty, an apple eighty or satsuma thirty, ish, a hundred in a standard sweet potato but that's before it goes near a fryer.

James and I go for the hash browns and nachos to share, a Pepsi Max for James, a bottle of water for me, and a wrap each: me chicken, him steak. He insists on paying, saying there's still plenty of Billy's budget left. There are several free tables so I let James lead and pick one.

I congratulate myself that my eyes don't wander to his bum then realise I had no inkling to do so until after he'd sat and I found I was self-congratulating. Duncan's I look at all the time, especially when he's in his scrubs, which he sometimes wears at home just for me. The thought makes me smile.

"Penny for them," I hear in the distance that is across the table.

My mind scrambles. "Sorry, just a joke I heard on the radio on the way in."

"Ooh, I love jokes. Do tell."

Oops. "Sorry, forgotten the punchline but I remember it being funny."

"Okay," he says nonchalantly as he takes one of the hash browns. There are six, just like the picture, all perfectly symmetrical. They must have a machine and part of me wants to ask the manager but I resist. I've been geeky enough for one month. A month and a day.

James and I chat about the state of the UK and US governments and swap ideas for how they can be improved. It's really nice to have a normal conversation, albeit about politics, and before we know it, our food's gone and it's time to get back to the office. We've not been an hour but the sooner we get back, the sooner I can hit the M1. Oh the joy. Commuterville on a Friday afternoon.

"Thank you," I say to James as we reach the top of the stairs between Phil and Owen's 'offices'. I want to touch James on the arm, only as a show of gratitude, but I don't want to risk spoiling the level we've left things.

We're side by side and he goes to lean in but clearly thinks better of it and steps back to compensate. "You're very welcome, my lady," he says and makes a sweeping gesture.

I laugh and beckon him through the door first.

"Oh contraire, my lady, beauty before age." James has the upper hand on both of those but I don't complain. I bow slightly and go ahead, nodding and smiling to Owen as I pass his cubicle. He's on the phone, chatting to someone, and I swear he's blushing so I'm hoping it's Greta. I pick up speed and almost run down the corridor, bypassing the kitchen although I could do with a cold drink, so I can get to Greta's desk before Owen's call finishes. Sure enough, she's on the phone giggling and blushing. I don't know for sure but hope that two and two only equals four on this occasion.

Back at my desk, wearing a grin I can't help, I type up my final report. It doesn't mention food as that's all done but is a 'how my month went' summary. And it went very well. Of course I'm not going to mention my ups and downs with James, that's only for him and me to know, but it's certainly been a learning curve, as life usually is.

And I return to my shopping list. If there's one thing this month has taught me, it's not only about how healthy we keep our bodies, it's mostly so we live longer and are happier doing it, but our mental health is just as important if not more so. What's the point in having a trim body if we're unhappy? The whole James – I want to use the word 'affair' but that would be misleading – it was never going to be that. The whole James matter has taught me to value what I have. Not that I didn't before but love, life, goes deeper than skin. James does have beautiful skin, but the head and heart are what matter and given the choice of the two, who wouldn't pick the latter.

So, my shopping list consists of just three things: loving someone who can love you back unconditionally; a rewarding career where you work to live not live to work; a body and mind as healthy as you can make it without punishing yourself if you slip up. Tomorrow is another day, as Scarlett O'Hara so eloquently said, while lying on the stairs, eyes still wet from crying.

As are mine a few minutes later after Billy's gathered everyone around my desk and Hazel's presented me with a card. It's huge and has a variety of scrawled farewells, including one from a name I don't recognise (Sam) and I feel bad that I didn't get to meet him or her. Hazel also gives me a beautiful plant. It looks like the red Christmas one whose name I can never remember… Poinsetta? Poinsettia… something like that, but pinker and more 'flowery'.

"It's a Monet Twilight," Hazel explains.

"It's beautiful," I gush. I then get a round of applause at which I go bright red. Someone at the back shouts "Speech!" and I go even redder. I'm not one for being the centre of attention but I'm so grateful that I don't mind on this occasion, stunned though I am. I remain seated and say, "I don't know what to say, which is not like me." Someone to my right laughs. "But I will just say a huge 'thank you' to you all. I'm sorry if I didn't get to know you as much as I'd like to have done but I would like to say a special thanks to everyone who helped me with this project. In day order: James and Leah, the lunches."

I search them out, conveniently stood next to each other, and they nod. "Nathan, Monday evenings." He grins. "Frank, Tuesday nights… er evenings!" Frank blushes. "Greta Wednesdays." She, I'm delighted to see, is holding hands with Owen. They both blush. "Billy Thursdays."

"Sorry about the first one," he says, to which I shake my head. Ancient history and I got Lussmanns in exchange. I look around and don't see Phil so don't need to mention the Fridays that didn't happen. I'm not sure how he would have reacted anyway because things seem to have gone a little frosty again but I'll make sure I at least say 'goodbye' on my way out. Someone will need to let me out of the car park as I'll have handed back my passes. "And everyone else for being so lovely."

My colleagues murmur then filter back to their desks, leaving Leah hovering. "Hello," I say and wait for her to speak.

"Hi. Thanks for doing everything you did. You didn't need to, you know."

I'm a little puzzled because I was really just doing my job but her words mean a lot. I say a 'you're very welcome', smile and watch her leave. Nothing's been mentioned on either side about Charles doing his information gathering and it doesn't matter. We all make mistakes in life and this was tiny by comparison, even by the dressed fleas standard. No one died. No one would feel better if it were ever mentioned again.

I do my final report and sigh when I click ‘save’. Everything’s either been printed or is on the network for Billy or Nathan to prepare when they need it.

I had purposely put most of my things in the boot of my car when I left work yesterday so I wouldn’t have much to carry and it is simply me, my bag, card safely stowed, and plant.

Hazel escorts me off the premises. Although I’ve done nothing wrong, I can’t help feeling like a criminal. It’s a silly feeling. I’ve never done anything illegal… well, maybe a mile or two over the speed limit occasionally but nothing intentionally against the law. Donna ‘Goodie Two-Shoes’ Evans, that’s me.

I feel sad waving goodbye to Hazel as the barrier lifts for the pass she’s flashing at it. Although I didn’t get to chat to her as often as I would have liked, I feel she made all the difference for my stay at Hemel Hempstead. Without her brilliant idea of providing me with companions, it would have felt very two-dimensional rather than the four, if that’s possible, that it proved to be. I’ll send her something as a way of thanks, although I know she’d not expect anything. Whatever I choose, I’ll make sure it’s a really really bright colour. And Scottish. And loud. The thought of that banishes my blues and Duncan appears in my brain.

As I drive up the M1, in the inside lane, well back from the car in front, doing a comfortable sixty-five, I think about how quickly this month has gone, month and a day since I arrived. Everyone’s been so lovely and I’m pleased, no relieved, that James and I have sorted everything out. I did get to say a quick ‘goodbye’ to Phil and once he had peeled himself away from the screen, he said he was sorry to see me go, which was nice.

I feel I’ve left with a clear conscience, a small army of good friends, and the satisfaction of a job well done. Okay, so the brief was rather hazy but I did what was asked of me and as far as I know, spent more time in the office than I was expected to, getting ahead with my own work which is brilliant, and didn’t shame Veronica who returns on Monday. I can’t help but wonder whether James has told her about me mistaking him for her husband. I’ve still not seen a picture of him, the real husband. I looked on social media but he’s either particularly private or he doesn’t exist. Of course he has to, for there to be children, but one of life’s mysteries, I guess.

I’m almost tempted to come back to meet her, Veronica, but a phone call or email will suffice. I’m too eager to return to the

Northampton hub, catch up on everything I've missed and settle back at my own desk. In that respect, it has seemed like ages. It's funny how time can be so misleading; quick in one life, slow in another.

Chapter 90 – Home Sweet Duncan's Home

I can't tell you how pleased, no, delighted, beyond thrilled, I am to be on my way back home. Duncan's.

He's back from work already. He's texted to say he was cooking and asked what time I'd be there. We settled on seven to be on the safe side. If the worst comes to the worst, traffic wise, I'll skip popping back to my flat. I have my overnight stuff and my own part of his wardrobe so there's nothing I have to get. I'd only be killing time so what's the point?

The month has been a blur. It ended up not really being about the food I was eating or the places I went to but the interactions, the fun and laughter. Plenty of trials and tribulations along the way but it's shown me that life isn't all about what we do but who we do it with and I know, without any silhouette of a doubt, that Duncan is the man I want to spend the rest of my life with. I'd still love him to propose to me rather than the other way round but there's a leap year every four years so who knows.

I still have that in my brain when I pull up outside his house. I did have time to go to mine first but I didn't want to. He won't mind me being early. What am I going to catch him doing? Walking around his kitchen, naked wearing just his muscle-man pinny? A modern version of my mum's. Or naked. Wouldn't be the first time.

Wine. I should have bought some wine. Oh drat. He has loads but it would have been a nice touch. I'm nervous. Why am I nervous? I'm never nervous around Duncan.

Because I want to marry him.

I have a huge grin on my face at the thought of him wearing nothing but a pinny, or less, as I fish around in my bag for his key then realise they're on the same bunch as my main set which is still in my hand from when I batted the remote to lock the car. I tell you, my brain's going to mush. Even more than normal.

I'm about to put the key in the lock when the door opens, making me wobble a little.

True to form, he's wearing his pinny, the two-dimensional muscles rippling as he leans forward to give me the biggest of kisses. It's slow, tender, and continues for ages. We've not seen each other for two weeks, the longest we've been apart since we met.

"It's been for-effing ever," he says as he pulls back.

"It has," I say and follow him into the hall. The smell of cooking is subtle but it's there.

"It's only just gone in," he says and smiles at my snigger before he takes a sip of red wine. There are two glasses and the other is a little fuller than his.

"I love red wine," I say, "sometimes I even put it in the food." I frown as it didn't come out exactly how it was meant. My brain catches up. "I cook with wine…" I give up. Duncan knows what I mean.

He looks from me to upstairs, then back to me. "We have twenty minutes to kill…"

I smile and he steps forward, takes my right hand in mine and leads me astray.

Chapter 91 – Catching up with Izzy

Saturday 2nd June

And I thought hangovers were bad. I smile as Duncan rolls over and snores, settling thankfully with his face away from me. I'm also grateful that he's not awake so I don't have to tell him that I've been up twice in the middle of the night, head over the toilet bowl, trying to keep down the lovely meal he cooked. As far as I know he's been all right, sleeping straight through, or certainly snoring away when I've been awake.

I love chicken. I love chicken teriyaki, especially with new potatoes and mixed veg. Mixed anything is fine with me; I love my combos. But just the thought of it… My stomach churns and I slide out of bed for a third time. I can't get comfortable no matter how hard I try. It hurts to lie, hurts to sit, hurts to stand. So I head back to the bathroom, lift the toilet lid and kneel, waiting.

I'm also grateful that I don't have work today, or tomorrow… or Monday. William's given me the day off which is very kind of him. He's running a spare article I'd submitted before I went away and I can do my round up / welcome back kind of article for Tuesday's issue. Then back to normal on Wednesday. Right now though I'm feeling far from it.

I look at a waterproof clock at the end of the bath. 08:01. If Amazon made waterproof Alexas we'd probably have one of those in here too. I must admit I am a bit of a news nut so would ask her what's been happening while I've been asleep, awake, barely asleep, awake, and even less asleep before the final wake. Another world tragedy, another loss for Hollywood probably, so I can wait.

Next thing I know there's a knock at the bathroom door. I've fallen asleep and my head's freezing, cheek stuck to the side of the bath. Very dignified. Thankfully though I'm feeling better. I turn, flush the toilet, and go to stand. I'm not queasy, not a hundred percent, but semi-human at least. I open the door and there's Duncan, bed-headed but as gorgeous as ever.

"Missed you when I woke this morning," he says.

I try a smile and blow him a kiss. I've not brushed my teeth yet so don't want to inflict him with that kind of skin on skin. I think he can tell.

"Cuppa?"

"Please," I say except it comes out as a bit of a squawk. My mouth is so dry. Brushing my teeth then mouthwash, or the other way round, I haven't decided which, will help.

I go back in the bathroom and shut the door.

"Oh!" Duncan calls through the door. I'm mid brush so can't move or speak but just listen. "Your phone's out here if you're looking for it. Izzy rang. She's on her way over. For a catch up, she says."

Urgh. I normally love to see her but not feeling up to it.

I can then hear Duncan plod back to the kitchen. He's wearing his particularly noisy slippers. I only have myself to blame as I bought them for him for Christmas.

I spit and stare in the mirror. I don't look sick yet sub-human is about as good as I feel I'm going to get today. I keep staring and a light bulb finally goes off in my head.

I come out of the bathroom about ten minutes later, hands behind my back, deep in thought.

Wandering through to the kitchen, I'm greeted by a pair of Cheshire cats. I'm not sure I can handle this.

Izzy's acting weird. She's me on a particularly bouncy day. I, however, still feel like death. No, not quite death but I currently don't know how I feel. She steps forward and grins. I think I know that grin and that once I get back to normality, it's exactly how I will be feeling.

We scream as we hold up our hands. The brands are different but clutched between the thumbs and index fingers of our right hands are two pregnancy testers: mine showing two blue vertical lines, Izzy's showing the words 'Pregnant' and '3+' underneath it.

Oh… my… god.

Locations featured in The Serial Dieter

Chapters 1-3: The newspaper office, Northampton town centre.
Chapter 4: The office, Boots, the market, the office, all Northampton.
Chapters 5-6: Duncan's house, somewhere in Northampton.
Chapters 7-8: The Northampton newspaper office.
Chapter 9: Duncan's house.
Chapter 10: Duncan's house then the M1 motorway.
Chapter 11: Donna's mum's (Lesley's) house in Tring, Hertfordshire.
Chapters 12-17: The sister newspaper office, central Hemel Hempstead.
Chapter 18: Ristorante Alberto, Hemel old village then Subway, town centre.
Chapter 19: Subway then newspaper office, both Hemel town centre.
Chapters 20-22: The Hemel office.
Chapter 23: The office then Chiangmai Thai restaurant, Hemel old village.
Chapter 24: Chiangmai Thai restaurant then Asda, all Hemel town centre.
Chapters 25-26: Lesley's house, Tring.
Chapters 27-28: The Hemel office.
Chapter 29: The Hemel office then XC, Jarman Square, near the M1, Hemel.
Chapter 30: XC then the Hemel office.
Chapters 31-32: The Hemel office.
Chapter 33: K2 Balti House restaurant, Hemel town centre.
Chapter 34: K2 Balti House restaurant then Lesley's house.
Chapter 35: The Hemel office.
Chapter 36: Donna's aunt Jan and uncle Pat's, Tring, then Tring reservoir.
Chapter 37: Bluebells Tearooms, Tring Reservoir, Marsworth.
Chapter 38: Ivinghoe Beacon.
Chapter 39: Aunt Jan and Uncle Pat's then Lesley's house, both Tring.
Chapter 40: Tring Garden Centre, near Bulbourne.
Chapter 41: The Hemel office then Pizza Express, Hemel town centre.
Chapter 42: Lesley's house, Tring.
Chapter 43: The Hemel office then Subway, Hemel town centre.
Chapter 44: The Hemel office.
Chapter 45: The office, Lesley's, Lussmanns, The Old (HSBC) Bank, Tring.
Chapter 46: Lesley's house, Tring.
Chapter 47: The Hemel office then The Marlowes Café, Hemel town centre.
Chapters 48-9: Duncan's house, Northampton.
Chapter 50: Starbucks then charity shops, Northampton then Duncan's.
Chapter 51: Duncan's house then Frankie & Benny's, Northampton.
Chapter 52: Duncan's house.
Chapter 53: Donna's flat then Duncan's house.
Chapter 54: The Hemel office.
Chapter 55: Hemel office then Nando's, Jarman Park, Hemel.
Chapter 56: The Anchor pub, Western Road, Tring then Lesley's house.
Chapter 57: Lesley's house then the Hemel office.
Chapter 58: The office, Black Goo café, High Street, Tring then Lesley's.
Chapter 59: The Anchor, Tring.
Chapter 60: The Hemel office.
Chapter 61: The office then Chiquito, Jarman Square, Hemel then Lesley's.

Chapter 62: Lesley's house, the Hemel office, Lesley's house, Tring.
Chapter 63: Lesley's house, Tring.
Chapter 64: Lesley's, Costa, the Natural History museum, Lesley's, all Tring.
Chapter 65: Lesley's, Tring reservoir, Bluebells Tearooms, Tesco, Lesley's.
Chapter 66: Lesley's house, Tring.
Chapter 67: Hemel office then The Paper Mill at Apsley.
Chapter 68: Berkhamsted canal, the office, The Plough, Leverstock Green.
Chapter 69: Hemel office then Nando's, Jarman Park, Hemel.
Chapter 70: Hemel office, The Mogul at Hemel old town then Lesley's house.
Chapter 71: Lesley's house, Tring, Hemel office then Boxmoor Steakhouse.
Chapter 72: Hemel office then Duncan's house, Northampton.
Chapter 73: Duncan's house then Izzy's house, Northampton.
Chapter 74: Heather's café, White Elephant pub, Izzy's, all Northampton.
Chapter 75: Donna's flat then Duncan's house, Northampton.
Chapter 76: Duncan's house and Donna's flat, Northampton.
Chapter 77: Hemel office, The Mazza, Marlowes, Hemel then Lesley's house.
Chapter 78: Hemel office then Maramis, Marlowes Shopping Centre, Hemel.
Chapter 79: Hemel office, Smoky Boys American diner, Saint Albans Road.
Chapter 80: Hemel office then Ristorante Alberto, Hemel.
Chapter 81: Bluebells, Tring Reservoir, Marsworth, Hemel office, Lesley's.
Chapter 82: Lesley's, Tourist Information Office, National History Museum, Jan and Pat's house, all Tring.
Chapter 83: Tring Park, Jan and Pat's house, Lesley's house, all Tring.
Chapter 84: Lesley's house, Beefeater Crow's Nest, Lesley's, all Tring.
Chapter 85: Lesley's house then The Full House (Wetherspoon), Hemel.
Chapter 86: Hemel office then The Olive Indian Restaurant, Hemel.
Chapter 87: Hemel office then Toby Carvery, Hemel.
Chapter 88: Hemel office then the Opuz Kitchen, Hemel.
Chapter 89: Hemel office then Subway, Hemel town centre, the office.
Chapters 90-1: Duncan's house, somewhere in Northampton.

Rachel's books

Novels

The Serial Dater — 31 dates in 31 days

The Serial Dieter — 31 dishes in 31 days

with other 'Serial' titles to follow

Oh, Henry — the first in the Henry Houdini series

Short Stories

Various Henry Houdini long short stories

About the Author

Rachel Cavanagh was born a southerner and will always be at heart. She transplanted herself, indirectly because of her job at the time, to the East Midlands, UK, in the early 1990s and has dreams of 'retiring' to Sussex, further south than her original roots, where she'd love to write full time with a sea view.

Short stories have always been her first love. A regular at her local library as a child, she devoured novels (sometimes under the covers with a torch) but often returned to short stories. Inspirations include Roald Dahl and Kate Atkinson.

Rachel will always be grateful to her father, with whom she would love to have had more time, especially to hear about his working relationship with Mr Dahl. Rachel knew how proud her father was of her, and she will always be a daddy's girl.

You can find Rachel at https://twitter.com/RachelCavAuthor.

Note from the Author

Thank you so much for purchasing this book, or choosing The Serial Dieter as your Kindle Unlimited read.

I loved writing it and hope you enjoyed reading it… and its predecessor, The Serial Dater.

I'd like to take this opportunity to also thank all my writing friends for their ongoing support,
and to my fabulous beta readers: Amber, Ann, Deborah, Diana, Dorothy, Heather (yes, from Heather's café), Izzy (not Donna's!), Laurence, Rachel, and Renu.
They deserve far more credit than I can give them as they received a first draft in such a raw state it could have easily given them food poisoning so my multitude of thanks.
Also to my tireless assistant Caroline Vincent.

Oh, and the scene with the beagle and chocolate really happened to my aunt and uncle… who in real-life **are** an animal portrait artist and a professional photographer… and are actually Jill Fowler and Mike Bass – the couple mentioned who write books about Tring!

I love hearing from readers, especially with feedback.

You can either find me on Twitter at https://twitter.com/RachelCavAuthor), or via email: rachelcavanaghauthor@gmail.com, and I am always grateful for honest reviews.

Published by **August Publishing UK**

Made in the USA
Las Vegas, NV
18 February 2025

18338779R00204